I0787964

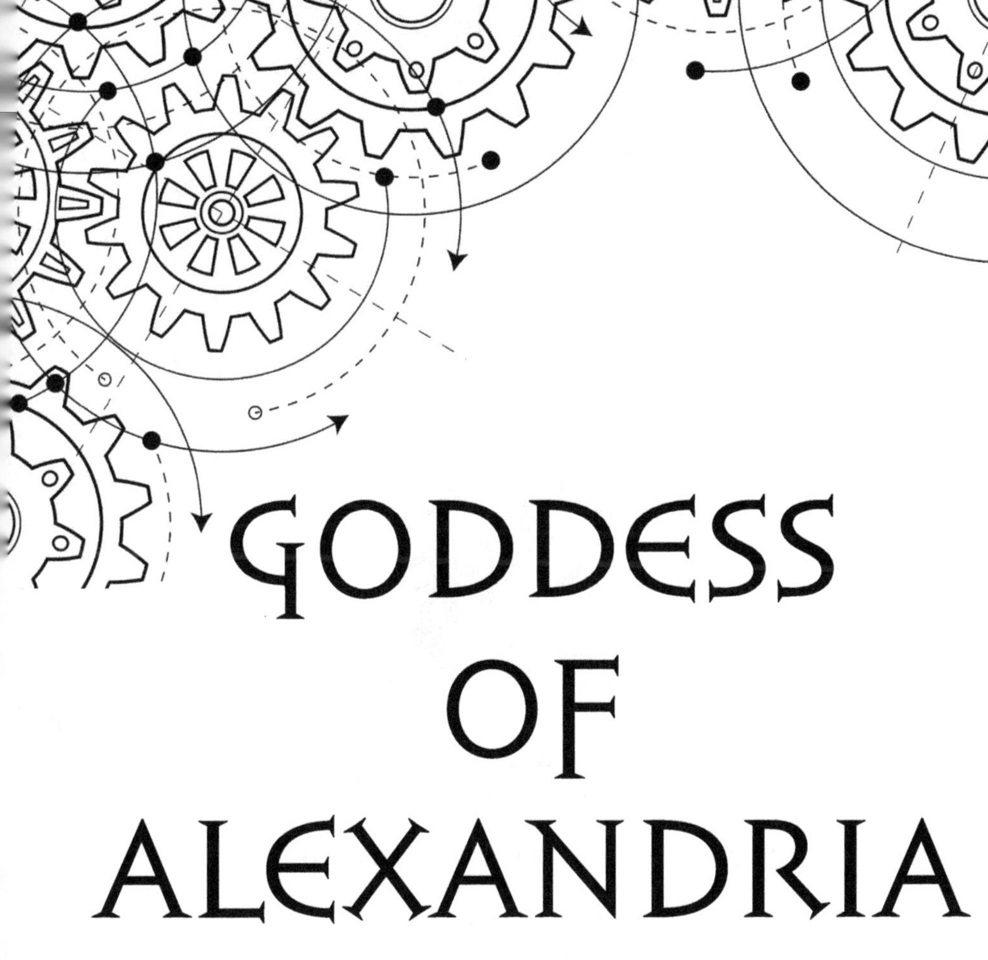

GODDESS OF ALEXANDRIA

Book Seven of The Alexandrian Saga

Thomas K. Carpenter

Goddess of Alexandria
Book Seven of The Alexandrian Saga

Hardcover Version
by Thomas K. Carpenter

Published by Black Moon Books

Cover design by
G&S Cover Designs

Chapter Headings design by Aleks49011

Discover other titles by this author on:
www.thomaskcarpenter.com

ISBN-13: 978-1-958498-17-0

ALEXANDRIAN SAGA

Fires of Alexandria
Heirs of Alexandria
Legacy of Alexandria
Warmachines of Alexandria
Empire of Alexandria
Voyage of Alexandria
Goddess of Alexandria

Other Books by Thomas K. Carpenter

The Dashkova Memoirs
Revolutionary Magic
A Cauldron of Secrets
Birds of Prophecy
The Franklin Deception
Nightfell Games
The Queen of Dreams
Dragons of Siberia
Shadows of an Empire

The Kingmaker Saga
The Stone Tree
The Crystal Bard
The Ghost Tower
The Champion's Prophecy
The Shadow Labyrinth
The Autumn Empire

The Hundred Halls Universe
SEASON ONE

THE HUNDRED HALLS
Trials of Magic
Web of Lies
Alchemy of Souls
Gathering of Shadows
City of Sorcery

THE RELUCTANT ASSASSIN
The Reluctant Assassin
The Sorcerous Spy
The Veiled Diplomat
Agent Unraveled
The Webs That Bind

GAMEMAKERS ONLINE
The Warped Forest
Gladiators of Warsong
Citadel of Broken Dreams
Enter the Daemonpits
Plane of Twilight

ANIMALIANS HALL
Wild Magic
Bane of the Hunter
Mark of the Phoenix
Arcane Mutations
Untamed Destiny

STONE SINGERS HALL
Song of Siren and Blood
House of Snake and Tome
Storm of Dragon and Stone
Sonata of Shadow and Thorn
Well of Demon and Bone

THE ORDER OF MERLIN
The Order of Merlin
Infernal Alliances
Tower of Horn and Blood

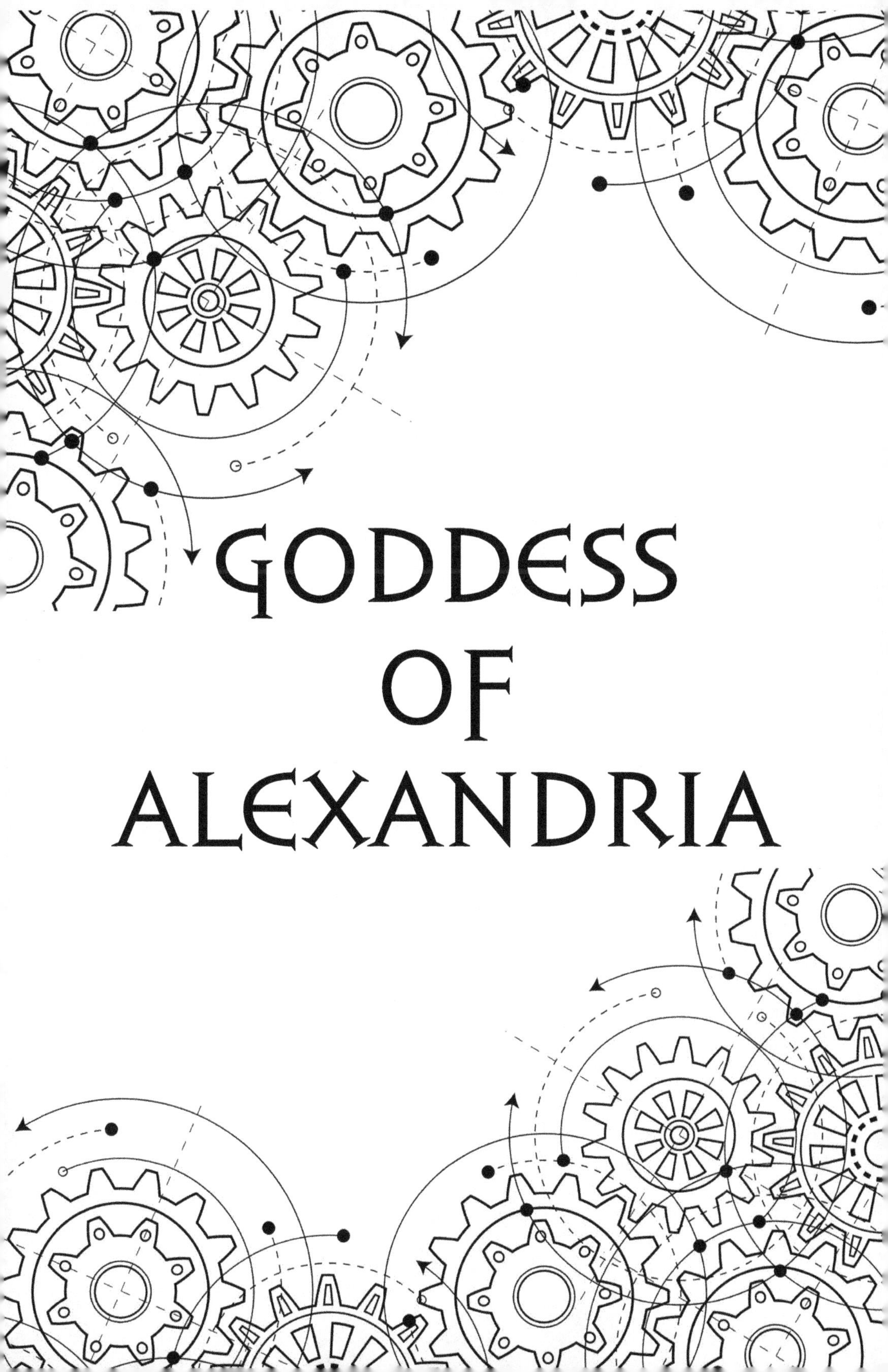

GODDESS OF ALEXANDRIA

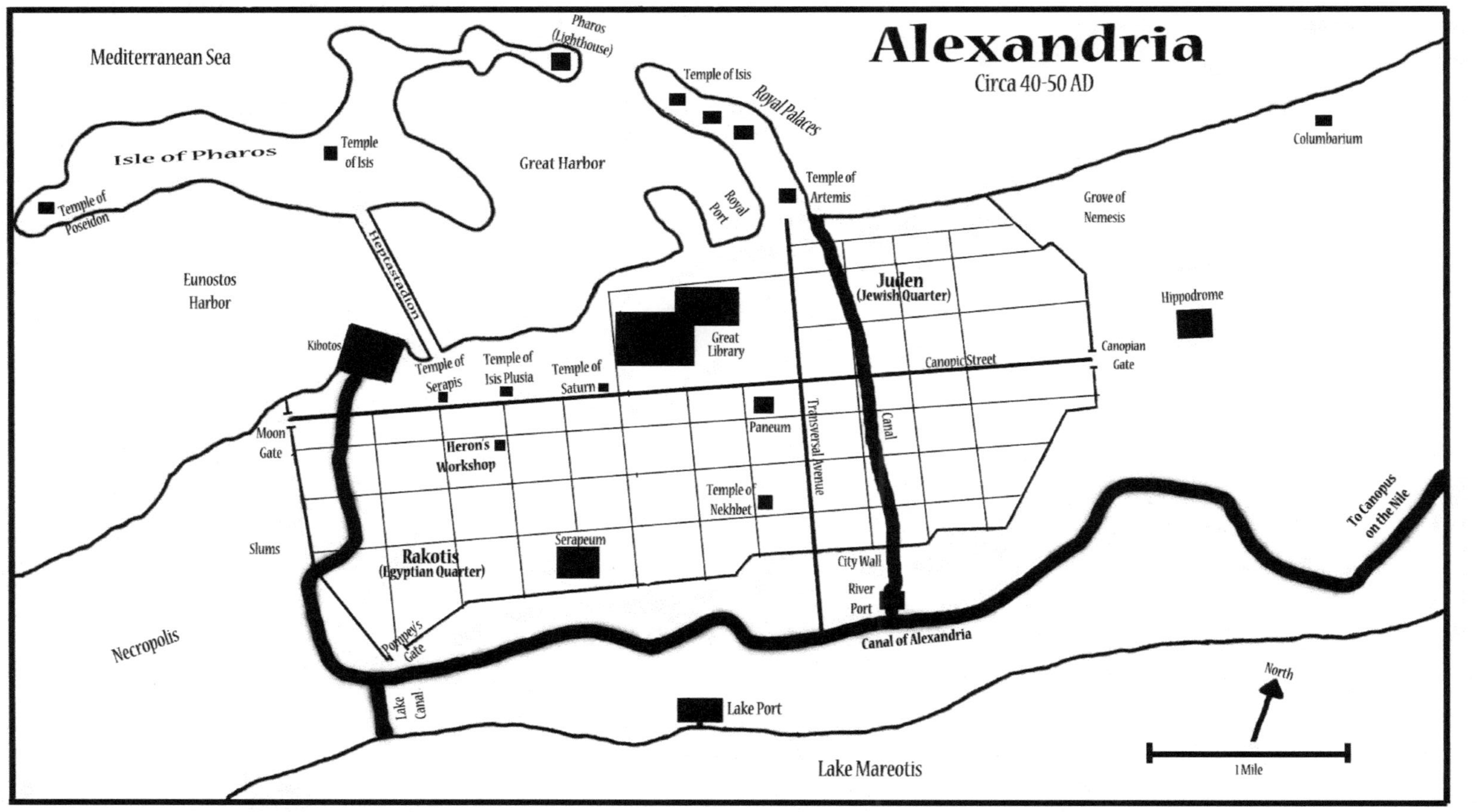

Alexandria
Circa 40-50 AD
Mediterranean Sea
Pharos (Lighthouse)
Temple of Isis
Royal Palaces
Columbarium
Isle of Pharos
Temple of Isis
Great Harbor
Temple of Artemis
Grove of Nemesis
Temple of Poseidon
Royal Port
Eunostos Harbor
Juden (Jewish Quarter)
Hippodrome
Heptastadion
Great Library
Kibotos
Temple of Serapis
Temple of Isis Plusia
Temple of Saturn
Canopic Street
Canopian Gate
Paneum
Moon Gate
Transversal Avenue
Canal
Heron's Workshop
Temple of Nekhbet
Slums
Rakotis (Egyptian Quarter)
Serapeum
City Wall
River Port
To Canopus on the Nile
Necropolis
Pompey's Gate
Canal of Alexandria
North
Lake Canal
Lake Port
1 Mile
Lake Mareotis

ONE

Night descended on the city of Alexandria, the molten iron of the sky fading to cold steel. Above the stone walls, towers thrust themselves against the dusk like spears from a returning army, though none reached higher than the Lighthouse of Pharos, its burning eye warding north.

Heron pulled the dark green robe around her body, feeling for the first time in over a year, substantial, rather than a ghost of a person. With a tilt of her neck, she flicked the stunted ponytail out from under the collar of the robe to keep it from tickling the back of her neck, while fingering the pugion, the spring-loaded knife that she kept in her sleeve for protection, a feeble weapon against whatever trials lay ahead.

"It's a wonder," said a pilgrim on her right in broken Greek while knocking the dust from his tunic.

Some of the pilgrims she'd arrived with in Alexandria had marched on ahead, to make the city walls before light had fled the sky, but others, like her, had stopped to admire the colors of the sunset hardening into night.

"It's the City of Wonders, a place of thought made action, a place like no other in the world," she said.

"I meant, it's a wonder that the Terrors haven't torn it down," said the man, nodding towards the Lighthouse.

Heron grabbed the man's arm, his earthy musk hitting her up close. "Terrors? What do you mean? Have you been inside the city? What's changed?"

The man, who had the body of a worker, broad shoulders and thick hands, yanked his arm from her grip and opened his mouth to rebuke her, when his eyes widened as he realized to whom he was speaking.

He backed away in jerky steps, catching a crack of dirt with his heel and stumbling. The man made a simple warding sign, two crossed fingers striking downward, and hurried to join the clump of pilgrims ahead, checking to make sure she wasn't following as he ran.

Heron rubbed her neck as she examined herself. The pilgrim hadn't recoiled from the sight of her face. He'd been looking at her robes.

"Terrors," she muttered, not daring to speculate what that might mean. It didn't matter. She'd returned to find Sepharia and flee to some other place. Maybe they could join a caravan and return to Sakrur, and enjoy the generosity of Queen Rembara. Sepharia would like the Queen.

Rather than hurry to join the others, Heron took a deliberate pace. It would put her at Pompey's Gate, the southwestern entrance into the Rhakotis District, after sun down, which would make it easier to blend into the crowd.

Once inside the city, she would make her way to her workshop. If her friends, or Sepharia, had survived, they would be waiting there.

The road took her around Lake Mareotis and into the slum city that leached onto the western wall of the city. The shantytown spilled further west along the dusty hard pack, bloated by refugees from the destruction of Rome.

Heron kept her head down as she passed the colorful tents of Thracian mercenaries. Their cooking fires delighted her nose and made her stomach gurgle in protest, and their laughing speech made her miss the company of others, for she had spent much of the winter secluded and before that, locked in a cage on the iron boat, *Petsuchos*.

Rather than make her way down the main road that the Alexandrian guards kept clear for trade and soldiers, Heron cut through the hidden, torturous paths that passed through the tent city. She wanted to avoid being noticed and catch the mood of the people.

Picking through the makeshift living quarters, thatched lean-tos, and mercenary pavilions, she heard a thousand native tongues filling the air: Greek, Roman, Persian, Thracian, Ethiopian, Sardian, Sindh, Ionia, Indus, and so on, until the babble became a steady hum in her ear.

In a shadowy space between fires, Heron came upon an Egyptian child poking at a hole with a stick. The dark-haired youth looked up at her with a gap-toothed smile.

"Greetings, child," she said, preparing to step over the hole and past the tent pegs that blocked her way.

Lantern light flooded into the space, making shadows march across the canvas tents, until Heron had to hold her good arm up to see.

"Get out of here!" growled a man in Egyptian.

He slammed his hilt against his scabbard in warning.

Squinting into the light, Heron replied in his language, "Apologies, just passing through."

The Egyptian man stepped forward and grabbed Heron's arm, squeezing hard enough to bruise. Heron fumbled for the pugion, hidden inside her robe sleeve, but his grasp made reaching it difficult.

He scowled and the muscles in his neck and jaw bulged. His breath stunk like rotten meat.

"I'll teach you to mess with my son, witch," said the man.

Heron reached out to push him away with her stump. When the

rounded end of her wrist stuck from the hem of the robe, the Egyptian man recoiled backwards, releasing her arm and tripped over the tent ropes to fall on his rear, somehow keeping the lantern from smacking into the hard earth.

Sitting on his backside, his eyes widened as he stared at her robe. Heron looked down, too, thinking she would see something fantastical blazoned on her chest, like a glowing ankh, but she saw nothing new.

Clambering to his feet, the Egyptian man yanked his son away eliciting cries from the child, and made a grave glance towards the city before yelling to his compatriots.

Heron pulled up the hem of her robe and fled through the dark spaces between the tents, hoping over ropes and latrine ditches in the dark.

A few hurried shouts followed her for a short time, but quickly fell back into the darkness. When she was certain no one was following, she slowed her pace, so she didn't injure herself, and spent the time contemplating the meaning of the man's reaction, especially the inexplicable glance into the sky above the city. Was he looking to the Lighthouse of Pharos for guidance?

When Heron came upon Pompey's Gate, her thoughts froze and she searched around, thinking she'd come upon the wrong entrance of the city. Then she remembered there'd never been a massive metal statue at any of the city's gates.

Gargantuan legs straddled the entrance, the crotch of the metal warrior higher than the wall. The lower half of the statue reflected golden light as bonfires burned in braziers. The upper half lay hidden in darkness, which explained why she'd not seen it upon approach.

Heron craned her head backwards to ascertain the identity of the statue. Her trembling heart seized the breath from her lungs as she saw the long snout protruding from the head of the statue.

Choking on her memories, Heron couldn't breathe and placed her fingertips against her lips. Two years ago. Two years ago, she'd instructed her workshop to create the statue of Ammon for Queen Amanitore of the Kushites as payment for their support against the Roman Empire. She'd developed a process that used the ghost fire jars to plate gold onto the statue's skin.

During the battles with Rome, and subsequent ruling of the city, she'd forgotten about this task.

In those busy years, the statue had been completed, but much to her dismay, had never been sent to the lands of Kush. Worse still, the head of Ammon had been replaced with Sobek, who leered over the slums outside the city.

The Egyptian man's glance into the sky became clear. He looked to the Colossus of Sobek. If she had any doubts about who controlled the city, they were erased by the transformation of the statue.

Rather than head to the gate, Heron stayed in the shadows and watched the traffic. Alexandrian guards in their stamped leather breast-plates and wielding gladii at their sides spoke to everyone, coming or going. They wore curious helms with the fronts molded into a shape that hinted at primal forces.

When a caravan wagon rumbled to the gate, pulled by a pair of roan horses, the guards spoke to the driver at length. He appeared to be Kush-ite and he argued with the guard before handing over a few coins. When they were done, one guard held the reins of the lead horse while the other examined the goods under the tarp. Satisfied, they sent the caravan into the city.

Heron checked her funds for bribes. She still had the coins she'd found in the temple along the river, but she shoved them back into her pouch.

She wasn't ready to give them up yet, even if it meant easy passage. She might need those coins to find Sepharia, or to flee the city once she'd found her. As much as it pained her to admit it, she'd only come back to rescue her daughter and then leave for calmer shores.

She waited until a group of men with fishing gear arrived at the gate to make her attempt to enter. The poorer folks in the Rhakotis District often relied on Lake Mareotis or the sea for their regular meals. Fish bit hard at dusk, but once night fell, the fishermen would return. They carried nets and wooden pails, stinking of fish.

Heron hurried to join the rear of the group, keeping her shoulders hunched and her head down. As the fishermen passed, shifting the tan-gled nets on their shoulders, the guards nodded them inward, the nightly ritual apparent by their familiarity.

The fisherman in front of Heron was tall with a loping gait. She positioned herself directly behind him, staring at his dirty heels, the filth earned on the muddy banks of Lake Mareotis.

Another dozen steps and she'd be inside the gate, one step closer to Sepharia. Her chest grew as tight as the Gordian knot.

As Heron passed the guard, he nodded, as he had for the fishermen and relief flooded into her limbs.

"Halt, priest," said the guard, not two steps further.

Heron stopped. The fishermen kept going into the city, leaving her alone. The gulf between her and the comforting crowds ahead seemed immense, like a yawning pit.

"Come here, priest," called the guard.

The act of hobbling in a forward motion had become smoother by time. Heron was used to the complexities of walking with a wooden leg, assuming she could point in one direction and move that way. Turning, however, was maddeningly complex with little side step movements, and always catching the end of the wooden stump, threatening to tip her sideways.

She felt like a horse trying to rotate in a small circle as she turned to the guard. He hooked his thumbs into the top of his leather waist guards, and tilted his head at her, reviewing her from wooden leg, to pink stump, to shoulder length feminine hair.

Like a coin spinning, her gut churned with worry. She swallowed and tried to smile, but it came out as a pained grimace, especially when she realized the helm was in the shape of a crocodile's mouth.

"I've never had a blessing from a woman Terror," he said, winking at his fellow guard. "Only seen a few of you, but never through our gate. Seems our large metal friend keeps the peace for you folks."

Heron looked back through the gate. A caravan waited to enter, its horses stamping and neighing, the driver craning his head to see what was holding up the line.

When she didn't answer and stared back with what she hoped was annoyance, the guard's joking smile faded until his lips thinned to white. Then he jerked his head towards the city.

Rather than make her wobbling rotation, Heron strode forward and circled around, forgoing the awkwardness. Once she'd fallen into the crowds moving through the streets, she contemplated the meaning of the exchange.

Who were these Terrors? Were they priests of Sobek? It would only make sense, as Lysimachus had named his god, He Who Dwelleth Amid Terrors.

She contemplated what it meant for the city that it'd fallen under the sway of the priesthood. How had the nobles allowed this influence? Once she'd found Sepharia, she would send inquiries to the Palace, to learn more from Polyxena.

Heron paused in the street and a Thracian trader in dirty leathers bumped into her. He mumbled a curse as he moved past, and Heron stepped to the side, huddling against a clay-brick warehouse that smelled faintly of musty wheat stores.

She'd forgotten about Agog's wife, the Macedonian woman who'd come to them four years back. How had the news of Agog's death affected her? Heron grabbed the front of her robe in mute anger. Though Polyxena had not married Agog for love, theirs was primarily a political alliance, it was another reminder of what the destruction of the Empire had wrought.

As Heron resumed her march through the streets, she pointed herself towards Canopic Street, the avenue that split the city in half, entering and leaving through the Moon and Canopic gates respectively. She didn't want to head directly towards her workshop, in case Lysimachus had spies lurking.

A pack of young boys in loincloths ran past, screaming and laughing, while dodging through the unexpectedly busy evening crowd. They seemed to be playing a game, and in their haste, one boy knocked a basket of hard breads from the hands of a stooped old woman in a soot-smudged stola.

The woman's wrinkled face soured into a scowl as she collected her fallen bread, dropping the round loaves back into the misshapen reed basket.

While Heron watched the woman collect her bread, the last boy ran past and the nature of the game became clear. The boy wore a scaly green mask with a long snout.

How could her city have changed so much in two years? First the statue, then the mention of Terrors, and now boys playing games with Sobek as their inspiration? How had the crocodile priest turned the soul of the city so quickly?

Heron hurried forward, stabbing her wooden leg into the dirt, as a heat rose in her chest. When the wind shifted, bringing with it not the crisp sea air, but of burning, her mouth opened in alarm. All around her she turned, but no one shared her concern.

Was fire not the greatest enemy of the city that housed the Great Library? And what she smelled was no simple bonfire. She could taste the flaky papyrus burning in some quantity. What sickness had befallen them?

Huddled against the fountain of Bast, Heron truly watched her fellow Alexandrians for the first time since she'd returned. Gazes burrowed into the ground, while shoulders hunched and brows tensed. The hurried sense of industry had been sapped from their limbs. They seemed more prisoners on a long march rather than inhabitants of the City of Wonders.

Even when she'd been drowning in debts, Heron had carried pride for the city on the crown of her head like a halo. The automatas that adorned street corners provided inspiration for thoughtful scholars and humble workers alike.

Behind her, the once active statue of Bast in her four forms lay dormant. The faces had been chipped by edged weapons and the water had been drained from the fountain. The hand of the Egyptian cat god had been snapped off. Even though the creation had been a design of Philo's, stolen from her workshop, its misuse made her jaw hurt.

A trumpet blast startled Heron. It came from the direction of Canopic street, the direction the crowds moved. To the east lay her workshop, but whatever was happening on the main avenue of Alexandria seemed more important.

Heron rejoined the crowd that grew denser the closer she got to Canopic street. Elbows jostled against her side as they packed together.

Braziers filled with greasy fires lit the wide avenue that housed the richest merchants. Marble buildings glowed with flickering light as shadows danced across their fronts.

Alexandrian guards kept the center of the street empty, except for a bald priest in greenish robes that meandered down the middle. But the crowd was not looking at the priest. They faced west and as she turned, the thump of the echoing drums kissed against the soft flesh of her neck.

A steam barge with wheels as tall as a soldier rumbled from the west. The brass shielding on the front displayed the horrible open mouth of a crocodile. A half-dozen priests in dark green robes encircled some poor soul held to the platform by chains. The crowd watched with muted interest.

Heron had been forced to attend an execution before, but the crowd had been elated, screaming epithets at the top of their lungs and throwing rotten vegetables as the prisoner went past. While certain rituals of a public execution were being observed - the dutiful priests, the gathered crowds, the long procession reminding the innocent the importance of adhering to stated laws - the *feel* of it was all wrong.

The crowd seemed maudlin to the extreme, much as if they attended their own funeral. But it wasn't quite that either. The people in the crowd were practically bored.

Rather than stay and watch the steam barge meander past, Heron moved back one street and then headed east. She had to go as far as Transversal Avenue, which was the other major cross street in Alexandria to reach the epicenter of the gathering.

By the time she reached her destination, she was covered in a light sweat, which made her robes itchy. The assembled spilled into the secondary streets at the massive cross street between Canopic and Transversal, which hosted festivals regularly throughout the year.

At the center of everyone's attention was a raised platform on what appeared to be a pyramid with the top cut off. Alexandrian guards ringed the pyramid and a few priests milled about the platform, gathered around a headsman's block, which was a heavy wooden stump with axe scars in the center.

Heron pushed through the crowd to get closer, but she didn't make it far before her way was blocked. She tried in other locations, but each time, the crowd grew so dense that she couldn't pass.

The drums of the approaching steam barge grew near and she was covered in a damp sweat. Heron tried pushing ahead, but a noxiously perfumed merchant in silks elbowed her back.

She hung her head in frustration. She needed to get up front to see what was happening. Why would everyone in the city, and it certainly felt like everyone in the city, given the heat rising from their pressed bodies, leave the cool confines of their brick homes to witness an execution so joylessly?

Staring at the fabric of her green robe, Heron remembered the reaction of the pilgrim on the way to Alexandria. She shook her head, hating to rely on its symbolic nature, but having no time for other actions.

In what she hoped was an authoritative tone, Heron boomed out her voice, "By He Who Dwelleth Amid Terrors, let me pass!"

The perfumed merchant's wide-eyed realization of who he'd just struck with an elbow blanched his face bone-white.

"Apologies, priest," he muttered and vacated the space she'd wanted to move through.

While the rest of the nearby crowd's reaction wasn't as overt, the invoking of Sobek's name drew the desired effect. Like a river around a boulder, the crowd parted and she strode ahead, keeping her pink stump in plain view.

She made it to the front of the crowd, having to use Sobek's name twice more, but most seemed to sense her presence and faded away from her. The powerful reaction was eerie and Heron quickly realized, could be quite addictive.

When she made the street, an Alexandrian soldier in leather breastplate and gladius moved to help her past the barrier, but she shook him off. The soldier nodded and moved on, continuing his circuit around the half-pyramid.

The approaching drums set a rhythm for her heart and nearing the end, both sped up. The steam barge rolled inexorably towards the execution platform under the watchful eye of the Lighthouse of Pharos.

The empty sky was a funnel that seem to focus the city's attention down to this point. If Heron had believed in the gods, she would have expected they were standing behind the curtain of the stars to watch.

When the steam barge rolled into place, shuttering momentarily as it kissed against the half-pyramid, Heron had a sudden terrible premonition about the identity of the prisoner.

The priests of Sobek in their dark green robes marched towards the pyramid, the woman - Heron caught glimpse of long blonde tresses - in a pure white stola followed along as if she were a queen as much as a prisoner. The wall of priests blocked her view until the woman stepped upon the ramp that led to the execution platform.

Sepharia! She was alive!

Heron had to resist with every inch of her being not to rush onto the pyramid and close her arms around Sepharia, smelling the sweetness of her hair.

Lightness filled Heron's limbs at the knowledge that her hopes had not been dashed upon the rocks. That Sepharia had not been lost in Rome.

Her daughter glowed with radiance, like the Goddess Diana, her skin seemingly bathed in milk. Sepharia held her chin high, and when she reached the summit, a man dressed in the ceremonial attire of the god Sobek took her hand.

The crowd made a hushed intake of breath on the appearance of the man-god. His brown arms flexed beneath the mask that covered his head down to his shoulders. The long green snout was benevolent and wise, not at all the horrible opening stinking of rotten meat and containing bits of old flesh caught between the teeth like she remembered when Petsuchos had crawled upon the stone altar in the temple of reeds.

Sobek carried a golden ankh and wore a beaded loincloth of sea stones and coral. Heron knew it was not Lysimachus beneath the mask, because Sobek had two hands and his skin was the golden mocha of an Egyptian.

Sepharia was led to a place before the scarred stump. She gazed at the crowd in a clear and direct manner, sweeping across the many upturned faces in a graceful review.

The man who was Sobek strode to the front of the platform and stamped his ankh staff downward, the impact booming across the crowd like thunder, silencing the murmuring like an axe strike.

"Faithful Alexandrians!" he called out, his voice echoing against the marble buildings. His tone carried the weight of a monument.

"Nine times I have brought you here to witness the powers of Sobek! Nine times you have seen the miracle from my hand. Today marks the Tenth! Do not be afraid, for Sobek controls the waters of creation, and anything is possible with him."

The man-god Sobek wandered around the edge of the platform. Heron couldn't keep her eyes off him. Her mind reverberated with the words *waters of creation* in remembrance of her dreams on the *Jörmungandr*.

"Again, I bring you my daughter to prove the depth of my sacrifice!"

Shouts erupted from the crowd, calling out a name Heron couldn't quite hear. She turned this way and that, trying to catch the shape of the names, but the praise-givers trampled over each other in their enthusiasm.

Finally, not far behind her, a man shouted, "Heron!" and she spun around expecting to see Lysimachus or an Alexandrian soldier advancing on her.

Instead, a simple worker in a pale gray tunic raised his hand to the heavens. He was looking not at her, but at the man-god Sobek upon the platform.

A wave of dizziness passed through her and she stumbled against the woman on her right.

As if wax had been pulled from her ears, she could hear their shouts clearly. They yelled, "Sobek" and "Heron" and "*Michanikos*". Heron even heard "shapeshifter" called out once.

They thought it was she upon the stage beneath that mask. Was it not apparent that it was not her? How could they believe such lies?

Her heart answered right away with damning precision: *it was you who taught them to believe such untruths with your miracles.*

The realization shed light on the mystery of why the city had allowed the priests to come to power. Heron placed trembling fingers to her lips.

When the cries of "Sacrifice her!" rose up like dark wings, Heron refocused on the half-pyramid platform. The robed priests formed a circle around the edge. Sepharia was bent over the scarred stump without restraints. From Heron's vantage point, she could see the back of her daughter's calves and the way she held onto the wide rim of the base.

The man-god Sobek, the horrifying perversion of Heron's legacy, took position at the head of the block, holding his ankh staff high like a banner. He lifted it above his head with both hands, and gave it a violent shake, and the ankh transformed itself into an axe head.

Heron heard the words spring from her lips, crying out in defense of her daughter, as the man-god Sobek brought the axe down in a sweeping arc.

"Sepharia!" cried Heron, her voice rising feebly to stop the blade.

The axe bit into the stump, separating Sepharia's head in one, brutal strike. As the robed priests rushed to form a circle around Sepharia's lifeless body, the god Sobek reached down and lifted the head high to display it to the crowd, eliciting a sickening cheer.

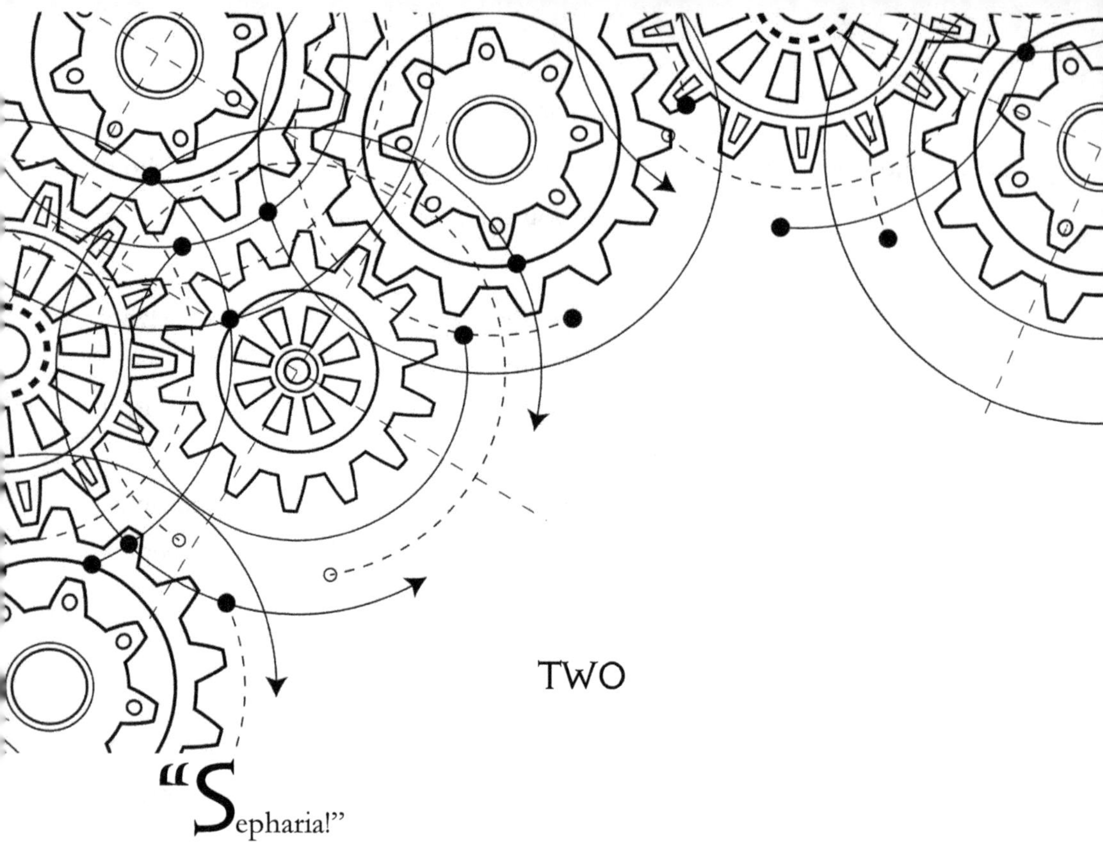

TWO

"Sepharia!"

The name leapt from Heron's lips a second time, part cry-for-help, part evocation in hopes that it could somehow summon Sepharia back from the dead.

How could she have come all this way only to be witness to her daughter's execution?

Heron's limbs trembled with the weight of the event, like a stone the size of the city had crashed into the earth. Heron reached around her, trying to grab something or someone to keep from collapsing, but the crowd had moved away from her, sensing some sickness, or repelled by her dark green robes now that the execution was complete.

"Sepharia!"

Her cry carried over the crowd, descending on the half-pyramid with vengeance.

One of the priests who had been bent over Sepharia's body turned and a chill went right through Heron as if she'd been stabbed with an icicle.

A pair of beady eyes fixed on her with bright, remorseless anticipation. Lysimachus stretched out his stump in her direction, the palest of grins fixing on his lips in a grimace.

"Collect her."

At the corners of her vision, she caught the nearest Alexandrian soldiers moving to intercept. Two of the priests started climbing down from the half-pyramid.

Heron hesitated, feeling held to the spot by Sepharia's body, but when the soldier to her left pulled his weapon and moved straight towards her, she fled, running right into the barrier of the crowd.

"Let me through, let me through," she cried, pushing at elbows and shoulders, trying to squeeze in.

She glanced over her shoulder to see the soldiers were close. She could hear footsteps and the jangling of chains.

"Lord Sobek demands you move!" she yelled.

The crowd did not part like before. They barely even acknowledged her shout, shuffling forward like cattle. The slow flood away from the half-pyramid had made them less malleable to her needs.

Desperate, Heron shoved her stump against the cheek of the man in front of her, and he flinched away, giving her an opportunity to squeeze in.

She kept up her cries of "Lord Sobek" and "this priest of Sobek demands you let me through" and combined with the touch of her stump, she forced her way forward.

She barely made it into the crowd before the soldiers reached her location. The closing of ranks behind Heron stymied the soldiers, so they began roughing up men and women to get them to move.

Heron slid past the sweaty bodies, squeezing between fat merchants and temple whores. She was a smooth rock in a bucket of mud and each time the soldiers neared close enough to grasp, she squirted out, one step ahead.

At the side streets, the crowd separated, leaving room for Heron to dart forward, always in a half-stumble, bouncing off people in a desperate scramble.

Heron came upon a merchant caravan that had been moving down the side streets to avoid the execution. The horses plodded towards the Emporium pulling wagons stuffed with clay jars that reeked of salty *garum*.

As a soldier reached out to grab her, Heron threw herself between wagon wheels. The iron-banded wheel bumped over her wooden stump, wrenching her knee, but not enough to keep her from scrambling out behind the wagon and heading up the street before the horses behind trampled her.

She made it down the next street before the soldiers realized where she'd gone. Cries of alarm followed as she turned the corner and ran into the body of a centaur.

For a moment, Heron feared witnessing her daughter's execution had unwound her reason, and she staggered against the man-beast that stared at her with grave ambivalence.

"Halt, citizen," said the bearded centaur.

When the creature moved its metal arm, the gears ticking through their paces like tiny hammers beating on a drum, Heron knew it for one of her designs.

The dream of an automata that could operate on its own, those metal soldiers Agog had come to Alexandria for, could never be achieved. But in Rome, she'd realized that men and machine could be married together into a formidable weapon. She'd forgotten about her creation left in the villa in Rome. Now, it stood before her, refined and deadly.

In her haste, she hadn't heard the low growl of the steam mechanical, but over her hurried breaths the machine rumbled against her chest. The metal centaur stepped forward, powered by the movement from the soldier inside, metal hoof scuffing against the dirt.

The machine stood taller than a warhorse. The soldier was protected by metal armor across his chest and neck. The front legs bent in a running stance, while the back legs had been replaced with iron-rimmed chariot wheels. Only the soldier's face shown beneath the Roman-style helmet with a crimson plume that gave the impression of a mane.

The centaur tilted his head at the cries of the soldiers giving chase. Then he reached out, his metal arm clicking and grinding obscenely, fingers articulating like a drunken spider.

Heron ducked under the arm and fled down the street. The metal centaur might one day be a beast on the battlefield, but the design wasn't made for pursuit and capture.

Checking over her shoulder to catch the location of the Lighthouse, Heron realized she was headed southwest into the Temple District. She ducked into a private courtyard with a well and hid behind an old olive tree with a trunk shaped like a hundred up-stretched arms bound and frozen in the wood.

The soldier's hurried shouts eventually passed her location, while she tried desperately to calm her heavy breathing. When she was certain the soldiers wouldn't come back, she drew water from the well and wiped the sweat from her face with a wetted hand.

Heron privately thanked the winter stay in the Temple of Sobek and the long journey to Alexandria for giving her the stamina to escape the soldiers. Had she come straight to the city without rest, she wouldn't have made it five steps without collapsing.

Standing in the darkness with only the Lighthouse to provide illumination, Heron placed her fist against her forehead and squeezed her eyes tight.

"Sepharia," she whispered, the pain leeching into her bones until the ache was a heavy weight.

How had Lysimachus known she was going to return to Alexandria?

The execution felt like a trap, except she couldn't understand how he'd known to pick that moment to spring it? Unless everything she knew about the world was wrong and that the gods did exist and Lysimachus did have the favor of the god Sobek, he couldn't have known she'd returned to Alexandria.

Her intention had been to return to find Sepharia, if she was alive, and then leave with her daughter to safer shores. But now that Sepharia was dead, Heron's escape felt like a pyrrhic victory.

On the long journey to Alexandria, a part of Heron had wanted to stay in the city that she'd made her home in. The City of Wonders. With Rome's influence turned to ashes, Heron might have filled that space with science and reason.

Sepharia had drawn her back to the city, but Heron was no stranger to hubris. She'd changed the world before and she could do it again.

Heron had let that part of her smolder in her chest, until her daughter could be found. But now Heron wished she'd never left Queen Rembara's Palace. Somehow, returning to Alexandria had caused Sepharia's death. If she'd never come back, Sepharia could live on in memory, the truth never settled by observation.

The darkness provided a comforting cloak while she wrestled with her decision. In the end, she made the choice as a practical matter. With no friends or allies alive, her daughter dead, and Lysimachus in firm control of the city, she had no choice but to leave or be recaptured by the priest of Sobek. She rubbed her arm and shivered away the memories of the seeping pit beneath the temple and the tortures Lysimachus had inflicted.

Heron waited for what she thought was an hour before leaving her hiding spot. South was the safest course. She plodded that direction, staying to the shadows, for what did the light have to offer her anymore?

Cutting up an alleyway, she came upon a wide, empty space between the Temple of Eros and a sturdy brick building with sweeping arches. The former was a long, low building with thick incense rolling from its chimneys, while the latter housed a Thracian mercenary company that made its home in the city.

But Heron was interested in neither of these. Instead, the spot between them, filled only with gravel and grass, drew her attention. For it had once housed the Temple of Nekhbet, before she'd pulled the whole structure down, rescuing Sepharia.

Heron stared at the empty space, squeezing her hand into a fist and then stretching the fingers outward like a cat.

None of the others had dared to build on the spot after what had befallen Nekhbet's temple. And nothing she could do would rescue Sepharia now.

When she couldn't stare at the spot any longer, Heron made her way to the canal that split the city north and south. After the encounter with the soldiers, she didn't dare try the gates. The canal was the next best way to leave the city, she hoped.

At a place behind a residential structure, Heron climbed down the stone-stacked wall covered in ivy to the water's edge. The wall was slanted and the stones spaced with enough room to place her foot, that she made it down without incident. In the northern part of the city, the nobles kept the wall steep and smooth, but the southeast part of the city housed the lesser merchants who cared more about earning coin than the intricacies of city maintenance.

It had a fishy smell, which was better than the shit smell it had when the water was low and the sewers leaked into it. But for now, the Nile fed the canal, and it'd not yet begun to flood, so only the lower half was full, leaving a path on either side. In another month, the water would be halfway up the second stone wall.

The water left the city through a huge metal grate, which Heron hoped to squeeze through. She'd toured this section once many years ago and her memory was sketchy, but she recalled thinking that it seemed an easy spot for saboteurs to sneak into the city.

Reaching the city wall, her hopes were dashed. It seemed the grate had been reinforced with an additional layer of bars. Judging by the lack of moss over the arch and the gray mortar that wasn't quite blackened by the rising and falling of the Nile, she guessed it'd been improved before the Romans had attacked the city. With a dry laugh, she considered that she might have ordered the improvement herself in preparation of the defense of the city.

Heron stared at the reinforced grate for a while before heading west. There was only one other way she knew to leave the city, but it came with a price.

She hadn't made it one block from the canal before the sound of a steam chariot rushed onto her street. Trapped against the wall, Heron had no place to run and the vehicle sped to her upon sight.

"Halt in the name of the Empire!" shouted a male voice from the steerage of the steam chariot.

A bull lantern flooded over her. Heron blocked the light with her forearm, careful not to use her stump.

"Plato have pity, I'm not moving," she mumbled under her breath, and then louder: "Greetings, good soldiers. In the name of Sobek, how can I help you?"

Blinded by the light, Heron didn't see the soldier approach until he'd grabbed her arm. He pulled up her sleeve, revealing the stump and then leaned down to check the wooden leg.

"It's her," said the soldier. "The gods have blessed us today. Lysima-chus said five talents to the soldiers that capture Sobek's bride."

Heron struggled against his grip, trying to pull away. "I'm not her, whoever you think I am. I'm a priest of Sobek. Let me go before our god answers this transgression with vengeance."

The soldier chuckled and yanked her arm as if he were pulling a reed from the water.

"I don't care what you think you are. You're Heron the Maker, and the High Priest of Sobek wants you in the Palace."

An iron manacle clamped around her wrist.

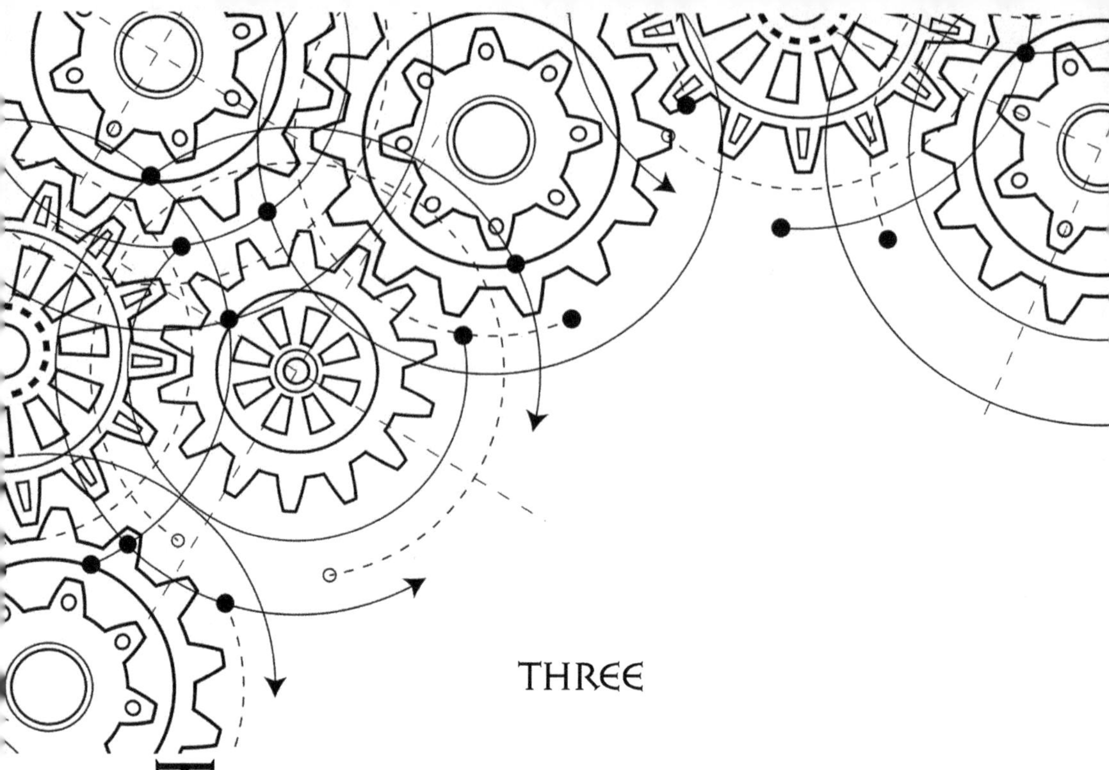

THREE

The steam chariot rattled across the flagstones with Heron chained to the pipes. Cool desert air had snaked up from the south, chilling Heron's face, still damp with sweat.

The glowing fire chamber on the mechanical put a band of heat across her back. The manacle bounced against her wrist bone as she tugged on it.

The steam chariot was manned by two soldiers. The pilot faced forward while the second, a scrawny youth barely old enough to hold a gladius with greasy hair and a patchy not-beard gawked at her.

"Five talents, Pontos," shouted the young soldier, a smile slapped haphazardly on his face. "That's a house and a wife and enough left over to thank the gods for this good fortune."

"To the Underworld with your wife, Artis," said Pontos from the steerage, yelling over his shoulder. "A brothel spends gold better than a wife."

They passed through the Temple District and the halls of the gods whipped past. Statues of painted gods and goddesses, virulent deities lording over the street, caught the reflected light from the Lighthouse, kissing their faces with faint fire.

Heron clenched her jaw until it hurt. Steam hissed out behind her and she had to resist the urge to thrust her stump into it.

"You won't spend a deaneries," said Heron, her voice etched with razors.

"You hear that, Pontos? She says we won't spend our gold. And why is that?" said Artis, laughing, though when he saw the look on Heron's face, his eyes glistened with worry.

Heron had carefully positioned her body so that she was facing to the side. Her right arm, trapped in the manacle, stretched out from her body, back towards the piping.

"Because you chained me up to the steam mechanical," she said, feeling a perverse joy as the words slipped her lips. "The very machine I invented. Didn't you think that I might turn it against you?"

Artis' hand went to his hilt. His brow bunched up as he looked past her to see what mischief she might have caused.

Heron waited until he'd stepped back a pace before she kicked her foot out, not towards the steam mechanical, but to actuate the lever that would bring the vehicle to a screeching stop.

The brake slammed into place, stopping the vehicle as if it'd hit a stone wall. The momentum yanked her against the chain, sending white-hot pain through her shoulder and wrist. It felt like someone had dipped her shoulder in lava.

Squinting through the stars in her eyes, Heron surveyed the damage from the sudden stop. Artis, the young soldier who'd dreamt of a wife, lay motionless on the cobblestones ahead, dark liquid leaking from his skull.

Pontos had rebounded against the steerage and wheezed on the floor of the steam mechanical. The impact had likely crushed his chest by the way he clawed at the air above his mouth, trying to capture more life-giving air.

Heron stretched her foot out and hooked it under his arm and dragged him backwards until she could reach his waist. The pressure turned his gasps into the wheeze of a man trying to suck mud from a swamp.

Leaning down with her teeth extended, she captured the ring that held the manacle key, tasting the rusty iron ring on her tongue. Then she transferred the key to her good hand, the one trapped in the manacle, and after careful maneuvering, unlocked it.

She shook the life back into her fingers, relieved she hadn't broken her wrist when the steam chariot slammed to a halt.

Standing over the soldier, she quickly decided his fate. It wouldn't do her any good to let Lysimachus know she was still in the city. Heron slipped the sturdy dagger from the soldier's belt and held it over his convulsing form.

"Apologies, Pontos," she said, meaning every bit of it. His eyes widened with the realization of what she was about to do.

Heron slashed the blade across his neck and then pushed him over the side of the steam mechanical onto the cobblestones. Tucking the blade into her belt, Heron released the brake and let the pistons push the steam chariot forward.

The street was wide enough for a turn, so Heron made her way south and east, thankful another patrol hadn't happened upon her.

She rolled westward through the city as the bells of deep night rang. Heron kept to the side streets, moving across the open spaces with alacrity. She caught sight of a Centaur meandering up the street, but he had his back to her, so he couldn't see, even with the dim lanterns that hung on the occasional street corner.

At each turn of the steerage, her shoulder burned, causing her to grimace, while her wrist throbbed. Nearing the Serapeum, Heron caught wind of the burning smell again.

The Serapeum was the daughter library of the Great Library that Ptolemy had built centuries ago. Originally, it'd been a temple dedicated to a new god—Serapis.

Standing bow-legged outside the marble doors of the structure was a stone bull, the Apis bull. In centuries past, the place had housed an oracle, but now the walls had become a library dedicated to learning. Heron had always thought that knowledge was an oracle, of sorts, so its repurpose had been fitting.

But the Serapeum was not her destination. That was further west in the heart of the Rhakotis District, in the places even Roman soldiers feared to march when Rome owned the city.

The scent of desperation hung on her frame, a scent that would do her no good in the halls of Black Omari. The Egyptian crime lord had long controlled the various illegal markets that circumvented the customs man. Even Lysimachus, when he'd collected the tax, had never dared oppose Black Omari.

The Serapeum marked the eastern edge of the Rhakotis District. The slums of the city would be safe from Alexandrian soldiers, but she would be presented with a new danger.

Rushing into his realm without a plan would be foolish at best. Even with a plan, she knew he could be capricious. And the score in the city had changed considerably since she'd last lived in Alexandria. For all she knew, he could have been replaced by a worse criminal, or he had allied himself to Lysimachus, and his crocodile god.

With the steam mechanical idled, Heron stood in the darkness for a long time considering her options. They were few and far between. It almost seemed safer to rush out Pompey's gate in the steam mechanical and hope she could outrun her pursuers.

Not that she had any faith in that idea. It would only take one steam chariot faster than hers to ruin the plan.

Black Omari.

She thought long on the crime lord. Even in the depths of her debts, she'd never considered taking a loan from him. If anyone could be worse than Lysimachus, it was Black Omari.

The last time she'd met with him, she'd come out alive, and mostly even. A win in any encounter with him.

But would he remember what he told her the last time they'd talked? She guessed he would, and that didn't bode for her next encounter.

Which meant she needed a plan that could get her out of trouble in a hurry, should she need it.

When she finally settled on one, she had to refill the steam mechanical before it would move again. The steam chamber had cooled until it ticked.

Heron put the steam chariot in motion, puttering towards the slums of the Rhakotis District. She had a plan. Not a good one, but a bad plan was better than no plan at all.

Black Omari's home was a towering villa with a ten cubit high wall surrounding it. Olive trees ringed his abode, but they'd been pruned liberally, so they couldn't be used to circumvent the wall.

Once Heron found a proper spot between two trees, she piloted the steam mechanical against the wall. Heron fed the fire chamber with as much fuel as it could fit, until sparks spit out the opening like a miniature fountain.

Then she adjusted the levers until she had set them, just so. The pistons churned until they made a beat like a drummer at full speed, except the wheels of the chariot did not turn. Heron left the vehicle, glancing back numerous times before she turned the corner, hoping that no one would disturb its rest.

At the entrance to the villa stood a hulking thug. Torch light flickered against his form, revealing rope-like scars on his neck. The thug's name was Dranis, and his presence confirmed that Black Omari was still in charge of the Rhakotis District. The black-hearted thug would follow no other.

Heron took a deep breath and stepped around the corner. Dranis fixed his beady eyes on her right away as if he knew she would be standing there.

There's no plan like a bad plan, thought Heron, unless you've got no plan at all.

Heron limped toward the villa and at each step, the thug's smile grew until it became a toothy cavern.

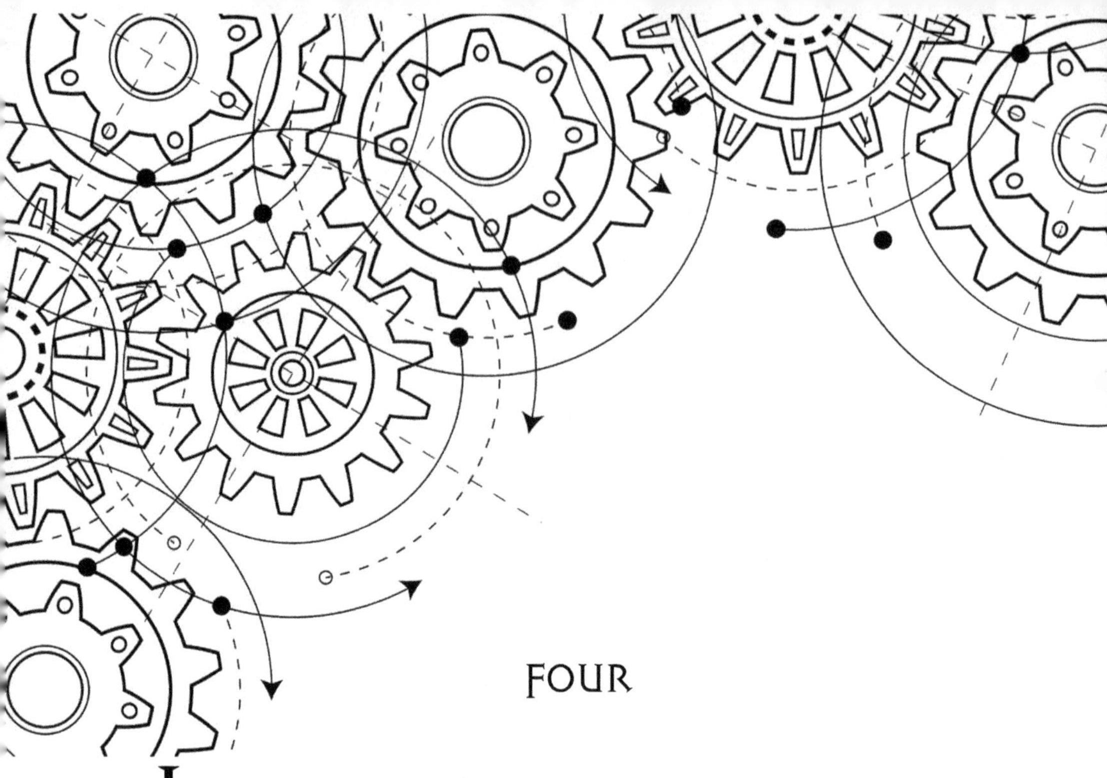

FOUR

Life in the Rhakotis District had never been easy for Heron. The other well-known workshops wisely stayed to the east of the Serapeum, not daring to set foot in the slums.

Before she'd developed a reputation as the Miracle Man, and her inventions were known as far north as Rome, she'd had to curry favor with the local Magistrate, a Roman who loved his food, by helping him with matters of the district.

When a particular problem of Magistrate Ovid's crossed paths with Black Omari, Heron had intervened, creating a *not profitable situation*, in the crime lord's words. Heron had escaped Black Omari's wrath, based on her good works for the district and a gift she'd brought, but he'd warned her never to visit his villa again, under threat of embalming—a promise not to be carried out while she was dead.

Another time, she would have struggled to remember the words of Black Omari. It had been years, maybe a decade, since she'd spoken to him. Time, and the many wounds she'd acquired, created a fog on the events of her life before the great fire of Rome.

But not that moment, not when she walked willingly into his lair. Black Omari's words had cut into her like a knife. Slicing themselves into her memory.

Debt is not paid. But only due if I see you again, with interest.

Dranis, the dung-breathed thug with rope scars on his neck, crossed his arms when she approached.

"Many years, Heron the Shapeshifter. Many years since you come to the House of Omari. He remembers," said Dranis, his lip twitching, as he nodded into the villa.

Heron knew that any perceived weakness would be punished harshly. The presence of the Magistrate upon her last visit had greased the events in her favor, since his death would have brought retribution to the district. She carried no official shield with her this time.

With chin high, she stared directly at him, "He's trained you well, Dranis. Does he let you lick his feet clean when he climbs out of the sewers each night?"

The bold statement brought the tiniest of flinches to Dranis' hard gaze. His grin turned cold.

"You were smarter when you were a man, shapeshifter. Not smart to play games with Black Omari," said Dranis.

"Even as a woman I'm twice as smart as you are dumb and I'm not here to play games. I'm here to offer him a deal." Heron let a secret smile trickle to her lips. "And I know you wouldn't tell him what I said, even if you wanted to. For being uglier than a hyena, you know Black Omari doesn't like bad news. He might take his wrath out on you as much as me."

Dranis bared his teeth like an angry dog. "Go on, woman. I'll take you to him. Let you hang yourself on your words."

He moved to grab her arm, and she thrust her stump out of the robe like a ward. His callused hands scratched across her forearm as he recoiled like a steam catapult.

"I've killed a god for less and losing that hand was worth it," she said.

The growl that came from his lips gave her pause, but he marched into the villa, expecting her to follow.

The ferocity of her words surprised even her. In her chest was a ball of emotions, pulsing with rage. *I grieve for Sepharia in the only way I know how, destruction.* Yet, she knew her time would come, if she did not reign it in. But that time was not now. Not yet.

Black Omari's villa rivaled the tomb of an Egyptian god with colonnades lining the entrance and miniature stone sphinxes to either side of an ebony door so black it absorbed the torch light.

The door opened as they approached with no attendant. To any other, its opening might have been seen as proof of Black Omari's semi-divinity, but Heron knew it for what it was—a trick.

She didn't need tricks to know that the old Egyptian was a dangerous man. His long rule in the Rhakotis District was proof enough.

At the opposite end of the atrium, a brass-geared Osiris stood guard with crook and flail. The Egyptian god of the dead.

Heron paused before the statue, touching the knotted end of the flail with her fingertips. Oh, what a simpler time when she'd made that statue for the crime lord.

The thug Dranis led Heron into a circular hall, ringed with statues that had once made their home in Memphis. Some of the painted sculptures had been rescued from the Old Kingdom and bore scars from their long history. Last time, Black Omari had been in a loquacious mood, and he'd bragged about some of them being over two thousand years old. Heron didn't expect that same treatment this time.

Black Omari appeared on the far side of the room through a door lit with shadow. Time had etched itself in the man's face, yet nothing about him indicated frailty. He was an elderly lion with the scars to prove his prowess and no other challenger dared his extensive territory.

Heron noted the differences between Black Omari and Dominitus. Both were of the same age and ruled in the ways of secrets and informants. Black Omari's name derived from the idea that the shadows of men were known as the watchers of Osiris. While she'd never feared for her life in Dominitus' presence. Here, she felt the sharp edge of Black Omari's reputation pressing against her neck.

Despite the opulence of his villa, Black Omari wore a simple pleated skirt and a beaded vest that exposed the coarse gray hairs on his chest. He was lean and his gaze held the weight of the pharaohs.

"You fool to come back," said Black Omari in thick Egyptian-accented Latin. He smacked his lips before speaking again. "But I know you not fool."

"Nor can I believe that you would welcome the influence of the crocodile god in Alexandria," she said.

His nostrils briefly flared.

"Peculiarities of old Alabarch not concern deal with me," he said.

Heron limped into the center of the room, fingering the pugion in the sleeve of her robe, feeling the presence of Dranis in the doorway behind her.

"That was a different Heron you made a deal with," she said, lifting her chin and staring directly into his black eyes. "That one was a simple workshop owner, trying to make good on the needs of the district. I speak today as the head of an Empire."

Black Omari's dry chuckle filled the circular room. The statues seemed to lean forward in interest.

"Maybe empire of dust," said Black Omari. "And now, shapechanger, your secrets revealed, your miracles denounced, your prospects set to flame. You hold nothing. Maybe, you stay away from Alexandria, better."

Heron propped up a smile and wandered to a statue of some ancient pharaoh with an ornate headdress and holding an ankh.

"How appropriate," said Heron, tracing her fingers along the jackal-like features on the statue's face. "Your villa is a monument to ancient Egyptian glory, just like your little empire in the Rhakotis district will become when Lysimachus consolidates power and decides to root you out."

"You nothing to offer," said Black Omari, narrowing his gaze. "One broken woman in borrowed robes. You alone."

"I have allies in the south, waiting for my return," she lied. "I will admit, I underestimated Lysimachus' hold on the city. I thought to sneak in with a small group and rescue my daughter so Lysimachus had no hold on me when we attacked. Her death changes everything."

When the sharp, cutting laugh exited Black Omari's lips, quickly followed by the thug joining him in amusement, Heron knew she had erred, but not how.

Her nerves were still raw from witnessing her daughter's death, exhaustion and fear had dulled it to a slow throb. The laughter at her misfortune was like salt rubbed into the wounds, at first.

Then Heron came to the realization that Black Omari and his thug weren't laughing at Sepharia's death. The crime lord had a dark soul, but he wasn't mad. In fact, his association with Osiris suggested otherwise. Osiris was the god of the dead. Reverence was his relationship to the end of life, not mockery.

As laughter fell upon her ears, echoing through the circular room, Heron saw the truth of her error.

"Oh, I *am* a fool," Heron muttered under her breath.

She turned to them, sensing the thug had moved closer, but he was still stationed in the doorway, the only exit from the villa.

"Sepharia is alive, isn't she?" asked Heron, and in her head, she thought, *and I had no reason to risk coming here.*

Black Omari clasped his hands in front, a smile leaking from his pursed, wrinkled lips. She was missing something else, she knew, but decided speaking would only further endanger her, if she wasn't in grave peril already.

"No," said Black Omari, "you right of it. She gone through Gap of Abydos, riding River of Death in the Meseket Boat made of amethyst and emerald, jasper and turquoise, lazuli and gold. In three days. Three days, your daughter risen again. Three days alive. Again."

Memory came to Heron like a dream. She said the words in a trance: *"Nine times I have brought you here to witness the powers of Sobek. Nine times you have seen the miracle from my hand. Today marks the Tenth. Do not be afraid, for Sobek controls the waters of creation, and anything is possible with him."*

"Yes. Yes," said Black Omari. "You heard. Ten times. Now eleven. He holds waters of creation. Gift of life."

Heron opened her mouth to refute the old Egyptian, but saw the light in Black Omari's gaze and closed it instead. He believed the gift. And if he believed it, so too would the rest of the city.

But Heron knew the truth. Lysimachus was using her miracles against her. Somehow, he'd tricked her, and the rest of the city, into believing that Sepharia was being executed each time.

Heron rubbed the spot next to her forehead, trying to erase the ball of tension. Miracles had always been performed in the temples. No one had ever thought to do them in public, but how ingenious of Lysimachus. That was how he'd gained control of the city. He'd made them believers, even if they didn't respect his crocodile god. It explained the crowd's somber acceptance of the events.

The thug, Dranis, stared at her with what could only be anticipation, with lips slightly parted, and fists flexing at his side. She could smell his body odor and his awful breath from across the room.

She'd never needed to come to Black Omari's for help. Sepharia was alive. The emotions in her chest were held in conflict, one part expanding in joy, the other contracting with the expectation of her coming death. Black Omari was not planning on letting her leave.

"You want what Lysimachus offers, don't you?" asked Heron.

Black Omari's eyes betrayed him, widening, as he licked his lips.

"I am old man. Older than you think. I enjoy my power. If he offers waters of creation, waters of life, then maybe time come out of darkness," said Black Omari.

Heron rubbed her arm absently. Even though she knew it was a lie, she couldn't refute the miracles, not in a way that would make Black Omari believe. If she'd had something substantial to offer, she might have had a chance, but Lysimachus' power had invaded even the darkest corners of the city.

"Are Osiris and Sobek not opposed? How can you embrace your god's enemy?" she asked, glancing upward briefly, hoping that the steam mechanical outside would explode soon, to provide her with the opportunity for escape.

"When it time for Meseket Boat, I go with Osiris, but Sobek offers freedom from journey."

The thug took a step towards her. He was being held back by his master, but when Black Omari gave the word, Dranis would take her. Death or trade to Lysimachus, she wasn't sure.

"I am not alone," she said, feeling time down to the grains. "My allies wait outside and if I do not emerge from this villa soon, they will take action."

Black Omari chuckled lightly, and lifted his hand to her as if he were offering a gift. "Lies, shapeshifter. You essence of lies."

"Remember what I did to Rome," she countered, willing the steam mechanical to explode, as Dranis took another step. "The fruits of destruction are within my grasp. If they do not see me soon, they will unleash them upon your villa. First a warning, then annihilation. Do not oppose me. We could be allies."

Black Omari tilted his head and his eyes glistened. The hand that he'd held out to her, he slowly closed into a fist, one finger at a time.

"You no allies. Only alone. Stupid woman. I see you come. I know your trick. Steam mechanical outside. I sent men after you come. They take it for me. A gift."

The air fled Heron's lungs. She backed against the stone pharaoh, her wooden leg clicking against the marble floor. Dranis advanced on her with fists held to his sides. He looked hungry.

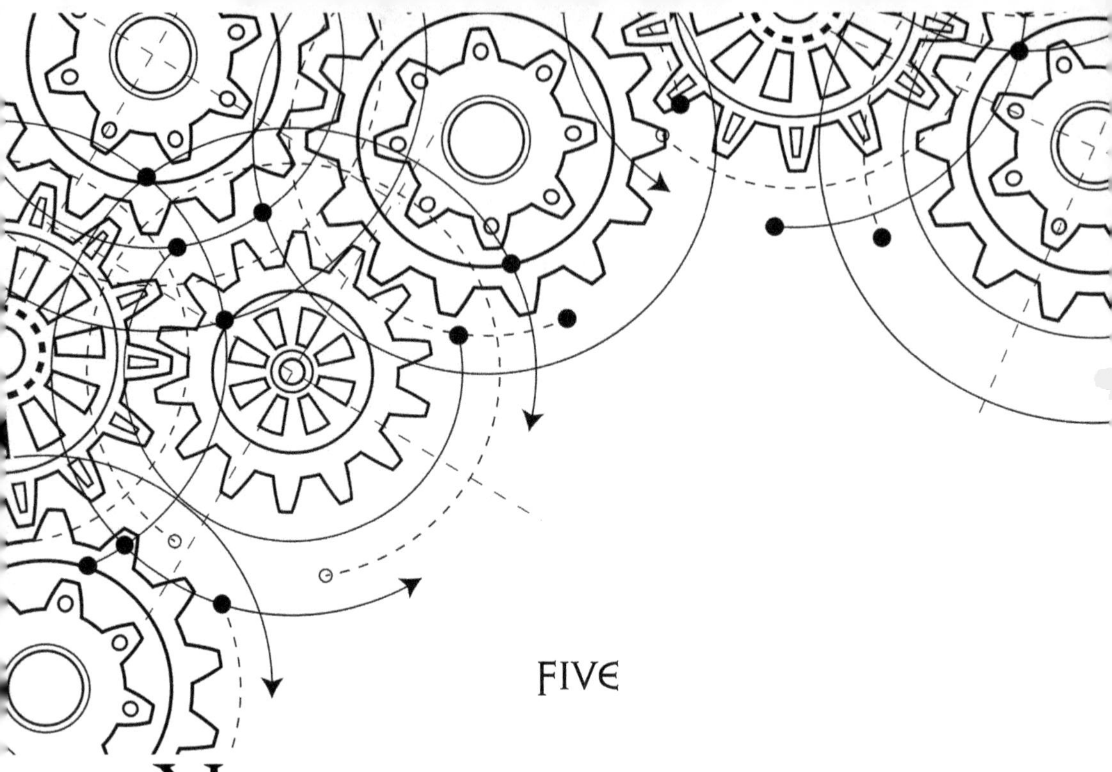

FIVE

Nothing hurt as much as knowing she'd been so irrevocably wrong. Except Dranis advancing on her, ready to throttle the life from her body.

She knew Black Omari wasn't going to trade her to Lysimachus by the way the thug's lips were parted. She could see by the lust in his eyes that he was going to enjoy killing her. The words she'd spoken to him upon entering the villa hadn't helped, nor the previous visit, so many years ago. She'd made a fool of him now and then.

The stone pharaoh cradled against her back, tipping a hair as she leaned into it. The pedestal was as high as her knees. Heron wrapped her hand around the staff.

She glanced to Black Omari, hoping to see restraint in his gaze, but he watched passively, stroking his chin.

The pugion inside her sleeve bumped against her wrist. She palmed the weapon and kept it held against her leg. Dranis' horrid breath washed over her. He was a man in a killing lust, breathing heavily.

When Dranis stepped close enough to grab her, Heron thrust her arm out against the thug's stomach and released the hidden blade with a click. Dranis flinched and grabbed her wrist, slowly looking down.

The blade had gone into his stomach as far as the curve of the tip. Dranis squeezed, putting pressure on her wrist until she released the pugion. The blade fell limply against his stomach before clattering to the marble floor. A blot of blood formed on his tunic.

Dranis released her wrist before setting his meaty hands around her neck. Rather than look into his eyes, Heron stared at the pugion, lying spent between their feet.

My invention failed me, was the only thing she could think about as the hands around her neck began to squeeze. His thumb jammed against her larynx, bringing spit to her lips.

Heron clutched at the staff with one hand, while her stump pushed at Dranis' chest. Spots formed in her vision. The statue of the pharaoh rocked against her back.

Using the stone staff as a lever, Heron leaned back, tipping the statue as far back as it would go before falling over. Then at the moment the weight shifted to the front, she yanked on it.

The statue, which was taller than Dranis, tipped forward. The weight of the stone pushed her against the thug, breaking the grip of his hands from her neck. Her face smashed against the rope scars on his neck, smeared with sweat.

When Dranis grunted and lifted his arms to stop the statue's descent, Heron let her knees buckle and slipped beneath his outstretched arms.

The statue caught Dranis right in the chest and slammed him onto the marble floor, bones crackling like reeds upon impact.

Black Omari watched with open mouthed horror. Heron looked to him and then Dranis, wheezing blood bubbles beneath the ancient stone statue.

She thought briefly of attacking Black Omari, but the blade on the floor had no handle, and even with his advanced age, she wasn't sure she could overwhelm him physically.

So she fled the room, her wooden leg pounding against the marble like a drum, as Black Omari looked on. The jarring impact of the wooden leg hitting the floor pinched the buckles against her leg, but she ran on, knowing that once the crime lord awakened from his stupor, he would send other men after her.

Outside the villa, she didn't dare the entrance. It was likely other men were stationed at the gate.

Into the olive grove she went, holding her arm and stump before her as she ran blindly into the darkness, her eyes reflecting the ghosts of flickering torchlight. She tripped over a gnarled root, twisted her knee, and went spiraling into the dirt.

Stunned, she lay a moment, blinking away the misshapen lights on her vision, tasting salt and dirt. Heron checked her surroundings as she heard shouts from inside the villa.

Scrambling to her feet, she looked like a newborn foal, but no one could mock her in the darkness, and even if so, mockery was a better course than strangulation.

At the wall, she quickly realized she couldn't climb the ancient olive trees and even if she could, the branches weren't near enough to the wall to enable her escape.

From the front of the villa, lantern and torch lights bobbed in loose formation. They were still deciding which way they thought she might have gone. It was clear without Dranis' direction, the other thugs were lost.

Heron put the wall on her right and ran forward, using it to keep vertical.

At intervals, she risked glancing backwards, catching the bobbing lights spreading out into the olive tree grove. Muffled shouts followed.

When her wooden leg caught a raised edge, Heron tumbled to the ground, knee hitting metal before shoulder slammed into the rocks. Shocks of pain went up her leg. Heron rolled to her side, sucking the blood from her palm.

In the darkness, she saw the faint outline of a sewer cover that ran from the back of an out building. She'd stumbled upon the sewer connection between the villa's latrine and the street. The out building had been hidden by darkness.

A quick whiff confirmed her estimation. The rotting fecal matter beneath the covering put off an awful stench, even worse than the thug's breath.

The iron plate behind the building was used to cover the main trench that went into the sewers. Occasionally, such trenches needed to be cleaned out when they clogged.

The lights of pursuit had made it through the olive grove. She was at the back of the estate. Heron gave a long exhale and shook her head.

Then she dug her fingers into the key hole on the plate. A lever was usually used to lift the iron plate, but she didn't have time to find the rod that was probably hanging on the inner wall in the out-building.

She strained against the weight of it, but was able to lift it until it was tilted on its side. Without the covering, the stench rivaled the latrines of the Underworld.

Heron suppressed a gag, coughing a breath that shot from her clamped lips. Then she stepped into the hole, feeling the sewer mud envelope her sandaled foot. Crouching into the hole, she let the iron plate slowly close over her body until it clanked into place, making her cringe.

The sewer trench was barely tall enough for her to crawl on her hands and knees. Heron crept forward, mud sucking at her limbs as she struggled through. The passage had to lead to the sewers, but she feared a grate might block the way, as it had at the canal.

Not a length from her entrance to the trench, footsteps clanged across the iron plate. She'd been trying to hold her breath, but the startling noise, unsealed her lips and the overwhelming odor conjured bile into her mouth.

The men were standing above the sewer, discussing which way she might have gone, not realizing she was right beneath their feet. Heron's vomit reflex overcame her fear and she convulsed, shooting stomach acid from her lips.

With wet eyes, and snot dripping from her nose, she waited to hear them opening the sewer lid. But to her relief, they moved on.

Heron shuffled forward, spitting and gagging as she went until she bumped her head against a round opening. The way wasn't blocked by a grate, but upon investigation with her hand, it appeared the hole might be too small for her to pass.

Heron pushed her head against her shoulder and snaked her arm through first, then using her hand against the other side of the hole, she pulled her way through. The stone edge cut against her back, but the sewer mud provided lubrication to slip through. She had a moment of worry when her hips caught on the opening, but she grunted and pulled hard, thankful she had a slight figure.

Inside the main sewer line, Heron scrambled to her feet. She felt around the walls and ceiling to confirm what she knew. In previous years, she'd supervised major repairs to the sewer systems for the Roman Empire, though it'd never been profitable, since the Roman officer in charge of the project funneled most of the gold into his funds, leaving her to manage it at one third of the expected cost.

Looking back, she supposed she should be grateful. If the officer had not used the project as his personal coffers, she'd be stuck on the other side of the opening, blocked by a thoroughly impassible grate.

For the most part, the sewer system, much like the streets of Alexandria, were as orderly as an army. The major sewer lines crisscrossed the city going north to south, and east to west. Once she figured out which street she was under, she'd be able to traverse the city without being seen.

The bigger question was, what was she going to do now?

Eventually, rescue Sepharia, yes, but she needed allies. Zeno had told her Dominitus would be in the city, though she'd seen no sign of him. Something about the Dutiful Octagon, a place she'd never heard of. It was more likely that the Senator had fled the city when he realized that Lysimachus and his crocodile cult had taken control.

The practical answer was that she needed a bath first. She shuddered to think of what clung to her legs and arms. She'd find no allies looking or smelling like she did.

A bath could be found in the sea, or one of the canals. The sewers and the canals sometimes overflowed into each other. But the sea seemed a safer place. If she made her way north and east, she could reach the Great Library by the sewer system. If there was anywhere in Alexandria she could find allies, it would be in the Great Library.

Heron placed her stump against the wet wall on her left and prepared to head in the direction she hoped was north, when behind her, something large splashed into the sewer water.

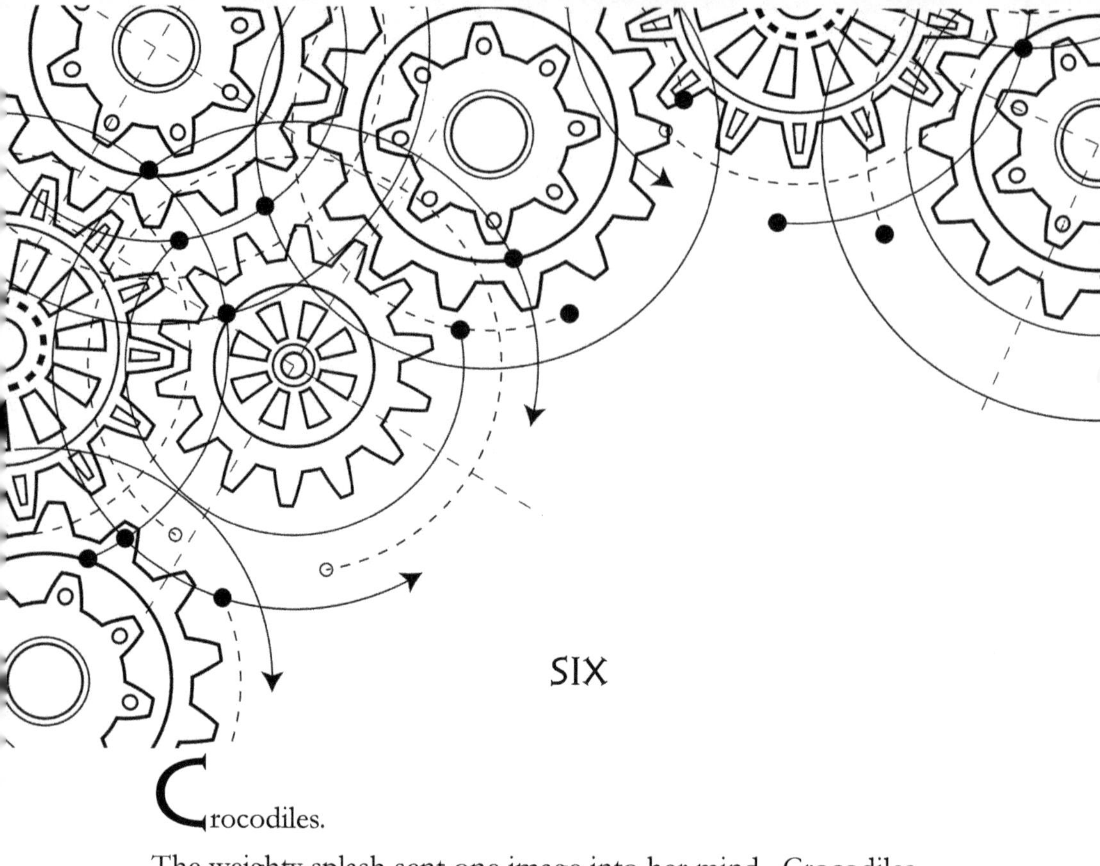

SIX

Crocodiles.

The weighty splash sent one image into her mind. Crocodiles.

The Alexandrian canal system ran from the city to the tributaries of the Nile. The city used it to move goods by barge to trade routes connected to the Red Sea.

While the canal system allowed for the easy transfer of goods to the Nile, it also provided a path for the occasional curious crocodile to make its way to Alexandria.

It was rare, but sometimes the creatures swam up the canal in search of food, especially during the flood season. At least twice in her memory, children had been snatched from the water's edge by a crocodile that had made it past the grates. Probably they had come up when they were slender enough to fit through the iron bars and then grew fat on the rats and rubbage thrown into the sewers.

Heron thought she heard a snort, felt breath against the back of her calf. She didn't wait to find out and burst forward, keeping her stump against the wall to keep from falling over unseen obstacles.

Labored breath filled her ears, so she couldn't tell if the creature, or whatever it was, followed her. She didn't care to know.

The time she'd spent in the pit of Sobek roared into her mind, until a crimson glare filled her eyes, despite the darkness.

The map in her head disappeared in a haze of stumbling and splashing through the water. She ran for a long while, each time she thought about stopping, the itch of teeth against the bare flesh on the back of her legs forced her to continue as if she were an automata geared to run forever.

It was only when she ran into a dead end, a grate set across the sewer, probably to block entrance to one of the old Empire's offices, that she could convince her legs to stop.

Heaving terrible breaths of fear, Heron clung to the grate, hanging her weight upon it. Heartbeats pounded in her ears, blocking all sound. Her right leg stung with the cuts and scrapes she'd endured during her flight through the sewers.

When at last her heart had calmed, Heron felt faint vibrations through the iron bars. The vibration rose and fell randomly. Heron meditated on the pattern until she realized it was the passing of wagons above her on the street. With the mystery solved, she left the dead end, keeping the wall against her stump.

Once she started moving, the darkness pressed in around her. Like ink stains, she felt the blackness etch onto her skin. It took all her will not to start running again.

"It's only darkness," she whispered. "We fear what we don't understand."

It seemed like a good thing to say, but once she was done speaking, the urge to flee flooded back in. Heron wiped her face on her forearm, careful not to use the part of her arm that had been doused in sewer mud.

"I need to stay calm. Running again will only get me hurt. It probably wasn't even a crocodile. A large rat, maybe. I was lucky to not knock myself out running into a wall."

Speaking felt good, even though it would give her position away should a crocodile actually be lurking in the darkness. But she decided that running was worse.

"At least, Sepharia's alive, right? Though, I've smelled better." She slipped into silence as she traversed a shallow channel, careful not to linger in the water too long. "But how did Lysimachus do it? How did he make the crowd think her head had been cut from her body?"

Something else was nagging at her thoughts. When it came to her, it turned her stomach sour, even worse than the vomiting.

"Why was Sepharia helping him? She could have fought. Yelled something out. My miracles required the absolute cooperation of everyone involved. Why would she help him?"

When the answer stayed hidden in the darkness, Heron kept speaking, "But even if she is helping him, for reasons I can't understand, I need help to get her back. Why couldn't Hoth be here, or Zeno? Why'd they all have to die, or leave me?"

A weight settled on her shoulders as she trudged through the darkness. At the edge of her perception, the memories of the temple lurked like a crocodile.

"Maybe Sepharia's helping him because Sobek is real," she smirked. "Oh, how the gods would laugh if they existed. How many trials can they put someone through and that person still not believe? If they were real, I could imagine them betting on me, throwing their silvers down, guessing when I might finally break. It'd be a cosmic joke worthy of an oration from Socrates, though I'd prefer Aristotle, since Socrates was an arrogant arse."

Heron splashed across another shallow canal when she noticed a faint nimbus ahead. It took a moment for her to realize she was seeing light.

She followed the source, turning twice before she could hear a strange rumble, like stones being thrown together.

It wasn't until she came out into the daylight that she realized it was the sea. The channel at the center of the sewer passage ran down a ramp, staining the crashing waves with black waters.

Across from her position, the white stone buildings on the Isle of Pharos reflected the morning light until they were a pale glare. Further east on the Isle, the Lighthouse stretched into the sky, first on a square base hundreds of cubits high, and then the observation layer, a building with eight sides, held the beacon level up like the fabled Atlas. On the Heptastadion, the land bridge that connected the island to the city, a wagon being driven by a pair of white robed priests made its way across, the snaps of their whip lost to the gentle crash of waves upon the shore.

She'd come out near the Moon Gate, west of the Kibotos, an artificial port that connected to the canal. Head-sized rocks covered the beach. Behind the sewer exit, a cliff wall extended upward. Above the crashing waves, the early morning traffic headed out the Moon Gate could be heard clattering across the cobblestones, shouting to each other and cracking whips at their teams of horses.

Heron made her way to the water's edge, staying on the high side of the currents that swept the contents of the sewer south of the city. Standing in knee high, rolling waves trapped by the inlet, Heron scrubbed the gunk from her arms and legs, using salt water and sand.

The robe, once green, was stained black. While picking the filth from her fingernails, Heron caught the smell of burning parchment again. A huge stone wall blocked her view to the east, but a trail of smoke rose into the sky, somewhere in the vicinity of the Great Library.

When she was as clean as her circumstances would allow, and ignoring the grumble in her belly and the way her tongue stuck to the roof of her mouth, Heron headed back into the sewers. With her location confirmed, she knew exactly how to reach the Great Library, where she hoped she might find allies.

After a nearly straight shot beneath the city, Heron came out of the sewers behind the Temple of Saturn. The halls of the Roman god nearly butted up against the warehouses controlled by the Great Library. From them, scroll runners would take the offerings from the ships and have them copied by scribblers.

It seemed a fresh memory that she'd taken Agog to the docks to show him the mechanism of the Great Library and explain her thoughts on the fires that had burned them.

When Heron rounded the corner of the temple, her heart froze and her limbs struck dumb as if she'd been wrapped in chains. A bonfire had been built on the docks in a wide brazier, twice the length of a man.

Instead of runners carrying armloads of papyrus scrolls from the ships into the warehouse, they carried them from the warehouse and dumped them into the fire.

Soldiers with crocodiles stamped into their leather breastplates watched the men amble from the open doors. A scraggly runner in a soot covered tunic took a laggard pace, which wasn't enough for one soldier, who cracked a whip at the man's feet until the runner hurried forward.

Both of Heron's knees buckled when the armload of scrolls went spilling into the crackling fire, crisping to crimson lace that floated into the air on smoke and heat. Tears fled from her eyes in disbelief.

Kneeling on the stone, face numb and fingers trembling, Heron didn't hear the soldier approach until he was only paces away. His lips soured into a frown as she turned to him. He placed his hands on his hips and spread his elbows wide, the crocodile helm casting a split shadow across his face.

"You're coming with me," he said.

SEVEN

"What?" Heron muttered, glancing behind her to see the sewer entrance was too far away. She'd barely be able to reach her feet before he could grab her.

"You're coming with me," he said, his lip curling back. He could have cut her with his eyes as they narrowed to thin slits.

Heron patted her waist, expecting to find a blade. The soldier's brow hunched into a knot.

"Are you deaf?" he asked.

Heron swallowed, trying to unstick her tongue from the roof of her mouth. She shook her head.

"Good," said the soldier, rubbing the back of his neck. "Seems half of you crocodile priests are imbeciles. Come with me."

She rose and followed. He glanced over his shoulder when her wooden leg hit the dock, but made no mention of it.

Nearing the bonfire, the heat made itself known against her face. When another runner approached with an armful of scrolls, she wanted to rush over and knock them from his hands. They flaked and curled with fire as they slid down the inside of the brazier. As each layer of papyrus exploded into flame, it revealed the ink lettering beneath, only moments before the blaze claimed the next section.

In mere moments, Heron watched irreplaceable knowledge turn to smoke and ash. Her eyes ached with the loss, stinging from standing so close to the brazier.

If only I had a machine that could copy these scrolls faster than they could burn them.

A hand touched her arm. The soldier. He looked at her as if she were a witch, or about to turn into a winged serpent.

"The water pump," he said, nodding towards a wagon covered in brass containers and bright gears. "I thought the high priest sent you to fix the water pump."

"The water pump?" she said, stumbling in the direction of the wagon.

"Yes, it needs to be fixed. We have orders to keep it working in case the fire gets loose. We spray the dock near the brazier from time to time, to keep it wet, but in this heat and from the constant burning, we have to spray it often."

"And how long have we been burning?" the words left her mouth in a dream.

"A couple of months now." The soldier straightened his breastplate. "Maybe since winter. Without the scholars attacking us, we've gotten a lot more burnt. Hang a few robed men and the rest fall in line."

"Since winter...?"

She'd wastefully spent the winter recovering when she should have been back in Alexandria. Months of burning? If she'd been tied to four horses and whipped it would have hurt less.

"It doesn't matter, though. We just need the pump fixed. Wouldn't want the whole city to burn on account of these scrolls," said the soldier.

"No, we wouldn't," said Heron, stumbling to the water wagon. Her limbs had turned to lead. She leaned against a wagon wheel and buried her face in her elbow.

When she composed herself enough to turn around, she realized the soldier was staring at her. She blinked away the daze and turned back to the broken water wagon before the soldier realized she'd not been sent by the high priest.

The water wagon had a steam mechanical on the back end and two enormous brass pots on the front, stationed like towers at the corners of a walled town. A wide leather hose snaked across the dock and down a hole into the sea. The wagon could pump water and send it out a second leather hose that lay curled like a snake between the wagon and the burning brazier.

Heron pulled herself onto the wagon, using the wagon spoke for a step and a brass pipe for a handle. Hitching her wooden leg over the side took three tries until she'd rolled onto the platform. The soldier had a smirk on his face when she dared to glance back.

For all the effort expended climbing onto the water wagon, it took her exactly one second to determine the root cause of the problem. The valve connected to the leather hose that siphoned water from the sea had been turned off.

Heron surveyed the other levers before deciding how she was going to *fix* the water pump. It would do her no good to sabotage it, since she wanted it to protect the city from being burnt to the ground. But she couldn't leave without taking action.

"I need to run the steam mechanical to understand what's wrong," she said, as she started it up. The soldier looked skeptical until the mechanical roared to life. Clearly, he hadn't thought she could actually start it. While the mechanical gathered steam, Heron surveyed the streets that led down to the docks.

Horse-drawn wagons moved in a sluggish tromp, less of them than she was used to seeing. The docks were barren, too. Only a few of the piers had ships tied off to anchor. The sounds on the docks were normally filled with industry, but today, only the crackling fire could be heard.

Even the white walls of the Great Library seemed listless and gray. Black stains collected at the corners of the walls and the patchy clouds above seemed to hold a haze over the city. The dome at the end of the Curiosity Rooms had broken out windows where colored glass should have reflected the sun. The whole structure looked like an old man too tired to wake from his slumber.

A rage filled her chest. She barked out to the soldier, "Grab that leather hose." She motioned to the other soldiers nearby. "Point it near the brazier, I'm going to turn it on."

Crouched down, Heron could see the wear marks where the lever had been set. To keep the hose from flailing away, the water pressure was kept low. Heron had no intention of being helpful.

When she cranked it on, the water pump made a gurgle, as air passed through the diaphragm inside the brass towers. Then, the hose bulged until it undulated away from the soldier and began spraying wildly all over the dock.

Heron jammed the lever into place, and bent the thin metal around the pipe to keep it from being turned off. The soldier shouted for her to stop it, but she threw her hand and stump into the air as if she didn't know how.

Each time the hose whipped past the brazier, steam hissed from the metal. One particularly virulent direct blast made the wide disc pop, sending fire and ashes in a cloud, as the instant cooling deformed the brazier.

The other two soldiers ran to help their compatriot. The runners, silently trudging to dump the next load, looked to her in confusion. Heron waved them back towards the warehouses and they dutifully scurried back, quicker than they'd approached.

While the soldiers fought the leather hose, Heron dumped more fuel into the fire chamber. The hose was the mythical Lernaean Hydra, and the soldiers could not slay it. One even pulled his gladius, determined to cut the hose in half, but it whipped around and knocked the blade from his grip, punching him in the face with water.

The brazier had taken enough hits that a huge cloud of steam rose above the docks, spreading out like a haze. Heron recognized that the events on the docks would quickly bring others and she needed to leave before she was recaptured.

As she dismounted the wagon, a touch more graceful than climbing on, the first soldier grabbed her arm.

"Make it stop," he shouted, spraying spit across her face.

She was about to fall into the confused scholar routine, when she noticed a host of movement on the finger of land that held the Palace. A tight formation of soldiers wearing crimson and gold gear were attacking the main buildings.

Heron pointed in the direction of the Palace. "We're under attack! Quickly! Gather your men and go!"

The soldier hesitated, glancing at the swirling hose spitting water in all directions, before yelling to his mates. The trio of soldiers went running for their horses, which were stationed nearby.

Even as the crocodile soldiers rode off, Heron could tell the attackers at the Palace were already fading away. The three soldiers would arrive late to the battle, as would any other defenders.

Heron pulled her robe around her body and hurried past the warehouses to the merchant district behind the Great Library. By the time she made it to the corner, the untended hose had put the fire out, leaving a billowing column of steam to roll into the sky. It wouldn't keep them from burning scrolls forever, but at least it gave her time to think of something else—but she needed allies.

Entering the merchant district, she remembered one, should the tavern still exist. Heron made her way towards the tavern named Cassandra's Tears, quickly but carefully, keeping an eye out for soldiers and priests, and wondering who it was that had attacked the Palace.

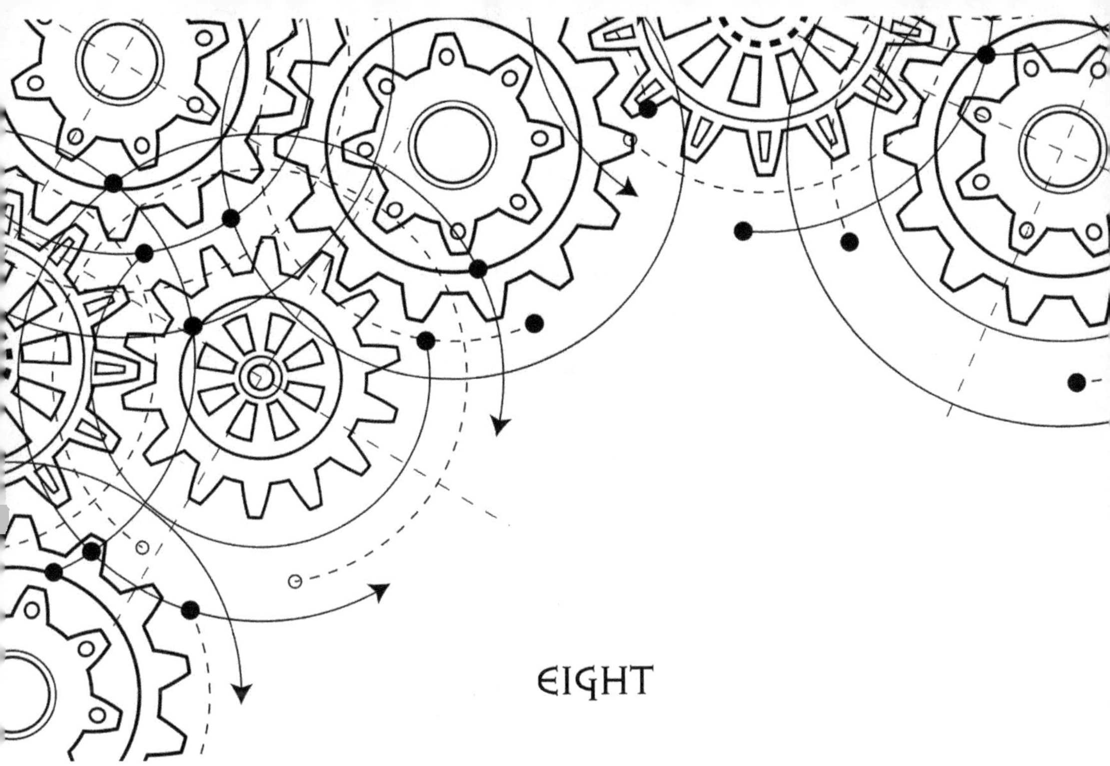

EIGHT

Warped windows obscured the inside of the Cassandra's Tears. No lights flickered from the interior, nor did even one sound emanate from the timbered walls.

The street was desolate. Not even the clatter of a wagon could be heard in the distance. The only sound intruding was a lone seagull patiently circling.

Heron gently tapped on the heavy door, using the meat of her palm, hoping the rattle against the frame would bring Arethussa. When she could wait no longer, Heron gave three swift raps and waited.

With her ear pressed against the wood, Heron thought she heard shuffling feet. Heron placed her lips against the crack where the door met frame, and called out in a loud whisper: "Arethussa. Arethussa, are you there? Open up, if you can. It's a friend."

The handle rattled and the door opened all at once, leaving Heron to fall unceremoniously into the room. She crashed to her knees and looked up in time to hear a crossbow click into place.

"Away with you, priest. I don't care about your scaly god. Come back again and I'll put a bolt through your neck," said a woman with dark hair, wispy and unkempt, making a wild halo around her head.

"Arethussa. It's me, Heron."

The crossbow dipped away from Heron's face. "Heron? By the gods, it's true. You *are* a shapeshifter."

Heron expected revulsion and the return of the crossbow to her face, but Arethussa threw the weapon onto the nearest table and swept Heron into her arms.

"The door," Heron muttered, patting Arethussa's shoulders as she enthusiastically gave a smothering hug. "We should close the door."

Arethussa snapped upright as if a spring had been loosed. "Yes, the door."

With the lock in place, Arethussa helped Heron to her feet.

"Why are you wearing their garb? I know you cannot be in league with them," asked Arethussa, biting her lower lip. "And your friend. The one you brought with you last time. Where is he?"

A shock of memory went through her gut. She tried not to flinch. "Jarngard. He's dead."

Arethussa's face screwed into a knot, lines marking the repetition of the familiar emotion. "Apologies."

"Don't be." *I've grieved enough for everyone.* "I have bigger problems, now. Tell me everything you know."

Arethussa looked around, nose wrinkling in disgust. "What is that smell?"

Heron swallowed. "That's me. I had to escape an unfortunate situation by crawling through the sewers. I cleaned up in the sea as best as I could."

Arethussa grabbed Heron's hand, the warmth and pressure felt calming. "Before we talk, you must clean up. Have you eaten?"

"No," Heron confessed.

Arethussa pushed Heron towards a bar stool. "First food, then a bath, then we talk."

Protests otherwise were quickly ignored and soon, Heron found herself inhaling a piece of stringy spiced meat that had slender bones and tasted like boar that had been raised on scraps. Heron didn't want to complain and instead busied herself chugging her mug of ale. By the time Heron finished eating, the hot bath was ready.

Before Heron could open her mouth, Arethussa had pulled the robe away. Naked and shivering, Heron tried to cover her breasts and pubic hair.

Arethussa rested her chin in her hand, brow heavy with thought. Her sea-blue stola expanded as she took a deep breath.

"What have they done to you?" she asked. "I'd hoped the stories were just that. Stories."

The will to answer seemed to wilt from Heron's lips. Arethussa knelt before Heron and began undoing the buckles that held the wooden leg to her thigh. Then she helped Heron climb into the steaming water which stung the pink flesh on her stumps.

Heron held her breath and dipped below the surface, letting the water surround her. When her heartbeat became a great pulsing drumbeat in the void, she broke the surface.

"I feel dizzy," said Heron, stretching her jaw.

"Beer and the hot water."

Heron nodded limply as her body wanted to dissolve into the warm bath.

She expected Arethussa to have left, but the tavern owner surprised Heron with a washrag and soap. The woman set to scrubbing Heron's neck right away.

"I'd like some flesh left when you're done," said Heron.

"Did you roll through the sewer or swim in it? It's hard to tell."

"I didn't have time to be careful. And then there was..."

Heron wasn't sure she wanted to bring up the crocodile in the sewer. It was entirely possible that it'd been her imagination.

"There was what?" asked Arethussa.

"Nothing," said Heron. "But tell me about Alexandria before I fall asleep."

"What do you want to know?"

Heron cupped some water in one hand and splashed it in her face. "I've been away from the city for almost two years. Tell me about Alexandria. Tell me what you know of the survivors of Rome. Tell me everything."

Arethussa set forth in a patient voice and preceded to tell Heron everything, and when something wasn't clear, Heron asked questions until she understood.

When she was finished, Heron realized it was worse than she'd thought. The cult of Sobek had arrived the previous summer, when Lysimachus had returned to Alexandria and begun his miracles.

At first, Arethussa explained, the crocodile priest had been mocked. But even she knew something was different, when scholars in her tavern began discussing the resurrections of Sepharia. Even the gas sniffers and rock lickers from the Great Library, the ones who could barely be bothered to put on clothes or wipe their privates after the latrine, took notice of the crocodile priest.

Arethussa couldn't quite explain when it was that Lysimachus took over the city. But the first scholar wasn't hung until the winter solstice. Then, a period of unrest took the Great Library, and afterwards, the crocodile priests started burning scrolls.

By this time, the city was firmly in Lysimachus' control. At the seventh miracle, everyone in the city was forced to attend. There were dissenters, of course, but after a few hangings everyone came out for the eighth miracle.

Of the miracles, Arethussa knew little. Despite the warnings, she'd stayed in her tavern, since she had no business left with the Library all but shut down. But each miracle was said to be different from the last. Sepharia had been killed and resurrected in numerous ways, each time brought back from the dead, to show the power of the crocodile god.

Finally, it was known, that at the twelfth miracle, during the Festival of the Nile when the flooding of the great river was celebrated across the city, something wondrous would occur. Wondrous to the followers of the crocodile god, and Heron suspected nothing she would think was wondrous.

Arethussa knew nothing else about the comings and goings in the city. She stayed to the merchant district, trading coin and favor for food. She had heard about a rebellion, soldiers in Roman garb attacking the crocodile soldiers, which Heron confirmed with her own sighting, but nothing else.

Arethussa hadn't heard of the Dutiful Octagon either, and thought the name too odd to be an establishment of drinking. Heron agreed, though she had no experience of such places.

When the water got cold, Heron was helped into a cotton robe while Arethussa picked through her closet for suitable attire. She pulled out each item, while Heron shook her head.

"What about this lovely saffron stola?" Arethussa asked, holding up the gauzy fabric while biting her lower lip.

"And fall on my face every time I took a step. I can't recall the last time I wore woman's clothing," said Heron. "This is pointless."

"We could cut your hair again and I have some tunics from when I ran that school?" asked Arethussa.

"No. I'm not cutting my hair. The tunic, yes, but I don't want to hide anymore. If I'm going to get Sepharia back, then I'm doing it as a woman.

No more lies."

A gleam sparkled in Arethussa's eyes. "I should have seen it before. That you weren't really a man. I was quite smitten at the time, if you must know. Even so much as lighting candles at the Temple of Eros. But then you stopped coming around. You could have told me."

"A secret isn't a secret if people know," said Heron, running her hand through her thick hair to dry it. "Knowing would have put you in danger."

Arethussa thrust her chest forward. Even though the woman had wrinkles around her eyes and the corners of her mouth, she was still a beautiful woman. The marks of age only enhanced her beauty, deepening it.

"I would have gladly put myself in harm's way for you."

Heron rubbed the edge of the robe, feeling the threads along the hem. "Would you do so now?"

Arethussa rushed to Heron's side and took her hand. She knelt, bringing a blush to Heron's cheeks. Then Arethussa kissed Heron's hand.

"Anything for the *Michanikos*. The heart of Alexandria."

Heron swallowed. Such devotion usually met with an unfortunate end. She'd left so many friends in her wake.

But she had no other way to get Sepharia back.

"I'll need your help. It'll be dangerous."

Arethussa brightened, her rose-red lips parting in a smile. "Are we going to get your daughter?"

"It would be my heart's desire. But, no. We start small. First, we need to stop them from burning more scrolls. We have time until the next miracle. In another month, right?" Arethussa nodded. "Then the scrolls it is. Do you have access to any equipment? I have an idea, but it'll take time to prepare."

"The other merchants in the area owe me some favors. I could probably get you just about anything you want," said Arethussa.

"A steam mechanical?"

Arethussa shook her head. "No. Not that. But short of that, about anything else."

"Ah, well. That's good enough." Heron squeezed her hand. "First, I need some sleep. But I'll give you a list and my remaining coins. Maybe you can start working on it. And then when I'm rested, only a few hours, don't let me sleep too long, we'll begin."

"How are we going to stop them?"

Heron tilted her head. "I'll tell you after we get the supplies. For now, I need sleep. My eyes are lead weights."

"By the gods, do you promise?" said Arethussa with a grin, tongue resting against her teeth.

Heron squeezed her hand into a fist as a flush of rage radiated through her chest. Arethussa flinched and her face paled.

"Not by the gods," said Heron, her voice shaking with anger. "By the will of our humanity, as women. First, we stop the burning, then we get Sepharia, then we take back the city."

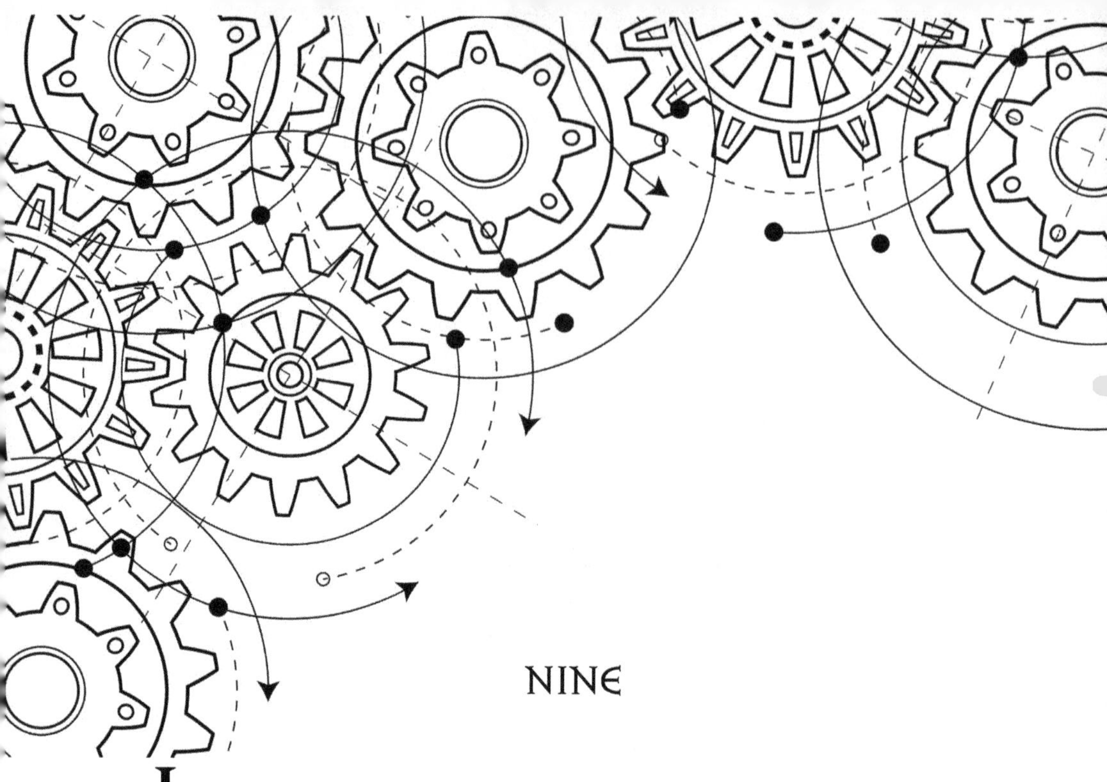

NINE

It took three days to find enough wax. Not any wax would work, otherwise they would have melted down every available candle, which were as common as flies.

The kind of wax Heron needed could be melted down and poured onto parchment to form a thin layer. It wasn't until Arethussa inquired with the Temple of Isis that they found the right wax.

Not all temples made their home in the Temple District. The Temple of Isis, in particular, was frequented by the merchants that passed through the city. Not to light candles and pay homage, but to spend time with the priestesses of Isis, some who wore blue faience beaded fish-net dresses and painted their lips bright red. The wax was poured on naked flesh, or so Heron had been told.

Melting and pouring the wax took another day, but by this time, the other preparations were complete. They waited until evening, for reasons of stealth and ambiance.

The wind was favorable for the plan, blowing northeast from the desert, bringing a hot wind that left beads of sweat on every brow. Earlier in the evening, Heron had climbed the old Roman Customs building, by way of a ladder on the back.

The building was on the docks away from the street. Its darkened halls once teemed with activity, as the Roman government took census of goods and services sold in the city. Now, without the trade that normally blew through Alexandria, it sat quietly on the edge of the piers, built on pillars that had been driven into the harbor, and surrounded by the wooden dock.

From the flat roof, she peered over the edge at the circle of firelight in the middle of the dock. Heron decided if there were gods and demons, then the conflagration was a demon from the Underworld, jealously eating the knowledge of this world. It was painful knowing that for three days, irreplaceable scrolls had been turned to ash.

She hoped she could put an end to it, but staring down from the building top, she had doubts. Heron pinched the bridge of her nose and muttered to herself, "This will work. This will work. Just don't burn down the city and do their job for them."

The water wagon had been positioned away from the burning brazier. The soldiers, three of them, had moved it further back after the incident with the hose.

Once the soldiers were done spraying down the dock, Heron watched the blob of darkness that contained the water wagon. Behind it, a piece of the night shimmered. Heron was too far away to see it clearly, but she knew that it was Arethussa sneaking down the slope from the upper city.

While Heron had been preparing the distraction, Arethussa had been lurking under the docks with a handsaw. For three days, she'd been cutting angled notches out of the wooden pillars that had been driven into the soil beneath the water.

Each night, Heron had massaged the life back into the tavern owner's arms. Arethussa had cried the first night, and Heron had offered to take her place in the morning beneath the dock, but Arethussa shook her head tightly, refusing such succor.

On the third day, they rode the little rowboat together, and wrapped the chain around the dock posts. The only thing they lacked was a steam mechanical, but the soldiers had provided her one. They needed to hook the mechanical to a spindle that they'd positioned beneath it.

Without a hand, Heron lacked the dexterity to make the connection, so she trained Arethussa. If it didn't work, she doubted they'd get another chance.

With Arethussa in position, Heron sparked the first candle to life. Then she placed the stub onto a web of thread beneath the waxy bag and held it until it expanded and lifted gently from her fingertips.

As she watched the first floating lantern drift into the open air above the docks, a crooked smile hitched the corner of her lips. What Lysimachus had perverted beneath the Temple of Sobek, she could reclaim.

It wasn't until the fourth floating lantern was in the sky that the soldiers noticed. Even from her vantage point, the ghostly lights glided as if they had thought and wings, making brief surges.

Heron knew it was the winds blowing over the city, pushing on the waxy bags, that made them move. But to the soldiers, they had no such knowledge, and when their cries of alarm carried up to the top of the customs building, her heart ached.

The soldiers moved after the floating lights, pointing and making fearful noises, questioning their misfortune to be stationed upon the dock this night. Heron glanced upward, to the crimson glow of the Lighthouse, which was no different than the floating lanterns, except that the soldiers understood it.

The runners, with armloads of scrolls, stopped to gawk. The soldiers moved further across the docks, until they'd entered the empty piers that had once housed so many ships.

At the water wagon, a dark shape moved behind the brass containers. It would take more than a few minutes to unhook the pistons from the mechanical and connect the chain that went through a hole in the dock.

Then they would only have to wait until the soldiers had to water the wooden planks for the pillars to be ripped from beneath the dock. It wouldn't stop them forever from burning scrolls, but it would make it harder, and until Heron could somehow take back the city, it was all she could do.

When the bag lights floated over the harbor, and the soldiers could not follow, they lost interest and began wandering back to the bonfire. Arethussa was still on the wagon and if the soldiers returned, they would see her.

Heron lit two more bag lights and let them ascend into the night sky. The first four were moving toward the Palace and from Heron's perch, looked like ships on the horizon.

Heron was about to light a third when the clatter of horse hooves brought her attention back to the south, towards the city. Coming down the street that led from the upper city was a group of horsemen.

The approaching party was a mix of soldiers in dark green tunics and brass helms, and priests in dark green robes with hoods pulled over their heads. Soldiers at the front and rear carried lanterns.

Heron clenched her jaw so hard it brought stars to her eyes when she saw the bald priest at the head of the column.

Lysimachus.

He must have seen the floating lights from the upper city, and knowing what they were, came to investigate. The shadowy shape on the water wagon was still dutifully working. The street circled around and past the wagon. When the soldiers brought the light, they would see Arethussa and capture her. Lysimachus would not be kind to the tavern owner. Heron squeezed back a tear thinking about what horrors awaited Arethussa.

Heron couldn't let that happen.

Before Lysimachus' party could reach the wagon, Heron took the rest of her candles, placed them on the edge of the building and lit them. When it was clear the light wasn't going to be enough, she dipped the sack with which she'd carried her supplies into the flame until it became a burning beacon.

The horses plodded inexorably towards the bottom of the hill, where they would see Arethussa. Not one head had jerked up to see her standing on the top of the Custom's building with a bag full of flame.

So Heron stepped to the edge, took a deep breath, and called out in a voice that could command armies:

"I am Heron of Alexandria."

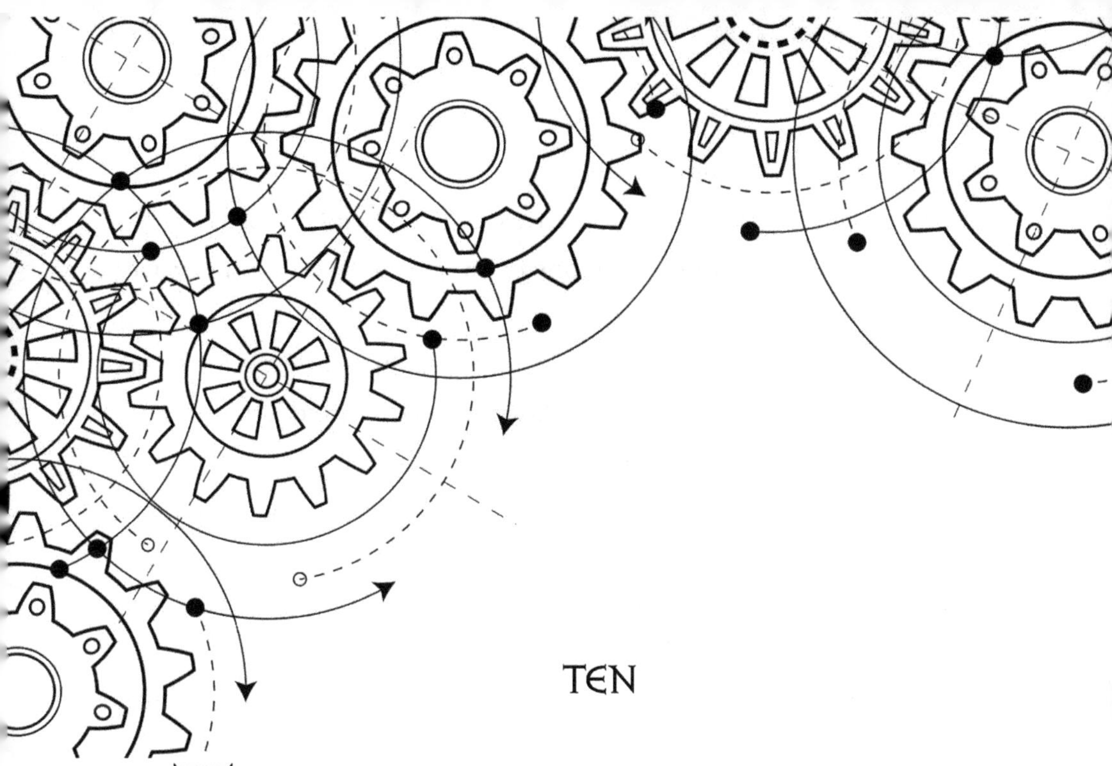

TEN

The whole sky seemed to cast its disapproving celestial gaze upon Heron, standing on the edge of the Customs Building, the echo of her voice still ringing in the air. It felt like tiny pinpricks of light from the stars needling her back, while the beacon from the Lighthouse blinked incredulously.

Flames licked at Heron's fingers from the burning bag, so she threw it over the edge. The flames wheezed before engulfing the fabric and making its way to the planks below like a falling star.

Lysimachus pointed his horse towards her. The cacophony of hooves upon the wood were the drumbeats of her impending execution.

The bald priest's mount sauntered before the building. The other soldiers and priests glanced to Lysimachus for guidance, but he gave none.

Then he noticed the fire burning in a pile on the wood and motioned for one of the soldiers to put it out.

"How careless of you, Heron of Alexandria," said Lysimachus. "You place the knowledge of the Great Library at risk with your fire. Do you plan to burn down Alexandria, too?"

"Says the man destroying that knowledge daily," said Heron.

Lysimachus turned his horse in one complete circle, clattering hooves dancing on the wood.

"That? I'm not destroying knowledge. I'm culling lies from the Great Library. The lies that do not place He Who Dwelleth Amid Terrors at the center of creation, his rightful place," said the bald priest.

Heron choked on the realization of what he was doing. She put a hand to her throat.

"Yes, you see," he said. "Don't worry, good Heron, your works will be revered. The steam mechanical, sparkpowder, the other weapons you've given me. These are the tools I will use to forge an Empire that will cover the whole world."

"There are other libraries! Other places of knowledge. You can't destroy them all!"

Lysimachus held his stump up for all to see. "Cutting away the chaff makes things stronger. I was once an addle-minded fool, until my lord Sobek gathered me in his waiting mouth and took away that which made me weak. Just like he did for you. Think of all you have accomplished since he took your hand, your foot."

"You took my hand," shouted Heron, her gut twisting. "Your cursed pet took my leg and now it's dead. Just like you will be when I'm finished."

Heron was glad she was standing upon a high place with little light to illuminate her, otherwise they would see she was shaking from head to toe like a reed in a storm.

"Come down, Heron of Alexandria," said Lysimachus. "When you do, I will give you a place of honor, just like your daughter. She sees that Sobek is the way. The true god to bring his light to the world."

"You lie, priest. Sepharia would never willingly help you. You've got her locked up, chained until you put her on your sick displays," said Heron.

Lysimachus laughed, and it was the laugh of someone in control, of a parent laughing at a child that had spoken its first words of rebellion. The crowd of priests and soldiers laughed with him, though not as openly, not as sure.

"You've always misunderstood the world, Heron. To you, it is wheel and lever, triangle and parabola, pyramid and tower. These are just patterns imprinted in the world by the gods. Born from the waters of creation," said Lysimachus. "You will never truly see until you accept He Who Dwelleth Amid Terrors as your inspiration."

"I will never."

"Your daughter did," he said.

Heron spit over the edge. "Lies."

Instead of answering, Lysimachus turned his head and spoke quietly to his priests. One of the priests on a roan horse sauntered next to Lysimachus. When the priest flipped back her hood, Heron's knees buckled.

"Sepharia!" said Heron, the name jumping from her lips.

"Come down, Mother," said Sepharia, in a level voice. "Come down and join Lord Sobek. You were always meant to be his champion. Can't you see that?"

When Lysimachus spoke his pious words, the hearing of them was a vile experience, as if she were rolling in week's old rubbage, or the coagulated blood of a sacrificed goat. Sepharia's melodic voice put a spike right into Heron's chest, a silky wedge that slipped right past her defenses.

"No," whispered Heron. "You can't. I don't understand."

"Come down," said Lysimachus, his beady eyes fixed on her. "Come down and be reunited with your daughter. I prefer you come willingly, rather than by force. There is no escape."

Heron scratched at her neck with her good hand, drawing blood, and glancing around feverishly. She tried not to look at the water wagon, to see if Arethussa was finished. At the corner of her vision, she caught movement in that direction.

Heron bit her lower lip. There would be no escape for her.

"I'll jump," said Heron suddenly. "If you send your men after me, I'll jump and put an end to this existence."

Heron thought she caught a flinch from Sepharia, but when Heron looked down, the same flat expression was on her daughter's face.

"Jump if you'd like," said Lysimachus. "While I would welcome new inventions to spread the word of Sobek, even if you did not press one more quill to parchment, we have enough of your bounty already. But I do not think you would jump. Eventually, you will come to see the glory of Sobek and join his side."

The bald priest made a motion and two soldiers hopped from their horses.

"Go around to the back. There's a ladder on that side." Then he looked up to her. "Remember, I was once the Alabarch, I know every secret in this city. You wouldn't have hidden from me for long."

Heron paced along the edge, glancing at the water. It was too far to jump without landing on the dock, a certain death at this height.

"Sepharia, please," said Heron. "Why?"

Her daughter said nothing, while Lysimachus glowered. And all the while, runners dumped more scrolls into the brazier, burning away history, silencing opposition to the crocodile god forever. Heron could taste the ash on her tongue.

Heron checked the ladder. The soldiers had found the bottom and the first had started to climb. She had no weapon. Only a few nubs of candles, flickering in the breeze.

Heron looked down at Sepharia to study her face. She didn't appeared drugged, her features were calm.

Would it hurt that much to go down and join with her daughter? Maybe she would find a way to escape later. But what if Lysimachus had truly changed Sepharia? Then joining with her would only make it worse. But was death the better alternative?

"Lysimachus," said Heron suddenly, before she lost her nerve. "I will...I will..."

The words were left floating through the air when the water wagon roared to life. Every eye turned back to see a dark shape leave the wagon and start running up the street to the upper city.

Lysimachus calmly turned to Sepharia and nodded backwards. "Take care of that."

"No, Sepharia," shouted Heron, but her daughter either did not hear or did not care. Sepharia wasn't an accomplished rider, but she handled the mount well enough to reach the fleeing Arethussa quickly.

While Sepharia rode, Heron willed the steam mechanical to gather enough steam to matter, but she knew there wasn't enough time. The pistons had to work up to speed and even from this distance, she could hear their laggard pace.

When Sepharia reached Arethussa, Heron had the hope that she would lean over and scoop up the tavern owner and take her to safety. Those dreams were dashed when Sepharia pulled a mace from the inside of her cloak.

Sepharia took Arethussa in the back of the head with the weapon. The woman crumpled to the cobblestones, her lifeless form hitting like a sack dropped from the Lighthouse.

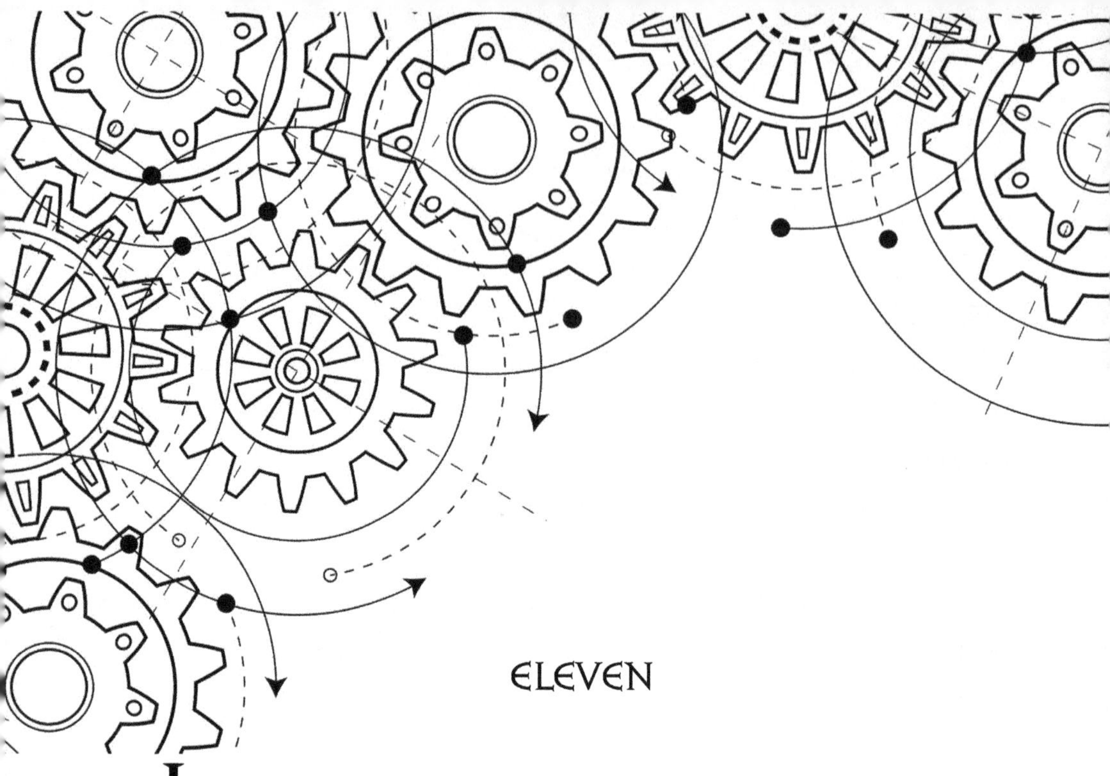

ELEVEN

In better days, before the burning of Rome and after the taking of Alexandria, Agog had told her about the cold north. He called it names like Ever Winter, and the White Lands, and spoke frequently of days so cold a man could freeze into ice two steps from his door.

He spoke of the danger of numbness, when the cold turned fingers and noses, and sometimes whole limbs, into inanimate objects. Heron knew the cold of the north hadn't swept down upon the summer city of Alexandria, yet, it seemed ice formed around her limbs, locking her into a stasis that might go on forever.

In some other world, beyond the ice, she had a daughter that had once loved her and worshiped at the altar of knowledge. Not the imposter on horseback below.

When she took her first breath after Arethussa's felling, a sharp pain formed in Heron's chest like a knot of rope stuck in her throat. Heron beat at the space between her breasts, trying to bring the world - one she once knew and understood - back.

"Sepharia."

A scuff and a clank of metal brought her around. A soldier had poked his head above the edge. The gladius in his hand clanged against the iron strut.

Using someone else's body that couldn't have been her own, Heron floated across the roof and kicked the soldier in the face with her wooden leg. He'd looked up in time to see her swinging back, his face frozen in the horrible realization that she could move faster than he'd thought.

She blinked and the soldier's lifeless body lay on the planks below. The second soldier gazed up at her and began climbing in earnest.

Heron ran back to the other edge. Lysimachus had left his men and trotted on horseback towards a rendezvous with Sepharia near the water wagon. The priest would probably instruct Sepharia to disable the steam mechanical.

The other soldiers had dismounted. Two more prepared to climb the ladder, while the other was nearly to the top. She wouldn't surprise this one.

Heron moved to the edge. It was too far to the water. The only thing left to decide was death or capture.

Looking back to the steam wagon, she wondered why it hadn't worked. Either the mechanical didn't have enough power, or Arethussa hadn't hooked it up correctly.

The second soldier poked his head above the edge with a short sword in his hand, ready to defend himself from her wooden leg. When he saw she was too far away, he quickly climbed to the roof.

Death or capture.

Which would it be?

Then a faint vibration made itself known through the structure. Heron wasn't sure she felt it until she noticed the soldier staring at his feet.

On the dock, the priests and soldiers were staring at the dock, looking down as if the world serpent was about to burst through. Sepharia had only just climbed on the wagon and Lysimachus was shouting at her. The soldier on the roof shook his sword arm and advanced on Heron in a wide legged stance.

When the first pillar beneath the dock gave way, the sound was like a tree being broken in half by a giant. The next break followed a second later, and then the avalanche of wood crashing into the harbor, followed by the screams of men and horses, was all she could hear.

The building shuddered, dancing the soldier on his feet, so Heron darted past him, running straight for the edge. She leapt without looking, closing her eyes, only to feel the cool embrace of water right as she caught her breath.

A timber slammed into her thigh as she flailed beneath the surface. Another section of wood hit her across the back, almost releasing the breath from her lungs. More wood piled overtop before she could regain the surface.

Feeling along the bottom of the pile, Heron scratched at the wood, dragging herself along as her chest turned to fire. She was at a dead end, everywhere around her was more wood.

So she dove further down, kicking off planks and pulling herself through the tangled and broken dock. When it felt like she couldn't hold her breath any longer, she moved laterally, hand over hand, and then kicked off, but the kick was weak and she had no momentum.

Heron scrambled upward, one-handed strokes growing weaker as she struggled. It felt like her chest was going to explode and all the water of the great harbor would rush in.

When her lips could stay closed no longer, she broke the surface, sputtering through, half-coughing, wheezing, taking in a mouthful of water. She opened her eyes to find herself in a maze of wood and beams. From other parts of the broken dock, men moaned, and a horse screamed like a demon unleashed.

She put a hand to her chin which stung in the salt water. In the faint light from the Lighthouse, she could see watery blood, running across her hand. More shouts reached her location. The collapse of the docks brought soldiers from the upper city. Heron started pulling herself through the wreckage.

It wouldn't do her any good to get caught by the soldiers looking for survivors, so Heron thrust into the harbor, swimming away from the broken docks. Her swimming gait was half-splash, half-paddle, and noisy, but the soldiers had her on volume, shouting, "Is anyone alive?" and "Someone shine a lantern here!"

When she made it to a little piece of dock that hadn't fallen into the harbor, she clung to the slimy post like a barnacle and looked back to the shore.

The thoroughness of the destruction brought a bit of pride with equal doses of worry. She was getting too good at destroying things. From the scroll depositories to the Custom's Office, mangled planks stuck from the water like the back of a porcupine.

The dying horse had been silenced, and bodies were being dragged from the water. Heron counted herself lucky that Sepharia had been on the street side when the dock fell in. Even across the black water, Sepharia was easy to see with her blond hair falling across the dark green robe. She was looking across the harbor.

After wiping the sting from her eyes, Heron pushed off from the post and made her way to the northern side of the Great Library with uneven paddling. When she climbed onto the hillside nearly an hour later, she collapsed on the rocks and caught her breath.

Then she made a circuitous route back to Cassandra's Tavern, and pushed her way inside with trembling hands, ready to collapse again. But she didn't allow herself. If they identified Arethussa's body, they would know where to find her. Heron gave herself enough time to change clothes into something less conspicuous and grab supplies before she would leave again.

Arethussa had a closet of men's clothing that she'd kept in case someone had ever questioned that she had a Roman husband. The truth was that she was single, but Heron had helped her file the documents with the Roman Empire, picking a Roman name at random. Having an absent husband had allowed Arethussa to run her tavern without interference.

It'd been over a decade since Heron had helped Arethussa, but she still remembered the name they'd picked for her Roman husband.

Casius Attius Tremulus. As good as name as any. He was supposed to be a one time member of the Equestrian class. Arethussa had even acquired the appropriate gear to complete the illusion, and updated it when Alexandria broke from the Empire.

Heron donned the simple tunic, then wrestled the leather jerkin over her chest and cinched the belt tight to remove the slack. She tied her hair into a knot and tucked it under the helmet.

She had no weapon, but a backpack full of hard bread and salty sausages. The coins she'd brought from the village were spent, but Arethussa had a secret stash. After much deliberation, Heron claimed the coinage for her own and set out, prepared to find a new hiding spot in the city.

Taking the first step out the door, Heron tripped over a body and crashed onto the cobblestones, jamming a finger on impact.

Lying in a heap in front of the door was Arethussa, a patch of dried blood across her neck. Heron put her ear to the woman's mouth to find that the Arethussa was still alive.

Then she looked in both directions to make sure no one was coming to get her.

But who had brought Arethussa? Or had she gotten up and made it back to the tavern before collapsing again?

Before anyone else came along, Heron dragged Arethussa's unconscious body inside and shut the door. The slamming rattled the brass
implements that hung on strings from the ceiling.

Heron squirmed out of her disguise and then got on her knees and
put her ear to Arethussa's mouth. Faint breath like mist was coming out.

Content the woman was still alive, Heron dragged her into the little
bedroom behind the tavern proper and lifted her onto the bed. Then she
grabbed a wet rag and cleaned the dried blood from the back of Arethussa's head.

When she was sure she'd done all she could do, Heron pulled a chair
into the room. While she waited, she contemplated the mystery of how
Arethussa had gotten back to the tavern. Had she stumbled back on her
own two feet? Or had someone brought her back?

The former didn't seem likely and the latter made Heron glance over
her shoulder and wring her hand against her tunic. It seemed doubtful
that she had unknown allies, which left open a possibility that made her
shudder in warning: what if Lysimachus was testing her?

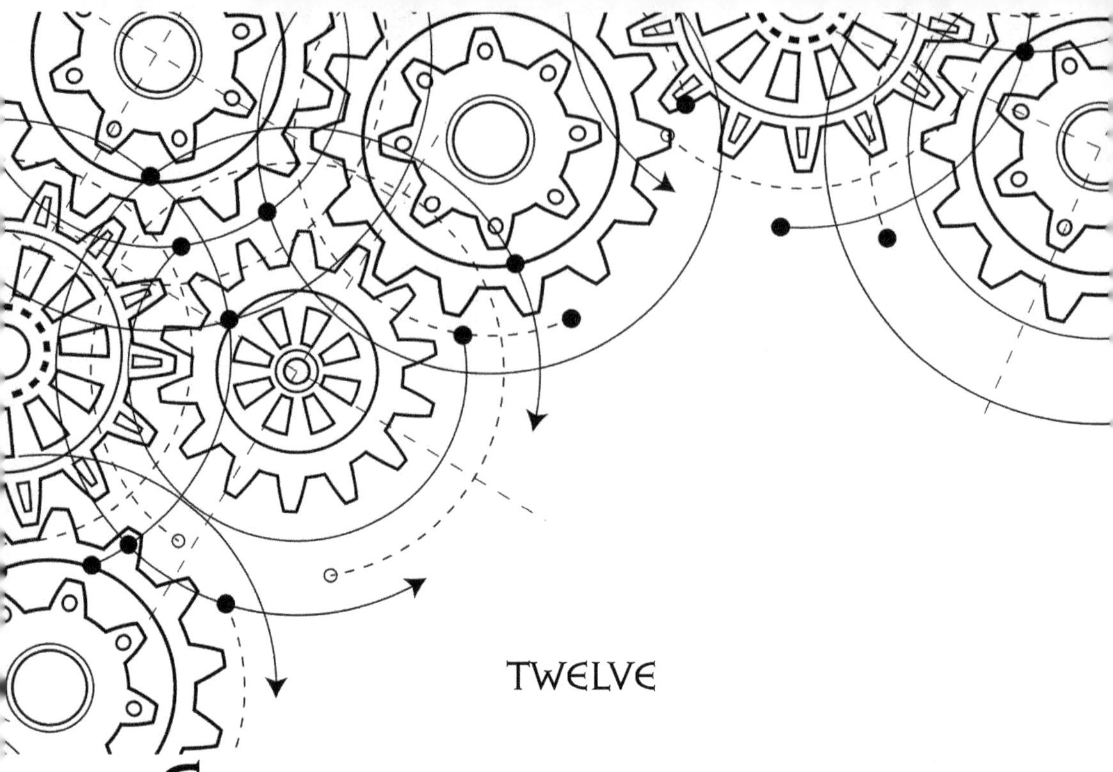

TWELVE

Standing outside the marble doors of the inner Palace, carved with the likeness of Alexander the Macedonian riding into battle, Sepharia shifted on her bare feet, trying to relieve the ache in her soles without drawing notice. She'd been standing on the stone for an hour and her arches threatened to cramp.

Despite her fidgeting, the crocodile soldiers standing guard kept their gazes on the columned hall that led up to the double doors. Their toothy helms glimmered in the greasy light of the oil lanterns.

The soldier on the right's stern-lipped grimace matched the missing finger on his hand that curled over the brass hilt of his gladius. The flesh was pink and cracked, sign of a recent removal.

The other soldier had all his digits and Sepharia caught him glancing at her whenever she looked away. They were both Alexandrians, probably from the Rhakotis District, by the scars on their hands. The full fingered soldier had a nose that had been broken and never fixed, listing to the right. He had dirty black hair, brown eyes, and a pleasant face.

A heavy pounding sounded from within and the two soldiers leapt into action, yanking the heavy doors wide, as one of the Terrors marched out, his dark green robes swirling around him. Sepharia flinched when she thought it was Lysimachus, but realized her mistake when she looked at him closer.

The Terror ignored her as he stamped down the hallway, eliciting angry echoes. Sepharia noted the missing hand on his arm, the same side as Lysimachus. The man could have been a close relative of the old Alabarch by the resemblance, but his eyes were larger.

"Enter, O Bride of Sobek," Lysimachus called.

Sepharia pulled up the hem of her stola and short-stepped into the inner chamber. It'd been months since she'd been inside the room and much had changed since the last visit. The fresco of Amun on the wall behind the dais had been chipped off, leaving scarred stone. The tapestries and statues that filled the wide space had been removed. The wide marble hall was empty of furniture except for a wooden chair on the dais.

Lysimachus waited for her from his seat. Two soldiers stood behind him, staring absently into space. On the marble floor in front of him was a crocodile. The beast lay a few steps from the dais, its scaly ridges reflecting the dim lights. Sepharia moved to a location right in front of Lysimachus, which was near the crocodile's open mouth.

Lysimachus had what she could only assume was a smile on his thin lips, though she wasn't sure she'd ever seen one before. Maybe it wasn't a smile, but the pleasure of an owner whose pet had successfully performed a trick.

Near her bare calf, the hissing breath of the crocodile washed across her skin. In the belly of the beast, a low growl formed. Sepharia kept her gaze on Lysimachus.

"I am pleased, daughter of Sobek," said Lysimachus.

"Yes, Will of Sobek," she replied quickly.

He tapped on his lips with his fingertips, glancing at the crocodile. The beast could lunge forward and take her leg off below the knee if it so chose.

"Such loyalty comes with its rewards," he said.

Sepharia kept her face neutral, despite the memory of the mace crunching into that woman's head filling her mind like cloying black smoke.

"Sobek controls the waters of creation," said Lysimachus, "the very pools from which life itself sprung. While the other gods mocked him, throwing him from the garden, he knew what he had wrought. Now, his time ascends, and with it, a new Empire under his name."

Lysimachus licked his lips, pulled a piece of bloody red meat from a wooden bucket next to his chair and threw it to the crocodile. The beast snatched it out of the air, its toothy maw making sickening smacking noises as it devoured the treat.

"What do you wish as your reward?" asked Lysimachus.

Sepharia inclined her head. "It's enough to serve you, Will of Sobek."

The priest rubbed the armrest on his chair with glee. "How things have changed from our journey. To think what a defiant young woman you were, always trying to escape. I asked Lord Sobek many times if I should offer one of your limbs as punishment, but each time his answer preserved you."

She hid her discomfort with a swallow, keeping her gaze on the edge of the dais. A piece of the stone had been chipped, probably from when the statues of the gods that had been removed. It was easier to think of the stone breaking, than the punishments Lysimachus delivered to those they encountered on their journey.

She tried to fix the shape of the chip, the sharp v of the stone, in her mind, rather than the screams that Lysimachus had summoned from his victims with a blade. She tried, but those memories had been branded into her mind.

"You need not linger on your past transgressions," said Lysimachus. "I've tested you time and time again since we've arrived in Alexandria, and you've passed every one."

"Yes, Will of Sobek," she replied.

"A reward," he said. "You must ask of one."

"Immortality," Sepharia said suddenly, looking up into his beady black eyes.

"I have given you this gift already," said Lysimachus, waving his hand at her, his lips curling downward. "Ask another."

"Then the secret of it," she said.

He eyed her with a coolness that bordered on disdain. "That, you have not earned. Ask another, and this time make it something I can give you."

The agitation in his voice let her know that he wanted something he could actually offer, so he could feel like a benevolent master. She wanted to say: give me my father, or kill yourself, or something else to infuriate him, but decided against it. She was still alive and sometimes that was enough.

"I could use some time in the garden," she said. "I grow tired of my room and my guardians won't let me leave. The flowers in the garden are wonderful this time of year."

His gaze narrowed for a moment as if he was deciding how she might use this request against him, but he quickly relented and nodded his head.

"You may have this, once per day, in the garden," he said.

"My thanks, Will of Sobek," she said, bending at the waist in a deep bow.

She didn't wait for him to dismiss her and lifted the hem of her stola to scurry out of the room. The crocodile made a lazy snap as she moved away.

Sepharia was about to leave the room when he called after her. She froze and waited for his instruction, her muscles tensed, her breath held between her teeth.

"Your loyalty will be tested again. Do not fail me, not even once. I do not think Lord Sobek will be so kind should it ever happen again."

Sepharia nodded and continued from the room. Still alive. Alive was better than dead, for now.

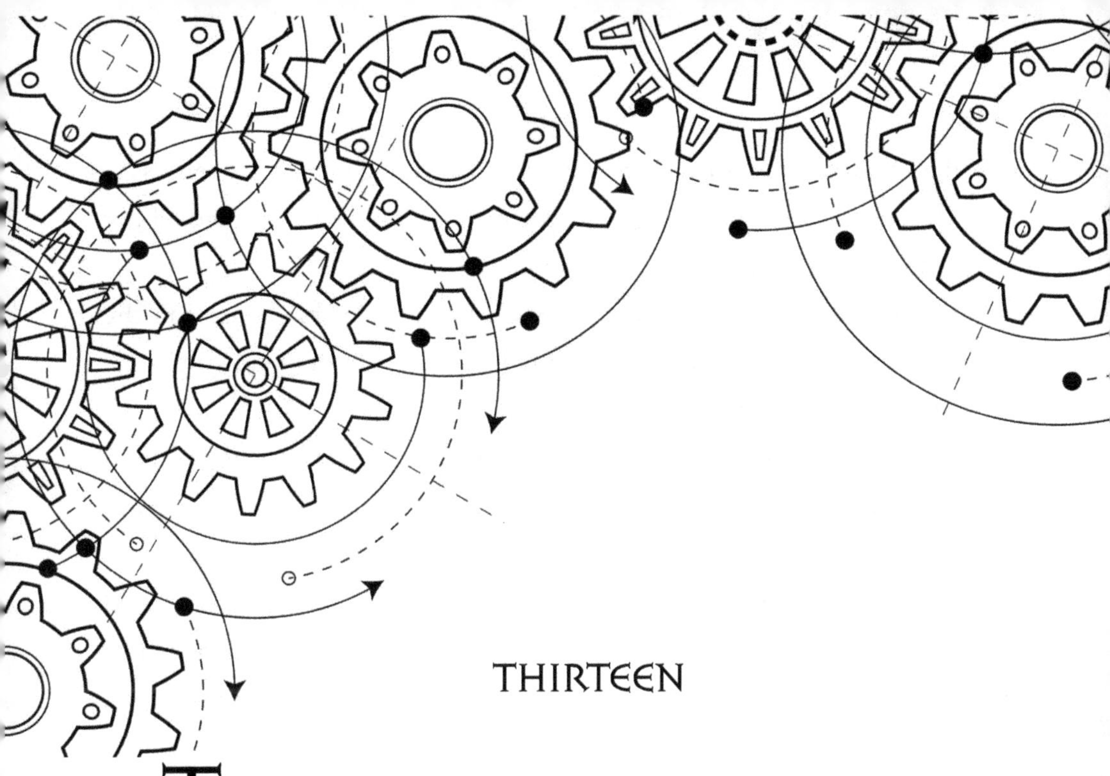

THIRTEEN

The events at the docks played across Heron's mind as she watched Arethussa recover over the course of a week, the slow rise and fall of her chest in tune with movements of the sea. Heron imagined the docks at low tide, the broken structures like skeletons of a wooden giant, slain and fallen into the rich silt that lay at the bottom of the harbor.

A terrible itch formed at her temples, a thought that lodged itself like sand in the teeth. Heron worried at the grit, trying to free itself from her mind.

It wasn't the way Lysimachus had shown up at the docks, almost as if he'd known where she'd be. Nor was it the indecency to not even feign surprise when he'd seen her shouting from the rooftop.

It was that he'd brought Sepharia with him. Could Heron really believe that he just happened to have her daughter with him, all coiled up in a robe so he could unleash his horrible surprise, if by accident?

And to double that feeling of frustration and pain, like hitting yourself with a hammer a second time after swearing you'd be careful, Lysimachus had flaunted his control of Sepharia by sending her after Arethussa.

Heron hadn't seen any signs of torture on Sepharia. She had all her limbs, no scars were visible. How had he done it?

Heron knew it could be done. She'd been under his control in the Temple of Sobek. She'd have done anything to make the pain stop. Everyone broke in the end.

But had he broken Sepharia's will? It didn't feel that way. When Heron had looked into her daughter's eyes, they hadn't been lost, or distant, just neutral. Of course, it'd been night with only lanterns to see by. Still.

Each time she reviewed the scene in her mind, she found her hand bunched up into a fist. Not a fist, but a maul to break the memory like a mirror. All Heron could see was herself after being tortured under the temple.

Sepharia had been broken, that's the only thing Heron could accept, which was its own set of problems.

When Heron couldn't take sitting and watching Arethussa lie on the cot, making breaths so shallow that Heron had to check the tavern owner's pulse every now and then to make sure she wasn't dead, the inventor scoured the tavern for parchment and ink.

A quill and a few rolls were stuck under the bar. Holding the writing utensil felt awkward, and she had to regrip multiple times before she dipped the end into the ink. A fat bead the color of night hung on the end, so she dabbed it off and sniffed, hoping the sooty smell would calm her by bringing back memories of the workshop, but the restlessness in her limbs went bone deep.

Once she finally set the tip to the parchment, she realized she didn't know what she was going to draw. Was she writing a letter? Or was it a new design?

Letting her frustration flow out onto the papyrus, she sketched a circle. Then in the middle, she made little jagged lines. Her fingers danced along the paper, end of the feather waving in maddeningly short strokes, until Heron realized what her mind was unconsciously drawing.

It was the double dragon carving she'd been given by the craftsman in Sakrur. One in fire. One in water. She'd lost the one he'd carved for her, but the image was imprinted into her mind.

Once the design had been replicated, Heron searched the storage room for a piece of carving wood. She couldn't find anything soft like birch, but Arethussa had disc shaped pieces she used to set candles on.

After gathering the appropriate supplies, Heron checked on Arethussa, dripping water into her mouth and massaging her throat to make sure the woman didn't choke. She didn't dare give her food.

The disc of wood she bound to the table using the cork press she'd made for Arethussa many years ago when she'd first opened the tavern. By latching the press into place, she held the wooden disc motionless.

Then Heron drew the double dragon design on the surface. It took almost a full day, but using a carving knife, she chipped at the surface, removing wood until she'd replicated the gift she'd lost in the Red Sea.

After blowing the shavings from the carving, Heron checked on Arethussa to find the woman sitting up in bed. Dark circles ringed her eyes and a gray tint turned her skin to ash.

"Are you well?" asked Heron.

Arethussa blinked, her high cheekbones looking gaunt. Then she closed her eyes and swayed against the wall.

"The world spins, yet I am still. What madness has afflicted me?" whispered Arethussa.

"You were struck in the back of the head. You're lucky to be alive. A bit of madness is an easy bargain to strike compared to death," said Heron.

She poured water into a pewter mug and brought it to Arethussa, helping her hold it while she sipped at the liquid. When the woman was finished, Heron set the mug onto the floor.

"What do you remember of that day?" asked Heron, tucking the wild strands of dark hair away from Arethussa's face.

"That day? You mean it isn't the same one?" asked Arethussa, lip quivering, while eyes passed in and out of focus.

"Two days since," said Heron. "It's important. Do you remember it? Or how you got back here?"

Arethussa placed her fingertips against the corners of her eyes near her nose and rubbed, making little concentric circles. After a moment, she gave a tiny shake of the head, making her hair dance.

"I remember running and horse hooves," said Arethussa. "Nothing else."

Heron let her frustration tug the corners of her mouth downward. It felt like weights had been draped onto her body.

"Is it important?" asked Arethussa, eyes still closed.

"I don't know. I thought you were dead and I escaped through the water. After returning, I prepared to flee, but found you on the doorstep. You either got up and made it back on your own two feet, we have a secret ally, or Lysimachus is playing with me."

"Why would he do that?" asked Arethussa.

Heron got up suddenly and went to the window. The streets were empty and only a lone trireme coasted into the harbor. She couldn't even hear the sailors on the ship. It was as if the sound in Alexandria had been sucked away.

The only thing that seemed the same was the Lighthouse of Pharos. The square walls at the base shone against the sun, whiteness like the sand of the deep desert. The main tower rose above the walls, making them seem like a child's creation in their tininess. The third level had eight sides, holding up the beacon on top.

On Pharos island, the priests of Poseidon tended the temple. White robes moving against the verdant green lawns from which colonnades sprung. Along the walls of the temple, caryatids of mermaids held up the angled roof.

"He wants me to be Sobek's champion. To help him create an Empire dedicated to his god." Heron turned and held up her stump. "He was the one who did this. In his temple. For a time, I would have done anything he asked to make the pain stop. It could be that he thinks he has some hold on me."

"Does he?" asked Arethussa, wide-eyed.

"No. But he does have my daughter. He has Sepharia and it appears he has some—" she almost said hold but didn't want to admit it out loud, "—way to control her. When she performed his miracle in the street, I thought it was a trick. That she really wasn't on his side. But then when she spoke to me, bade me to join them...and then she was the one to take you down. She could have killed you. How can I make sense of that?"

"If you said that Lysimachus was able to make you do anything. Why not with Sepharia?"

"But how? She has no marks on her. She could have rode away on the horse. But instead, she tried to kill you."

Arethussa's chin sunk to her chest. "What if she believes him? That he's resurrecting her from the dead? Wouldn't that make you believe?"

Heron slammed her fist against her leg. "He cannot control death. No one can. It's a trick."

"But what if she doesn't know that? What if he's fooled her, too?" asked Arethussa, and then she shrunk against herself. "Or what if he can control death?"

"You don't believe him, do you?" asked Heron.

"We cannot know the mind of the gods."

Heron went back to the window. The warm sea air was stifling.

"It doesn't matter," she said eventually. "Belief or not, I need to save her. I cannot let Lysimachus keep my daughter."

"What can we do? We have no weapons, no allies. I can barely move and if I do, I think I might vomit."

"We have allies in the city, if we can find them," said Heron. "Dominitus is here. That could be those soldiers in Roman colors that attacked the Palace. I can't be sure, but I believe he wouldn't let Lysimachus keep the city."

"And how do we find them? I've never heard of that place you called the Dutiful Octagon," said Arethussa.

"Nor I."

Heron pounded her fist on the windowsill, looking past the Lighthouse towards the sea. How things had changed that she wished to have the Roman Empire as an ally, broken as it was.

"What if it's a word puzzle?" asked Arethussa. "The kind in which you mix up the letters to make other words."

"I've thought of that, but it doesn't make any words that I know of. Unless it's some sort of code."

They shared a silence for a while, Heron rolling the phrase Dutiful Octagon around in her head.

Arethussa politely cleared her throat. "What if it describes something?"

"Like what?" asked Heron. "I don't know anything that's in the shape of an..."

The words trailed away as she looked to the third level of the Lighthouse. It was an octagon. And the Lighthouse was a structure of duty, guiding ships to shore safely.

Heron pushed a hand through her hair and let a hint of a smile form on her lips. "I think I know where they're hiding."

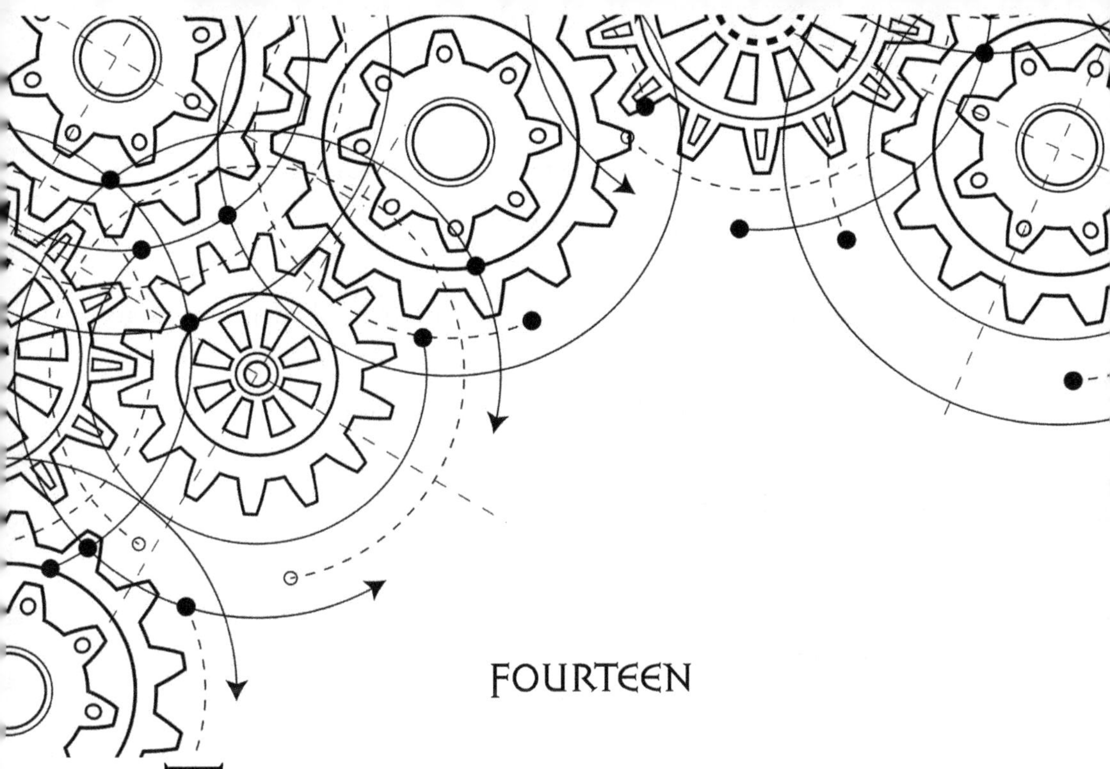

FOURTEEN

The flowers of the garden paled in the bright sun, their scents empty and frivolous. She'd scarcely been sitting on the stone bench for twenty minutes before she called for the guard to bring her back to her chambers.

It'd been a mistake to think that a change of scenery would lighten her heart. The colorful garden had only reminded her that she was a prisoner.

The approaching guard was not the one who had brought her to the garden. It was the one she'd seen outside the inner chamber at the Palace. The soldier with the broken nose and scarred hands.

"Where is the other guard?" she asked.

The soldier cleared his throat. "Goric asked me to take his place while he went to the privy. He didn't think you'd be done so soon."

She blocked the sunlight with her hand. The soldier didn't have the righteous stare of the others. He seemed almost embarrassed that he was attending her.

"What's your name?" she asked.

"Abeden."

He glanced furtively towards the far side of the garden where another guard watched from the shadows.

"I shouldn't be talking to you," he said.

Sepharia offered a coy smile. "That's a nice name, Abeden. Let's start walking back to my apartment. We can talk along the way."

Abeden marched ahead of her, so she hurried to his side. He tried to speed up, but she tugged on his elbow.

"I don't bite," she said.

"You're the Bride of Sobek," he said.

"I still don't bite." She stopped him with a gentle tug. They were standing in an old gallery. It was the same one she'd encountered Vestalis in. "You're from the Rhakotis District."

His brow furrowed. "How did you know?"

"I grew up there, of course, I would know one of my own," she said with a smile, which Abeden returned, though he quickly squashed it, checking over his shoulder.

"We should go," he said, pulling on her arm.

"Why haven't you given an offering?" she asked. "Most of the other soldiers have at least chopped off their smallest finger."

"You shouldn't ask me that," he said, continuing to tug. She dug her heels in.

She looked into his brown eyes and he looked away.

"Well, then," she said, hurrying ahead, leaving him behind. Rather than move towards the exit on the far wall, she went left. It would bring her back to her apartment, but by a different route.

"Not that way," he said, running after her. Sepharia picked up her hem and ran ahead. The hard slap of his sandals followed her. She darted into one of the libraries, surprised to find that the scrolls and books in the room hadn't been burned.

The guard, Abeden, came in right after, breathing heavily. "You shouldn't be in here. Even I shouldn't be in here."

Sepharia shrugged. "No one told me I couldn't. We're taking the long way to my apartment," she said, but didn't move towards the exit.

On the table in the corner of the room, Sepharia spied an unrolled scroll next to a quill and a pot of ink. A gasp escaped her lips when she saw what was on the parchment. It was a sketching of a naked Lysimachus. Notes were annotated along the margins, but she didn't get a chance to read any of them. Abeden grabbed her by the upper arm and dragged her out of the room, back the way they'd come.

"I'm taking you back to your room, right now," he said, his voice cracking with a mix of fear and anger.

Sepharia dutifully followed, not trying to pull away, even though his grip hurt. When they finally made it back to the apartment, she rubbed the feeling back into her arm.

When he slammed the door, the sound of the bar sliding into place, locking her into her apartment, Sepharia slumped to the floor and put her face into her hands.

Her brief escape had been foolish. She wasn't sure why'd she'd bothered. No one in Alexandria could save her. And it wasn't like she even understood why Lysimachus would have drawings of himself naked. She wished she'd seen the notes. They might have explained the sketches, or maybe she didn't want to see them at all. The parchment might have no other significance other than more proof that the former Alabarch was a sick and twisted man.

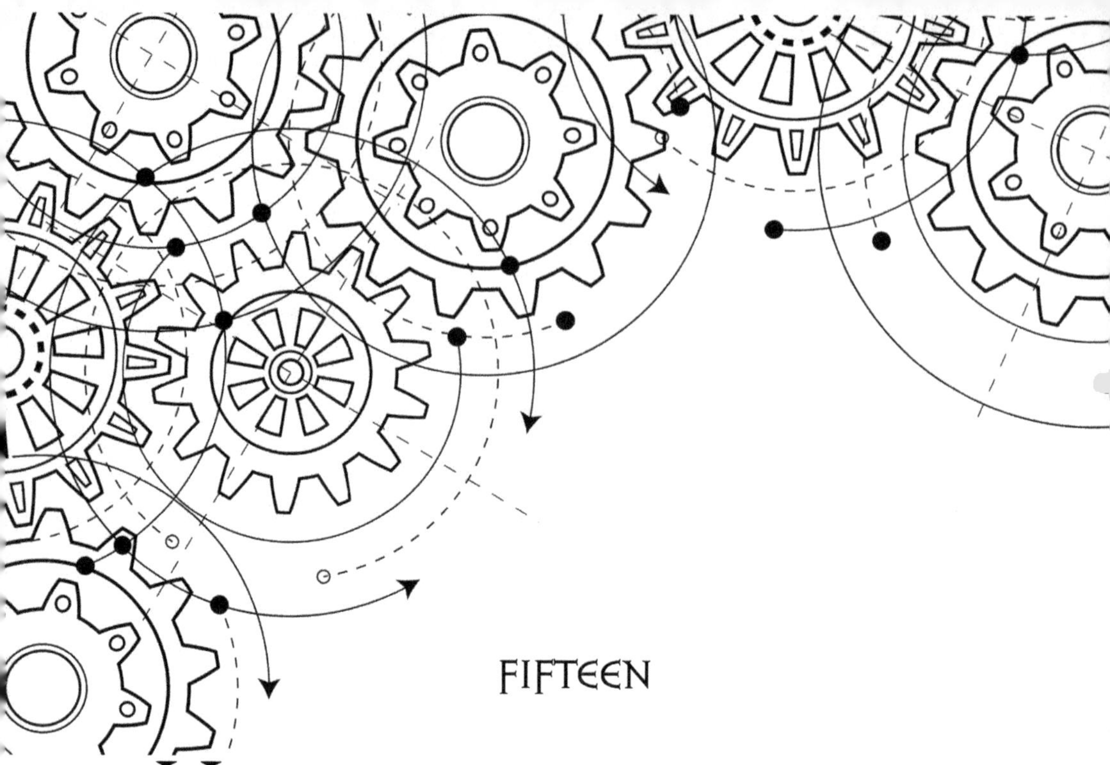

FIFTEEN

Heron's hand was shaking as she gripped the reins, but that was no surprise. She tried to hum a tune, a Macedonian one she recalled from her youth, but it only came out in fragments. Mostly guttural noises from her throat and if anyone had been nearby they might have thought she was clearing phlegm.

They'd already made two visits to the Lighthouse, the first to scout and the second to prepare an escape, but this time, she was going to reveal herself to Dominitus' men. Had this meeting occurred two weeks ago, before Black Omari, she would have marched into his chambers, desperate for allies. But her dealings with the crime lord had taught her caution.

To the west, the sun bled into the sea, sending brilliant pinks and oranges across the water and reflecting shimmering jewels on the Temple of Isis directly ahead. Heron kept her face angled to the east so she wasn't blinded.

The wagon bumped over the threshold at the end of the Heptastadion, the land bridge that connected the island to the city. Arethussa had

bribed a merchant to let them bring supplies to the Lighthouse. The beacon required constant feeding to stay alight and behind her in the wagon
was a full load of chopped wood that shifted as the wheels rattled.

The city kept a garrison on the island, soldiers in Alexandrian garb,
but the taking of the city by Lysimachus had hollowed out the army and
the island was lightly held. Heron suspected that Dominitus had replaced
the men in the garrison with some of his own, but she couldn't trust it.

The soldier at the end of the road waved her down, so Heron pulled
on the reins until the two draft horses plodded to a stop. In watching the
traffic going to and from the island, Heron had noted that the soldiers
rarely stopped the wagons. Rarely. It was just her luck that today one of
them was trying to do his job.

The approaching soldier had Egyptian eyes with the broader face of
a Persian and the nose of a Thracian, a true Alexandrian if she'd ever seen
one, in that he was a little bit of every nationality. And maybe that was why
he'd stopped her, because he wasn't one of Dominitus' men from Rome.

"I haven't seen you before," said the soldier, squinting into the sunlight. "Pull your hood back and let me see your face."

Heron hesitated and glanced back towards the city. The soldier followed her gaze, a perplexed look perched on his brow.

"Show your face, boy," said the soldier, his hand on his hilt. He
rubbed his smooth jaw with the other hand.

Keeping her stump safely in the sleeve of her robe, Heron pulled back
the hood with her other hand, careful not to dislodge the bandages.

At the sight of the gauzy fabrics wrapped around her neck and the
lower half of her face, the soldier stepped back away from the wagon. His
lips soured as he regarded her misshapen hump.

"By Sobek, what's wrong with you? Why are you wearing a leather
glove? And those bandages?"

Heron croaked out an answer, "The swelling of Khonsu."

The soldier took another step backwards, his face in a rictus of curled lips and contorted muscles. "Why would they think to let you out?"

"Sobek has healed me," said Heron. "And they cut the worst away from my body."

She nodded downward as if to indicate there were more bandages and more wounds.

The soldier made signs with his fingers, warding away whatever bad spirits she might be carrying. His curiosity drained, he motioned her on.

After snapping the reins, she made for the lower level, wishing the leather garments beneath the robes breathed a little more. She felt like a ball of sweat beneath the leather and the closer she got to the Lighthouse, the more her heart climbed into her throat. By the time she passed through the gate, she had to pound her hand against her leg to keep the trembling to a minimum.

Unlike the soldier at the end of the Heptastadion, the others quickly noted her bandages and looked away, fearful that whatever ailment had befallen her, might leap through the air and onto them, should they stare too long. Truthfully, the method of infection was unknown to Heron, but since she didn't actually have the disease, she wasn't worried.

Once inside the base, horse hooves and nervous nickers echoed against the stone. The archway led into the center of the Lighthouse to a warehouse that housed the stores of wood for burning. Lanterns burned with an oily glow and cast multiple shadows across the rounded archway.

The workers at the lift moved to greet her until they saw the bandages and the hump. Heron made non-committal grunts and limped away from the wagon.

She made her way to the service stairs and began the slow plod upward. Normally, the wooden leg would sound against the stone, but Arethussa had sewn a boot onto it as a disguise.

Reaching the observation level in a light lather, Heron caught her breath before entering the wide room that often served as a marketplace for tourists. But the taking of Alexandria by the priest of Sobek had dampened such enthusiasms, despite the swelling of refuges outside the walls, so the lively chatter that normally graced the observation level proved absent.

Heron thought she would have to search the backrooms and hidden halls to find Dominitus, but as soon as she took one step inside, a very Egyptian looking attendant with mocha skin and almond shaped eyes wearing a beaded tunic and sandals met her at the entrance.

"Greetings, Heron of Alexandria," said the attendant in accented Greek.

The words caught in her throat, as her gaze wheeled around the room. The level was sparsely populated, except for a couple of tables near the windows. Normally on a summer day, the level was jammed with merchant stalls and tourists, but today it could have been mid-winter. The attendant waited patiently before speaking again.

"Master Dominitus would like to speak with you."

"*Master* Dominitus?" she asked, putting heavy emphasis on the Master.

But the attendant didn't rise to her bait, and instead, motioned to the far side of the level. Sitting at a table along the city-side was Dominitus. He raised a hand in salute.

Heron didn't like that he'd known who she was. It made her plan more precarious. For all she knew, the plan or Arethussa had been discovered. Heron's gut twisted even more when she realized that no one stared at her, wrapped in gauzy bandages, as she made her way across.

"Greetings, Heron. Are we imitating the mummies of the pharaohs, or is it just a disguise?" asked Dominitus. "And I doubt I've seen bigger humps on a camel."

He sat with his fingers steepled, head turned so he could see with his clear eye, not the right one that had a milky glow to it. His back arched a little, so his shoulders hunched, and Heron guessed that his lips might have contained a grimace of pain, if it weren't that he was enjoying his surprise.

"I'm dressed like one, but you look the part without the bandages," said Heron.

The wrinkles on his face deepened as he grinned. "The years haven't changed you."

Heron opened her mouth to refute him, but a rattling noise saved her the trouble. They both looked to the center of the level where the open hole was ringed by columns. The lift carried a load of wood upward to the beacon, moving through the observation level with steady jerks. In years past, they'd had to haul them up by hand, but she'd installed a steam mechanical at the top before she'd left Alexandria for Rome, saving the workers from the dangerous labor.

"They've changed you," said Heron. "And what's this Master business? No longer a Senator?"

"Not while the Empire is no more," said Dominitus, his gaze level, his lips pursed with thought, before his eyes brightened. "What news of Cultri do you bring?"

Her hesitation was answer enough, and Dominitus wilted against the chair, the fire in his eyes dimming.

"He saved me, more than once, and for that, I thank you," said Heron.

Dominitus nodded and then whatever mourning he carried on his diminished frame, it was gone. Heron noted how quickly he shed the loss of his servant and friend, like a snake molting old skin.

"What happened after Rome?" asked Heron.

The former Senator looked out the window to the city. Though light still shown through the windows that ringed the observation level, the city was drenched in shadow. Only the tips of the tallest towers and the upper half of the Colossus of Sobek blazed orange with sunset.

"When the city burnt," he began, glancing momentarily at Heron, "I knew we had to get to Alexandria, to flee ahead of the refugees. Without stores for winter, the city would turn to chaos, and it did. I have estates along the coast, so we fled there and collected whatever wealth I could before chartering a ship across the sea to Alexandria. Not before sending Cultri to aid you, of course."

"Why did you?" asked Heron.

He rubbed his wrinkled hand across the surface of the table, until it met with an opaque glass filled with dark liquid. He let his fingers dance along the curve of the glass like a lute player.

"Though many curse the excesses of the Empire, like it or not, the peace and stability it provided made up for its faults. Without it, the world will descend into chaos. Though you seemed unsuited, at times, for political gamesmanship, your inventions might help tame that chaos, solve the practical issues that will plague this new world bereft of Rome."

"And the Empire of Sobek? You do not approve of it?" she asked.

Dominitus made a clucking noise with his tongue that reminded her of Agog. "A theocracy is a different kind of chaos. One that I would not wish upon the world."

"Then what do you wish upon the world?" asked Heron.

"Peace, law, order, stability. What most men want, but fail to account for."

Heron pulled the bandage away from her neck. "What about your Ceres cult? Or Dis Pater? Or whatever god you stamped upon your movement?"

His pinched mouth soured before he spoke, "You speak of these things with distaste, but you should think otherwise. That society helped guide the Roman Empire through many trials and crises. Without it, Rome would never have stayed an Empire for as long. Ask those who starved away the winter if they would have their Empire back? I think we both know the answer."

"It's easy to say this when you and your kind sat at the mouth of the cornucopia, feasting on the fat of the land," said Heron.

Dominitus raised a trembling fist and slammed it onto the table, spilling wine from his glass. His rage seemed unfit for such an aging body and it appeared, by the way he wiped the spit from his lips with the back of a liver-spotted hand, that his emotion had gotten the best of him.

"Why are we arguing when its Lysimachus that holds the city? Why must I ask again and again?"

The shakes that had plagued her limbs earlier had faded, leaving Heron in an abnormally calm state of mind. She wasn't sure if it was numbness or exhaustion, but she looked at her steady hand before answering.

"You need me," said Heron. "As you said, Lysimachus and his crocodile cult hold the city. I've been watching the island for the past few days. I know you don't have the troops to take the city. It's why you've been making those hit and run attacks."

Dominitus didn't answer at first. He rubbed the stubble on his chin, visibly pondering her words. When he spoke, a shard of ice formed in her gut.

"I haven't played my cards too openly," said Dominitus, "unlike yourself. I don't want to tip Lysimachus off that we're on the island."

The former Senator seemed to be mulling something. Heron gathered she'd made a mistake, but she couldn't figure out what it was.

"Even if you're hiding troops elsewhere, you can't have enough to take back the city," said Heron.

"Then why did you come here, if not to band together?" asked Dominitus.

"I wish to band together, but only if we're at the same purposes. What good is a revolution if we turn at each other at the first taste of victory?"

Dominitus sipped at his wine, leaving his lips blushed with red. In the fading light, it almost looked like blood.

"What do you offer?" he asked, his gaze like a drill into her chest.

Heron thought about her answer carefully, but it seemed she was still missing something. It felt like they were having separate conversations.

"It's not what I offer. It's what I want for my help. Will you rebuild the Empire on the back of slavery? Or will you turn away from it?"

The cutting laugh that issued like a knife from his parted lips made Heron flinch.

"You speak of Empire while we hide? We should be banding together, using our forces as one," said Dominitus. "Not sneaking around wasting time destroying the docks."

Heron put a hand to her chest. "You knew that was me?"

His lips soured. "By the gods, of course I knew it was you. So did Lysimachus. Why do you think he was burning those books? He wanted to lure you out. You're all fools to have engaged him there. We watched the whole charade from here. You could have been taken, and then we'd have no chance."

"So you admit you need me?" asked Heron.

Dominitus slapped his palm on the table, shaking the glass. "Admit? Why are we wasting our time stroking your ego? Of course, we need you. And so does Lysimachus. If he can get his hands on you, he'll have an overwhelming technological advantage. With you, I hope we can turn the tide on him. That you can cook something up, some new warmachine to break his hold on the city, or that maybe you already have in your secret workshop."

"Secret workshop? Are you mad? I've just been trying to survive the city. And why would I make new warmachines after Rome? And—"

The words fell from the cliff of her mouth as she saw the way Dominitus was looking at her. And then the answer to her earlier confusion came like a swelling wave into her mind.

Dominitus wasn't behind the attack on the Palace. That was some other group, and based on his reactions, Heron guessed that it could be Vestalis. Or at least she hoped it was. That would explain why the Senator kept mentioning banding together, and that he was confused about her mention of the attack on the Palace.

As Heron came to her realization too late, Dominitus motioned for his guards. They grabbed her by the arms before she could protest.

"Vestalis doesn't even know you're in the city, does he?" asked Dominitus.

While confirmation of her friend's existence was comforting, her current situation was less than.

Dominitus leaned back in his chair, steepling his fingers. "With you, I can not only counter the influence of the crocodile cult, but you can help me figure out his secrets of immortality. While he holds that advantage, we will not prevail in the end."

"Immortality? I doubt it. A trick, if anything," said Heron.

Dominitus gazed out at the sea. "Then you have not seen what I have seen. He's executed your daughter time after time, bringing her back each one."

"A trick, I say," she said.

"Why not real? Your machines would be a miracle to a man who knew nothing else? Maybe he's found some elixir. What about the ambrosia of the gods?" he asked.

"A fool's notion," she said.

He scowled. "I am no fool. But it doesn't matter. If you cannot help me unravel the secret of his wards against death, then I shall provide some inspiration."

Heron looked to the city, awash in darkness, and cradled her stump against her chest. From one mess to the next, it seemed her return to Alexandria was going worse than planned.

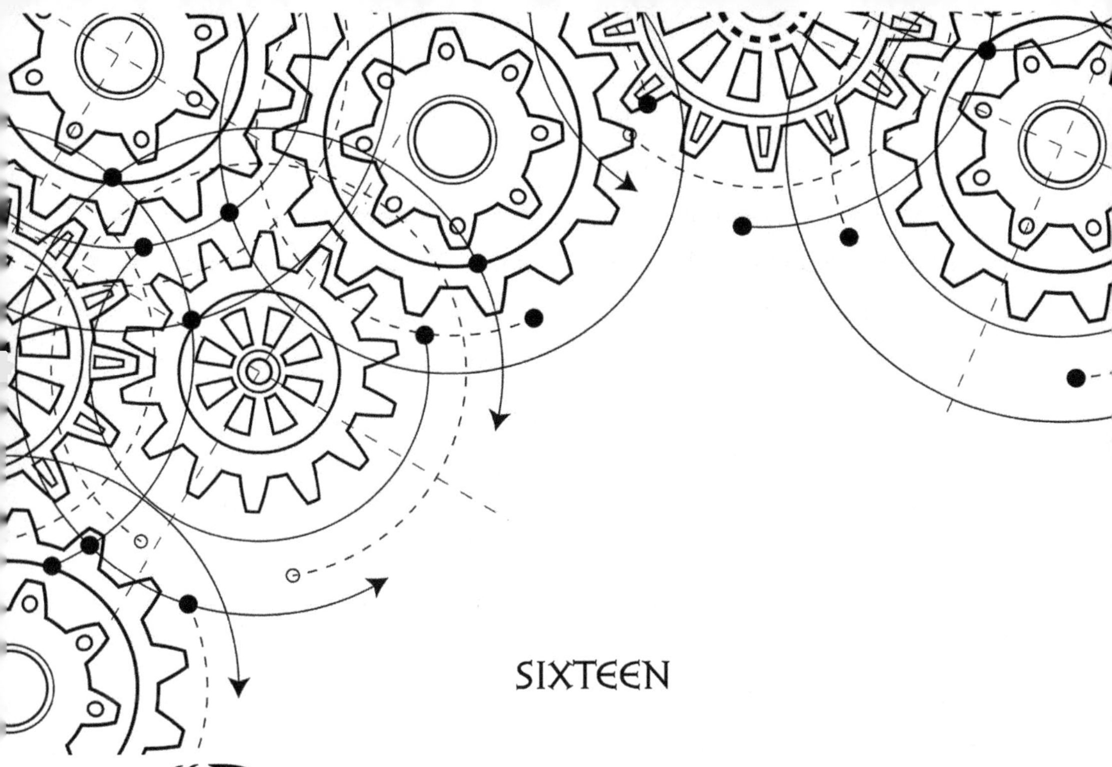

SIXTEEN

"Didn't you learn from the destruction of Rome?" Heron shook off the grips of the two guards, keeping her expression neutral.

Dominitus raised an eyebrow. "Callous about wanton destruction? Do you seek to rival the gods?"

"The gods, no. I'm a practical person, is all. Do you think I would come here without plans?" she asked.

The shuffling feet of the guards looking around the level made her smile. Dominitus snapped his fingers at them.

"Don't let her play you like a lute, you fools. She's bluffing. All this talk of being practical is nonsense, camel dung, I say. If you'd been prepared, you'd have known that Vestalis was in the city, and you'd be with him rather than begging at my table."

His jaw had taken a hard line, and his eyes gazed at her with as much respect one would give a milk cow. The way he held his shoulders, straight back, showed how he was used to having power over other people. They'd called him the Hidden Emperor in Rome. A name she hadn't forgotten when she came to the Lighthouse.

"Apologies, Dominitus, for giving you the impression that I was unprepared. While I am quick to make mistakes, I'm also quick to learn from them. A visit to Black Omari taught me much," she said.

Dominitus snorted derisively and looked away to the darkened city. "A bluff."

"Bluff or not, I ask you one last time, will you renounce slavery in the rebuilding of the Empire? If you do, I shall join your side without comment, and labor industriously, until we take back the Empire. Like you, I see the wisdom in laws, and peace, and stability. But not at the price of chains."

He gazed at her with cold eyes, like shards of ice, and even the milkiness of the one eye did not diminish his contempt.

"You know nothing of Empires. Nothing of ruling. There will always be winners and losers. To have anything less would invite anarchy," said Dominitus.

"Then I will take my leave," said Heron with a shallow bend at the waist.

The guards moved to corral her as she peeled away the leather catch inside the sleeve of her robe. As the guard to her right reached out to grab her, Heron jabbed her hand against his arm.

The high, willowing scream from the guard froze the other. The first guard held his arm to his chest as if it'd been severely burnt. Heron put her gloved hand out towards the second guard and he backed away. When she looked to Dominitus, he practically fell backwards in his chair trying to get away.

With the guards momentarily stopped, Heron ran for the center of the level in a half-gallop. The boot sewn to her wooden leg didn't give her a feeling of control.

As she reached the hole at the center of the room, she recovered the brass rod attached to her arm. The shock from the ghost fire jar in her backpack had done its job. Now, she needed to get away quickly before they decided to recapture her, or stab her through the chest with a sword longer than her arm.

Heron pulled the pole she had tucked into her boot out and used it to catch the rope at the center of the hole. The rope was part of the pulley system that lifted supplies up to the beacon level of the Lighthouse.

While she pulled her contraption from a hidden pocket in her robe, the guards, at violent urging from Dominitus, pulled their swords and approached her.

The confusion on their brows was evident. Why would she run to the center of the room rather than the stairs? The jump would kill her, at a height of nearly two-thirds of the Lighthouse.

But their misunderstanding was her gain. Heron used the time to connect the contraption to the rope that she'd trapped in the elbow of her left arm. Then she yanked on it twice to make sure it was properly seated.

The guards stayed spread out, to keep her from running. They were almost near enough to poke her with a sword.

Heron examined the contraption one last time. The two pullies counterbalanced from either side of the rope in an S-pattern. If everything went as calculated, she'd slide down the rope, connected to the contraption by a harness around her shoulders, and land safely at the bottom in less than ten seconds. If not, they'd be pouring her broken body into a sack to bury in an unmarked grave.

"For Alexandria!" she said before jumping into the pit.

The wide-eyed soldiers quickly disappeared as her stomach leapt into her throat. The pulley wheels against the rope screamed on the way down, burning hair thick in the air. Heron barely had time to get a breath before she hit the ground, heels first.

The impact jammed her legs into her hips and her chin snapped against her chest, as she bent in two and went over front ways. As she climbed to her knees, stunned, but alive, she found herself ringed by the workers who had unloaded her wagon.

No one was moving. They'd turned to stone for all she could tell. Heron repressed a grimace and climbed to her feet, brushing past the immobile workers and hobbling towards the tunnel as fast as she could go, which wasn't fast.

Every step felt like her hips were grinding to bonedust. She bit back tears and kept moving, ignoring the straps around her shoulders that had been loosened by the fall. She must have miscalculated the tension between the pullies, or they'd become loosened by the force of friction. She hit much harder than she'd calculated.

Still, she was alive, and sometimes, that was all you could hope for.

Reaching the north side of the Lighthouse, Heron made for a stretch of rocky beach not illuminated by any torchlight. She imagined that Dominitus would expect her to escape the way she came in, by wagon over the land bridge.

The slope on the beach was steeper than she'd expected. Heron used the boulders to back down the slope, listening for shouts over the crash of waves behind her.

When Heron reached the bottom, the sea splashed against her legs. She teetered on a rock and searched the night sea with her light-blind eyes.

The skiff swelled out of the gloom like Charon's boat. Arethussa helped her onto the bow and they pushed off with a pair of oars as the wooden hull bounced on the rocks beneath the water.

"It went as expected?" asked Arethussa, taking up one side of the oars.

Sitting on the wooden bench, Heron tried to find a comfortable sitting position, but her hips burned with each adjustment. Eventually, Heron gave up and gritted her teeth as she yanked on the oar handle, propelling them into the dark waves.

"Next time that I tell you I'm going to jump off the upper level of the Lighthouse, tell me to recheck my calculations and add a little extra for error."

"Yes, *Michanikos*," said Arethussa with a smirk.

"Or rather, I should think, remind me that I am not meant to fall through the air like Icarus."

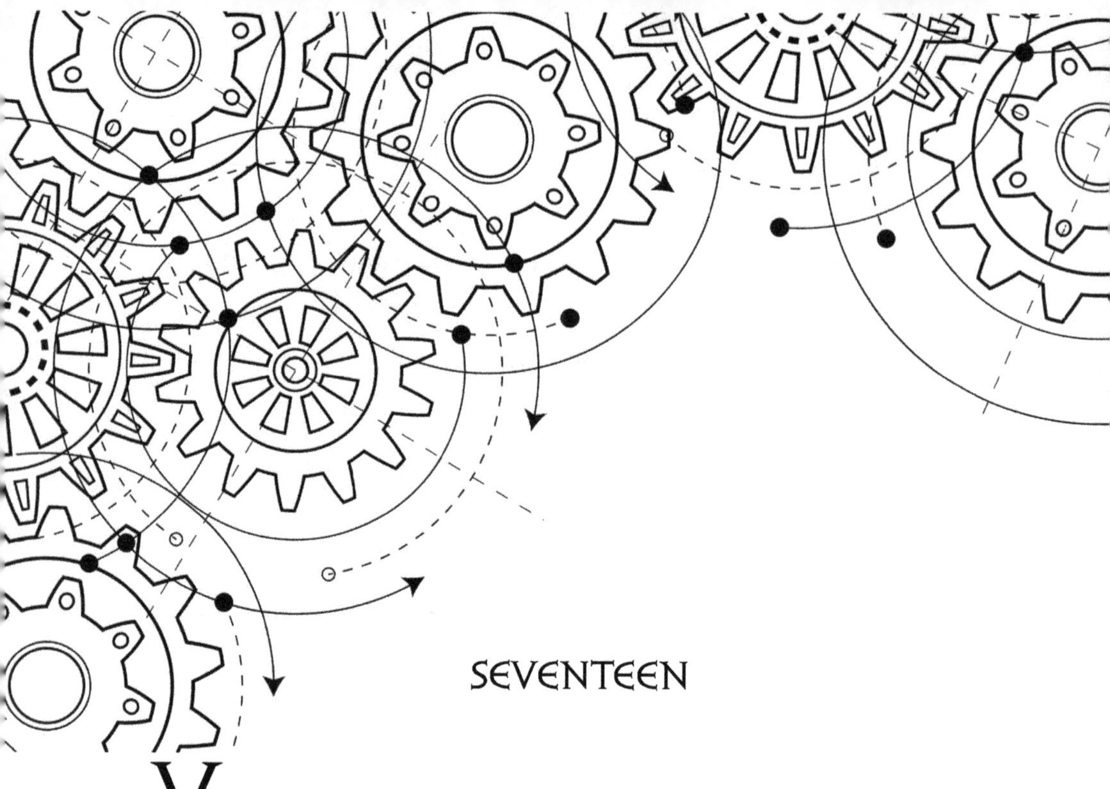

SEVENTEEN

Vestalis put the blade to the man's neck, leaving a red line beneath the beard. The crocodile soldier, one of the true believers Vestalis reckoned by the missing digits on the left hand, stared back with impunity.

"If you're in a hurry to visit the Underworld, then clamp those lips tighter," said Vestalis, pressing the knife until the skin threatened to split wide, "but if you value your mortal breath, then speak clearly and tell me when the next patrol is due."

The soldier, in leather breastplate stamped with the sigil of the crocodile god, glanced to the dead men lying in the dirt. The summer heat had turned the warehouse into a furnace and a rivulet of sweat ran down the soldier's cheek, right through the patch of dirt on his face.

He swallowed before speaking, "The captain tells us to vary our routes and times, on account of the attacks. Yours, I assume."

Vestalis let his lips tug towards the earth, but only for a moment. He couldn't afford to let his emotions betray his true thoughts, which bordered on despair.

He looked around the room to the band of fighters he'd assembled in Alexandria. Less than a hundred remained from when he'd first entered the city a few months ago and he'd only dared to take thirty on this raid.

Vestalis shook his head. The crocodile cult had proved to be more resilient that he'd expected, though he'd realized his mistake when he'd learned that Lysimachus, the former Alabarch, was at its head. The man could squeeze gold from stone and he'd hired the best mercenaries in the area, while the rest of his ranks swelled at each miracle.

"When is the next patrol?" asked Vestalis, bearing down on his words like a horse at the bit.

The soldier blinked heavily. "I told you. We vary our routes and times."

Vestalis glanced to the hang-dog faces around the room. In taking out the last patrol, they'd lost four more soldiers, including the big Roman, Maximus, the one they called the Bear. He knew the men wanted to take their flawed victory and head back to the rally spot, but Vestalis wanted to hit the crocodile soldiers one more time before they left the Juden district for other parts of the city.

But was he pushing his luck? He missed the battle-counsel of Agog, who knew how much to push, how much the men might bend, and when they would break.

Too few of the Northmen remained, not that Vestalis thought that Agog's revolution still mattered. The battle for Alexandria was about keeping the last vestige of civilization intact. The refugees of Rome, spilling in all directions, had created chaos like throwing a wasp nest into the middle of a wedding.

So Vestalis marched the crocodile soldier to the heavy wooden pillar in the center of the room.

"Calder, come here."

The Northman was one of the half-dozen left in his contingent. The others had either died in Rome, returned to the North, or joined nearby mercenary bands. Calder had beefy shoulders, pale hair that swept to the middle of his back, and the nickname of the Butcher.

"Yes, Captain."

The Northman appeared like a wisp, blood splatters on his neck and chest from the earlier battle. The crocodile soldier startled, letting a breathy hiss escape his lips.

"I need an answer," said Vestalis. "Quietly."

Calder stared back with a half-lidded gaze. When Vestalis had first met the Northman warrior, Vestalis had thought he was bored, or an imbecile. After watching him on the battlefield with his double-axe, Vestalis had different ideas about that emotionless stare.

The Northman grabbed the soldier by the neck, forcing the man's mouth open, and shoved a bloody rag into his mouth. Then, quick as one might lasso a horse, he wrapped a second rag around the soldier's face so he couldn't spit the first out.

"Calder, how is—"

The words barely left Vestalis' lips when the Northman slammed a knife through the soldier's hand that was pressed against the pillar. The muffled cry was absorbed by the rags and a tangy scent filled the air as urine ran down the soldier's legs.

Calder slipped the rag from around the soldier's face, and removed the one in his mouth. Spit glistened across the soldier's lips as he heaved whimpers of agony.

"Speak," commanded Calder.

The crocodile soldier looked to Vestalis and then Calder, his spirit fractured by the dagger blow. Then he looked to the knife pinning his hand to the wooden pillar as if he couldn't understand why it was there.

"Speak," said Calder, "or I slice bits from you like roasted pig."

The soldier vibrated with pain, his face moving through the contortions of agony. "Victory street," he said through gritted teeth. "Hepton's patrol. He likes to watch the washer women in the canal. Told me so. He always goes by Victory street."

"When?" asked Vestalis with a raised eyebrow.

The soldier shook his head. "I don't know. I said, random. Maybe now, maybe later."

"Do you have a guess?" asked Vestalis.

The soldier was breathing shallow, his lips quivering. Calder bent the knife, putting pressure on the wound. A guttural cry came from the soldier's throat.

"The washer women only work at the top of the day. So he takes his patrol there early in the route, rather than later," said the soldier.

"What about numbers? How many in his patrol?" asked Vestalis.

"Ten?"

"Any Centaurs? Or Manticores?"

The soldier shook his head vehemently. "No. The Will of Sobek does not let us use his best weapons."

Vestalis rubbed his salt and pepper chin stubble. Lysimachus, or the Will of Sobek, as he was known by his followers, kept a tight leash on his best weapons. While the crocodile priest held the city and the military, he'd lost the workshops when he started killing scholars and burning books. So any mechanical weapon damaged couldn't be repaired.

Another reason Vestalis wished that the *Michanikos* had survived Rome. With her - it still made him shake his head in wonder that he was a her - they stood a better chance to retake the city with their inferior numbers.

Vestalis tilted his head at Calder in question. Calder nodded.

"May you find peace in the afterlife," said Vestalis and turned to his troops as Calder slit the crocodile soldier's throat. "One more fight and then we'll take a few days off. Leave the dead, we'll send back others to get them later."

Vestalis moved to the sewer entrance and the men stashed their water pouches and collected their weapons. They moved like one of Heron's automata plays, rehearsed, and stiff. He almost changed his mind about one more fight, but he'd rather not show indecision.

They marched in single file through the sewer, feet scraping against stone more than Vestalis would have liked. Calder took the lead, holding a lantern for illumination, showing muted reflections on the damp walls. Vestalis hadn't gotten used to the stench, breathing shallow and through his mouth whenever they passed this way, but it was better than getting caught by a couple of Manticores on the streets. Even one of the famed steam chariots could decimate his side.

Coming up on the eastern side of the canal gave them limited options for ambush. The sewer system was split by the canal, so the yearly flooding didn't push water back into people's homes.

Calder scouted a deserted courtyard between a patch of buildings. The city, despite its overflowing refugees, seemed emptier every day. The courtyard was further away from the sewer entrance than Vestalis liked to fight, but the arched bridge across the canal made for an advantageous ambush spot.

Sentries were posted on either side of the courtyard, so the men lounged against the brick walls, picking dried blood from their weapons, or speaking in hushed voices. Vestalis wondered if they'd found the right spot, since he didn't see signs of the washer women, but Calder assured him the stones at the edge of the canal had old, caked lye and tallow ash scattered across them.

His fears were assuaged when a group of five women in sturdy brown stolas and carrying baskets, their voices like sharp stones rebounding from the surrounding buildings, came into view from the western side. They passed a common well, which had a red scarf tied around the lowering rod indicating it was contaminated, and climbed down a ladder to the canal.

"He didn't lie to us about the washer women, at least," said Vestalis.

Calder, who was lounging in the shade of the wall, picking his fingernails with a bone-handled curved knife, twitched with displeasure.

"I wasn't calling into question your methods, good Calder, but I'd rather see things with my eyes to know they're true," said Vestalis.

The Northman lifted his chin, his eyes reflecting the coldest ice, and made a sucking sound across his teeth. Vestalis took the sound as: *if that's the way it must be, so be it*, and went back to watching Victory street.

He didn't have to wait long. The sounds of marching boots, like slaves chipping rocks with hammers, as the hobnails impacted against the cobblestones, gave away the approaching patrol.

The sky was a hazy blue, the kind that killed whole caravans in the deep desert, and the sun had reached its withering apex. Vestalis sheltered his eyes from the blazing light as he leaned into the street to catch sight of the patrol.

The sounds of boots disappeared, as the women in the canal erupted into a chorus of laughter, splashing water at each other. The smell of lye became an irritant in Vestalis' nose.

Vestalis motioned to Calder to listen to the street, but the Northman soldier was already crouched to the ground, his ear pressed to the stone. Vestalis watched his face for signs of recognition. They could take the Alexandria patrol in ambush, but not if a Manticore rode with it.

When Calder gave a shake of the head, Vestalis breathed a sigh of relief, though it did nothing to reduce the tightness in his chest. He dismissed it as battle nerves. Even after all these years, he still felt like a fresh recruit each time he prepared to cross blades.

His seasoned warriors needed no instruction. They flexed their arms and regripped their weapons, hardening their stares for the coming fight. A few in the back had eyes closed, mumbling prayers to the gods. Any edge in a battle he supposed, and offered a few words to Mars, the Roman god of war.

As the patrol approached, Vestalis and his men faded into the courtyard, out of sight. The soldiers passed the entrance to the courtyard, helms shaped like crocodile mouths bobbing with their marching step. The anticipation of spying on the soaked forms of the washer women bright on their murmuring lips.

With the big Roman dead, Calder led the charge. His axe was the prow of a ship, bursting through waves, splitting men and armor and bone from skull.

Vestalis caught a soldier under the arm with his sword, a longer variant that had reach on the common gladius. The old Roman didn't stop to admire his work and kept moving in the wake of the man they called the Butcher.

Surprise had netted them over a dozen corpses, and dead men didn't fight back. But the patrol leader, Hepton, was a cagey warrior and rallied his men into a knot of steel and shield, backing up to the bridge to give them defensible position.

They had the crocodile soldiers two to one, but the wall of swords turned the battle into a standoff.

"For Empire!" cried Vestalis.

Swords sparked in the heat wavering air.

If they didn't finish the ambush, the patrol could follow them to the sewers endangering their movements.

Vestalis pressed harder. A blade nicked him in the arm. Blood ran into his grip, making the hilt slippery.

Two more fell on his side. They couldn't get through the wall of steel.

Out of the corner of his eye, Vestalis caught the flagging blows, swings made of damp effort rather than focused intensity. He'd pushed them too hard, too far. The second fight of the day and after marching through the merciless sewers had left them drained.

Hepton's patrol seemed lively and fresh. Eyes glinted with the spark of victory.

Even though they outnumbered the crocodile soldiers, both sides knew the eventual outcome of the battle. Two more of his men fell and the other side pressed its advantage.

Vestalis prepared to call for retreat, to fall back to the sewers, when he felt a familiar rumble in his chest. He knew where to look, even before he saw them.

Two Manticores coming from the western side of the canal provided unassailable backup to the Alexandrian patrol.

Stepping backward, blocking rather than striking, Vestalis turned to run when he saw the second patrol come around the corner, trapping them on Victory street.

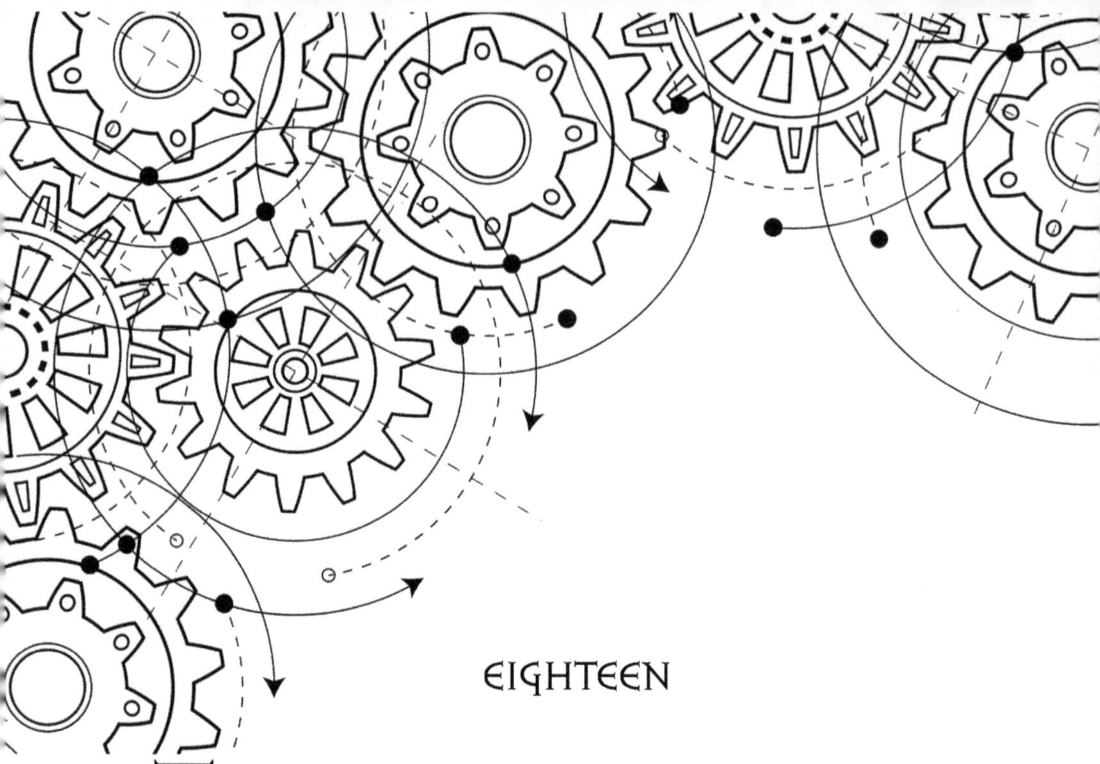

EIGHTEEN

Terror bloomed in the hearts of his men, like a plague of rottenness, hollowing out their will, until they were mere husks going through the motions of their pre-death.

Eyes bulged like fruits squeezed in a gauntleted fist. Nostrils flared wide until they seemed almost split, flayed. The stench of their fear was palatable, a bitter shock of adrenaline-filled sweat that communicated only one thing: flee.

Vestalis' chest hardened into iron until he could hardly breathe. His sword arm turned to water with each blow it blocked, the relentless impacts scattering his thoughts.

Which way to flee?

If he were the first to break, he might stand a chance of escaping. He sensed the others thinking the same thing.

His band's tight formation loosened like a net expanding in the ocean.

"To me! To me!"

The voice was his own, but it sounded like someone else screaming it.

Why would he stay?

The answer returned right as a crocodile soldier kicked at his knee. Vestalis bent his leg, deflecting the blow, and jabbed his sword forward.

I'm their Captain.

The words echoed through his head and he wanted nothing to do with them. He was an old man, had fought his wars. Why was he skirmishing in the middle of the Alexandrian streets?

The second patrol was moving to trap them and there was nothing they could do. If they broke now, the first patrol would cut them from behind, and if they somehow fought past the bridge, the Manticores would annihilate them in a hailstorm of arrows.

"To me!" he cried, and the men tightened further, swords clipping to sparks.

The last vestiges of their strength were fading fast.

Vestalis slipped on the bloody stones, falling to one knee. His opponent lunged in to split him with his sword.

Calder's axe took the man's hand off at the wrist.

Vestalis fought through the confusion in his mind. They couldn't stay where they were.

Move to engage the second patrol? Or push through towards the bridge and take their chances with the Manticores? Maybe the Manticores wouldn't fire on them if they were mixed up with the crocodile soldiers?

"To the bridge! To the bridge!" cried Vestalis.

With purpose flooding through his veins, Vestalis found a second reserve, and took the fight to his opponent. Fear could sap a man's strength, but it could also give it back.

The crocodile soldiers, confident in their growing victory, had broken formation and engaged in individual skirmishes. Vestalis' side, still outnumbering the others, broke the patrol like a reed over the knee.

One crocodile soldier fell off the bridge, his skull splitting like a melon when it hit the stones of the canal.

As the second patrol crashed against them, Vestalis rallied his men at the bottleneck of the bridge, taking the spot the first patrol had occupied previously.

The fresh soldiers battered them like the pistons on the steam mechanical, relentless and ungiving.

"Push into 'em!" shouted Vestalis, knowing the only thing keeping the Manticores from splitting them with arrows was the second patrol.

A soldier came at him. Vestalis caught the man's wrist after deflecting his sword and they wrestled. Vestalis spit in the man's face and kneed him in the fruits, pushing the soldier against the legs of another, until he fell backwards. A sword to the gut ended his fight.

A brief hole in the battle left him without an opponent. Vestalis spied the Manticores, waiting on the other side of the bridge like carrion birds.

If they lost, well, it wouldn't matter and they'd dump the bodies in a hole. But if his side won, they would get a reward full of arrows.

He had to get to the Manticores to give them a chance to escape, but the only way to stay alive was to stay engaged with the second patrol.

Vestalis cursed himself for not listening to his gut. He'd pushed their luck too far and look what it'd gotten them.

He was about to offer his shouts to the gods, whomever bothered to be watching, and charge the Manticores, hoping to surprise them before they could fire on him, when he caught a flash of movement behind the right-most steam chariot.

To his unbelieving eyes, the soldier at the arrow launcher flew backwards from the platform, as if a god had flicked him off, and slid feet first towards the well until he bounced over the stone-lip and disappeared.

Vestalis looked to the sky expecting to see the god Mars or some other battle-hungry deity flowing down on a cloud, but only the merciless sun held court above.

Calder punched him in the shoulder. "What you gawking at? Get back in the fight!"

Vestalis tried to swallow but his mouth was so dry, his tongue stuck to the roof.

"I saw..."

He felt like a lunatic.

At least until he saw the female shape climb upon the back of the Manticore and put a knife in the pilot's neck. When a second woman, long black hair and missing a hand at the end of her arm, took control of the arrow launcher, his heart cheered.

The soldiers on the other Manticore soon found themselves feathered and bloody. Steam burst from the holes in the chambers, as the arrows split bronze like wet papyrus.

The soldiers of the second patrol saw the tides change against them, and broke to flee, which exposed them to the Manticore, sending its missiles over the bridge in a lazy arc of death.

When the battle was done, Vestalis counted his men. Only eight remained, but eight was more than zero, and considering the odds, he knew he'd been lucky to survive.

Or maybe not lucky at all.

Vestalis, covered in a half-dozen wounds, mud and shit caking his boots from the trek through the sewers, and exhaustion like a plague on his bones, moved to greet the two women, one of whom, he had to blink a few times to make sure she wasn't a mirage.

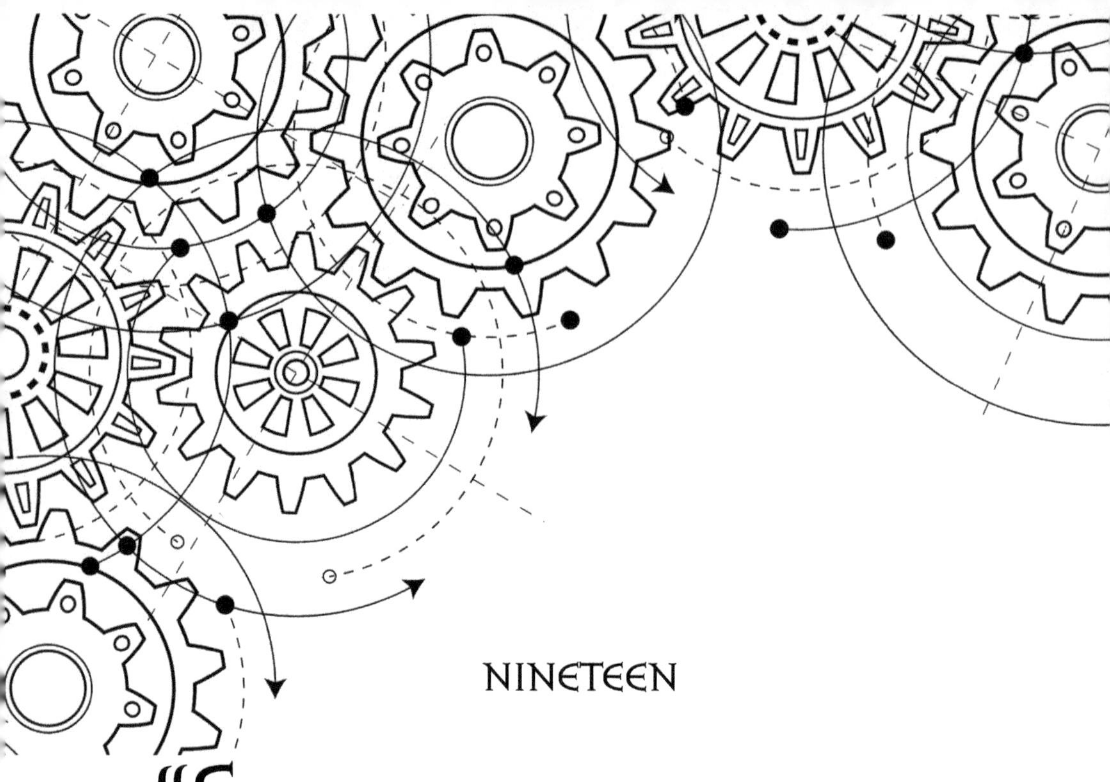

NINETEEN

"Something in your eye?" asked Heron leaning on the frame of the arrow launcher.

Vestalis reeled on his feet, and Heron thought he'd never looked older. What had once been salt-and-pepper stubble was nearly all gray. He looked like an old dog whose muzzle had turned. His bald head glistened in the burning sun, steam rising skyward. If she threw him into the canal, she thought the water might boil.

"How?" asked Vestalis in one short, out-breath, as if it were the only word he knew.

Her whole faced ached with a smile, spilling into her chest until she vibrated with laughter.

"Do we have time?" she asked.

Vestalis leaned on his sword as if it were a cane, his shoulders drooped as he took huge, cleansing breaths. The weight of the battle was still draped around his shoulders, and as he shook his head, Heron realized how many of the dead soldiers on the bridge were his.

Heron swallowed her grin. "Apologies. I didn't realize."

"No," he said, wiping blood from his neck, but mostly smearing it. "You saved us. But we have to go now. Another patrol could be along at any moment."

Heron patted the arrow launcher. "We have this now."

His eyes creased and he shook his head again. "We should get moving. Get down from there, so you don't get hurt."

She couldn't quite understand why they couldn't take the Manticore with them, but followed his directions, waving Arethussa off when she hesitated.

Vestalis nodded to the big Northman carrying a two-sided axe. When the blade slammed into the brass chamber, releasing a cloud of steam, Heron cried out as if her child had been murdered.

"We can't take it with us and we don't want to leave it," said Vestalis. "Let's go."

The small band moved one street up from the bridge, to the west side of the canal. They entered the sewers by a set of stone steps. One of the soldiers produced a hand-held lamp and it was given to the Northman at the front, a man she'd heard named Calder.

A little bit after they entered, the rumble of steam chariots passed over head. Heron counted at least seven, which would have been enough to wipe them out.

This time, with light and companionship, the sewers weren't so frightening. Arethussa made retching noises occasionally, but kept moving despite her discomfort.

They marched beneath numerous cross streets and Heron marked the passage by the round dump holes that lined the main avenues, only having to leap out of the way once when a bucket of refuse slid through the hole. With light and a map of the sewers in her mind, she guessed where they were headed before they reached their destination.

"The Serapeum?"

Vestalis turned his head and grunted an acknowledgement. His right arm clung to his torso as if he were holding rocks in his stomach.

"Are you well?" she asked, touching his shoulder.

"Alive," he replied. "Better than some."

Heron thought they might return to the streets to enter the Serapeum, but then they passed through a ragged hole cut into the earth, held up with timbers and stone. They had to step around the pillars, which Heron surmised were placed there to keep the tunnel from collapsing.

The tunnel led to a wide room that held a faint musty scent. The walls wept with moisture. Empty scroll racks had been shoved into one corner of the room, leaving space for dozens of bedrolls, many of which would stay empty.

"Did they——?" she asked, nodding towards the empty scroll racks.

Vestalis unloaded his scabbard onto a table and splashed water into his face. Arethussa grabbed a jug of water from the table and brought it around to the men, giving Heron a glance that said *go ahead I'll be fine*. She seemed right in her element, as if she were back at the Cassandra's Tears.

Vestalis led her from the room while the remainder of his men collapsed on scattered bedrolls. Heron quickly became lost as Vestalis made many rapid turns. She didn't know the daughter of the Great Library, the Serapeum, as well as she would have liked. They kept scrolls on history and geography more than science and mathematics, leaving less need for her attendance.

Upward leading stairs, painted with quotations from history's greatest thinkers, led them to the main lecture hall, a place Heron recalled from years ago when she gave a speech on the importance of testing theories. But when she entered, she didn't recognize it, because the floor was covered with hundreds of racks, overflowing with scrolls, until they looked like porcupine nests.

"When Lysimachus began his war against the Library, scholars smuggled what they could, replacing those documents with empty papyrus," said Vestalis.

Heron's face grew flush with excitement. "You mean they're not burning anything of worth?"

Vestalis' jaw pulsed. "Not all was saved. But some. There are other locations in the city like this, including the Soma of Alexander. But if we lose the city, a little scroll hoarding won't matter. He'll find them and burn them eventually."

Heron pulled the hair away from her face. It was sticky with sweat from the humid air. In some ways, she missed her male cut.

"Then we must not lose the city," said Heron.

The old soldier wiped his forehead with the back of his hand. The skin that wasn't splattered with blood seemed gray. He looked to her with a gaze that had once held steel, but now seemed rusty with misuse.

"We have few troops left and I lost two dozen more today in my arrogance. I expect more to defect in the night. Seems each time I wake up, there's another empty bedroll," said Vestalis wearily.

"You shouldn't whip yourself. You're doing the best you can," said Heron. "But do you have any steam mechanicals? Any equipment we might put to good use?"

"Some, but what about you? The last I saw you, you were being dragged out of the Senate. What happened? How many men have you brought with you?"

Heron glanced at the floor before answering. "Only myself."

"Then where have you been for the last year and a half?" he asked, raising his voice and catching himself halfway.

She opened her mouth to speak, but it was too painful to explain. "Surviving. The Romans hunted us down."

He seemed to accept her answer with a reluctant nod, though she could tell he wouldn't be satisfied long. But how could she explain that Hoth had rescued her with over a dozen ships and no one would return? It was Rome all over again, with her playing the part of the destroyer.

"What of the workshops? Have they come to your aid?" she asked.

"Some were killed, others fled the city."

"Nektam?" she asked, but he responded with a grim bunching of the lips. "Show me your equipment, then. Give me some bit of good news."

"Apologies, *Michanikos*, I'm short on good news." He paused, a faint twinkle leaping in his eyes. "Though I do have one thing to show you that might bring you some joy."

"Only one?"

He twisted his lips to the side. "Maybe two."

He led her to a smaller lecture hall down from the one packed with scrolls. She smelled the coal dust before she stepped into the room and expected to see a steam mechanical in the room.

She did see those, more than a couple, including the parts from four or five, scattered around the room: broken and misshapen pipes, wheels snapped in half, pistons unhooked from gears, buckets of gears, and so on. Men in scholar robes moved through the equipment, poking and prodding as if it might reach out and bite them.

Heron thought the old soldier might have been mistaken about bringing joy until she heard a booming voice from the other side of a wall of shelves.

"I'm not Vulcan, you withering old goats, and I don't shit fire out of my arse. So if you want it fixed, find me a proper furnace!"

Heron almost tripped over her wooden leg in haste to witness him. Her Master of Foundries stood wide-legged before a trio of wrinkled sages, his bald head darker than she'd ever seen it, wearing desert gear rather than the leather smith's loincloth she was used to him wearing.

"I'll find you a proper furnace," she said.

Punt spun around, the barrel-chested blacksmith moved like a dancer, and upon gazing at her, he rubbed his eyes with his palms.

"I thought the mirages would stop once I left the sands," muttered Punt.

"Good Punt, my eyes scream joy upon seeing you. You don't know how many times I have missed you," she said, holding a hand across her heart.

Punt rubbed his jaw and looked at her sideways. "I...uhm, I've missed you."

"You're still not used to me being a woman, are you?"

A storm cloud gathered over his brow. "Knowing and seeing are two different things."

The comment hit her in the gut. "I'm not a shapeshifter, if that's what you mean. And I've always been a woman."

He nodded, but she could see that even though he'd known since the ride to the Temple of Alexandria, it still weighed heavily on him.

"Where's Plutarch?" she asked hesitantly, conjuring reasons for his absence in her mind.

Punt's face drew grim. "On errands."

Heron opened her mouth to ask, but his demeanor suggested otherwise.

"I look forward to the moment of seeing him," said Heron. "My journey was long and arduous. How did you survive the burning of Rome?"

"Once it started, we fled the city immediately, having no ties. But even our fear wasn't enough, at times," he said, staring at his hands as if they were covered in blood.

"Have you returned to help free the city?" she asked.

He tilted his head as if to say that he would, though his heart wasn't in it.

"I feel that, too, good Punt. But I must save Sepharia. I can't leave her with Lysimachus," she said.

"Is it possible?" Punt asked.

The truth was a cut across the chest, bright searing pain that made her heart seize. How could she think that she might rescue Sepharia? They had no troops, no workshops, nothing other than a few squads of men, and a bunch of wrinkled old sages hiding from the crocodile priests.

"I don't know yet," she said. "But I'll figure something out."

Vestalis, who'd been quiet during the exchange, spoke up from the doorway. "We need to figure something out soon. Lysimachus' hold on the city grows stronger each day. I fear after his next miracle, his hold will be unstoppable."

"What can be made, can be unmade," said Heron.

"Then I hope you have some good ideas," said Vestalis, "because I'm all out—"

An explosion rocked the Serapeum, shaking dust into the air. The withered old sages bleated like lambs, while Vestalis cursed the gods.

Wide-eyed, they shared glances, until a soldier came stumbling down the hall, crimson blooming through his tunic, until he collapsed at their door.

"They blew the gate up! Manticores and Centaurs! And something worse in the smoke, the Crocodile God!"

When he turned, Heron could see the arrows sticking from his back. He'd been hit with an arrow launcher.

Vestalis' sword sung from his scabbard right as three soldiers with crocodile helms rushed around the corner at the end of the hall.

When Punt grabbed his warhammer, leaned against the stack of scrolls, Vestalis nodded in Heron's direction.

"I'll hold them off. Take her to Plutarch," he said.

The blacksmith grumbled, but grabbed her by the arm and began dragging her down the hallway.

"We've got to stay and help him," she said, wedging her hand against the open door, but her fingers slipped away as quickly as she gained purchase.

The crocodile soldiers advanced on the old equestrian.

"Vestalis!" she cried. "Don't sacrifice yourself for me."

He lunged forward with his blade, forcing the first soldier to stumble into the second. "Who said I was going to sacrifice myself? Go, now!"

As they disappeared around the corner, amid the clash of steel, Vestalis' last command sounded like a zephyr chasing after them.

"Punt, make sure you close the door behind you!"

The blacksmith grimaced as he heard the words, but Heron was too busy trying to figure out how Lysimachus had known they were at the Serapeum to make his attack. The coincidence seemed too strong.

They made their way into the lower level, Heron having given up her resistance and collected Arethussa before they left. The tavern owner appeared flush with concern, cheeks like bright apples.

"What's happened? Everyone ran out after the explosion," said Arethussa.

"No time," said Punt, pushing them both through the tunnel that led to the sewers. Punt handed Heron a lantern and motioned for them to move down the passage. "We need to get you to the Soma."

"You can't close that behind them," said Heron. "Then no one will escape."

Punt replied through gritted teeth, "I'm not closing it behind them."

Then he moved back into the room and Heron thought he was going to grab a backpack, or another weapon for them to use, but then he turned around and struck the middle timber with such force that it cracked and the center of the tunnel slumped in. Once the movement of earth started, the rest collapsed and the pair of them had to flee the billowing dust.

TWENTY

Sepharia was climbing from the tiled bath, water sluicing from her naked body, when she saw her father through the window, standing at the far end of courtyard. Heron stood motionless, as if she didn't actually exist, gazing across the rows of bushes resplendent in purple and white flowers that smelled like lavender.

In her stillness, like a watcher of birds, Sepharia let the water drip from her body, beads escaping from elbows and nipples, tickling the cool flesh. She made no motion toward the plush towels hung by the door and kept her gaze on Heron, who like a mirror, watched her in turn.

This Heron had longer hair than the previous ones, similar to the one she'd seen that night on the top of the Customs building. She wore a cream stola, beaded with emerald stones, making it appear she was a Lady of the Crocodiles. Her left hand was hidden by the folds of the garment, but when she lifted her arm to block the sunlight from her eyes, the stump was visible.

Sepharia clamped her eyes closed, pinching her face into a point.

"This is not Heron. This is not Heron."

When she opened her eyes, the woman was gone. Sepharia didn't know what was worse, seeing the copy of her father, or opening her eyes and finding the woman gone, as if she'd only been a mirage.

The first bothered Sepharia more than the second, for that meant that Lysimachus was maiming poor women who happened to look like her father. To what purpose, Sepharia didn't know except to infect her with madness.

Each one seemed so real, so perfect, as if the scribblers from the Great Library had composed her father in mid-air with only their ink-tipped quills. That thought was worse than the others, because it led her mind down the pathway towards the next miracle, to the next demonstration of Sobek's power.

A knock on the door sent her scrambling for the plush towel. She wrapped it around her body, hating its seductive touch.

"I'm here," said Sepharia.

One of Lysimachus' priests, Dagius, a Thracian who'd sworn his life to the crocodile god after the third miracle, the one in which she'd been drawn and quartered, ducked under the doorway.

He was an odd priest, a mountain of muscle that tried to shrink into the dark green robes the followers of Sobek preferred. He had all his limbs and digits, at least. Though she knew his *sacrifice* from when he'd taken off his robes to show her, as if she'd wanted to see it. The craters on his back where flesh had been scooped out like sand from a dune made her jaw tense thinking about it.

"The Will of Sobek wants you in the chapel," said Dagius, trying not to look at her.

"Then leave me so I can dress, or am I to march there wearing nothing but my naked flesh?"

The big man blushed, a contradiction to his brutish past. Sepharia had seen his scars from his life as a mercenary and she doubted he'd not forcibly taken of womanly flesh after battle. But unlike her captivity with Vima, the priests of Sobek treated her like a fragile object that might be shattered if dropped.

Dagius turned his back. "I will wait, Bride of Sobek. But hurry." The priest's deep voice was a drum being beaten in the darkness.

Sepharia wrapped the stola around her body, wishing it was any color but the dark green that matched the robes of the priests. As she dressed, she glanced out the window, unsure if she was expecting to see Heron again, or even if she wanted to.

She followed the lumbering priest through the halls of the Palace. The opulence from her previous residence had been erased by the priesthood. Lysimachus funded his efforts with the treasures that had graced the marble halls. They passed an alcove that had once held a gilded vase with deep blue scrollwork and an image of Alexander the Macedonian riding across the plains on Bucephalus. Sepharia couldn't recall when it'd been sold, but she mourned its absence each time she came this way.

Passing beneath an archway decorated with tiled frescos, Sepharia noticed the mold creeping across the surface, a common sight since the servants had been banished from the Palace. When the priests spilled, or trailed damp robes across the once-mirror surface of the marble floors, the wetness festered.

Even before she reached the chapel, the area once known as the Sun Room, Sepharia sensed the rot. A cloying richness of vegetation choked the air, but not like the clean, orderly gardens of the Great Library. When she'd visited the rows of potted plants in the Botany Hall, the air had been sweet on her tongue. This air expanded in her mouth and nose and throat until she gagged.

As they passed through the Green Room, the place that had once held the feast for Agog's wedding, her step faltered. Ahead, between the columns that separated the rooms, vines exploded onto the walls like ink that had bled onto parchment.

The chapel was dim, muted splashes and eternal drips, filling that failing light. Each step turned to lead until she was standing in the center of the Green Room, unmoving. She knew the price of fleeing, but what would they do if she refused to go forward?

Sepharia didn't have to find out. Dagius made a grumble in his chest, like a leashed dog growling, and Sepharia found the courage to move her feet.

The room that had once been the Sun Room had been transformed into a sweltering nightmare. The tiled pool in the center of the room had been expanded, except it wasn't a pool at all, but a swamp, as mounds of earth had been dumped into the room.

Insects buzzed through the bleak and shapes moved in the darkness ahead, beyond the ridge that kept the water from flooding into the Green Room. The room was the belly of a chthonic leviathan, carved out and deposited in the Palace. The completeness of the transformation sent shivers through her limbs.

A voice startled her. "Greetings, Sepharia."

She knew better than to answer Lysimachus, who stood right inside the swampy room to the side. She hadn't seen him because he blended into the foliage in his dark green robes. Sweat beaded on his bald head, though he seemed unaffected by the smothering heat.

"As the Bride of Sobek," said Lysimachus, "you must prove your worthiness to him, before He Who Dwelleth Amid Terrors can accept you as his wife."

"What if I don't want to be worthy?" she asked, raising her chin.

It seemed that Lysimachus had expected this reply, because his lips twitched in recognition.

"You will be worthy, or Heron will take the punishment."

On the other side of the room, a shape appeared, the woman who looked like Heron. Sepharia bit her lower lip, she should have known something like this would happen as soon as she saw the woman. Was it Heron? Sepharia truthfully didn't know. She didn't *think* so, but Lysimachus had been testing her with events that couldn't be real, yet felt that way when she passed through them.

Sometimes, the falseness of Heron was like a warped mirror, and Sepharia knew it right away. But other times, like the night of the docks, she'd almost believed it was really her father on top of that building and wanted to stray from the script that Lysimachus had fed her before they'd arrived.

"What do you want me to do?" asked Sepharia, wanting to get it over with as quickly as possible.

But a splash somewhere ahead, between her and Heron, sent a flood of primal fear through her mind. Her heart shrunk with the knowledge of what had made that splash.

"Walk to her," said Lysimachus. "And let your fear be a ward to Sobek's children."

She shut her eyes and clenched her fists. She muttered under her breath, "I could run, run and run, and never stop. They can't catch me if I run."

But when she opened her eyes, her legs did not move.

"Walk to her," said Lysimachus, the threat of punishment woven into his words. He'd shown her too many times that there was always punishment, though usually not for her, and that was worse.

It took some effort, but she was able to move one foot forward, onto the slope of mud and grass.

"Before she goes, Dagius," said Lysimachus, "give her your knife."

The big priest moved to her side and shoved the hilt into her grip. The wooden handle had been carved into a crocodile head. Sepharia hated holding it, but the idea of moving through the swamp without a weapon was worse than carrying Sobek's symbol.

Sepharia took one last look at Lysimachus, who watched her with beady eyes. For a moment, the thought of turning on him and driving the blade through his neck almost overcame her sense of self-preservation, but she knew that if she failed, the consequences would be catastrophic.

Lysimachus nodded towards the swamp. She set her shoulders squarely forward and willed her other leg to move. The mound upon which she stepped shifted beneath her sandal, so she reached down and removed the thin coverings. Bare feet would find better purchase in the soft soil.

The mound rose and then descended into the water. Sepharia pushed a frond away from her face using her free hand. She kept the dagger at the ready, gripped for downward stabs.

She shuffled her feet forward, cool mud squeezing through her toes. The water went up to her ankles when she stepped in it. Grassy mounds rose from the water in various locations, blocking sightlines.

A splash not far away brought a cry to her lips, which she immediately regretted. Something moved through the water between the mounds, the shape hidden by the depth ahead.

"It must be a trick. It must be a trick."

She said the words, but did not believe them. Or at least her trembling hands did not.

"He's killed me before and brought me back. How can this not be the same?"

She found her gaze was locked onto the surface of the water. She dared a glance up, to see Heron on the other side. The room hadn't felt so large before, but now it seemed as long as the coliseum.

Sepharia kept moving, passing an earthy mound covered in grass, gentle ripples cascading away from her across the dark waters. As she made it to the other side, a foul scent rose up, bringing bile to her throat.

With her legs refusing to move, Sepharia searched the water for the source of the smell. Lurking beneath the surface, something pale was stuck in the mud. With her outstretched toe, Sepharia pushed and it released from the muck, rising to the top. It was a half-eaten arm, bloated from the water, but undeniably real.

At that moment, something moved in the water towards her from the right. An angled-v disturbed the surface. Sepharia lunged forward to escape only to sink into the water to her thighs. The creature turned and headed straight for her.

When a lumpy snout broke the surface, Sepharia jammed her knife into the exposed flesh. The blade barely bit through the tough skin, but it forced the crocodile to turn away.

Fear flooded through her body, a crimson haze tainted the air. Sepharia waded forward, head swiveling around, searching for more crocodiles. She heard other splashes at different points of the room. It sounded like they were converging on her.

She reached an earthy mound, and climbed up the side, grass slapping at her face as she pulled herself up, clawing into the soil. Reaching the top, she jumped to her feet, right as a mouth snapped at the area her feet had been.

The crocodile slithered through the water, its body and tail undulating across the surface before it submerged again.

She was over halfway across the room. Heron stood motionless on the other side and at first, Sepharia was confused, until she saw the bonds holding her to a timber sunk into the soil.

If she made a mad dash through the water, she could reach the landing on the other side before the crocodiles could reach her. But she wasn't sure she knew where all of them were. Sepharia circled the mound, trying to spy their location, feeling at all times like one would come up the other side and crunch into her feet.

With a burst, Sepharia leapt over the water, falling face first, mud and bugs splashing into her eyes as she lost her balance. Righting herself, she thrust herself through the water, hearing nothing but her own splashing, knowing that those beasts could be on her.

She raged through the water, arms wheeling through the air. She reached the muddy landing and climbed upon the ridge, checking behind her for crocodiles.

Her chest heaved with breath, the efforts of escape burning through her limbs. She held the dagger in a trembling fist, ready to stab it into anything that came on shore.

When nothing came out of the water at her, Sepharia allowed herself to untense, if only so she didn't pass out.

"I'm here," she shouted over the swamp. "Now what do you want?"

Once again, Lysimachus' voice startled her. He stood nearby, but too far for her to reach. He must have moved through hidden paths in the room while she struggled through the water.

"You must kill Heron," said Lysimachus.

Sepharia looked upon the woman bound to the pillar. Sepharia's eyes were puffy and bloodshot from the filthy water, but she could see enough to know the woman was not her father.

"That's not her," said Sepharia, hearing her own voice crack.

"Do not despair," said Lysimachus, ignoring her comment, "I will give her back her life even after you take it. Remember, I control the Waters of Creation."

"It's a lie, a trick," said Sepharia.

Lysimachus raised an eyebrow. "A trick? Have I not shown you time and time again that I hold the power of eternal life? Dagius, come here."

The big priest pushed through the foliage to Lysimachus' side.

"Give me your hand," said Lysimachus.

Dagius obeyed and Lysimachus produced a dagger from the folds of his robe. Before Sepharia could wonder what he would do, Lysimachus put the knife to the smallest finger and sheared it off the hand.

The big priest muffled his cries, but even the hardened soldier couldn't ignore the pain.

Lysimachus held up the finger before tossing it into the swamp. A faint plop swallowed the digit.

Then he pulled a water pouch from beneath his voluminous robes and poured it over the bloody hands of the bent priest.

Sepharia could not take her eyes from the scene and when it was over, she'd realized she'd missed her chance to attack.

"Show her your hand," said Lysimachus when he was finished.

The big priest held out his hand, showing the smallest finger intact.

She started to say, *it's a lie*, but she couldn't get the words out and choked instead.

"Kill Heron," said Lysimachus. "And she might live. If you don't, I will let her die forever."

Sepharia looked to the knife in her fist. What harm would it be to put the knife in the woman's chest, if Lysimachus could bring her back? But to do so, would admit that he did control the Waters of Creation, she realized.

She glanced to Heron and then back to the knife. She wasn't trembling anymore, but that seemed somehow worse.

"Kill Heron," said Lysimachus. "Kill her, so that Lord Sobek might bring her back."

Sepharia moved to the woman. Stood close enough that she could smell the stink of her fear. The woman who would be Heron kept her gaze on her feet.

"No, I won't," said Sepharia eventually, dropping the knife into the mud. "I won't do it."

A stifled bubble of relief escaped from the woman's lips.

"You won't save her?" asked Lysimachus.

"I won't kill her."

"Then Dagius will."

Sepharia thought the big priest would put his blade into the woman, but instead, he lifted the timber out of the mud as the woman began to scream. His arms bulged as he stepped through the mud, sucking at his feet, as he moved towards the water.

He launched her bound form through the air and she screamed until she hit, sending brackish bug-filled water up in a plume. Interested splashes followed as shapes in the water moved to investigate, followed by terrible thrashing as they tore her apart.

TWENTY ONE

While waiting for the scouts to return, Heron paced around the tomb of her ancestor, her steps bright echoes in the marbled room. As she made her circuitous route, she couldn't help but glance at the scenes of the great man carved into the sides of his final resting place. He'd been a conqueror, a creator of Empires, and seeing his tomb reminded her that she'd helped recreate his Alexandrian vision, if briefly.

She wondered what it'd be like to speak with him, to hear his thoughts on what mistakes she had made along the way. Sometimes, she paused and put her hand against the cold stone, wishing for his counsel. For who did she have left? Almost no one.

The battle at the Serapeum had decimated Vestalis' troops. A trickle had made it back to the Soma, none bearing news of Vestalis or Punt. Beneath the Serapeum was a second, more hidden, entrance into the sewers, and those who had escaped had taken that way.

The weight of events pressed onto Heron's shoulders, so she escaped to the outside, passing a few soldiers and sages carrying scrolls along the way, surprised to find night greeting her upon exit.

The Soma of Alexander faced north, so the beacon fire of the Lighthouse was a flickering eye through the sentinel branches of the great Sycamore tree. Heron thought she saw a white light blinking from the beacon level, facing south, but it ended as soon as she noticed it.

The rest of the city, marked by faint lights, could be seen from the rise, as the eastern side was higher than the west and the Soma had been built on a hill. Surrounding the Soma was the noble district, the Broucheion, and its torturous streets made for an excellent buffer against the spies of Sobek.

From out of the darkness, soldiers appeared, limping and carrying one another. A bald, broad-shouldered man carrying a warhammer and holding up a fellow soldier with bloody bandages across half his face, came up the hill.

"Punt!"

News of their return brought helpers from inside the Soma and the surrounding buildings. The injured soldier on Punt's shoulder was taken away by men in gray robes. The strong voices of Arethussa and Plutarch could be heard organizing the chaos, the pair of them marshalling forces to care for the wounded.

"Vestalis?" she asked, touching her lips with her fingertips.

Relieved of his burden, Punt sagged heavily against his warhammer, steel resting in the grass. Staring into the distance, he rubbed his jaw as if he were trying to erase some memory.

"Punt? Are you well? What happened to Vestalis?" she asked, touching his shoulder.

The blacksmith startled, eyes flaring open. "It's been a hard day."

"Yes, yes. But Vestalis?"

At that moment, two men went past, carrying a stretcher. The motionless form of the old Roman soldier was upon it, his chest covered in bandages.

"He's alive," said Punt, before she could ask. "Barely."

"What happened after you closed the tunnel?"

Punt rubbed his eyes. "Only the gods know. Battles were fought in the hallways, in the auditoriums. But that was better than facing their warmachines in the open." He shook his head. "When we made those damn things, I never thought I'd be on the other end of one."

"How did you escape?"

He shook his head. "Luck. One of the blasts from the steam launchers put a hole through the wall and a group of us, including Vestalis, made a break for it."

Heron was about to ask another question when Punt collapsed to his knees, holding onto the shaft of the warhammer. She retrieved a water pouch and brought it to the blacksmith. When he was sated, he sat in the grass, head in his hands.

When Punt seemed rested enough, she asked, "How many men survived? We're going to need everyone we have if we're going to take the city back."

The normally stoic blacksmith choked out a derisive laugh. "Take the city back? At this point, I'm thinking about how to safely retrieve Astrela and leave Alexandria. Plutarch will come, too. I'm sure our talents could be used in Parthia, or Indus. Somewhere far away from this crocodile god."

The words burned Heron's ears like acid and she rubbed the side of her head to erase the pain.

"Leave? We cannot leave. If we do, Lysimachus will erase the knowledge contained here and plunge the world back into a stygian darkness. And I cannot leave Sepharia, not in his clutches. I must save her, somehow."

"Heron," said Punt quietly. "I have followed you time and time again and you've never let me down. But I cannot see how you can save us from this. Lysimachus has all the advantages: soldiers, mechanicals, the city. What do we have?"

"We have us," said Heron, touching Punt's arm. "It's not that I'm a woman is it?"

He lifted his chin and stared at her, the whiteness of his eyes catching an orangish glow from the Lighthouse, contrasted against his mocha skin.

"No," he said. "At first, it did, and once it became common knowledge, it bothered me again. But I couldn't imagine working in anyone else's workshop."

"But you're going to leave the city?"

The pained smile on his lips was tortured by the thoughts passing through his eyes. "I'd hoped you'd come with us. But I can see that you can't."

A prickly flushness overtook her body, as if a swarm of bees had politely stung her and the venom coursed across her skin. She turned her head away, staring at the blotches of light scattered across the city.

"You see that?" she said. "My city is wounded. There should be light blossoming from every street. Now it looks like mange on a tired dog."

"Apologies," whispered Punt. "I know this hurts you."

She went to clasp her hands together, but when the one hand hit the stump, she remembered that Lysimachus had taken the other. A surprised cry left her lips.

"Curse that man, Lysimachus. He's taken everything. My limbs, my daughter, my city. I cannot leave. I must right this."

"But how? You've nothing left. Not even a workshop."

At those words, the fever across her skin broke, leaving her faint.

"Even my workshop," she muttered, and then grasped Punt's arm, squeezing. "You must stay. Help me take it back. I don't know how I'm going to do it, but we'll find a way."

Punt wiped a hand across the dome of his bald head and when it reached the nape of his neck, Heron knew what his answer would be.

"I'm leaving tomorrow at dawn," he said. "First to get Astrela, then head east. I don't think you will, but if you change your mind, I'll meet you at the ruins of the old coliseum outside the city. We'll wait for you until evening."

Punt, her blacksmith and oldest friend, stood up, patted her arm, and trudged into the darkness. Heron pulled her knees to her chest, wrapped her arms around them, and squeezed until the tears blotted out the world.

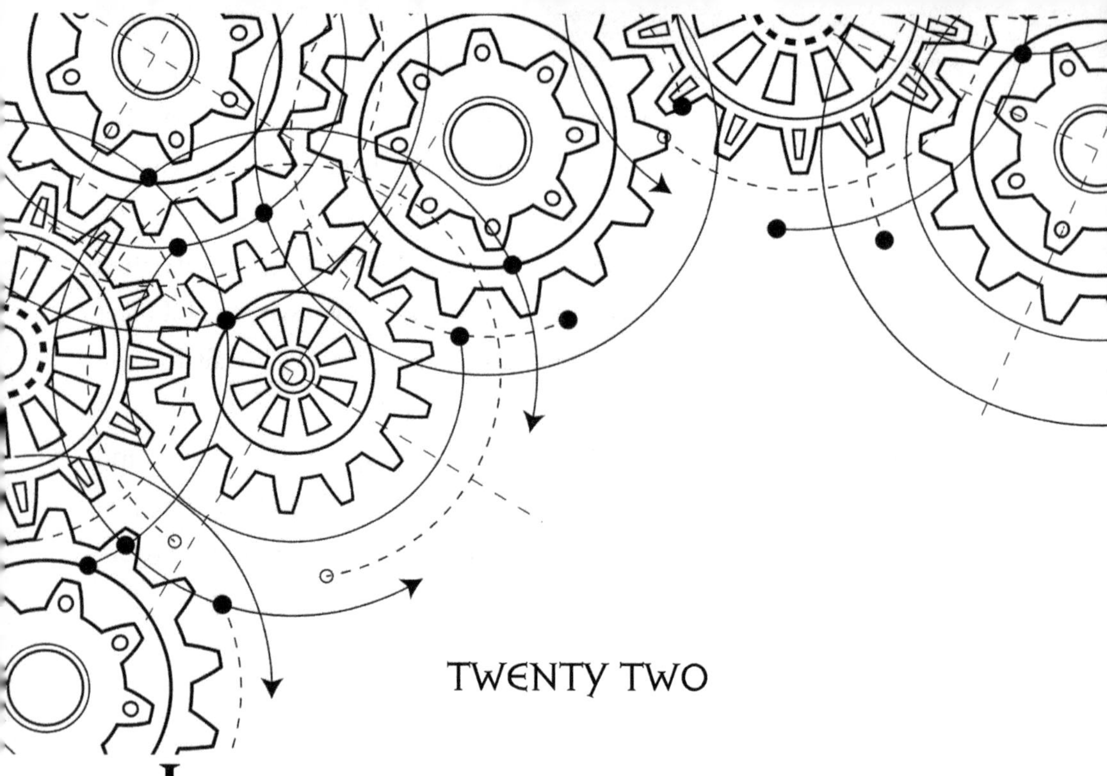

TWENTY TWO

It was a blessing that her workshop was guarded around the clock by crocodile soldiers. Without a way to reenter, she'd changed the plan to occupy Nektam's old workshop, which was hers too, in a way.

Heron ran her fingers across the cracked stone of the hearth, gray ash with flecks of black iron sitting in the belly of the furnace. The smithy was three times the size of the one Punt tended, with two openings and a separate chamber for loading fuel.

With a team of blacksmiths, one could produce top quality iron or steel at ten times the rate of her workshop. It was no wonder that Nektam had become the ship builder for Alexandria.

Heron pounded her fist on a pillar, shaking chalky dust on her arm. The platform had once held a steam mechanical for keeping the furnace hot, but it'd been removed some time ago, possibly after Nektam had been executed for opposing Lysimachus.

"You look like a woman considering her former lovers," said Vestalis from the archway.

He leaned against the brick wall, his arm in a sling, a yellowed bruise across his jaw, and a scab on his lip.

Heron smiled and patted the stone. "No, not former. Maybe a little jealous of a marriage I arranged. I built this workshop for Nektam when his old one was destroyed."

"And now you've come home to claim it," he said.

"Claim? No. And we won't be restarting the furnace, as much as I'd love to smell its coal fires burning. That would let Lysimachus know where to find us."

Vestalis had a maudlin smile. "I meant only that you seemed content here, more relaxed than I've ever seen you. In Rome, I thought you might snap the table in two by staring at it."

The sound of crates being ripped open with tools made them both glance to the workshop through the archway. It'd taken two days, but they'd moved a couple of wagon loads of supplies to Nektam's in preparation.

When Vestalis looked back, Heron met his gaze and they stared at each other from across the foundry. Nothing was said in that moment, because nothing needed to be said. They both knew how much the way forward would test them and their shared gaze was confirmation of the commitment.

"So how do you propose to take the city back?" he asked, checking back into the workshop.

"First, we get Sepharia back."

Vestalis responded slowly, "Apologies, Heron, I mean you no disrespect, but isn't that walking right into the trap he's set for you? Wouldn't it be safer to focus on the city, finding troops, purchasing whichever mercenary groups Lysimachus hasn't already bought? Trying to get Sepharia back could be seen as selfish."

"It is selfish," she replied. "But I plan to use getting her back to our favor."

"How?" he asked, gaze askew.

"How did Lysimachus take the city? How did he go from one priest dedicated to his sick god to an army of believers?"

Vestalis thought for a moment. He tried to scratch an itch with the hand in the sling but realized his mistake and used his other fingernails to relieve the irritation. "One miracle at a time."

"Exactly, one miracle at a time."

Vestalis narrowed his gaze. "Do you mean to discredit him?"

"He's been too smart for that to work. It's much easier to make people believe than it is to dispel their belief. Because, in the end, belief is exactly what it is, belief. It requires nothing else than commitment from the believers."

"Then why haven't the Temples done this before? How has he done what the others could only dream of? It won't be long before the Temple of Sobek is the only religion in the city, and one year ago, they didn't even have a temple."

"Because the temples only wanted one thing—gold. Lysimachus had that once, but now it doesn't interest him," she said. "So he's focused on making people believers rather than trying to take their gold. He's done that by convincing them he has special powers straight from his god. Not everyone believes him, but enough, and specifically, the right people do."

Vestalis let a short laugh burst from his lips. "It took the Customs collector to figure out what the temples never could."

"Which makes him more dangerous, because he knows why he's in power, and he's doing everything to solidify it," she said.

"So how are we going to take it from him?"

She had to work herself up to even say it and he sensed her discomfort by tilting his head. "We have to use their superstitions against them."

An eyebrow went up on the old Roman.

"It pains me to even suggest it. The Great Library has done the world wonders in dispelling the idiocies propagated by fools and now I'm preparing to go against everything the Great Library stands for and double those falsehoods."

"I suppose you're going to tell me how? We only have a week until the next miracle. Is that what's in those scrolls?" he asked, nodding towards the elongated knapsack.

She grimaced. "Not entirely. Most of that is another project, one I can't commit to without more resources."

He lifted the arm in his sling. "I would help your workers, but I'm as useful as a Thracian at cooking."

"I don't need you for that. I'll play the foreman when I'm not making new drawings," she said.

"You'll have time for both?"

She sighed. "Sleep is rather unnecessary, don't you think?"

"Then what I am doing?"

At that moment, a crash startled them both. Heron's heart raced to full until Vestalis gave a little shake of the head, indicated something had fallen in the workshop.

"I need you to protect us. And not in the way you think," she added, when his eyes narrowed. "We're going to need to make noise at times, creating the equipment I need. But if we're too loud when a patrol passes, they'll discover us. I need you to set up watchers and signals, like you did with the army on the march to Rome. You give the signal, and we'll stop working, even speaking if that's what it takes."

"The sounds of your work will travel. I'm not a miracle worker," he said.

"Arethussa can help. She ran a secret school in the back of her tavern. She probably knows ways to make the walls quieter."

His face grew tight. "You have neighbors. They might talk. Especially for the rewards Lysimachus is offering."

"I don't have time to worry about that," she said. "You'll have to figure it out. You always do."

"I'll do what I can." He gave a reluctant nod. "So what's this miracle that will save Sepharia and change Alexandria, again?"

Heron cleared her throat and stared at her feet.

"You don't know?" he asked.

She looked up, cheeks turning red. "I do. But not the details. If we had a couple steam mechanicals, I'd have more options, but we don't, so we'll have to make do. The rest I still have to figure out."

Vestalis was a hard man, but even this admission, knocked him back, widened his eyes.

"So Lysimachus has every resource in the city, including thousands of loyal troops and the very technologies you invented, and we have a vague plan and some rope and pulleys?"

As he spoke, the ridiculousness of her ideas seem to crystallize into midair and then shatter by the force of his question.

"I know..."

The words deflated in her mouth, bereft of air and sense. She thought to herself: *Am I mad?*

Then a voice from the other side of the foundry, through a separate archway with the carved likeness of Hephaestus in the stone above the opening, carried to them like a bell being struck.

"You can do a lot with a rope and pulleys."

At first, Heron thought the voice was a woman's, which only confirmed the identity of the speaker.

"Plutarch!"

Two men in desert cloaks and travelling gear came through the archway, one tall and reed thin, the other like a barrel of dark muscle.

"You came back?" asked Heron.

"See," Punt grumbled, "even she can't believe we'd be so foolish to return."

"Fools, the both of you," she said, laughing. "But glad fools."

Heron hugged them both, which Plutarch accepted gracefully, while Punt stiffly patted her shoulders. She gave Punt an extra squeeze.

"I hope you got some sleep on your little vacation outside the city," she said. "We have much work to do."

Punt raised an eyebrow to Plutarch, who had his arms crossed and a playful smile on his lips. "Not a moment's rest. Not one. I suppose I should have expected it."

"Maybe I shouldn't ask," said Heron, "but why did you come back?"

The pair shared a glance that spoke of strange things.

"We heard a story from the caravan trader we'd contracted to take us east," said Plutarch. "A story about you."

Heron swallowed. "Do I want to hear this?"

Plutarch winked. "It was a story about how you flew from the top of the Lighthouse to the bottom without injury. Is this true?"

"Like you said, you can do a lot of things with a rope and a pulley," she replied.

Plutarch gave Punt an I-told-you-so glance, while the blacksmith rolled his eyes.

"Well," continued Plutarch, "the trader spoke of the Goddess of Alexandria coming back to kick the crocodile priests from the city. He seemed as excited as Zeus in a thunderstorm, and he's from Parthia, not Alexandria."

It felt like her chest was caught in a vise. Part of her was thrilled because she'd worried the whole trip around Africa that she'd be named the Destroyer. But another part, the rational part that gave lectures at the Great Library, saw this new image destroying the very ideas she wanted to spread.

She'd been planning a miracle to turn the Alexandrians back to her side, but not by placing herself on a divine cloud. It was like balancing a pea on a knife and either way, she'd be cut.

"We'll have to use what we can to our advantage. We have little time for anything else," she said eventually.

But the others seemed not to have the same reservations as she. They nodded in agreement, she could almost say, eagerly. But that was to be expected. They'd taken losses, and plans had been ineffectual thus far. She provided a way out of the mess, even if it would probably get them all killed.

"I make no claims for your safety," Heron reminded them.

"When have you ever?" responded Vestalis, to nods from Punt and Plutarch.

"What shall we do now, O' *Michanikos?*" asked Plutarch, bending at the waist in a superfluous bow.

The smile she gave them wasn't just a smile. It was like another moon in the sky, brighter than the original, maybe even as bright as the sun. She had to hide her parted lips with a cupped hand even to speak, her joy at being reunited with her friends so great.

"Plutarch, take the scrolls in that knapsack to the Soma. You'll need to find the scribblers, and sages, and as many wood carvers as you can find. The rest you'll figure out from my instructions. I want you to stay in the Soma and complete that, no matter what happens to us at the miracle. Your work is more important than what we're doing."

Plutarch collected the knapsack.

"And Punt," said Heron.

The blacksmith groaned in recognition.

"You have a workshop to run."

He grumbled. "But that's Plutarch's job."

"He has other things to do." She smirked.

"Apologies, good Heron. Instruct me in my tasks," he said, with no shortage of sarcasm.

She paused and waited until the three of them were staring at her. "We're going to make a building fly."

TWENTY THREE

The week passed like wildfire and as promised, Punt didn't sleep but a few nods between jobs in the workshop. The arches of his wide feet ached like they'd never ached before. Punt thought that someone might have slipped needles in the soles of his sandals, needles that went right into the heel of his foot, because tendrils of pain went up his calves at each step.

He was not unused to working on his feet as preparing and pouring molds could take a whole day, from mixing the binders for sand at daybreak, to knocking the flashing from the castings when they cooled late at night. It wasn't until he collapsed on the bed next to Astrela that he would realize his exhaustion.

But acting as foreman had provided no distraction, so the aches and pains he endured walking between the many tasks in the workshop collected on his mind like leaches from a boggy swamp. Which only made the assignment he'd been given that much more painful.

Punt crouched in the darkness of the side street near the Moon Gate and examined the object of his task. Towering over the city, at a height only exceeded by the Lighthouse of Pharos, the Colossus of Sobek made for an imposing sight. Its brass legs straddled the southern entrance to the city, facing the slums that crowded against Lake Mareotis.

The giant crocodile head seemed obscene on the body of what had once been the statue of Ammon, though its green skin from the corrosion of the bronze was appropriate for Sobek. The colossus held a great golden staff in one muscled green arm, which Heron had designed to raise and lower when the rains filled the catchers inside.

The door in Sobek's foot faced east along the wall, giving Punt easy access to the interior of the statue. The opening had corroded shut and Punt had to wedge a tool in the gap to pry it open.

Inside, Punt found the steam mechanical rusted with disuse. He might have been disappointed, except he wasn't expecting to find one at all, which would have made his task many times more difficult.

Punt relocated a dozen barrels, each the size of a beer keg, inside the leg, along with a sack of tools and a lantern, which he lit and set safely away from the barrels. When he was finished, there was barely enough room for his bulk.

Using his warhammer, Punt sunk a hooked spike into the earth, and wound a rope around it and then the interior door mechanism to keep it from being opened. He wouldn't be going out that way when the task was over.

With the patience of a river, Punt meticulously went over the steam mechanical, picking off rust with his fingernail and moving the pistons by hand to confirm they still worked. Then he opened one of the carefully marked barrels and poured the chunks of coal into the fire chamber, stopping frequently so the dust didn't build up in the air. If it weren't for his need to see, Punt would have quenched the light and waited for a good, long while before relighting it, but he had other things to do and no time to spare.

Next, Punt poured two barrels of water into the steam chamber, splashing handfuls on his face as the interior of the statue heated up. Even without a window, Punt could tell the sun had come up by the warm bronze on the eastern side. By mid-day it'd be a furnace. Punt hoped the statue wouldn't cook him before nightfall at the time of the miracle.

He worked over the steam mechanical for a while, wiping his bald head with a damp towel to keep the sweat from stinging his eyes. As the heat grew inside the interior of the statue's leg, the other nine barrels began to tick, the iron bands expanding as the material inside grew.

Punt put his calloused hand on one of the stoppers and considered releasing the pressure. After a moment's thought, he decided it was better to keep the substance inside the barrel.

When he was certain the steam mechanical was in good working order, as much as he could tell without test firing it, Punt unhooked the pipe that went up through the leg to the top of the statue and blew in it to make sure nothing had built a nest inside, or had otherwise clogged the tube.

The steam mechanical and tube had been built into the statue's leg so the moving arm could be tested by pumping water into the upper chamber. The steam mechanical could also pump other substances if needed.

He hooked the pipe back to the steam mechanical and took a break to eat and drink some hard bread, nuts, and water he'd brought with him. Punt was careful not to bump into the wall with his shoulder as the bronze skin of the giant statue could sear a mark into his flesh.

As he ate, he stared at the barrels, the thick stench of their contents making him a little dizzy. Not all that hungry, Punt left his bread, wrapped towels around his hands, and climbed up the ladder to the upper door.

The ladder didn't go all the way to the top, since the middle section of the statue was filled with gears and the giant buckets that moved up and down. When it was time to go to the top, Punt would have to exit to a ladder on the exterior of the statue and climb to a new door on the chest of Sobek. Once inside the upper section, he could finish his task by rerouting the pipe to its new location.

But that wasn't why he had climbed the ladder. He made his way to the door so he could get a breath of fresh air. The black tarry stuff in the barrels, Heron had called it pitch, was putting off an odor that was giving him a headache. He wasn't supposed to make his way to the upper section until night since the outer ladder was in plain sight, but he had to risk opening the door a little, or he'd pass out.

To his luck, a breeze was blowing to the southwest, which seemed to force the fumes into other parts of the statue's interior, or suck them out completely. Punt wrapped the towel around the rungs and hooked his elbows over them so he could rest.

To the northeast in the city, at the foot of the Great Library, a scaffolding was being built. The next, and eleventh, miracle would take place in front of those hallowed halls of learning, a message from Lysimachus, Heron had thought.

Punt muttered prayers to the gods: Bes for luck, Thoth for wisdom, and Set that he wouldn't visit any storms upon them. As the blacksmith leaned on the highest rung inside the Colossus of Sobek's bronze leg, he realized that if lightning struck the statue, he would have no way to avoid the death it would bring.

But his fears quickly evaporated, much as any bead of water did on this bright Alexandrian summer day, because the season for storms wouldn't come for another month and the sky to the east was as pale as milk with only a faint finger of a cloud daring the sky.

No, the gods would smile on them for once, he decided. They had no love for Sobek and would aid them in the quest to bring down the croco dile god. As Punt watched the scaffolding at the Great Library grow like weeds from rich soil, he knew this to be true, knew it in his bones.

But then again, when had the gods ever cooperated for Heron of Alexandria?

TWENTY FOUR

Titus Claudius Vestalis, once the head of the largest merchant house in Alexandria and former equestrian class of the Roman Legion, leaned against the cracked brick of the Bast Inn, picking his teeth with a stalk of wheat he'd plucked from a passing wagon.

The crocodile helm sat uncomfortably on his head, like an uneven crown, but at least it kept the sun from his eyes, a welcome bonus on this blinding white day. He tried to rub the soreness from his jaw where he'd taken a shield blow to the face only to wince in pain from his shoulder. The dislocation had been reset a week ago, but he still felt like it could come loose at any time.

"Patrol coming," muttered Calder in broken Greek.

Vestalis glanced to the hastily dyed hair on the big Northman raining out from his helm. The old Roman wasn't sure how the disguise was going to fool the patrol, especially when the Northman was twice the size of a typical Alexandrian.

"Walk now," said Vestalis, breaking down the street, his knees crackling as he forced himself into a stiff march.

A voice of command came after them, "Halt, in the name of Sobek! Halt! Halt!"

Vestalis gave a reluctant glance to the side street, before turning back to the patrol. He made the soldiers come to him, rather than meeting them halfway, which left the patrol leader steaming by the time they reached him.

The patrol leader was an Alexandrian noble, one Vestalis had seen before. Gratis, he remembered his name. The man was built like a damp parchment, his chest nearly caved in for lack of muscle. What he lacked in physical strength, he made up for in accruements. His gladius had a jeweled hilt, a ring of rubies pressed into the pommel, and he wore golden jewelry around his wrists and neck. Even his eyes were painted in the Egyptian style. When Vestalis was in the Roman army, they called men like this a soldier of the theatre—a man who looked good on the stage in a uniform, but died at the first press of battle.

"Are you deserters?" asked Gratis, his cheeks bright red from his rapid march.

"No, Captain," said Vestalis, "bad plums last night. We both had to stop and take a shit and our patrol left us. We're hoping they might come around again."

The soldiers began to laugh, their eyes rolling in condemnation, which only made the patrol leader's cheeks redder.

"Have you no discipline?" asked Gratis, poking at the sloppy belt line on Calder. "And what zoo does this beast come from?"

Vestalis half-shrugged, instantly regretting it, and wheezed out an answer, "His mother was a Thracian and his father a bear."

Gratis narrowed his brow and licked his lips, tilting his head at the big Northman. The other soldiers had chuckled at his joke about the bear, but Gratis was less amused. When the patrol leader's gaze flickered to Vestalis, a spark of recognition registered there, making the heart speed up.

"Soldier, have I seen you before?"

Vestalis let his helm tilt down to partially obstruct his face. "Probably, I've been a soldier in Alexandria longer than most."

Gratis did not look away and kept his gaze on Vestalis, who wanted to wipe away the bead of sweat trickling down his cheek.

"Your face. It's familiar," said Gratis. "I can't place where, but I've seen you before."

The patrol leader leaned in, looking under the snout of the crocodile helm, his face so close, his breath tickled against Vestalis' stubble.

Vestalis moved his hand closer to his hilt, feigning an adjustment to his belt. Calder was behind him, so he had no idea what the big Northman was doing. If they had to fight, they'd best be the first ones with their swords out. The odds were overwhelmingly in the patrol's favor, but Vestalis had no intention of being captured and tortured by Lysimachus.

"Are you sure you..."

Gratis' question was interrupted by the sound of water loudly spraying against the brick. Vestalis knew exactly what it was the moment he saw the soldiers holding back laughter. Gratis spit all over himself in bluster as he stepped to the side to address Calder.

The big Northman had lifted his tunic and was pissing against the side of the Bast Inn. Now that he had the patrol leader's attention, he began to moan softly in relief. Urine pooled in the cracks between the cobblestones and rivulets ran towards Gratis' sandals, forcing him to sidestep.

"Jupiter's balls, soldier. Have you no discipline? Away from that wall and cease your urination," said Gratis.

Calder made a guttural moan and shook his leg slightly. "Can't stop..."

Vestalis wished the Northman wouldn't have spoken, his accent was clearly not Thracian, but Gratis didn't seem to notice as his nose wrinkled in disgust. Even Vestalis couldn't help but crack a smile. This little demonstration was typical camp humor, but Gratis had clearly never been on march, so he wouldn't understand.

"Stop your pissing, soldier. Stop!"

Gratis forcefully tugged on the sleeve Calder's tunic. Everyone in the patrol knew what would happen next, except Gratis. Calder turned, his stream of urine arcing through the air, until it slashed across Gratis' legs and then his pristine tunic, marring it with the pungent liquid.

The patrol leader jumped back and started patting at his legs and tunic as if he'd been cut with a blade.

"By all the gods above and below, what have you done?"

Gratis' cheeks were already bright red from the stiff march and energetic invective, but when he looked to his soldier's faces, ballooning in the effort of containing their laughter, his eyes turned gray and his blotchy red skin turned a deep shade of crimson.

"Amanitore," said Gratis, addressing the soldier nearest him with a voice as pale as the sky. "You have charge of the patrol while I return to my villa for the day. This heat has taken a toll on me."

Gratis marched away from the patrol, arms shivering in revulsion as he kept trying to wipe away the stain. The patrol burst with laughter when Gratis was out of earshot.

The new patrol leader, Amanitore, gave a half-nod toward the back of the lines. "Join us for the rest of the route today?"

"Gladly," said Vestalis, moving to the back of the line.

The rest of the patrol gave Calder bright eyed nods of appreciation. Any concerns Vestalis had about being discovered were assuaged by the Northman's demonstration of piss humor.

They fell into line as the patrol moved out, marching down the street, and quickly Vestalis' new concern became surviving the day's heat. It'd been a long time since he'd been an infantryman and he still wasn't recovered from his injuries.

Vestalis gave a knowing nod to the cagey Northman as they neared the construction at the Great Library. Joining a patrol had been one thing, getting in with the guard around the evening's miracle was another, but if they were going to have any chance of getting Sepharia back, they would have to find a way.

TWENTY FIVE

The Great Library was a bit of a misnomer. Visitors to the storied structure expected a singular monument like the Lighthouse of Pharos, or the pyramids of Memphis. The Great Library was the descriptor, but it did not describe the physical structure.

While the city streets of Alexandria had stayed mostly true to its founder's vision, keeping straight and orderly, the Great Library - erupted from the distracted minds of its scholars - was a sprawling complex that contained many levels and buildings, some like the Serapeum and others the book depositories on the docks.

Heron had once encountered a growth of mushrooms in the corner of a scroll room. A crack in the floor had let moisture in and at least three kinds of fungus grew. The bulbous and spiny mass climbed over itself, multi-hued with bright spores glistening in the damp that had come up from the earth.

To Heron, as she gazed at the complex known at the Great Library from atop the Hall of Curiosities, it was a lot like that. The building hadn't been guided by a single visionary, rather a multitude of bumbling architects, each one well meaning in their construction.

But visitors required a point of focus. A lens to place their eye to weigh the history against their imagination. So the keepers of the Great Library had built a grand entrance, white marble stairs climbing majestically to a columned atrium.

It was this location Lysimachus had chosen for his next miracle. Scaffolding and tarps protected the design of Sepharia's execution mechanism from prying eyes. Workers scurried over the construction, while a couple of mechanical Centaurs and dozens of soldiers stood guard. Further out, the sounds of Manticores prowling echoed like unruly beasts against the confined streets.

"Do you think me a monster for what I have unleashed on the world?" asked Heron.

Arethussa, who'd been crouched behind the crenellation, raised an eyebrow as if she didn't understand, but Heron caught the brief widening of the eyes indicating concern at the question.

"*Michanikos*, what do you mean?"

Heron tried to release the tightness in her chest by taking a breath. "Call me, Heron. I'm not a machine."

"Apologies."

"Do you think me a monster?" asked Heron. "For destroying Rome? Creating these machines that deal death so easily?"

"The monsters are the ones that use them," said Arethussa, nodding towards a clump of green-robed priests conferencing at the base of the scaffolding.

"You didn't mention Rome," said Heron.

Arethussa blinked, her lips bunching up. "I was not there. I have no opinion on it, except that war is the oldest profession. You didn't invent that."

Heron rubbed her stump absently. Sometimes when she looked at it, she couldn't believe it was her arm without a hand.

"Do you think it'll work? My plan?" asked Heron, nodding towards the crate of props they'd brought to the roof.

The tavern owner, either because she was actually considering the question, or politely feigning the motions, took a long while to answer.

"It seems like it should," said Arethussa, as the westerly winds blew dark hair into her face. "When it does, what will we do next?"

"I have ideas, though none fleshed out." Heron glanced over her shoulder towards the Lighthouse. "We have allies if we want them. Alexandria isn't completely held by Lysimachus and his priesthood."

"Can you trust this Dominitus?" asked Arethussa.

"Not at all. While Lysimachus holds the city, we have aligning interests. My intention isn't to take control for myself. I seek to liberate Alexandria from Sobek, though I would prefer Vestalis to rule rather than Dominitus."

"I hoped you would rule," said Arethussa.

Heron wiped the sweat from her neck with a towel. "In Rome, I learned the price of leadership. My curiosity was quenched there."

A breeze picked up, racing cooler air across the roof of the Hall of Curiosities. Heron shook her hair, enjoying the wind against her damp neck. It pleased her to have long hair like Arethussa.

"Will the pulleys work in the rain?" asked the tavern owner, looking east.

Heron bit her lower lip as she stared at the blotches of cloud forming. "It could cause complications. Especially since some of the ropes are protected and others are in the sun. It's getting later in the day. We can only hope there isn't enough time for a storm to gather before the miracle."

Arethussa seemed to accept the answer, though Heron had not been entirely truthful. The miracle she'd devised was made of wood and painted canvas. They'd spent the night putting up the structure that had been built in pieces in Nektam's workshop. Water in the form of rain could complicate things, but the winds would be worse.

Already, the stiff breeze that formed in the afternoon heat worried Heron. The "miracle" would make it appear the Hall of Curiosities was being lifted in the air. The reality was they'd be lifting a wood and painted canvas structure that looked like stone into the air, projecting the image that the building was floating. A miracle that could only work at night and from afar. But if the canvas caught the wind and swayed the structure, the illusion would be shattered.

As Heron waited for evening, she kept glancing eastward. Each time she did, it seemed there was another tusk of cloud stretching out towards them. Summer storms were rare in Alexandria, but when they did come, they came fast and hard.

"Do you pray to the gods?" Heron asked Arethussa.

The raven-haired tavern owner glanced skyward. "At times, when necessary."

"Do they ever listen?"

Arethussa tilted her head. "Occasionally."

Heron fixed Arethussa in her gaze, trying to ignore the towering clouds forming in the distance, painted with bright oranges and reds from the setting sun. "Then pray for the storm to go north over the sea."

TWENTY SIX

The bronze skin of the Colossus could be touched without flinching and its soothing warmth reminded Punt of a hearthstone after the fires had been banked.

In the city, Punt witnessed crowds moving towards the Great Library. Lights flickered along the avenues, like sparkling water flowing to the next miracle.

The sun had set, leaving the toothy maw of the giant Sobek statue and the upper half of the Lighthouse awash in bright hues. To the east, darker colors formed as mountainous clouds, purple with energy, rolled towards the city. Lightning crackled through the clouds, looking like veins of an elder god. Punt stared at the coming storm, shaking his head and muttering.

"Not dark enough," he said, glancing to the ground where a half-dozen soldiers milled about the gate.

He looked to the storm, bloated with rain.

"Dark enough," he decided.

Punt climbed down to the floor and sparked the fire on the steam chamber, so the mechanical could begin heating up the water while he worked in the upper statue.

Then he made his way back to the opening and leaned out the hatch.

The wind pushed on his stocky body as he made the climb, hand over hand to the next opening. He looked down once and regretted it instantly when the world whirled around his head. Punt closed his eyes to make the vertigo disappear.

"Don't do that again," he told himself. "Never was much for heights."

He made the opening that formed in the chest of Sobek. The green corrosion on the bronze reflected enough light on Punt that he felt like the whole city could see him.

The door, when he tugged on the handle, proved to be stuck. He'd brought his knapsack of tools, but the wedge he'd used to open the bottom door was inside the foot.

Punt wiped his hands on his tunic. They were getting sweaty. He gripped the handle and pulled as hard as he could.

When the door gave way, he flew backwards, and his hand slipped from the rung. The earth pulled at his back like a hungry animal.

He slapped his hand out and caught the rung with his fingertips, giving him enough time to swing his other arm around and grasp the ladder. With breaths shaking from his lips, Punt clung to the statue until he had composed himself enough to move again.

A platform was right inside the opening, so Punt climbed in, checking to make sure no one had saw him, before closing the door. The guards had missed his climb as they were pointing eastward toward the storm.

He lit a lantern and light bloomed into the cavernous space. Gears the size of wagon wheels hung in a steel frame connected to pistons and levers that stretched from the platform at the bottom of the chest to a massive bucket near the head. Iron rods as thick as a man's arm formed the bones of the statue.

The edges of the holes in the crown of Sobek's head reflected the sunset as crimson half-moons. When it rained, the water would fall through those holes and fill the bucket. The additional weight would push the bucket down, lifting the lever that controlled the arm holding the staff.

Using the lantern, Punt found the pipe that snaked from the foot to the head. A ringed platform went around the inside of the chest, allowing Punt to move to another ladder. He climbed up to the final platform inside the head and above the bucket.

The upper section of pipe had a bird's nest built into it, so he disconnected it and pulled out the twigs and grass with his hands listening for sounds of the storm.

When a deep rumble broke against the sky, making the whole statue vibrate, Punt increased the pace of his work. Not only did he have to be ready for Heron's signal, which would come as the miracle began, but he needed to be out of the statue before the storm struck.

Punt rerouted the pipe to stick from the crown of the statue and while he worked, the statue, cooled by nightfall, made loud ticking noises as the skin contracted. Then he pulled a second lantern from the sack and fixed it to the top with ropes, before lighting it, praying to the god Amun that the wind wouldn't extinguish it.

With his task complete, Punt took one last look at the storm which threatened to overtake the city. A buffet of wind slammed into Punt's face, making him squint, right before lightning crackled above his head.

Punt hurried down the ladder, moving at a pace that surprised himself. He had to get down to the leg hatch to watch for the signal to start the steam mechanical. A signal he hoped would come soon, because he didn't want to be in the statue much longer.

When he reached the hatch in Sobek's chest, the door resisted his efforts. Setting his backpack on the platform, Punt pushed with both hands, but the door didn't budge.

Thinking he might be tired from the climb, Punt wiped his hands on his tunic, shook out his arms, and prepared to push again.

Punt strained against the hatch, groaning with the effort, his feet sliding backwards as he put his muscle into the task.

The door didn't budge.

Another rumble of thunder crashed against the statue, this one so close Punt was sure the storm was right over head. At the end of the thunder, the statue made a loud tick, the tightening of the skin like a boom in the interior of the chest.

The cooling bronze skin had wedged the door shut. Now, he couldn't get down to the lower section to start the steam mechanical. And if lightning struck the statue, he'd be a dead man. Punt slammed his fist against the door and the sky answered with a bang.

TWENTY SEVEN

The crocodile helm had worn a blister into the back of his head. Vestalis rubbed at the sore, trying to keep the helm from slipping over it, but the storm had brought with it damp air and every part of his skin was covered in beaded sweat.

Vestalis stretched his neck and nodded towards Calder, who stood on the other side of the platform, one foot forward and his hand resting on his hilt. The big Northman could have been asleep on his feet by his relaxed pose, but Vestalis knew otherwise. The sleepy countenance was a mask.

The crowds stayed behind the barriers and the silence of so many people unnerved him. Vestalis didn't know exactly what had quieted them, but the crowd was a sea of faces, blanked of emotion, and staring at either the storm or the implements of execution on the platform.

Vestalis had spent some time himself staring at the twisted iron structure when the tarps had first been removed. The purpose of the giant X was not readily apparent, which worried Vestalis, because they had to intervene before Sepharia was fastened to them.

A crackle of lightning startled the crowd, making them collectively stoop. Vestalis felt like the rain could come pouring down at any moment - he could smell the sharp metallic scent in the air - and its arrival would complicate things. He checked the dark shape of the Colossus of Sobek. He thought he saw a flicker of light on its crown, but that could have been his hopeful imagination.

When a murmuring wave traveled through the crowd, Vestalis knew Sepharia's procession was on its way. He resisted the urge to check down the street for fear of giving away that he was not one of Sobek's men. It'd been surprisingly easy to convince the other soldiers to trade jobs, giving Vestalis and Calder ones around the platform, which said much about the Alexandrian military's support of Sobek.

Movement on the platform startled Vestalis. No one had been standing there moments before. Now, a dozen Terrors stood in a circle around the twisted metal X. A thirteenth priest waited at the edge for the procession to arrive.

Vestalis realized the thirteenth priest was Lysimachus, the moment he looked right at him, his beady eyes fixing him in his stare. Vestalis looked away, too late he was afraid, for he'd known the Customs Man when Alexandria was owned by the Roman Empire.

If Lysimachus had recognized him in that instant, Vestalis wasn't aware. Though it'd seemed that the high priest of Sobek had looked right to his location as if he'd known he would be there.

Vestalis had no time to contemplate further, the procession bearing Sepharia had arrived. When Vestalis' gaze fell upon Heron's daughter, his palms grew damp. Sepharia had been crucified on a wooden crossbeam that matched the twisted iron X on the platform. Her head hung down, hair covering her face. Wounds wept on her hands and feet where the spikes had been driven into the wood. Now, it wouldn't be as simple as rushing on stage when everyone was distracted, grabbing her, and disappearing into the crowd. First they would have to remove her from the wood, assuming that didn't injure her further.

He looked to the Hall of Curiosities, knowing that it was too late for changes in the plan. He would have to improvise.

The Terrors of Sobek flowed to the steam barge when it connected to the platform and unhooked the crossed beams. They attached it to the twisted iron X using clamps and then moved to the edge of the platform, each facing outward.

Vestalis stared at the contraption, rubbing the salt and pepper stubble on his jaw. Then he glanced to the crowd, to a knot of conspirators, sages from the Great Library who were to receive Sepharia and carry her away once they'd rescued her.

"Faithful Alexandrians!" Lysimachus called out, his voice breaking through the still pre-storm air.

He paused and waited for acknowledgement from the crowd, but the onlookers only stared back with muted compliance.

Lysimachus let a nearly imperceptible frown tug at the corner of his lips before gathering himself and forging ahead.

"Ten times I have brought you here to witness the powers of Sobek! Ten times you have witnessed my miracles. Today marks the eleventh! Do not be afraid, for Sobek controls the waters of creation, and anything is possible with him!"

It was then that Vestalis realized what was different from previous miracles. Before, Lysimachus had cloaked the executioner in a Sobek mask and named her Heron to fool the masses. This time Lysimachus had taken the platform to speak to the crowd. Did that mean he'd anticipated their plan?

"Again," Lysimachus called out to the crowd, "I bring you Heron's daughter to prove the depth of my sacrifice!"

An explosion from the direction of the Hall of Curiosities startled everyone, including the Terrors and Lysimachus. Twin balls of flame floated into the sky, stagecraft of Heron's devising.

Between the balls of flame, multiple bull lanterns shown on a figure standing at the edge of the Hall of Curiosities. Vestalis heard the murmurs of Heron's name from the crowd, even before she'd spoken.

Heron had dressed in a golden gown, her dark hair resplendent against her shoulders. Her hair appeared longer at this distance. She held up her stump to silence the crowd and then spoke and the wind carried it down to them, and Vestalis could hear every word.

"Do not believe this interloper. He brings pain and death. He brings darkness. He brings terror. He does not care for you as I have," said Heron.

The crowd responded with cries of confusion, agreement, and condemnation. Some couldn't understand why the two were opposed, while others greeted Heron's appearance with joy, weeping openly. Vestalis found his own face relaxing into a smile.

But Lysimachus had not moved a muscle and his contentment made Vestalis wary.

"Tonight marks the end of Sobek's brief reign of terror in Alexandria," Heron called out. "Tonight, I demonstrate my powers so you know that Sobek has no sway here."

A bolt of lightning streaked across the sky as if it'd been thrown by Zeus himself and struck the Lighthouse, spraying fire into the air. The sound of pounding rain approaching followed right after.

TWENTY EIGHT

Some moments were made for rage. In the middle of battle, a stoutly wielded warhammer could rip a shield from a man's arm. Or in the foundry, a section of iron had to be beaten and flattened until it could be folded for strength.

Though every vein on Punt's neck, every muscle on his arms and chest, and every essence of his will wanted him to unleash his fury on the stuck hatch, this moment was not one of them. Rather, Punt examined the crease where the door met the statue, finding the two overlapping, with the door wedged on the inside of the door, while the hinges were on the outside.

The hatch wouldn't open no matter how hard he hit it. He'd dislocate his shoulder before breaking through. Only the sunrise would save him by heating up the statue until the opening was larger than the door.

Punt rested his head against the cooling metal, feeling the minor pings as different sections shrunk. Moments later, a thunderous drumming erupted on the surface of the statue, starting first on the eastern side before covering the whole surface. Punt was inside the world's largest drum.

"The gods mock me with this rain," said Punt, looking up to the holes in the statue. The rain was cascading into the bucket.

He put his fingertips to his temples and tried to remember the construction of the statue. It seemed there was a way to bypass the flooring to reach the lower section without having to use the outside ladder, but he couldn't remember if Heron had actually put that into the statue, or it was his imagination.

He had to try something, so Punt climbed down to the waist of the statue, where the massive gears for the bucket were housed. A loud click announced that the bucket had moved downward one tooth. As the rain filled the bucket, the gears would turn and the statue would lift the staff outside.

Using the lantern, Punt examined the platform, looking for cracks. The gears ticked two more times while he searched. The crack he eventually found was not in an ideal location. It was centered directly beneath the bucket.

If the space between the platform did lead to the lower section of the statue, it would be closed off when the bucket filled and reached the bottom.

Growling to himself that Plutarch had gotten the easy job, while he was being overworked, Punt ducked through the struts that held up the gears and started working the crack.

He fit a rod between the two platforms and leaned on the tool to bend the wooden platform. It curved upward until the wood bent, sending the rod out of his sweaty hands to roll across the platform.

Punt scrambled through the struts after the rolling rod, catching his knee on a piece of iron. He barely managed to retrieve it before the gear snapped the rod. Punt rubbed his knee before returning to the crack.

While he was climbing back in, the gear clicked a few times. The bucket was about a fourth of the way down and it would move faster the further down it went, giving Punt less time than he would have liked.

Jamming the rod in the gap, Punt wrestled it back and forth, trying to pull the nails from the wood. He was able to make enough space to put his hands, so he positioned himself on one half, while pulling the other.

The edge of the platform had been formed oddly, so it cut into his hand as he strained to lift it. The clicking of the gears came at a more regular pace.

Punt refused to let himself look up and stayed focused on the task beneath his fingertips. Either the platform was going to come up, or his arms were going to rip right off, that's what he'd decided.

The nails fastening the platform whined as they were pulled out of the structural beams. The clicking sped up, coming one after another like a chain anchor being pulled up through an iron ring.

He wasn't sure how much longer he had, so he gave it one last grunt, nearly ripping the platform in half and revealing a space inside. The giant bucket filled with water was right above his head and clicking downward to smash him against the beams. Punt grabbed the lantern and jumped into the hole as the bucket slammed onto the platform, shaking dust into his face.

He was trapped in a space between the two halves of the statue. Mice scurried in the darkness, nests of twigs spilling from corners.

Getting out of the center space was easier than getting in. Punt kicked the ceiling of the lower section open, right near the ladder.

He reached the bottom of the statue and put his hand near the curved steam chamber. He could feel heat radiating from the bronze surface. Punt dumped more coal into the fire chamber before reaching for one of the pitch barrels.

A tap on the barrel let him know the pitch wasn't under pressure, so he uncorked it and poured it into the pumping chamber. The fumes from the noxious black liquid nearly overcame him. Punt staggered against the steam mechanical, narrowly avoiding burning his leg.

In quick order, he poured the nine barrels of pitch into the pumping chamber of the steam mechanical. By the time he was finished, Punt was holding his breath and trying not to retch.

Punt was about to turn the valves that would begin pumping the pitch up through the pipe and out the top of the statue, when he remembered he'd roped the door shut so no one could bother him. He cut the rope and loosened the door before starting the pistons. Once they started hammering, the noise would surely bring the guards.

Punt turned the valve handle and hit the door with his shoulder, bursting into the pouring rain. Behind him, the steam mechanical made a clatter that rivaled the gods in battle.

Clearing the rain from his eyes, Punt took two steps from the door when he ran into a group of crocodile soldiers headed towards the Moon Gate.

TWENTY NINE

Sepharia couldn't remember the spikes going into her palms and ankles. Peering through her tangled hair, hanging from the crossbeams, Sepharia stared at the iron rod sticking from her hand.

"I must have blacked out," she whispered, as the steam barge came to an abrupt stop, jarring her against the spikes.

If she doubted the spikes before, she doubted them no longer. The agony ripped through her. She tried to catch her breath, to cry out and ask the pain to stop, but even that was too much. Sepharia could only mutter, spit bubbles forming on her lips.

The crossbeams were lifted by a group of Terrors and carried to a twisted metal structure. The pain was a shield that kept her from seeing beyond the edges of the platform. She knew the crowd was there, witnessing her death, again, but she couldn't see them.

Lysimachus was there, leaning into her vision. His eyes had no color to her. They were watery steel.

"It'll be over soon," he said, as if he were her father, and he was merely pulling a thorn out of her foot.

She smelled the figs on his breath. She remembered figs, too. She'd eaten them, eaten cheese and bread. Lysimachus had come to visit her. Then she remembered nothing else.

Lightning flashed across the sky. She saw that. The sheer whiteness of it was a stain against her vision.

Then Lysimachus was speaking. He'd never spoken before. Usually he let the priest dressed as Sobek speak. It was different for a reason, this time. She knew it was different. She just didn't know why.

When the reply came, she squinted until she could see. Beyond the platform was the entrance to the Great Library. Sepharia had visited those steps before. Had even snuck into its halls dressed as a boy. Now, she was nailed to a cross, ready to be executed by Alexandria's former Alabarch at the foot of those stairs.

"Tonight marks the end of Sobek's brief reign of terror in Alexandria," cried a voice. Sepharia searched until she found it, a shape upon the Hall of Curiosities. She lifted her head, despite it feeling like a hundred stones.

From the crowd, calls of: "Heron!" and "*Michanikos!*" fell like soothing music on Sepharia's ears.

"Tonight," Heron called out again. "I demonstrate my powers so you know that Sobek has no sway here."

"No," muttered Sepharia, the words coming out like thick mud. "It can't be. Another trick. Like the Sun Room."

The woman on the Hall of Curiosities kept speaking. Sepharia found it hard to concentrate on the words with so much going on. Lysimachus was sending soldiers to climb the Hall of Curiosities. People in the crowd were shouting Heron's name, or Sobek's. Sometimes both as if they were the same person.

Sepharia tried to clear the hair from her face so she could see better, but her hand was trapped, nailed to a beam.

"Heron, run," said Sepharia, to no one except herself. "But you're not Heron. I can tell. This is another...trick."

Part of her wanted to believe it. That it was really Heron. But each time she'd gotten her hopes up, Lysimachus had crushed them mercilessly. How many times had Heron rescued her, only to find out that it was one of Lysimachus' men?

The Heron on the Hall kept shouting. Cries of alarm went up from the crowd when the rain started falling. Not falling, pounding into them as if they were nails.

Sepharia welcomed the rain. Despite the water in her eyes, the cool rain soothed the heat that was burning like a forest fire in her chest.

Something happened in the city behind her. Screams pierced the veil of falling rain. Faces turned that way, despite the commotion at the Hall of Curiosities.

Sepharia looked up in time to see Heron leap from the building that had grown to a height nearly twice of what it'd been before. Heron fell from what had to be a deadly distance, her landing hidden by the shops in front of the Hall.

The words came out her lips so faint and pale, they barely made a noise above the rain, "Heron, no."

And then, "Please, don't be Heron. Please be a trick."

She said the words because she knew that if it were Heron, that she was dead.

The sounds of swords clashing to the right drew her attention. Soldiers with crocodile helms were fighting each other. One of them had salt and pepper stubble, while another stood a head taller than the others. A Terror, one of Sobek's priests, stumbled backwards with a crossbow bolt in his chest to die against the twisted beam, pink blood running down the groove in the metal.

The world has gone mad.

The crowd had surged past the barriers, men crawled upon the platform. A man in a tunic with a dark beard took a sword in the gut when he got too close to the fighting.

One of the Terrors moved close. Sepharia expected to see Lysimachus' leering face when the Terror pulled the hood back.

Instead, a pair of familiar brown eyes stared back from behind dark hair soaked through with rain. The sky pulsed with lightning, shining its brilliance on her rescuer.

It was her father, Heron.

THIRTY

"One. Two. Three. Four. Five. Six," said Punt, pointing at each soldier in turn with his thick fingers. "I'm afraid there's not enough of you. Better scurry along and find reinforcements."

The crocodile soldiers glanced amongst themselves, peering through the pouring rain at the blacksmith. A few of them shook their heads or fingered the mostly dull iron blades at their sides.

The leader of the group was a pale easterner with a crooked nose and two blades on his hips. He had the gait of a mercenary, which meant he knew his business with his weapons.

"What were you doing in the statue? That's property of Sobek," said the mercenary, tilting his head with his hands resting comfortably on his hilts.

"Taking a piss. Rain gets the pipes flowing," said Punt. "Tried to squat, but it didn't come."

The others, ordinary soldiers, laughed, while the mercenary folded his arms across his chest. The best that Punt could hope for was to get a fight one-on-one with the mercenary. If they attacked together, he'd be dead after the first pass.

When the rain mercifully reduced to an annoying drizzle, the noise of the steam mechanical could be heard clearly, echoing from statue like a caged beast. The mercenary wrinkled his nose.

"What is that? Roltos, check it out."

"Aye, Thule," said Roltos, a scrawny soldier with long greasy, wet hair sticking from the back of his helm.

Punt took a step backwards, the warhammer bumping along the cobblestones. Thule the mercenary noticed, frowned, and nodded towards his companions to circle around to the sides. Two of them pulled their swords, so Punt leaned on the warhammer as if he didn't have a better place to be and rubbed the grip with his thumb, keeping his weight on the balls of his feet.

Roltos leaned into the opening and came back with sword drawn, his drenched hair splattered across his face.

"I'll be a crocodile's balls," said Roltos, wiping the rain away with a forearm. "The whole thing's jammed with barrels, and there's one of them mechanical beasts in there, humping away like a stallion on a mare."

"Barrels?" asked Thule. "The priest said to keep an eye out for barrels in the city. That they can rip a man apart faster than a lightning bolt from Zeus. He must be one of them raiding the patrols."

Mention of the raids brought the remaining swords from their sheaths, quick as snakes. Punt, despite his thick arms and broad chest, was faster. The warhammer went through the nearest soldier's face as he danced away from a strike.

One down, five more to go, and one of them a blooded mercenary.

As Punt danced in a circle away from their sword thrusts, he knew he'd have been dead already if it weren't for the slick cobblestones. The soldiers wore marching boots and the iron hobnail soles made for slick purchase. They danced like foals across an icy lake.

Punt might have taken the face off another or two, but he was too busy swinging his warhammer in a circling arc, keeping them off balance.

The mercenary, Thule, waited in back, his swords held eagerly. He was no fool, nor did he wear boots like the others. Punt kept the other soldiers between him and Thule.

Punt smashed the hilt of one soldier, breaking bones like twigs, and the soldier dropped his weapon and knelt onto the wet stones, screaming.

"Kill him, you idiots!" said Thule, shaking the rain-soaked hair off his face.

Punt kept his arms wheeling, his thoughts hopping around in his head like a bean on a hot pan, trying to figure out a way out. The tip of a blade caught his arm, leaving a bloody mess.

Suddenly, every rotation of the weapon made his arm scream in agony. Ignoring the pain, Punt lunged forward and caught a soldier in the fruits with the head of the warhammer. He didn't hit hard, but it was enough and the soldier collapsed as if his legs had been cut clean off.

Three left. Roltos and two others. Thule was still watching, waiting.

The battle to that point had been one of scrambling madness. Everyone falling over themselves either to kill him, or stay alive.

With one dead and two out of the fight, the pace slowed. Roltos and the two soldiers with him moved like predators, eyes glinting distant lanterns, as they cornered Punt against the statue.

Everyone was breathing hard. The rain had stopped and cool mist climbed from the stones like spirits released from the Underworld.

In a desperate ploy, Punt lunged again, the iron head of his warhammer thrusted straight out like a spear. The center soldier caught it in the midsection, *oohf*.

Roltos used the opening to try to take Punt's head off, which might have worked had Punt stayed in the same location. After he slammed the one soldier in the gut with his warhammer, he kicked out the iron-ringed shaft and blocked the slash of the other.

Punt ducked his shoulder into the first soldier's chest, the thrashed meat of his injured arm screaming in agony as he pushed, knocking the man to his back, while tripping the other to his knees. The maneuver worked in everything except escaping injury.

When he went by, the sword slash deflected into his side, piercing his ribs under his arm. The cut was deep enough to keep him from pressing on, scrambling through the streets to escape the patrol.

In fact, Punt could only take another three or four steps before he had to hold his arm to his side, as each pounding impact was like the sword

digging deeper through his ribs. Punt glanced down to the dark blood leaking from his side.

It wasn't a fatal wound, but it wouldn't matter, the remaining soldiers could kill him because he couldn't lift his warhammer to defend himself.

Like a hyena to a wounded prey, Thule decided it was time for his entrance to the fight. Thule kicked the soldier who'd fallen with the toe of his boot. The man scrambled to his feet and got behind Thule, along with the other soldier.

Roltos took position next to the mercenary, though it was clear he knew that Thule wanted to do the killing.

"You don't want to kill me," said Punt, trying to convince his arms that they could hold up the warhammer without pain.

Thule's lips rose to a sneer. "At least you acknowledge that you're going to die."

"Why kill me, when you can profit from my life?" asked Punt.

He wanted to wipe the water from his eyes, but he could barely move his arms. The meat on the right shoulder had been pulped, while the left ribs made any move pure agony. Punt blew air from his lips, trying to knock the water from them.

"Speak, and speak quickly," said Thule.

"I'm a companion of the *Michanikos*," said Punt.

Thule's eyes widened with the appropriate signs of gold falling into his pouch. The others, mere soldiers, looked on wearily, though they flinched at recognition of Heron's moniker. Roltos seemed to be weighing his allegiance to the crocodile god with his new friendship with the mercenary.

"I can show you the mysteries of her miracles," continued Punt, "which can give the gift of life, or death, should she choose."

Punt had never been one for words, that had been Plutarch's domain, but standing at the river's edge of death, seemed to loosen his tongue. He only wished his friend was here to see it.

"And are these mysteries profitable?" asked Thule, who still looked like he was trying to decide if it was less trouble to kill the blacksmith.

"What's more profitable than your life?" asked Punt.

Thule's jaw hardened in slow recognition that Punt had been stalling. His gaze straightened, washing away the brief gold lust, as he tried to figure out how his prey could turn the tables on him. Eventually, he shrugged his shoulders, and brought his blades level, ready to dispense death.

The truth was that Punt was stalling. He was delaying the mercenary and his three companions for as long as he could, which wasn't as hard as keeping his eyes off the upper portion of the statue that had lit up like a volcanic eruption.

Thule seemed to notice it first, the way the wet stones on the streets turned to gold, the way the sky brightened as if the dawn had come. And for Punt, it had.

Punt had been delaying so that the steam mechanical had enough time to pump the pitch to the top to ignite as it sprayed across the back of the statue of Sobek.

It was also why Punt had courted death with a risky maneuver to get away from the statue. Everyone standing near it would be immolated, as long as the flame at the top didn't go out.

By the time Thule seemed to realize that he didn't want to be standing near the statue of Sobek, it was too late. A waterfall of flame fell onto him and his companions.

While the crocodile soldiers screamed - their bronze helms melting in the fire, along with their clothes and skin and the breath from their lungs - Punt scrambled away.

Away from the pool of fire, Punt put himself out, not without considerable pain and before he moved on, he looked upon what he had wrought, to the Colossus of Sobek, wearing a cloak of fire, bringing daylight to the city of Alexandria.

It was the first time Punt had ever destroyed one of the creations he'd made for Heron, and it came with considerable regret. He watched the burning statue long enough to know the whole thing would collapse soon, destroying the region around the Moon Gate, and that too, made his heart heavy.

When he moved on, he did so with a limp and without his warhammer, like his burdens, it was much too heavy to carry. He made his way east to the Soma of Alexandria, where they agreed to meet after the raid on the miracle.

The city of Alexandria would never be the same.

THIRTY ONE

*I*t takes a lot to kill a god.

Heron watched the crown of the Colossus of Sobek erupt in flame. From this distance, it appeared the statue had been sitting on a volcano, and the eruption had blown the head off.

The destruction brought screams and chaos. One crocodile soldier, upon seeing the burning statue, dropped his sword and ran into the darkness with the fleeing crowds.

Killing Sobek permanently wouldn't be that easy. A god was an idea trapped in the minds of men. She could only hope to wrestle away Sobek's hold on Alexandria. Free the Great Library, so it would take the fight back to the gods again.

But first she needed to free Sepharia.

Buried in the robes of a Terror, Heron climbed onto the platform where Sepharia was being kept. Vestalis was fighting off two crocodile soldiers to her left, while further on, Calder took the arm off a priest who'd gotten too close.

Other fights, like scattered fires, surrounded the platform, as their supporters came out of the crowd once the crocodile soldiers had been sent to apprehend "Heron". Heron hoped that Arethussa was able to get away, once she jumped down from the Hall of Curiosities, using the same harness Heron had used when fleeing the Lighthouse.

As long as Arethussa could shed the wig and clothes, the soldiers, upon finding her, would not realize she had been the *Michanikos*.

Heron's heart nearly broke in two, like an iron mold cracking from rapid cooling, when she saw the sunken eyes of Sepharia, reflecting the pain of crucifixion.

"Sepharia," said Heron, pulling the hood away from her face.

The rain had stopped, while the fighting continued. The Alexandrians held the platform.

"Father?" asked Sepharia.

"It's me," said Heron. "We'll get you down. Save you from this."

Sepharia gave a wounded shake of the head, as if every movement was pain. "No. You can't save me. Only Sobek. Only him."

Heron examined the spike in Sepharia's hand. Something was wrong with it. It didn't seem right.

"We'll get you down and take you somewhere safe. Get this mad idea out of your head," said Heron.

"No," said Sepharia, as if she were a maiden trapped in a cave, doomed to live a lifetime apart. "I can't. The pyramid. I can't."

Heron pressed her forehead against Sepharia's chin and held her body to hers. "No, stop saying that. I'll free you. I came back because of you."

Heron looked into her daughter's eyes. Sepharia seemed dazed, blinked heavily, as if they were made of iron.

"Are you Heron?" asked Sepharia. "You seem like it more than the others. Not that it matters."

"The others?" asked Heron, slowly recognizing what had happened.

"Don't you see? It's a trick. Those haven't been me. This is me. I'm here to rescue you, if I can get your hands free. How did they put you on this? I can't believe Lysimachus would nail you here. It'll kill you."

"You've said that before," said Sepharia, lazily.

"It's me, daughter. It's me."

For a moment, clarity grew in Sepharia's eyes, like the sun passing through a lens until it became a searing point. The corners of her eyes creased as if she was remembering something.

"He's immortal," said Sepharia, the words falling over themselves. "He has a plan to live forever. He can. I've seen it. I figured it out. What the parchment meant. He can be immortal because—"

"Heron!"

The call of her name startled her, and sent Sepharia into a forced silence. Heron whirled around, almost falling. The sages were supposed to be on the platform, helping her remove Sepharia from the cross. She didn't see any of them.

She saw Lysimachus.

He stood on the platform, in a place that had been empty before. His robe was dry. A smile crept onto Lysimachus' face as he took solemn steps towards her.

"Greetings," said Lysimachus.

She eyed the dagger at his hip, wishing she'd brought a weapon. Heron wheeled around, searching for allies. No one stood near. It was her and Lysimachus.

"You can't hold the city forever," she said. "The people hate you and your god."

"Contrary," said Lysimachus, waving his hand around him, "you think all this will stop He Who Dwelleth Amid Terrors? Your petty fire in his statue? Your struggles to accept him only make him and the city of Alexandria stronger."

"Stronger? You're tearing it apart. Destroying knowledge, turning people against the Great Library. It's Alexandria that made the tools of your conquest possible. And now you're using it to kill my daughter over and over."

At the mention of her name, Sepharia lifted her head and mouthed words. Heron pulled on the front of her robe with a fist.

"But I bring her back," said Lysimachus. "I save her life, giving her the waters of creation, life given from Sobek. Like I saved her from the destruction you wrought in Rome. If it weren't for Sobek's intervention, she would have died at the hands of the Brethren. I saved her at the domus from assassins. And is it not you who are the destroyer? What have you done since you returned to your city, but knock down the docks and burn the Colossus? Will the people of the Rhakotis District rejoice your name now?"

The truth, that she had done so much damage to Alexandria, and that Lysimachus had saved Sepharia, quenched the burning rage in her chest until it crackled with brittleness. If someone had hit her with a hammer, she might have broken into a thousand pieces.

"No," she said, as much to herself as to Lysimachus, "I'm not a destroyer."

Lysimachus took a step closer, his gaze warm and inviting. He reached a hand out towards her, close, his fingertips hovering over her arm.

"Don't fight it, Heron. You could be Sobek's champion and live immortal. You could be reunited with your daughter, who has already accepted Sobek into her heart."

Lysimachus took a step closer, placing his hand on her shoulder. He gazed at her kindly, his bald head glistening in the torch light. The fighting had moved from the platform, a hush had fallen over them.

His nearness brought a prickliness to her skin, as if she'd been bathed in mint. Heron found it hard to breathe.

"Join me," said Lysimachus. "Together, with Sobek, we can transform the world in his vision."

A part of his offer, Heron hated to admit, sounded tempting. She'd been fighting for so many years without rest, that her soul was thin. It would be cathartic, to let herself go, to join with Lysimachus.

And in that moment, she understood her ancestor Alexander the Macedonian, when he lay on his deathbed after a decade of conquest and destruction, how he could have climbed to his feet to throw himself into the river. Part of it had been a vain attempt at becoming immortal in the minds of men, the other part, she realized in that moment, was sheer exhaustion.

Heron looked to her daughter, who she wanted so badly to reunite with, to free her from suffering.

"Yes," said Lysimachus, "the final miracle, we need not use her. Once you are in Sobek's arms, the final miracle during the Festival of the Nile can be a celebration of his victory. The first day of a new Empire under Sobek."

Heron looked into his beady eyes, reached out to embrace him, and grabbed the dagger from his belt. She sunk it into his chest.

"I would rather die than be his tool," said Heron.

His eyes widened with alarm, his mouth rounded in surprise. Lysimachus grabbed her hand that was holding onto the dagger.

Heron had killed men before, but never so close and personal. Never to sate a need for revenge. Her skin flushed into a cool sweat.

"Then die, you will," said Lysimachus, cold and impersonal.

His expression turned, stretched, until it was the rictus of a smile. The taste of victory soured in her mouth, though she didn't know why.

"Did I not tell you, that Sobek gives the waters of creation? Through him, I am immortal. As much as you desire, you cannot hurt me," he said.

Heron looked to the dagger buried in his chest. There was no blood around the hilt.

"No," she whispered, releasing the blade, that stayed in his chest.

"You cannot kill me."

Heron stepped away, and again. "No."

She glanced past Lysimachus' shoulder, soldiers were returning. Vestalis was shouting at her, they were falling back.

Heron stumbled off the stage, while Lysimachus stared at her with the dagger still in his chest, a grin so wide it could swallow her whole.

Then Heron ran, her wooden leg bouncing off the rain soaked cobblestones. She ran as if a great Nile crocodile was chasing her through the streets. She ran away from Lysimachus and toward oblivion.

THIRTY TWO

The sunlight bruised Sepharia's skin as she sat amid the summer lilies and red poppies in the Palace garden, listening to the fountains dribble water into their basins. Algae clawed at the stone with streaks of greenness as nature reclaimed its own, while wild grasses batted at the benches in the breeze.

Despite the heat, Sepharia felt a chill in her bones, as she rubbed the pale blotch on the back of her hand with a thumb. She rubbed and rubbed, and the white flesh remained, surrounded by olive skin.

She had another patch of pale skin on other hand, and matching spots on her ankles where the spikes had been driven into her limbs. Except she couldn't remember the spikes being removed, or the healing, and it'd only been three days since the miracle.

Sepharia remembered the rain, and Heron and Lysimachus' argument. Not the specifics, only that they had sparred with words. It was their quarrel that let Sepharia know that it'd been the real Heron, not an imposter, one of the many women Lysimachus had mutilated to look like her father.

The buzzing insects of the garden chased her from its rich embrace. It was growing wild, much like Alexandria, the biting bugs more than a nuisance.

Sepharia moved to the edge of the cliff looking over the royal harbor. Wooden stairs led to the docks. An iron ship floated in the water, orange stains streaking the sides, like more rot in the city.

She wondered how far her captors would let her go. They watched her at a distance. Guards were stationed at the atriums and hallways that led from the garden.

Black smoke was strangely absent from the city. Normally, foundry fires burned day and night, leaving a haze that trailed west in the constant winds. Even the fires from the burning of the Colossus had been quenched, though it'd been the rains that'd done most of the work.

Sepharia ran a finger along the fence. Years ago, she'd stood in this very spot, flirting with Jarngard. It seemed strange that he was dead, along with so many others.

It wouldn't take much to follow him into the afterlife. The guards would never reach her before she stepped over the railing and threw herself onto the rocks below. Death was certain from this height.

It was tempting. More than she liked to admit. Lysimachus had let her live in relative safety thus far. That could change at a moment's notice, especially with her father in the city. The priest of Sobek could decide to torture her, put her to the blade like he did Heron, to draw her father out.

Leaping from the cliff would be easy, safe. It would only take a moment of bravery. She could muster that if she needed to.

A gust of wind threw her hair into a frenzy around her face. She tucked the strands back, enjoying the sun warming her skin. Would it be the last?

The horizon was frighteningly empty of ships. Sobek's name kept merchants away, starving the city of trade and knowledge. Only a few fishing skiffs anchored along the coast.

Sepharia put her foot on the railing. Not a single guard was close enough to stop her.

By leaping to her death, she'd save herself from future torture, and free Heron from having to save her. Sepharia lifted herself onto the fence. The nearest guards appeared from the shadows and began a slow walk to her location, not wanting to spook her.

The complication that remained was the hostages at the pyramid. Lysimachus had promised to kill Polyxena, Bani, and the other nobles, if she tried to run. Would he count her suicide as escape? Would it matter if she were dead?

Sepharia stood on the railing, arms locked to hold herself up, letting the wind turn her hair into a banner. The guards closed the gap.

Contemplating her death, Sepharia found her heart surprisingly calm. Maybe it was spending the last year and a half with Lysimachus, wondering what he would inflict on her next, that had made her numb to her own death.

Before the guards could get any closer, Sepharia stepped over, placing the fence against her back. The guards stopped and looked to each other, unsure of what do to.

Sepharia privately smirked. Lysimachus had probably threatened the guards with torture if they let her get away. Her death was their death, and she would get the cleaner way out.

The stretch of land between the fence and the edge was no more than the length of a foot. Her toes hung over the cliff. She remembered the time she escaped from the Parthians, by climbing down the cliffside with Jarngard, Hoth, and Punt. The way down had been terrifying. Each time her sweaty fingers had slipped, Sepharia had been certain she would fall.

When one of the guards took another step forward, Sepharia tilted her head and gave it a little shake. His shoulders slumped with the realization that his life was in her hands.

Sepharia released her grip from the rail, letting her weight fall forward, before grabbing it again. She wanted to feel what it was like, that moment before death. If these were her last moments, she wanted to revel in it.

Or maybe she should wait for them to retrieve Lysimachus. Surely, they had sent runners to notify him. No, she decided. His threats might convince her not to do it, might invite him to put the blade to her.

If she was going to do it, then she needed to get it over with. Sepharia took a deep breath, maybe her last.

She looked back to the city, her birthplace and home. Alexandria. It'd been like growing up at the center of the world. She looked to the Lighthouse, the marble buildings of the Great Library, to the white walls that stood shining in the sun. Each monument reminded her of Heron: her father, mother, and protector.

Sepharia closed her eyes and thought about what it would do to Heron if she leapt. Heron had risked so much in the past to save her. Would she not do so again?

In the end, thoughts of Heron swayed Sepharia to return to the garden side of the fence. The guards looked visibly relieved, letting out held breaths, though they did not move back to their posts until she was safely in the garden.

Two guards stayed at the fence. It was doubtful she'd get another chance to end her life.

Sepharia looked back to the city, back to Alexandria.

"She'll come for me."

THIRTY THREE

Vestalis found Heron in the Soma asleep next to Alexander's tomb. The inventor had been inside the room for the last three days and it stunk like it. Mostly, Heron had been walking around the massive stoneworks, running her fingers along the carvings and muttering to herself.

"Heron," he called softly, almost embarrassed that he had to wake her up. "*Michanikos.*"

She stirred, lithe figure stretching and yawning like a dog at rest, her naked legs stiffening briefly before curling beneath her as she sat up. If he hadn't known her before, he would have said she was beautiful. It wasn't the changing gender that bothered him, but the hardness of her gaze, like reaching into a cotton sack only to find broken glass.

"There's no *Michanikos* here," she said, her voice oddly sure of itself, unlike the muttering he'd witnessed before. "No Heron, either."

Vestalis checked to make sure no one was within earshot. The rebellion was at its ragged end after the failure at the eleventh miracle. He'd done what he could to keep people away from the Soma, claiming that

Heron was working on the next plan to take the city back.

He'd been letting her recover after what happened between her and Lysimachus. Vestalis had been too busy fighting to see what it was, and Heron had refused to speak after they'd fled.

"You're Heron," said Vestalis. "Why would you say anything different?"

Her sober gaze gave him grave worries. It was the look of a prisoner who'd come to terms with their execution, or a scholar speaking on their topic of expertise.

"I'm not Heron. I'm Ada. Heron was my twin brother. I took his name when he gambled his life away," she said.

"Heron, don't speak this way. We're barely holding on. If the others hear—"

"Everything I've ever known is a lie," said Heron, her face twisting in horror, as if she was being sent into a dark cave inhabited by a terrible monster. "I killed him. Stabbed him. Put the blade into his chest." Her lips pulled back in revulsion, as if they couldn't even stand forming the words.

"Killed who? Was there someone in the tomb?" asked Vestalis.

"That day. The miracle. Don't you see? It was Lysimachus. I killed him. Stabbed him with a knife, right through his chest. He should have died," she said, shaking her head incredulously.

"Maybe you're mistaken. Was he wearing armor under his robes?" he asked.

Her cry was pathetic, tugged on his heart, even though he didn't know why.

"The blade went *in*. Right in his *chest*," she said. "Don't you know what that means?"

He checked the stone hallway again. If anyone came upon her, even her close friends, they would think she was mad. Vestalis didn't allow himself to think that, yet. Sometimes a battle unhinged a man, watching others die under their blade. Though he'd never heard of someone turning to madness for *not* killing someone.

"I don't know, Heron."

She slapped the stone with her palm. "It's Ada."

"I...I don't know," he said, finding it impossible to say the other name. Heron was the only name he'd truly known her by.

She kept talking, this time quieter, almost to herself. "Afterwards, I thought about it. What if the gods were real? What if I'd been deluding myself all along? Then I started thinking about other times, other instances when they might have been telling me the truth."

"The gods are real," said Vestalis, "how else did we get here?"

"Not that. Maybe I could understand that. It's that they've been speaking to me and I haven't been listening. And now, here is proof among proof that they are, and that I've been wrong. What if all the destruction I've wrought was because I wasn't listening to them? Wasn't taking their heed?"

"The gods let us war where they might. Who are we to know their mind?" asked Vestalis, rubbing his jaw.

Heron leaned back against the tomb and gazed into the ceiling, her mind going into the past. "I remembered a time, while I was lying here. I remembered a time, that a mystic gave me a prophecy, but I ignored it, because I did not believe such things. It was a time back at the beginning of this. Back when Agog had first come to Alexandria."

"And what was this prophecy?" he asked.

Heron composed herself as if she were reciting and her voice took on an eerie quality that made Vestalis shiver. "*And in your hand was a blur. A strange apparatus I could not lay my sight upon. And from this device, the world shook, and a crack formed traveling north, and floodwaters came down the crack, and its fury scattered men and women like seeds.*"

Vestalis frowned, not understanding. "That sounds like gibberish to me."

"Apologies, you couldn't understand. The device that was a blur was the aeolipile. And from its vision, I designed the steam mechanical. That invention is what gave Agog his advantage, so we took the battle to Rome, and the world did shake, first in battle at Antioch, and then when I destroyed Rome, and now men and women are scattered like seeds."

Vestalis stepped into the tomb. "I've heard you say it before that prophecies are lies that prey on the minds of weak fools. Listen to enough of them, and eventually one will sound like your reality."

Her laugh had holes in it. She put a hand over her mouth as if she was trying to keep it from happening, but it came anyway. Her eyes pleaded with him, to make it stop, as if he had that power.

"By the gods, Heron," he said, the words trailing to concerned softness. "I can't tell you what you believe in. You're the mistress of miracles. Maybe he figured out a way to trick you, I don't know, something, as smart as you are, you can't know everything."

The declaration made her unhinged mirth stumble on itself. She tittered into silence, eventually staring at her hand and stump, resting in her lap.

"I can't," she said, shaking her head, tears streaking across her cheeks and falling into her cupped hand.

"What about Sepharia?"

She pressed her lips together so hard that her forehead wrinkled. "She didn't want to come. She's his. I don't know how, but she's his. Sobek." And then quieter. "Lysimachus."

The realization drained Heron of color. She wrapped her arms around her chest and rubbed her arm as if she were cold.

"Apologies, Heron. I know this is hard...but, what will we do now?" he asked.

She speared him in her sights. "Abandon the city."

"You can't be serious?"

She blew a breath out her nose. "What choice do we have?"

"We must try something? Do something? I put my life into Alexandria, I don't want to abandon it now."

"Then what is your plan?" she asked.

"I don't have one, but surely, we can figure one out. The city is all I have left." He showed her his palms.

"You have your life. Your skin. Your limbs," she said. "Stay in the city and you won't get to keep those."

"I cannot believe the *Michanikos* would leave. I can't believe Heron, the great inventor, would abandon the city, the Great Library, with its wealth of knowledge, to Lysimachus and Sobek."

"I'm not Heron. I'm Ada. And I don't owe the world anything."

Vestalis shook his head. He couldn't believe what she was saying.

"I'm not leaving," he said, deciding in that moment. "Not right away. There has to be something good to be done first. Maybe we can smuggle the scrolls from the city. Bring them to a city that would welcome their knowledge."

"May the gods smile on your efforts," she said listlessly, "for they have never smiled on mine. I will leave the city alone, so I do not curse your efforts."

Heron leaned against the tomb, absently tracing the shapes in the stone with her outstretched fingers. Something deep inside her had been broken and Vestalis had no idea how to fix it.

"I will help you leave the city," he said. "But promise me you'll do it quietly. Your leaving will cut the hearts from those still here. Let me tell them you're in another part of the city."

Her face soured. "You would lie to them?"

"I would. Saving something of Alexandria is more important. I wish you would see that."

Rather than answer, she went back to tracing. Vestalis watched for a while, but when he realized she was done speaking, he left her, afraid that he'd spoken to the great Heron of Alexandria for the last time.

THIRTY FOUR

Ada left Alexandria through the bars of the canal, the same ones she'd tried to leave through a month before. Between the patrols, Vestalis had the iron bars broken, and in their stead, wooden poles replaced them.

No one sent her off. She passed outside the wall alone in the depths of the night when the sky was a bright splatter. Vestalis had said his terse farewells at the Soma, his disappointment a sharp edge to his words.

Her layered traveling robes weighed heavily on her frame, along with the act of leaving. Her sandal, and wooden leg, scraped the hardpack, knocking sand and pebbles loose as she made short strides.

She planned to head south, near enough to witness her pyramid, before turning east. Before his death, she'd promised Jarngard that they'd see the other side of the Indus river. It seemed a good as place as any for a destination, and she was doubtful that Lysimachus' new empire would reach her before her end of days.

Ada left the banks of the canal, which had risen due to the flooding of the Nile, and made her way around Lake Mareotis. Despite the summer month, the evening was cool, and critters were more active, so she kept her gaze focused on where she set her good foot. Stepping on a viper would end her journey on the first night.

By morning, when a faint nimbus painted the horizon, Ada left the lake's edge and headed straight south. There were no paths where she tread, which kept the likelihood that she would encounter one of Lysimachus' patrols low.

As she climbed a rock-strewn slope covered in wind-blown sand and brush, an ache formed in her thighs. The stamina that she'd built up heading north from the Red Sea had evaporated in the months she'd spent in Alexandria.

At the apex of the hill, Ada paused, the wind rustling her robes and she looked back to the city. The walls were a tired gray and haphazard scaffolding covered the southern gate. Without the workshops, the repair would drag out for months, maybe not ever to be repaired.

Ada watched while the sun broke the horizon, splashing its crimson light across the city. The red light of morning spilled around the walls and caught the towers and parapets in flame. Above the city, the Lighthouse of Pharos stood tall, though Ada worried that she could not see the beacon and blamed the morning light on hiding it.

When she could no longer stand to look at the city, Ada turned down the rocky slope, walking away from Alexandria. The hardpack carried her south, towards the pyramid which rose like a ghostly tomb through the heat haze.

A breath caught in her throat when she saw the golden tip of the pyramid shining like a beacon. Around the base of the pyramid, a city was rising like mushrooms in a damp cave.

The population of Alexandria had been moving south to the pyramid. The nobles of the city were probably being held captive in this new city.

As she circled east around the pyramid, careful to make her way through the stunted brush, Ada caught brief flashes of light emanating from the top of the pyramid. She'd seen these flashes before when she first arrived at the Soma. She observed them long enough to guess to their purpose and then moved on. Those were concerns that might have bothered Heron, but not Ada.

She moved slow, stopping frequently to wipe down the straps on the leg harness. The journey would be long and she didn't want to wear blisters into her thighs.

When she heard the throaty growl of steam chariots in the distance, Ada crouched against the earth, content that the haze would hide her.

During the heat of the day, Ada slept beneath a lone olive tree that had somehow survived outside of the city. It had no fruits and few leaves. Her rest was interrupted when a steam chariot patrol passed near enough she lay flat on the ground.

The patrol passed within a stadia, its green flags fluttering behind them, soldiers in crocodile helms reflecting in the blazing sun. When they were out of sight, Ada pulled a hunk of hard bread and dried meat from her pack and ate in silence, taking careful sips between to work the food down.

The moment she could no longer see the pyramid passed without notice. For a long time, she could see the whole structure and then she turned and it was gone.

Ada traveled with her mind comfortably blank. She knew Heron would have spent the days creating new inventions from thin air. Ada didn't find that exercise appealing. Maybe there would be a day in the distant future when she wanted to practice those skills again. Until then, she was content.

She planned on heading south to Memphis for a safe place to cross the Nile. If she took her time, she would arrive after peak flooding, though she might have to wait a few weeks until it'd passed, unless she could join a trading caravan heading east.

She had a few coins Vestalis had given her to pay the way, though she preferred to travel as a working customer. Her only concern was that her missing limbs would make finding a caravan willing to take her more difficult.

The first few days of the journey passed quickly. She woke in late afternoon, ate, cleaned her gear, and started walking again. The patrols she encountered less and less the further away from Alexandria she traveled.

At night, she found peace. The dome of the sky glittered so bright, it wasn't hard to find safe places to set her feet, and the slithering and skittering critters that posed her danger were easy to avoid.

Ada enjoyed star gazing as she walked. When she'd been Heron, she'd never found the time to simply be herself. There'd always been taxes to pay, miracles to devise, inventions to conjure from thin air. It was no wonder Heron had been a shell of a person. As Ada, she thought she might be able to recover, find herself in ways she'd never been able to before.

Each day, getting further and further away from Alexandria was freeing. Like bonds shuffled off - thread by thread, chain by chain - until she was as light as one of her floating lanterns.

She'd almost forgotten about the trials in Alexandria, the botched rescue of Sepharia, and the encounter with Lysimachus when she came upon a camp of soldiers in the night. She'd been craning her neck, trying to recall the lore of the astronomers about the shapes of the stars and what gods and animals they indicated, when she heard the muffled shout.

Ada froze and fell to the dirt, and keeping her body low to the ground, she raised her head high enough to see what had made the noise.

Ahead of her, a small camp had been formed and either she'd wandered onto an ancient road or the caravan deviated from the regular paths. The fires were banked, so she hadn't seen them upon approach. She heard the snorts of camels, their smell unmistakable.

By the number of tents, she counted at least thirty men. The shape of their language was unfamiliar, though she could not hear them clearly since the wind was blowing easterly. Shapes moved across the firelight. Ada studied them for clues to their origin.

She was staring at the camp when she thought she saw a man with pale hair enter a tent. The viewing had been brief and in reflection, she was sure her eyes had played a trick on her.

When she looked back, she could see a man standing next to one of the banked fires. His skin was as dark as midnight and not a pale strand upon his head. She'd been hopefully mistaken.

They were southerners. Traders from the deep deserts to the south. Ada suspected they would be heading north, not the direction she wanted to go.

When she saw the hesitant light of morning on the horizon, Ada decided to stay where she was, rather than try to move around the camp unseen. Fortunately, she lay in a little hollow, surrounded by dusty scrubs. If she stayed prone, she could wait until the caravan moved on before resuming her journey. Ada curled into ball, covered herself with her sand-colored robes, and promptly fell asleep.

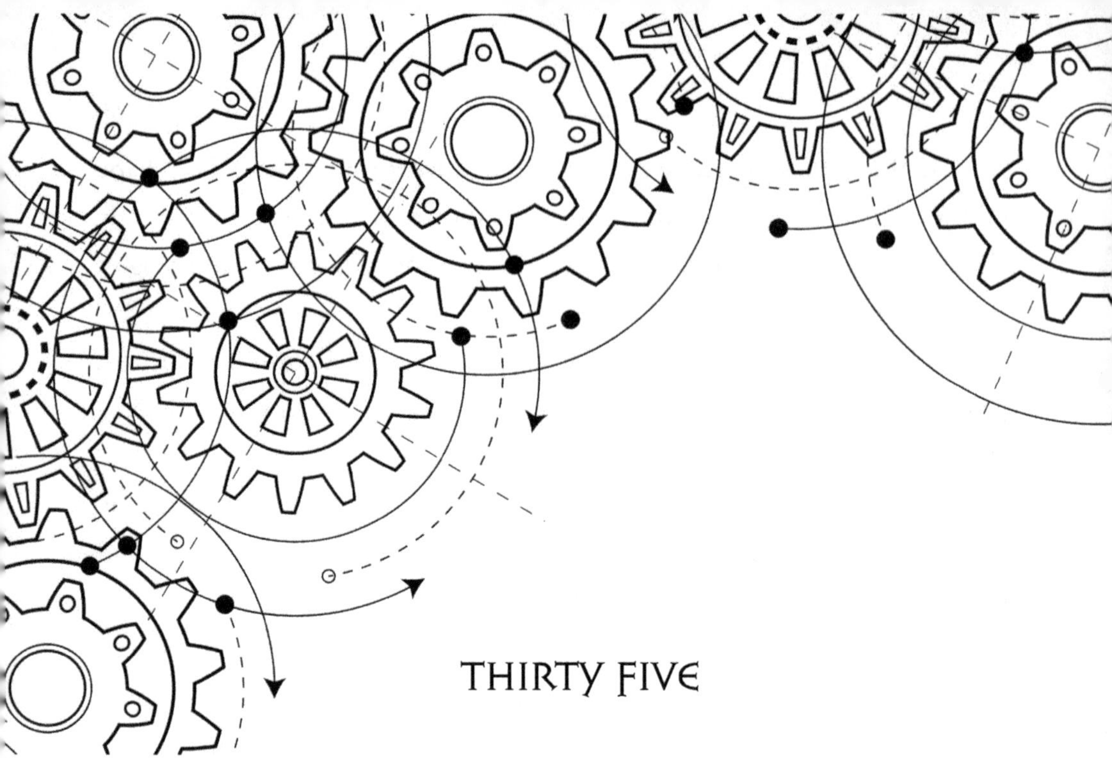

THIRTY FIVE

Hoth the Black ducked inside the goat-skin tent to find the stern-faced Kushite already awake, sharpening his curved saber, flashing his whetstone against the blade. First glance from Algoni was less than welcoming, his stern brow rippling. The Kushite Queen had warned Hoth that Bani's brother has lost his sense of humor fighting the tribes south of their empire.

"Greetings," said Hoth, stretching his chin when his words came out gravelly.

"Does your neck still bother you?" asked Algoni in Greek, moving the whetstone along the curve of the saber without looking at it.

The Northman touched the long scar that stretched from one collarbone to the other, passing dangerously close to his throat. If Zeno had cut him even a finger higher, he would have drown in his own blood on the swim back to shore.

"Only in the morning," said Hoth. "Are we traveling soon? Shall I give the word?"

Algoni had his head tilted as he swept the stone across the edge. When it kissed off the end, Algoni looked up, any emotions he held hidden by his mask of a face. The only hint to his inner workings were the beads of sweat resting on his shaved head, despite the cool morning air.

"Camels need rest. Carrying your equipment has taken a toll on them. They are not meant for such burdens."

Hoth turned his back to Algoni to look northwest, though he could see nothing through the thick canvas. "They can rest once we've made the shanty town outside of the city. But if you want rest for the camels, we should drill the men again. I'm not sure they're ready yet."

Algoni examined the edge of his blade before setting it down and grabbing the other, then with deliberate slowness, put the whetstone to it.

"These scales can defeat the Manticores as you say?" asked Algoni, frowning.

"Only if your men use them properly," said Hoth, "though I'd prefer we get to the city without having to fight. From there, we can make better decisions."

Algoni gave him a sardonic glance. "What does it matter? We know the crocodile lord holds the city and we know he holds my sister hostage."

Hoth held his tongue. He couldn't voice his concerns that he wouldn't find Heron in Alexandria. The last time he'd seen her, she'd been in the hands of their enemies. No trading vessels had seen the *Jörmungandr* reach the Red Sea. Either the iron ship had left for the east, or headed back around the continent. Neither prospect was good for the inventor. But he felt a burning need in his gut to get to the city and find out if he should start mourning Heron.

"I've been too long in the south," muttered Hoth.

Algoni lifted his head before Hoth heard them. They sounded like menacing beasts on the hunt. Hoth burst out of the tent as shouts of "Manticores!" went up.

The Northman ran to the back of the camp near the camels. They'd unloaded the scales there when they stopped for the night. Each one had been covered in a textured fabric the color of sand. When he saw the Kushite warriors grabbing the scales by the wooden handles in groups of four, Hoth ran towards the sound of the approaching Manticores.

The streaking steam mechanicals threw up billowing dust behind. Four of the deadly vehicles headed towards the camp, while one circled around.

Teams of Kushite warriors carried their scales to the north of the tents to a flat stretch of hard pack. Another group of Kushites carried lengths of chain, while a final set of pairs carried two-man crossbows with bolts as thick as his finger.

Algoni appeared at Hoth's side like a ghost, the curved blades dancing in his fists. His wide eyes stared down the approaching Manticores.

"You have your drill," said Algoni.

Hoth rubbed the coarse hairs on his chin. "Never easy, is it? Not one time." He looked up to the predawn sky filled with fading stars. "My efforts amuse you, eh?"

Algoni gave him a concerned frown, before settling his gaze back on their enemies. "Aren't you going to do something?"

The Manticores bumped across the hard earth towards them. The arrow launchers on the back were pointed towards the sky.

"Too early will be the death of us," said Hoth, glancing towards the lone Manticore that was circling around wide. He didn't have an answer to that one, yet.

"As will too late," said Algoni.

Hoth chuckled. "It's like bedding a woman, my friend. Too quickly, and she's not interested. Too late, and she's angry that you took so long."

"I don't have time for women," said Algoni.

"The world weeps for you." Hoth could see the helms on the soldiers bouncing. "Ready!"

The Kushites stayed true to their discipline and stayed standing, not one of them reaching to the ground.

The Manticores' formation began to change from an arrow point to a line, with the vehicles in back speeding up. They would create a wall of arrows that would decimate any infantry squad.

"Stay ready," said Hoth.

A few of the soldiers glanced back. They wanted him to make the call.

"Not yet, not yet," he shouted, and gave one last glance to the lone Manticore. Had the crocodile soldiers timed it right, Hoth's defense would be rendered useless. He thanked the gods that the crocodile soldiers had been impatient.

The Manticores bore down on them, only a few lengths away. When the arrow launchers came level and the pilots called out, Hoth gave his command.

"Now! Now! Now!"

The Kushites lunged forward, grabbed the leather loops on the huge flat pieces of steel and lifted them up, stepping behind the barriers as the whine of the arrow launchers keened through the air.

Hoth grabbed Algoni's arm and pulled him forward to hide behind a barrier as a wall of feathered death flew towards them. The impact of the many arrows sounded like a hailstorm on a copper roof. Bits of wood, feathers, and steel tips rained over the angled iron plates.

Three of the Manticores veered hard to avoid the scales, while the middle steam mechanical thundered straight ahead.

"Brace it!" shouted Hoth. "Center!"

The scale teams had been set in a semi-circle, three facing north, while one on either side angled to the east and west. The middle three teams pulled down the steel rods that were hinged on the underside and jammed the ends in the earth. The Kushites put their shoulders into the steel as the Manticore hit.

The vehicle hit the ramp and went flying over, one side angled poorly and when it landed, the front axle snapped and it went tumbling end over end, taking out tents and camp fires, while the soldiers on it were tangled in the destruction.

When the other Manticores split around, two going left and one going right, the chain teams launched their loads onto the ground in front of the vehicles. The chains had been woven into loose nets with extra loops and threads hanging off like gnarly, metal, curly hair.

The chain net on the left landed in a heap and the Manticore bumped over it. The right net deployed perfectly, landing in a flat blanket, and when the wheels ran over it, they grabbed hold and got lodged into the gearing. When the wheel came to a screeching halt, the backside lifting into the air and spinning around, it threw the men from the vehicle like an untamed horse.

The crossbow teams fired their massive bolts, aimed not at the men, but at the steam chambers. The first hit solidly, a geyser of superheated water splashing over the pilot, his screams heard over the din of battle.

The second shot missed and flew out into the desert. The team moved to reload the two-man crossbow, but the Manticore sent a quick volley of arrows into the men.

Hoth barely ducked behind the side scales. Another Kushite soldier took an arrow through the thigh and erupted in screams.

Three Manticores remained, though one was rolling to a stop a ways from their position. Without the steam chamber, it couldn't generate enough force to move the pistons. The soldiers climbed onto the other Manticore and they sped away to meet the other Manticore a distance from the camp.

"Readjust the scales over here. Reload those crossbows. Grab that net, we might need it again," said Hoth.

The men complied while the two Manticores sat unmoving. The soldiers on it were conversing amongst themselves.

"We can't let them return to Alexandria," said Algoni, blades still in his fists.

"I know. I know." Hoth shook his head. "If they leave and get more Manticores, we'll never make it to the city. We won't make it anywhere."

"We must take the fight to them," said Algoni.

Hoth tugged on the hair on the top of his head and stomped his foot into the dirt. "And people call me mad."

Algoni captured Hoth in his stony gaze. "You and I both know we cannot let these Manticores return to Alexandria. We die now or we die later, it does not matter to me."

"By the jarls," said Hoth, as the Manticores began to move again, not in their direction. "To the camels!"

As Hoth ran to the unruly mounts, the first Manticore circled around to head northwest, the direction of Alexandria, while the other idled, waiting for the rest of them to make their move.

"I hope you're enjoying this," said Hoth, to whatever gods might be listening.

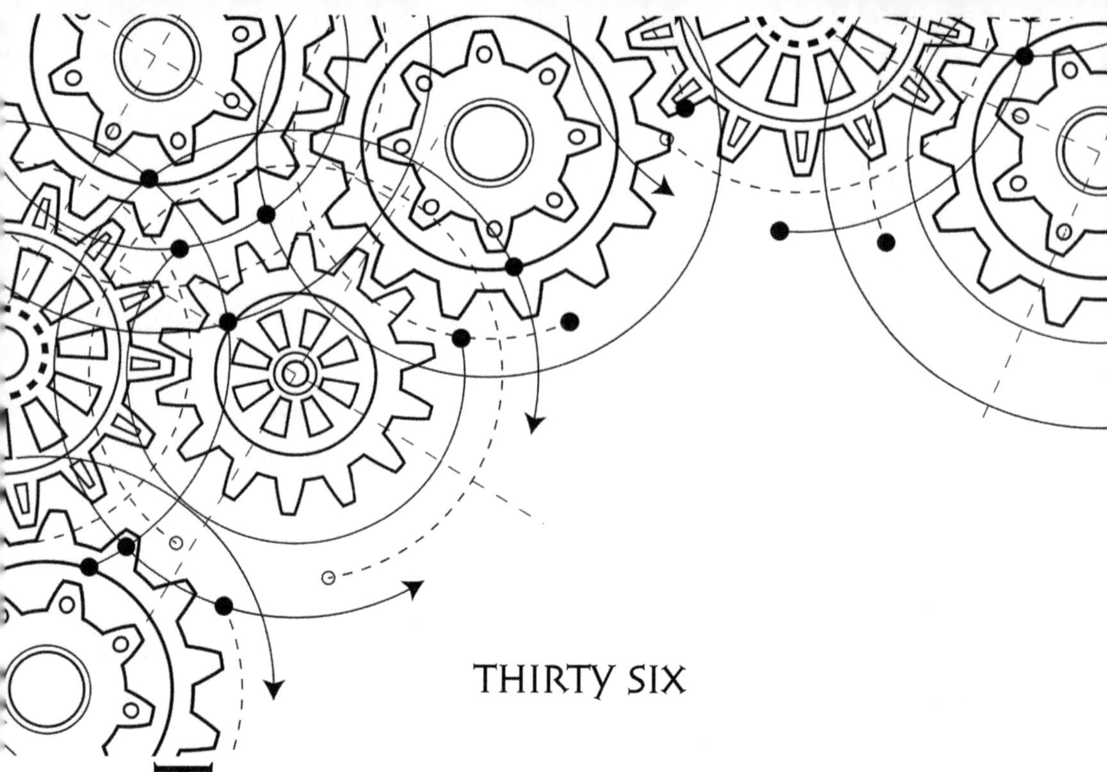

THIRTY SIX

The vibration in the earth woke Ada moments before shouts of "Manticores!" filled the air. She peeked her head from the covering, squinting into the rising sun to see men from the camp scrambling past the tents carrying huge stiff sheets.

She let out a gasp when she saw Hoth's tall frame striding through the camp, shouting orders at the soldiers. His pale hair formed a cloak on his back and he'd grown a beard that could have been a pile a straw on his cheeks and chin. The addition didn't change how she felt about him, though.

From the north, a group of five Manticores were headed towards the Northman. Dust streamed after them, catching the rays of the rising sun.

Ada wanted to stand up and shout for the fools to run while they could. How could they think they were going to survive even one pass from the deadly vehicles?

Crawling forward on her elbows gave her a better view of the upcoming battle. She cursed when the fifth Manticore broke from the others to circle around.

Putting a fist to her forehead and biting her lower lip so hard that she whimpered didn't get them to do as she wanted. "Why aren't you running?"

The sea captain was not only not running, but he seemed to be relishing the approaching steam chariots. Only he would look so unconcerned in the face of certain death. Which meant that he had a plan. He always had a plan. Not always a good one, but give him credit, he never went down without a fight.

Ada winced when the hum of the steam mechanicals reached a higher pitch and cheered when the Kushites lifted the metal shields in time to block the arrows. The rest of the battle happened so quickly, she barely had time to register the impact of the first Manticore after it flew over the barrier, when two others were quickly disabled.

Ada scratched at the dirt when the two men at the crossbow didn't get behind the barrier in time. She was so focused on making sure Hoth hadn't been hit, that she didn't see the other Manticore until it'd almost rolled over her.

The iron banded wheels skidded to a stop less than a body length from her position, crunching across the crusty earth. The crocodile soldiers were focused on the Kushites and the rapid destruction of three Manticores, so they didn't see Ada slip beneath the sand colored covering. She peaked through a thin crack to watch. The other remaining Manticore rolled next to the other, thankfully on the camp side, otherwise it might have run her over.

Ada pulled the knife from her belt and held it beneath the blanket. She tried to listen to what they were saying, but the men were facing the other way, and their voices carried in that direction.

While she waited, it occurred to Ada that she could slip out and kill the first two soldiers before the others noticed. She might even be able to speed away on the Manticore before the others could stop her. Doing so would probably save the men in the camp.

It would also mean that she'd have to return to Alexandria.

Ada stared at the backs of the crocodile soldiers from her hiding spot. She squeezed the hilt of the knife until her knuckles cracked. She wouldn't just save those men, she reminded herself. She'd save Hoth.

Ada almost climbed out to attack, before closing her eyes and gritting her teeth. It didn't help that she imagined Hoth taking a dozen arrows to the chest.

She wanted to save them, but when she moved to stand, she couldn't. It wasn't that she was afraid. It was something else.

The Manticores pulled away, the first headed northwest, while the second waited before heading south. Ada choked on the dust they kicked up when they left.

She saw Hoth running to the camels. He climbed onto a tall beast and helped one of the Kushites, a bare-chested man with richly colorful pants, onto the mount with him.

Every fiber of her soul wanted her to stand up and call to Hoth before he chased after the Manticore. But she didn't. Not because she might be seen by the crocodile soldiers, but that she might have to return to Alexandria, and that filled her with an unexplainable dread.

So she watched as the two men on a camel raced after the Manticore. Other camels with men followed, further behind Hoth, but none of them were even remotely close to catching up. The remaining men in the camp milled about and got into arguments about what to do, before grabbing weapons and setting off on foot in a northerly direction.

Fools, all of them. Hoth, especially. Eventually, those Manticores would realize the men were without their metal shields and turn around. One pass with the arrow launcher and they'd be worm meat.

Then the crocodile soldiers would come back to the camp to make sure there were no survivors. She didn't want to be within a league of the camp when they did that. With the Kushites out of sight, Ada gathered her gear and hobbled towards the southeast. It wasn't quite the direction to Memphis, but she wanted to put as much distance between her and the camp as possible.

Ada pushed on, even when the morning heat rose, leaving her undergarments soaked with sweat. The desert was a merciless plain, which was why she'd been traveling during the night and sleeping during the day. It was bad enough resting in the heat. Marching across the hard earth chaffed her skin against the straps on her leg.

Ada was limping along, imagining lying down into one of her fountains, even one of Philo's, since she wasn't that proud, when a noise made her flinch. She reacted first by instinct and then as she pulled the cowl of her robe away from her face, she grimaced and thought about throwing herself to the ground.

But it was too late. The Manticore had seen her and was headed in her direction, its bronze metal shield flickering out of the heat haze.

It wouldn't do her any good to run, so Ada kept hobbling in the same direction, hoping the vehicle would realize she wasn't one of the Kushites and keep going. Wasn't likely, but she had to try.

She flipped her hood back, too, in hopes so they wouldn't mistake her for a soldier. Revealing that she was a woman had other dangers, but she was willing to take a chance.

Ada bowed when the Manticore reached her. "Greetings, travelers."

The three soldiers shared exaggerated glances, owing to the elongated bills on their crocodile helms. She gave them a great big smile, trying to infuse a general sense of benignness. The soldier at the steerage removed his helm, wiped his glistening forehead with a piece of cloth that'd been tucked in his belt, and nodded his head in a westerly direction.

"You come from that camp?" he asked.

Ada blinked. It was the only thing she could do that wouldn't provoke the soldier. She wanted to tell him what a stupid question it was, but gave him a terse shake of the head instead.

"How can I believe you?" he followed up.

"What camp?" she asked.

The soldier in back spoke up, "Let's return to the city. This heat is worse than Vulcan's forge. She doesn't look like she was with them."

Ada thought they were going to let her go. The soldier at the steerage weighed the decision, pursing his lips into different shapes before coming to a conclusion.

"Better take her, just to be safe."

She didn't resist when they grabbed her. The first spoke up when she realized she was missing a hand.

"I think she's one of Sobek's," he said.

A chill passed through her and the soldier saw the fear in her eyes, which only confirmed his suspicions.

"Aye, she don't want to go back to him. Must be one of his pets that he cut on. Snuck away or something. Might be a reward in it for us when we bring her back."

Unlike the soldiers that had captured her when she first returned to Alexandria, these bound her on the back of the Manticore, away from any levers, or valves. Nothing within reach that she could create mischief with. The only thing she could reach was her nose to itch, if she leaned her head down.

As they sped across the hard pack, the soldier in back with her leaned down, putting his pock-marked face into her vision. "The priest isn't gonna be too happy to find out you run out on him. Might feed you to his crocs he got in his temple there in the Palace. Gonna wish you'd stayed in Alexandria, cause things gonna get real worse."

Ada buried her head in her robes. The memories of the pit beneath the temple came up through the cracks in her mind like bubbling pitch, no matter how hard she squeezed her eyes shut. Feeding her to the crocodiles? Ada pounded her head against her knees. That was the least of her worries.

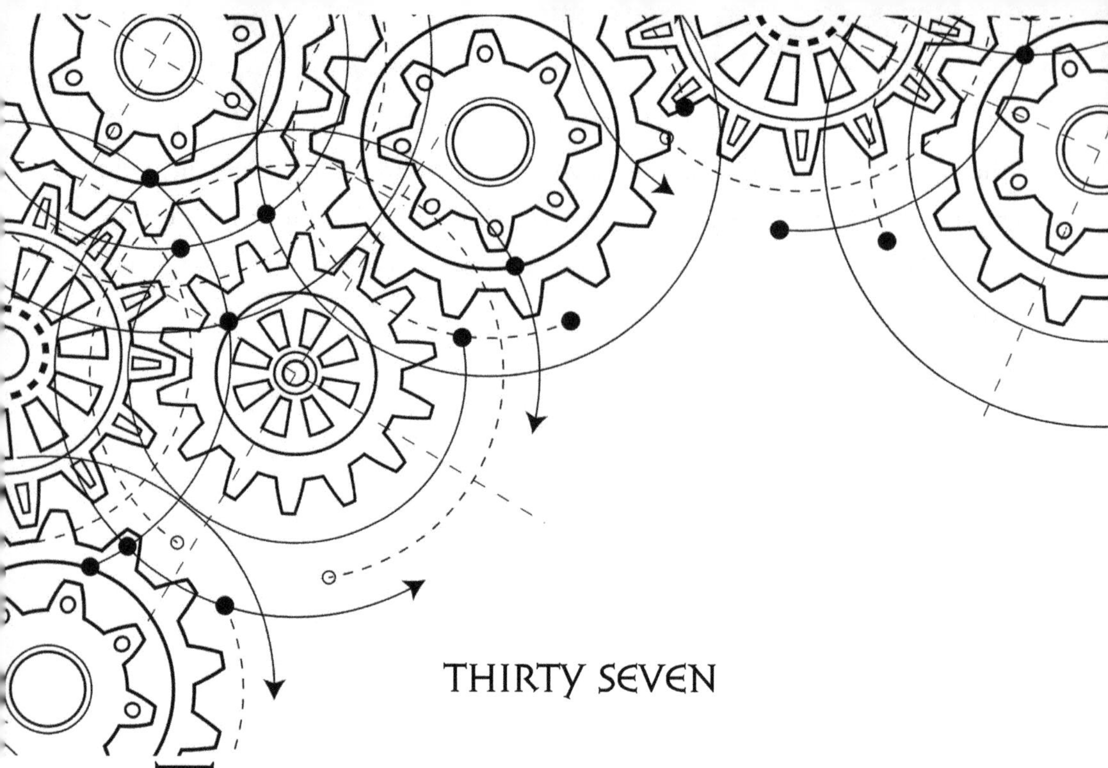

<h1 style="text-align:center">THIRTY SEVEN</h1>

The camel was faster than Hoth expected, even with two grown men riding between its humps. The camel could even keep up with the Manticore, though Hoth suspected it wasn't his mount's doing. But what the camel was not, was smooth.

Trapped against the front hump, with Algoni's bulk pressing him forward, each gallop crushed his manhood into the camel. After the first few minutes of chasing, Hoth was begging for the Manticore to turn around.

"Why won't...they attack?" Hoth shouted into the wind, catching dust on his tongue.

"Maybe they think more tricks," said Algoni in his ear. The Kushite had a saber on one fist, while the other grabbed onto the front of Hoth's tunic.

"Then why...not go faster? That Manticore can go...much faster," said Hoth, grunting with each impact.

Algoni tapped him on the chest and pointed forward with an outstretched arm. The Manticore was making a wide turn, kicking up dust in every direction. No other camels were within sight. Either they'd out-paced the others, or everyone else had gotten better sense.

"What do we do now?" asked Algoni, his shouted words tickling Hoth's ear.

"What do we—" Hoth paused as the camel's gait made him shift forward, further squeezing his fruits, "—do now? You're the one...who said we had to attack."

"We do," said Algoni, "but I didn't have a plan."

The Manticore was headed directly at them. The bronze shield on the front depicted a lion's head. Though he couldn't pick it out amid the glare and dust and heat haze, the arrow launcher on the back grew larger in his mind.

"Plan?" Hoth muttered to himself. "Freya's tits...I have no plan."

Hoth almost yanked on the reins to veer the camel to the right, but that would only expose them to being shot at short range. He had to think of them like ships. The faster he passed the Manticore, the faster he could put distance between them.

But passing the steam mechanical without being feathered with arrows was not a task he rather liked considering. If Heron were there, she'd know how to defeat the vehicle. Hoth wished he'd paid more attention to her ramblings about steam mechanical design. None of them were perfect, in the inventor's eyes, and each could be improved.

Then Hoth remembered a little fact about the Manticore, one that Heron had groused about during the war with Rome. The arrow launcher couldn't fire straight forward without hitting the pilot. They could arc the arrows over the steerage, but anything directly in front couldn't be hit. So they had a small window to get close to the Manticore, unless the soldier on the back knew his geometry.

"Curse the inventor and her maths," said Hoth the Black.

"What?" said Algoni behind him, but Hoth shook him off.

Hoth turned his head, "Ready your saber."

The Manticore grew closer, its traverse across the dusty scrub-dotted plain a miracle in Hoth's eyes, simultaneously taking forever to reach them and approaching so rapidly his breath was held between his teeth.

When the arrow launcher fired, it didn't release its arrows right away. First, a heavy whine filled the air, like the keening of a mechanical ghost. When Hoth heard the sound over the grunting of the camel and the thundering of the pistons, he kicked the camel in the ribs, willing it to fly like Mercury.

Hoth leaned into the hump, Algoni wisely pressing against his back, as the arrows sliced through the air above their heads like an executioner's axe. Hoth scarcely had time to cheer before he had to yank the reins so the camel didn't run into the Manticore. As they slipped past, Algoni swung his arm and Hoth heard a metallic impact. The Kushite Prince cried out in pain right after.

"My blade," he cried.

To Hoth's dismay, the soldiers on the Manticore lived, and the pilot was bringing the vehicle around while the second loaded arrows into the launcher. The third, one of the rescues from the other vehicles, crouched behind the pilot.

Hoth turned the camel, giving it a moment's rest from its headlong sprint. The Manticore was taking a wide turn as well, though not all seemed right on the vehicle. A white mist like a miniature fountain sprayed upward from the back.

"By the snows of the North, I hope that means what I think it means," said Hoth, kicking the camel into action toward the Manticore.

"What are you doing, my friend?" asked Algoni, "I'm without my weapon."

"And I'm without a plan and that's never stopped me before," laughed Hoth, his hair swirling around his face.

The camel and the Manticore raced to meet each other again. This time, Hoth veered perpendicular well before they passed and the soldier at the steerage, turned to come along side.

"What are you doing?" asked Algoni, the concern lacing through his words. "They'll rip us apart."

"Don't worry," said Hoth, spitting his hair out of his mouth, "I'm a ship captain."

The Manticore was running parallel and slowing, closing the distance between the two. The arrow launcher was pointed directly at them, loaded full.

"What in all creation does that matter here? We're going to die, you fool," said Algoni.

Nudging the camel toward the Manticore with his knees, Hoth passed the reins back to Algoni.

"What are these for?" he asked, as the heavy whine of the arrow launcher keened into existence, but instead of releasing its load, the pressure contained within spit out the cut in the brass line.

"You're the captain of the ship, now," said Hoth, as they were almost side to side with the Manticore.

"This isn't a ship."

Hoth hopped to his feet, steadying himself on the front hump. The soldier at the steam launcher was staring at the contraption, not understanding why it didn't work. The soldier at the steerage gripped the handles, glancing over his shoulder, his brow knotted in confusion as to why the launcher hadn't fired.

Only the third soldier, the one crouched behind the pilot, seemed to understand what was about to happen. He was pulling his blade free and standing upright, knocking his helm off with his other hand to career off the speeding vehicle.

"It is a ship," shouted Hoth, "if I'm boarding the other."

Hoth pushed off hard, leaping to cross the distance. Unlike a fixed ship, the camel reacted by veering the other way, much like it would if he were nudging it with his knees. Hoth flew through the air, and for a moment, he thought he would come up short.

He hit the platform behind the steerage and before the brass chamber of the steam mechanical on his knees. He would have tumbled right off, had the soldier not been standing in his way, short blade glinting in the morning sun. Hoth hit the man in the thighs with his shoulder, and he tumbled off backwards. An ungraceful exit, if Hoth had ever seen one.

A moment's hesitation cost the pilot as he dithered between his sword and the steerage. One of the first things Hoth had ever been taught about battle was that if you're going to do something, do it quick and with all your heart, no matter how stupid it seemed in the doing.

Hoth relieved the man of his weapon and made the end quick with a slice across the neck before throwing him from the Manticore. He captured the steerage in his other hand, keeping the blade at the ready, as it rocked and bounced, and kicked the speed lever into the dead position.

The soldier at the back was ready with his weapon when the Manticore came to a stop, but by this time, Algoni had retrieved the first soldier's weapon, and the two of them advanced from opposite sides.

When the soldier was dead, Hoth moved to rub down the camel as it wheezed from its efforts. Algoni stared at the Manticore, his dark skin glistening in the sunlight, cleaning the blood from his acquired weapon with the same short strokes he had put the whetstone to his saber.

"Looks like a cooking pot mated with a spider," said the Kushite Prince.

Hoth laughed. "Not far off. When next I see Heron, I'm going to have to tell her that one. It'll be worth a scowl."

"This inventor, Heron, the one I have heard so much," said Algoni. "How can it be that this one person do so much?"

"You can ask her that when we see her. I hope she's in Alexandria," said Hoth. "But let us not waste more time. We have to find that other Manticore."

Each one took the ride they were most comfortable with. Hoth was glad to be off the smelly camel. He much preferred horse flesh if he had to be mounted, and the Manticore was another thing entirely, reminding him of a ship on land. It didn't even bother him that the arrow launcher had been disabled by an errant saber.

The pair set off in the direction they thought the other Manticore might have taken. Prince Algoni took the lead on his camel, to give the illusion he was being chased. Hoth piloted the Manticore, wearing the crocodile helm and the bloodless tunic of the soldier who had broken his neck.

Hoth was fussing with the helm, he didn't know how those soldiers could stand the unbalanced weight on the forehead, when he saw the other Manticore.

As he'd guessed, the soldiers had circled wide around to meet up with the nearest trading road, the one that headed south to Kushite, and that they'd been avoiding on their way up towards Alexandria.

The second Manticore turned to join the pursuit and Hoth gave a terse wave and glanced behind him. The dead soldier they'd bound into a standing position had slumped over onto the launcher. Unless they were blind, the other soldiers would see something was wrong.

Hoth increased the speed, closing the distance on Algoni, hoping the lure of the chase would blind them to his deception. The other Manticore was coming at an angle, going faster to catch up.

Without moving his head, Hoth kept watch on the approaching vehicle. As far as he could tell, they hadn't spotted the dead soldier, but it was only a matter of time. They were coming up alongside.

The crocodile soldier on the back noticed first. He shouted to his companions, pointing at the dead soldier. Two other sets of eyes followed, so Hoth veered right, aiming the shield on the steam chariot at their back wheel.

The impact shattered wood and iron, sending splinters past Hoth's head. The other Manticore yawed wildly, before the axle dug into the dirt, whipping the vehicle to the side and then throwing it end over end.

The Manticore flipped twice before coming down on broken wheels, burning coals thrown in a wide pattern. The soldiers were no longer on the vehicle. Hoth put a sword through the only one that was crawling and Algoni did the same to the two others, though Hoth wasn't sure they were even alive.

Hoth was checking the dead soldiers for orders when Algoni called him over.

"They had a prisoner," said the Kushite Prince, "but I don't think it survived that tumble."

Intrigued, Hoth approached. The tone of Algoni's voice said that it hadn't been one of his men. So who could they have taken prisoner in such a short time?

Hoth saw the olive skin and long black hair first. The woman's body was slumped against her bonds. Blood trickled from her lips onto a knee. The legs were splayed out and on the end was an oddly shaped boot.

When he saw the stump, the words slipped out his lips in a cry, "Heron."

He threw himself forward and pushed her head back up. Her tongue lolled out of her mouth and her eyes had rolled into the back of her head. He'd killed Heron.

A chill wind swept through him as if every bone in his body had been replaced with ice. His hands and feet went numb.

"Oh, Heron, I didn't know. How did you get here? I'm so sorry," he said, touching her face tenderly with his calloused fingertips.

Hoth buried his face against her chest, digging his hands in her hair.

"You know this dead woman?" asked Algoni.

Hoth pulled himself away, wiping his sweat soaked hair away from his face. Pain had turned every muscle in his face into contortion.

"It's Heron. The inventor."

Hoth was looking up at the Kushite Prince when the body stirred beneath his fingertips. The sea captain looked down to see Heron's weary gaze, bloodshot and sore, regarding him with hollow indifference.

"I'm not Heron."

THIRTY EIGHT

Hoth arrived at Cassandra's Tavern breathless and footsore with Prince Algoni right behind. They'd been spotted by a patrol when crossing Canopic street and it took them numerous double-backs through side alleys and abandoned courtyards to lose them.

His heavy breathing was an intrusion into the quiet tension of the tavern and it didn't take him long to figure out why. An older white-haired male in the trappings of a Roman Senator sat in one corner with a darkwood cane across his lap, surrounded by a trio of personal guards in Roman livery, complete with the seal of the Roman Empire stamped into their breastplates.

Senator Dominitus, though it seemed odd to think of him that way since there was no Senate, was a deep pool, the surface of which could scarcely be disturbed, even with the largest of stones. In the North, men like Dominitus never ruled, but held positions of advisor to the King.

The Senator bivouacked in one corner, while Vestalis conferred in quiet tones with his men in the other. Hoth knew the man from their campaign against Rome, and trusted him implacably.

When Hoth had entered, Vestalis had only acknowledged him with a terse nod, his brow so stern and steadfast, a series of battlements could be built upon it.

The tavern had been chosen as a meeting place for security and mutual convenience, though Hoth found the brass implements from the Great Library that hung from the ceiling felt more like the nursery of a scholar rather than a location of negotiation that could determine the birth and death of empires.

Though Hoth felt a kinship with Vestalis, he did not join his retinue, instead keeping separate with Prince Algoni. Both sides were waiting for Heron to show up, and when she did, he suspected there would be mutual disappointment.

Hoth had barely spoken with the inventor since they'd returned to Alexandria. She'd been spending her time with Plutarch at a hidden location, hopefully working on a new weapon that would carry them against Lysimachus and his Terrors.

When Heron finally arrived, it was not through the front door, but from the back. Arethussa and Punt stood with her, though no one in the room noticed the others.

Since the discovery in the Roman Senate, when the whole world had learned that the great Heron was a woman, Hoth had been wrestling with the notion. While he'd known about her womanhood since that fateful ride in the sky, he'd spent much of his time after that away from her. It wasn't until their journey around Africa that he began to understand what that meant.

On the *Jörmungandr*, she'd been convalescing from her horrific injuries sustained in the burning of Rome and had been at the mercy of the available materials on the ship. With new resources at her fingertips, Hoth finally had an idea of who this person that called herself Ada was.

In contrast to Arethussa - who stood by Ada's side in a lavender stola, raven-hair modestly hanging in loose curls, cheeks blushed with color - the inventor was not in womanly attire. But yet, there was no denying that she was a woman. It seemed the inventor had chosen a unique path that straddled the various pieces of her.

Heron, or Ada, wore her customary tunic, the one he'd seen her wearing in the workshop so many times, except it was not a plain garment that exposed the usual ink stains, but a fitted fabric of deep azure, almost black. She wore a silver belt stamped with gears, an accoutrement that would have looked frivolous on someone else, but on her it was like a band of bright iron around her waist.

Her dark hair had grown long enough that it reached her shoulders. It was brushed back straight and contained with a silver band that matched her belt.

The wooden leg had been replaced with a mechanical one, and by the looks of it, an earlier version they'd rescued from somewhere, along with a mechanical hand. Their added weight did not seem to burden the inventor, who stood comfortably with her flesh and metal fingers clasped in front, the human and the mechanical, working as one.

Her gaze flickered upon Hoth for a moment, so brief and ephemeral that his heart doubled in time and he knew then that he'd never desired her more. She was Athena and Vulcan combined, a goddess of invention and the fount from which the new world had sprung.

Algoni moved to speak, but Hoth held him back with a gentle touch on the forearm. The Kushite returned a nod and moved to find a nearby chair.

A cleared throat crowded into the room, dispelling the weight of the inventor's entrance. Dominitus coughed into a cream cloth, wiping his mouth with the corner when the unpleasant affair was finished.

"Apologies," said Dominitus, sitting up against the back of his chair, his bloodshot eyes creasing. He tapped on the floor with his cane. "We should get this business started. If Lysimachus finds us here, then our little revolution is over."

"Agreed," said Vestalis, "we need to come to terms on how we'll split the Empire when the priest is overthrown."

Dominitus pounded his cane three times, quite vigorously, surprising Hoth. "Split the Empire? Are you mad? The Empire is the only thing that's held the world together these past centuries."

"Then maybe the Brethren should have thought of that before they started a war in Rome," said Vestalis, fingering the guard on his hilt, his mirthless gaze unwavering.

The old Senator responded in a crumbling voice, "I'm not the Brethren, nor was I during the rebellion. If you recall, they tried to kill me, too."

Vestalis stern lips ticked in response. "But you share the same goals. One Empire ruled by your shadow council."

Dominitus cleared his throat. "Our methods proved quite constructive, ruling over an Empire that lasted for over five hundred years. Only the inventor's machines and the previous Brethren's incompetence put an end to that."

The implication of Dominitus' words passed through Ada without notice. Hoth was surprised, only because she'd taken the destruction of Rome so personally.

Vestalis took a step, his shoulders back and his chin jutting forward. "Incompetence? An understatement, considering the destruction they wrought. Or maybe you name it incompetence because their stratagems did not overthrow the Alexandrian government."

The old Senator shook his head, jowls swaying, white wispy hair falling over his forehead. "I would have counseled them to accept the new rule and work to better the Empire rather than fight it."

"Easy for you to say here," said Vestalis. "How can you demand anything without significant resources to offer?"

Dominitus scoffed. "I have more to offer than you. The only thing you've done is destroy part of the city and cause more men to flee to Lysimachus' side."

"While our numbers were depleted, they've been recently bolstered by the Kushite Prince." Vestalis inclined his head toward Algoni. "And we have the *Michanikos* on our side, the great inventor, who has been laboring on a new warmachine to turn the tide against followers of Sobek. Tell him, Heron. Tell him what you've been working on."

Like a proud elder brother, Vestalis smiled at the inventor. She did not respond right away, throwing doubt into the old soldier's grin.

"I'm not Heron. That was my twin brother. I'm Ada," she said.

A moment of annoyance passed across Vestalis' face. "Apologies, Ada." He sounded like he was tasting her name. "But tell Dominitus that you have new warmachines for us, to take the fight to Lysimachus. Something to counter his advantage with the Manticores and Centaurs."

Ada looked at her mechanical arm, picked at an imaginary piece of dirt on one of the gears, and then raised her head. Her lips were flat, gaze distant.

"I'm not working on a weapon to win this war," said Ada.

Confusion knotted on Vestalis' brow. "What kind of weapon is it? And which war should we be fighting?"

"It's not a weapon at all. Not like you think of it," said Ada. "But my time making weapons is over. The battles I fight now are ones purely of the mind. It has taken too many failures to learn that I cannot change the world by killing my enemies."

Vestalis looked like Ada had snapped her fingers and made his clothes disappear. Hoth had never seen the man look so uncomfortable. Hoth had similar feelings, but he'd had time to reconcile the new Heron, or Ada, since he'd been the one to rescue her in the desert.

"By the gods, how will we take the city back?" he asked.

Hoth had almost forgotten Dominitus was in the room, but found his expression composed, as if he'd known about this revelation beforehand. Hoth knew better. The old Senator was a better liar than Vestalis, who had been visibly wounded by Ada's declaration.

"That's not my problem," said Ada. "I'll help you get my daughter back. And if that provides some distraction, then so be it. The rest of you can fight over the city without me. I'm done with war."

"But we need your ideas, Her...Ada," said Vestalis, holding his palms up.

Ada nodded towards Prince Algoni. "Look to your allies for help. The Prince can provide support, he wants his sister back."

Vestalis pounded his fist on the table. "We don't even know where the noble prisoners are being kept."

"At the pyramid," said Ada. "They're building a city around the monument. You'll find them there. But what I don't know is where they're going to perform the last miracle."

"In the Lighthouse of Pharos," said Dominitus, finally speaking up. "We barely snuck out of there before they brought in new soldiers, ones that wouldn't accept my bribes."

Ada bowed towards the Senator. "Thank you, Dominitus."

Dominitus gave a watery smile. "They also had wagons full of crates. Whatever miracle they're planning, it's going to be bigger than the others."

Vestalis frowned and pounded lightly on the table. "I thought you'd given up on Sepharia. That's why you left the city."

The accusation cut through the room, but Ada seemed unaffected. "I had. But it seems no matter how I try to avoid it, I must finish what was started many years ago when Agog first knocked on my door. It seems the gods wish an ending."

"I didn't think you believed in the gods," said Vestalis.

Ada smirked. "I don't. But it seems they believe in me."

Hoth cleared his throat, drawing pointed stares. "Which target shall we attack first? The pyramid or the Lighthouse?"

Before anyone else could speak, Ada said, "Both. The priests have set up a communication system between the two monuments using flashing lights. If you don't hit them both at the same time, they'll know you're coming."

Vestalis gave him a stern look, so Hoth cleared his throat. "Don't you mean *we*? If the last miracle is on the Lighthouse, then Sepharia will be there."

Hoth's stomach twisted when Ada looked at him. He felt like he'd been caught stealing food.

"I told you," said Ada. "I'm done with war, done with fighting, done being *Heron*. I'm getting Sepharia when you attack the Lighthouse, but I won't be with you."

Hoth rubbed the back of his neck. "I don't understand. I thought you'd be with us? And if you're not going to be in the attack, how will you rescue Sepharia?"

"Better yet," said Dominitus, his voice growing hard. "Why would we bother with the Lighthouse if the nobles are at the pyramid? Free them, and our allies won't be worried about hostages. We can take the fight to Lysimachus once they're free."

Ada took a step forward, glancing at each one of them. The bruising around her jaw from the flipped Manticore had faded to yellow.

"You'll take the fight to the Lighthouse because that's where Lysimachus will be. If you kill him, the war is over. This movement, this burgeoning theocracy, lives and dies on him," she said.

No rebuttal followed, though Vestalis jawed at the air for a moment, as if he had something to say.

"And I don't care what you do with the city afterwards," said Ada, before anyone spoke up. "That'll be your problem to figure out. But we only have three days before the last miracle, so stop wasting time bickering about the spoils of a war you haven't won yet. You'd better spend that time figuring out how you're going to take down those steam chariots. I'm not your miracle worker anymore."

Vestalis visibly recoiled from the admonishment, while Dominitus tilted his head slightly. Before Ada could leave, Hoth caught up to her, grasping her arm lightly.

She turned and stared at him passively, her gaze flickering across his face. "I'll help you get Sepharia back. Just say the word and I'll be at your side."

Ada gave him the courtesy of appearing to think about it, but he could see in her eyes a resoluteness that he could not touch.

"Apologies," she said. "I've made my plans already and they'll need you for the fighting."

He pulled his hand away as if her skin was hot steel. "I don't understand."

Her stern facade broke a little, enough that the corners of her eyes softened. She glanced to Arethussa and Punt, who waited at the backdoor of the tavern.

"I have things I need to do," she said, and his heart deflated.

She sighed and parted her lips. "But tonight, tonight, I could use your help."

"Name it."

"Meet me back here," she said, and when a grin formed on his lips, "dressed for stealth, not your usual whorish attire."

Hoth felt the vise around his heart release and put a hand to his chest in mock injury. "But my whorish attire is made for stealth. Sneaking through windows and away from angry husbands makes it a necessity."

The faintest of smiles ghosted to her lips, as if it hurt to have joy, before she nodded and left.

Hoth rubbed his fingertips across his lips, thinking about how much he missed holding her in his arms. Maybe if he was lucky, they could finish whatever job she wanted done, and they could have time together.

Then again, when had he ever been lucky?

THIRTY NINE

Sepharia recognized the guard when the door swung open, banging against the stone. His expression was flat. He motioned for her to leave with a nod of his head.

She glided to his side and put her hand on his muscled forearm.

"Your name is Abeden," she said.

He looked down at her, his once-broken nose appearing straight from her angle, and squeezed his lips until they were white as marble. Sepharia slowly pulled her hand away and when she did, he marched ahead.

"Lysimachus wants to see me, doesn't he?" she asked, speaking to the broad back of the soldier Abeden.

She tried to catch up to him, pulling up the hem of her cream stola, and scurrying forward, but when she did, he lengthened his stride. She intended to speak to him, implore him to give her a clue of what was ahead, when she saw the missing finger on his left hand.

There would be no answers from Abeden the guard. His loyalty had been tested when he cut off his finger.

Sepharia rubbed the white patch on the back of her hand with the thumb. None of her sacrifices had been willing. Lysimachus had drugged her or tricked her, or done whatever he could to obtain her help.

A feeling in her gut, she wasn't sure where it came from, told her this time it would be for real. The final miracle was in three days, and she believed it would be the end. The soldiers had been restless, edgy, like a cat trying to eat from a crocodile's mouth.

The walls of the Palace passed without notice, not that there was much to look at anymore. Once, the walls had been covered in paintings and tapestries, the alcoves filled with statues of Alexander and Caesar, the marble scrubbed so white it was brighter than the sun.

The rot had dug in. It was no longer a green haze at the corners of each room. Blackish verdant tendrils of mold streaked across the walls, fed by the hot, humid days. Each step was a guessing game, as her sandal could catch a spot of moisture.

She reached the inner chamber of the Palace, wondering why Lysimachus even bothered anymore. The room felt like a cave, rather than the proud seat of an Empire.

Sepharia realized she'd marched up to the dais too proudly when he glanced up from his scroll at her, his black pebble-like eyes squinting.

The priest of Sobek stood, using a twisted brass staff with a miniature head of his god on the end. A table was set to the side. A peculiar box with an opening on one side sat on it, staring at her with its open mouth.

When she looked back to Lysimachus, she realized her gaze had lingered too long on his little torture device. She knew his game, they'd played it so many times.

"Doubt," said Lysimachus. "Doubt fills your waking mind. I doubted once before pain set me free."

The way he looked at her sent bolts through her chest. Sepharia thought this moment would happen the day of the final miracle. She wasn't ready. Her hands burst into trembles, so she grabbed the sides of her stola, trying to still them before he saw.

It didn't work. He saw her fighting with the fear. He smiled.

"It need not be this way. With fear. Give in to Sobek and the fear will wash away like dust after a hard rain," he said.

"Lies," she said, "it's all lies. Tricks. Like my father's miracles. You can't fool me."

His face stretched wide, like a benevolent parent hearing his petulant child speak back to him for the first time.

"Your father. Heron. Yes, she made tricks for the temples. She even tricked me once in her workshop. Yes, I think you remember. You were there, too. Do you think I would stoop to mere tricks if I were messing with the daughter of such an inventor? Do you think me that stupid?" he asked, though Sepharia had no intention of answering.

She clasped her hands in front. The white scar on the back of her hand was too real. She rubbed it with a thumb.

"I don't know how you've done it, but it's lies," she said, her voice cracking at the end.

Lysimachus stared at her with absolute certainty. He had the gaze of kings and it withered her soul.

If she were Heron, this would have been easy. Her father didn't believe in the gods. But not Sepharia. In her own way, she believed. Like waking from a deep sleep and having a dream that she couldn't quite remember, that's what the gods felt like to her.

"How can you continue to deny Sobek's greatness, after he brought you back from death, time and time again?" asked Lysimachus, pursing his lips into a point at her.

"You drugged me," she said. "How could it be real if you needed to drug me?"

His smile twitched. "Because I care for you. I know you don't believe yet. You will eventually, but not yet. The drugs helped you survive the pain. Sobek can bring you back, but he can't dull the pain. Only I can do that."

The softness of his voice was a vice around her heart.

"No," she said through trembling lips.

"Behold my staff made of copper and brass," he said, projecting his voice as if he were speaking to a crowd.

He held the staff up in his good hand and threw it across the hall, a good ways behind her. Sepharia turned as the staff hit the marble, a loud clatter making her flinch.

When she found it, the stiff piece of metal had been bent into curves. Sepharia squinted, trying to get a good look at it, when the staff undulated away.

It wasn't a staff, but a snake. Sepharia spun around, trying to find where the actual staff had been thrown, but the floor was empty. The only other objects in the room, not by the dais, were the pillars which were too narrow to hide anything or anyone behind.

When she turned back to Lysimachus, his gaze held her with a heavy lidded surety.

"I don't believe it," she said, the words limping from her lips.

"Believe or not believe, I cannot make you, only show you the way. You have to walk to Sobek. You have to put yourself into his waiting mouth." He nodded towards the box. "If you do, the rewards will be great. For what is the value of a hand if you are dead?" Lysimachus raised his stump in salute.

Sepharia squeezed her eyes shut. "No," she whispered, shaking her head.

"If you deny me here, I can promise you the end will not be pleasant. I will make you watch everything you love burn," he said, coolly.

She hid her face in her hands. It wouldn't be that hard, right? To unhinge herself from reality? To give up what she thought she believed in? She'd been in his care long enough to know what he could do with his implements. She'd watched him drag out a death for weeks at a time. Giving in to him would spare her of that.

Part of her wished she hadn't changed her mind at the cliff's edge. If she'd leapt then, he wouldn't have control of her. But she'd stayed in this world because of Heron, a thought that seemed more foolish by the moment. How could her father rescue her now? Was Heron even in the city? Sepharia was observant enough to realize Lysimachus and his crocodile soldiers were winning. The rebellion hadn't even figured out that the real problem was the pyramid. And they probably wouldn't before it was too late.

Sepharia took a hesitant step towards the steel box. Then she took another, her knees feeling like they could give out at each step.

She found herself before the box faster than she wanted. She looked to Lysimachus, who nodded, a victorious grimace hiding on his sneering lips.

She knew he was right about one thing. The pain would set her free. She'd spent the last year and a half almost drowning in fear. It was like the time they'd been trapped in that underground cave filled with water, when they were searching for Archimedes' weapons. When they could only push their lips to the ceiling and breath whatever air remained, knowing that they would probably die soon.

It felt like that, but worse. Drowning would have been over in minutes.

The box would be pain, but not putting her hand in the box would be worse. She'd never get another chance.

Sepharia moved her hand towards the box, the tips of her fingers passing the threshold of the opening.

The sounds in the room increased in volume, as if her ears had been unplugged of wax. Lysimachus' breath came in hurried gasps, like a man waiting for a woman to undress. Somewhere in the room, water dripped. A cough echoed outside, a guard clearing his throat.

"He Who Dwelleth Amid Terrors awaits," said Lysimachus, "whichever way you choose, he will be there for you."

Sepharia wished for some crystallizing moment, that helped her decide, one way or another. Or washed away the fear, as if she were a hero in a tale, vanquishing the horrific monster with her sword. But there was nothing but fear. A black, miasmic tar that burned at her soul like acid.

She looked up at Lysimachus, her hand almost in the box, and smiled.

"May the gods curse your soul," she said, grabbing the metal box and throwing it at the priest. She leapt at him, claws ready to tear at his face, when the soldier at the dais intercepted her. He struck her to the ground with a heavy gloved fist, pain searing her vision like white light.

When she looked up, Lysimachus lorded over her, the two guards standing at his sides. A trickle of blood ran down his cheek from the metal box. She'd struck him true at least, though she doubted she would feel such pride later.

"You should have joined with me," he said.

Then he kicked her in the face.

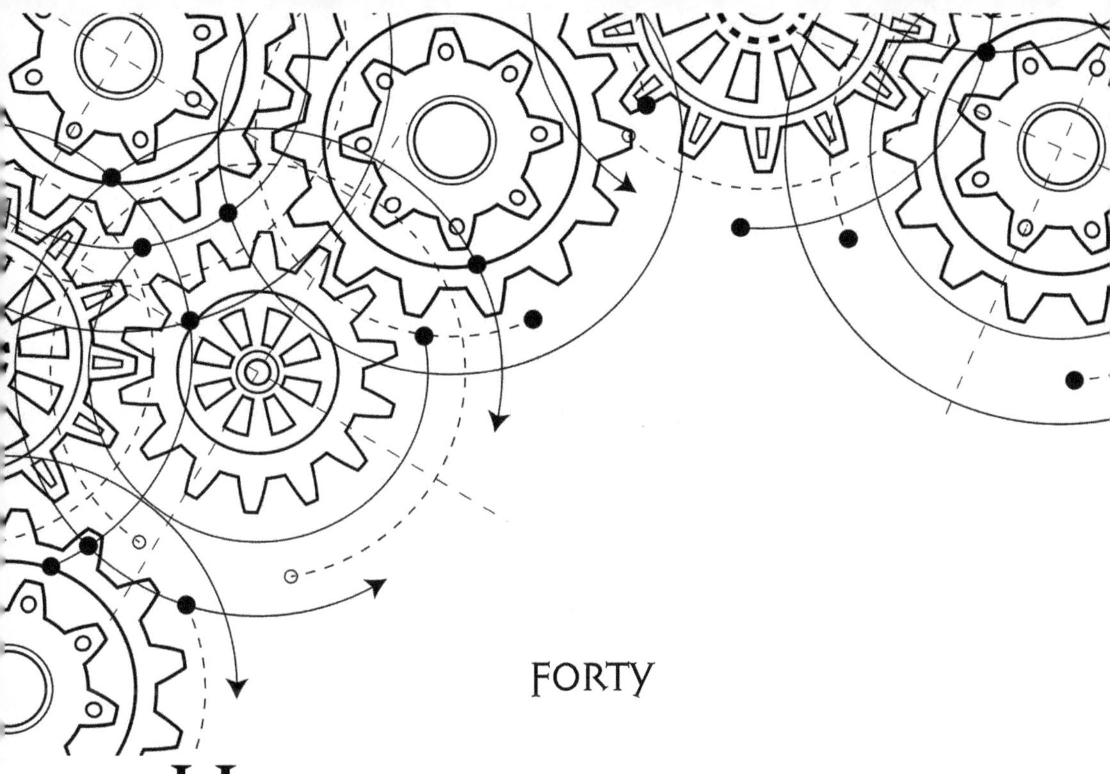

FORTY

Hoth had been walking through a tunnel beneath one of the warehouses, heading west, for what had seemed like an hour. The passage walls oozed with a wetness that Hoth knew from his previous times in the Great Library were a plague to be stamped out with powders and rags.

But the moisture persisted, because the Library was empty, the scholars dead, or scattered to the winds, and the books and scrolls burnt or turning moldy without their watchers to protect them.

Ada had sent him directions to their meeting place, though he thought she would have revealed herself sooner, which made him wonder if he were lost. It wouldn't be a bad thing to be lost in the Great Library. It was a peaceful place. Even now, the war with Lysimachus and his Terrors seemed a distant thing, maybe even a dream.

He passed through a stone door that wheezed with infrequent use. His breath caught when he realized how large a room he stood in. Above him, a domed ceiling painted with a scene of the gods smiled down on him with such beauty, he couldn't help but smile.

As Hoth lifted his lantern higher, to examine the details of the painting, he heard a click of metal against the stone. Ada stepped from behind a hidden wall, wearing her dark tunic.

"What is this place?" he asked, recoiling when his voice echoed.

Ada moved to a bench that he hadn't noticed before, and indicated the room with a wide sweep of her hand. Benches circled the room and behind each one, an inset fresco of a god stood.

"The Room of Debate," she said. "When the leaders of the Great Library could not agree upon a particular decision or bylaw, they would come down here and debate the matter."

"Why here? What's so special about this room?" he asked.

She put a foot on a bench, balancing on her mechanical leg. She seemed at ease with her limbs.

"When arguing above, each scholar presented his point of view. When they came here, they were expected to argue from the point of view of the opposition. Each scholar in the argument would take a seat at one of these benches. When they had expressed their views, they would rotate one seat, and argue from the point of view of the person that originally sat there. The gods on the wall helped keep order, so you knew who had sat where," she explained.

"Did this work? I can't say it makes much sense to me," said Hoth.

Ada shrugged. "Even when the decision was not changed, the scholars each came away learning something about the other side. The decision might not have changed, but the people who made the decision changed and that helped with the consensus, when it came time to present the decision to the rest of the Library."

"Why did you bring me here? Are we to have a debate?" he asked.

"No," she said. "I brought you here to be my scholarly assistant like you were when we researched the heir of Alexander."

"Aren't you worried about the guards?" he asked.

"Lysimachus pulled out of the Library. His focus is on the Lighthouse and the pyramid. The sages in the city have been removing more books, trying to get them to safety while he's distracted. His inattention is sure not to last long."

"But that's not why we're here. What are we here to learn?" he asked.

"We're going to learn how to live forever."

Ada didn't wait for him to respond and disappeared behind the wall. Hoth caught up to her in hallway.

"Why does the Library have all these tunnels?" he whispered, "I didn't think you scholars went for subterfuge."

A breath of amusement passed Ada's lips. "They're not for subterfuge. Only convenience. We scholars don't like to have to go outside unless we have to. Books and scrolls are our friends, didn't you know that?"

"No wonder you're a sexless bunch," said Hoth.

Ada didn't answer, which made him wonder if he'd insulted her. He thought he was being playful, but he didn't feel like he knew Ada, where before Heron would have laughed at his joke. Ada seemed more introspective, rather than Heron, who was unbridled genius burning at both ends.

She led him to a scroll room. A few lanterns had been set about the room already, which told Hoth she'd been here a while.

"What am I to do?" he asked.

She indicated a rack of scrolls with her mechanical hand. It whizzed and clicked as the fingers moved into a point.

"Start there, scan quickly, look for anything about immortality," she said.

Hoth turned to her. "What's this about? Why this? This doesn't seem like it's going to help us in the war."

Ada looked away, her face grimacing in pain. "This is my war." She paused and looked to him with bloodshot eyes. "Can you help me for once, without the questions?"

"Apologies," he said.

She moved to another rack on the far side of the room, away from him. Hoth grabbed a scroll off the one she'd indicated and unrolled it. He scanned the words, which he was much better at reading after years in the south, and found nothing pertaining to immortality.

He worked for hours, or it could have been minutes, or days, it was hard to tell in that windowless room, before he found a meaningful scroll.

"I found something," he said.

Ada appeared, a scroll half opened in her hand. "Tell me."

"It's about the Egyptian god, Thoth, and the *orme*, or white drops."

He paused and looked to her, but when she stared back, he continued, "It talks about the spittle of the gods, some white powder that the gods used for their immortality."

"Anything about actual properties, what the material might be, or if it actually exists?" she asked with a surprising amount of concern in her voice.

"It's only a scholar talking about some texts he found on a trip to study in Memphis. Nothing else." He paused. "Maybe it would help if you told me what you've found already."

She glowered for a moment and then relented. "Mostly the same stories about ambrosia, or manna, or other foods of the gods. They all say the same thing, but in different ways. Every culture has a story about immortality. Every pantheon repeats the same stuff. Why is this? Why do they all have it?"

"I don't know," said Hoth.

"Neither do I," said Ada, "but the answers it suggests worry me."

Ada wiped the hair out of her face and moved to the back of the scroll room. They continued for a long time, Hoth occasionally finding another mention of immortality. When he would explain it to Ada, she would scowl and shake her head, as if hearing about it pained her.

When Hoth thought he couldn't stand on his feet any longer, Ada appeared by his side, pulling the scroll from his hands.

"We're done," she said.

"Did you find it?" he asked, hopefully.

She shook her head. "There's nothing here to find."

Hoth glanced to the many racks of scrolls yet unread. Before he could ask a question, Ada left the room, and Hoth hurried to follow, grabbing a lantern on the way, since she'd left into the darkness. He followed her to the Room of Debate, grabbing her arm to stop her from marching out.

"Ada, stop, explain to me what's going on," he said.

She turned and looked into his eyes, the wrinkles around them relaying the weight of time on her.

"I sense a confrontation with him, with Lysimachus," she said. "It's why I can't leave. Why I can't escape."

"What do you mean?" he asked.

She shook her head tightly and looked at her feet. "A feeling. Nothing more. But it won't go away. This all began with Lysimachus, even before Agog banged on my door. He's been there through the whole thing. It comes back to he and I, as our true selves. One of us must die, and I'm afraid that's going to be me."

He shook her arm lightly. "Don't say that."

She looked up, and the pain reflected in her eyes made him recoil. "You don't know what I've been through. I'm tired of this. I just want it to end and I hope I can save Sepharia before I go."

She pulled her arm out of his grasp, gave him one last look, and disappeared behind one of the walls. Hoth stood for a long time in the Room of Debate, thinking about what she said, about what she'd gone through. All of it, from the beginning when she'd had to take her twin's place, to the destruction of Rome. In the end, he could only shudder, his understanding a pale shadow of her life, but enough to know what she intended in her war against the Lysimachus and his crocodile god.

She intended to die.

FORTY ONE

Three days passed. The summer heat baked the city like an oven. Even the sea was tamed by the heat, waves listless, shuffling back and forth as if they were too tired to move.

A heat haze hovered over the city. From his hiding spot near the Heptastadion, Vestalis thought he'd never seen the city without its characteristic black smoke. Not one workshop tended its foundry fires, not one bakery filled its ovens with fragrant bread.

Alexandria was a husk of its former self. The streets had been empty on their journey across the city. Not even the crocodile guards patrolled any more.

The people of the city, those that hadn't fled, had been sent to the camps around the pyramid. They called it the Crocodile's Tooth, or at least the soldier they'd captured had called it that before they wrung him for information and cut his throat.

No one they'd captured knew anything of note about what was going to happen at the Lighthouse, except that the Will of Sobek would perform his greatest miracle there. The soldiers claimed that only the Terrors knew what was going to happen, and they couldn't be found. Even the Palace, which had held Lysimachus' inner circle, was empty.

But what was a miracle that had no one to witness it? If the people had been sent to the pyramid, they should abandon the attack on the Lighthouse, or at least that had been Dominitus' argument. Vestalis had been want to disagree with the man they once called the Hidden Emperor, but his words swayed him. The value of the Lighthouse reduced considerably, except that Ada thought they might find Lysimachus there, and that she would need to rescue Sepharia.

The only clues they had to the nature of that miracle were the wagons that went over to the island. One of them contained Sepharia, riding in the back, face blanked of emotion. Had Vestalis been ready, he might have tried to snatch her then before she was on the island, behind a heavily guarded gate, but his men hadn't reached the warehouse yet. At least it confirmed she was there and that the rescue wouldn't be in vain. Even during the planning, Vestalis had harbored concerns the miracle at the Lighthouse would prove a trap.

Standing in the warehouse, Vestalis wiped his nearly bald head with a clean rag. He turned to Calder, who despite his Northern roots, seemed unaffected by the smothering heat.

"How many men do you count?" Vestalis asked.

"Forty, maybe fifty," said Calder. "They move between the Lighthouse and the gate, so it's hard to count them."

"The gate," muttered Vestalis.

At the end of the narrow land bridge between the city and the isle of Pharos, a gate blocked their way. It was a stacked stone and steel rod construction. In Caesar's time, it'd been used to keep the Alexandrians from taking back the city.

Vestalis rubbed his stubbled chin. "There was a land bridge like this at the city of Tyre when we marched north to Rome."

"I remember it," said Calder.

The old Roman soldier glanced at the squad of men sitting inside the warehouse in various forms of rest, some sitting with their backs against the wall, and others laying prone, catching a bit of rest before the battle.

"I don't think we have enough men," said Vestalis, under his breath.

"At least they don't have any steam chariots on the other side," said Calder.

"That worries me as much. Where have they all gone? I haven't seen any in the city, nor heard them, and you can hear them blocks away. Alexandria is a tomb."

Calder shrugged his broad shoulder. He wasn't a man bothered by those sort of things. A trait Vestalis envied. Vestalis saw all the possibilities, the problems, and potential solutions, and knew that they were going to come up short.

Their hasty plan, the one hatched in that tavern, with Hoth and the Kushite Prince, and Dominitus and his ilk, it seemed an ill-fit. Like trying to repair a wall with unfired clay.

"How will Ada reach the Lighthouse?" asked Calder, an amused twinkle in his eyes.

Vestalis sighed. The Northmen were enamored of the inventor, even more so that she'd been outed as a woman.

"I don't know," said Vestalis. "She wouldn't tell us. I can only assume by boat, or through trickery. She told us to attack when the sun reached the proper angle on this device."

Vestalis held up a brass contraption, something that looked similar to an astrolabe.

"How long?" asked Calder.

"Soon. Too soon." Vestalis rubbed the back of his neck. "When we took Tyre, we had the steam catapults and an army at our back. Now we have half their numbers and a gate to get through."

Calder nodded towards a massive shape under a tarp. "We have that. The *Michanikos'* invention. Shall we get it ready?"

Vestalis checked the position of the sun with the device, careful not to look directly at it. The sunlight reflected through a lens on the end and put a pinprick of white light along the shaft where it almost met the line etched into the brass that indicated the time. It was close enough.

After brief instruction, the men gathered up and removed the tarp from the steam chariot. Hoth had acquired the vehicle on his way to the city. They'd debated where best to utilize it, the pyramid or the Lighthouse, and it was only the need for stealth that swayed the argument. There was no way to get the steam mechanical to the pyramid without notice, and Vestalis needed a way to break through the gate.

When they were ready, Vestalis glanced at the hard faces of the soldiers with him. Whatever happened this evening, they would either be victorious, or dead. Maybe even both.

Outside the warehouse seemed cool in comparison. Vestalis didn't have long to enjoy the respite, they couldn't give the crocodile soldiers at the island gate warning.

In the safety of the alley between the buildings, they lined up the steam chariot for a straight shot across the land bridge. The sled was hooked to the back end and Vestalis took position at the helm, behind a modified shield that would protect him from arrows, or other missiles.

With his soldiers on the sled, and Calder hunched on the back of the steam chariot dumping more fuel into the fire chamber, Vestalis engaged the lever.

The steam chariot was slow to get moving with the weight holding it back, but by the time they hit the land bridge, bumping along the cobblestones hard enough to rattle his teeth together, the vehicle was moving at a dangerous clip.

Vestalis pushed the steam chariot as fast as it would go, aiming it towards the gate on the far end of the Heptastadion. They weren't a quarter of the way across when they heard shouts from the other side.

The crocodile soldiers, rather than stay and brace the gate, ran the other way, leaving the entrance to the island uncontested. Vestalis didn't have time to register his confusion. He had to be off the steam chariot when it hit the gate, or he'd be thrown to his death.

Holding the twin ropes they'd festooned to the steerage, Vestalis moved carefully to the back of the vehicle, stepping over blistering hot pipes, while keeping the steam chariot pointed straight ahead. When he reached the back, Calder helped him onto the sled and then joined him there.

The sled was worse than the steam chariot, bumping across the stones. He could barely hold onto the ropes. A couple of the men looked ready to lose their last meal.

When they were three-quarters across and racing towards impact, Calder cut the rope that held the sled to the steam chariot. Vestalis held onto the steerage ropes for as long as he could before letting go. They'd locked the steerage so it couldn't turn, but even a little veering would mean the improvised ram wouldn't hit the gate true.

Vestalis worries were misplaced. The steam chariot ran straight across the last stretch and hit the gate with overwhelming force. Stone and steel blew across the ground, one tumbling stone making it to the base of the nearby Temple of Isis. The force of the impact would have killed any soldiers waiting behind it.

Without the steam chariot pulling it, the sled slid to a uneventful halt and the soldiers leapt over the side and ran onto the island. Vestalis shared a glance with Calder, who seemed unconcerned by their easy entrance to the isle of Pharos.

Vestalis formed his men up into a defensive position, using the heavy

Roman shields they'd brought on the sled in expectation of a counterattack. It wasn't long before he realized the crocodile soldiers weren't coming, which seemed worse.

He looked back across the land bridge. The way was open. They could turn and leave if they wanted. The inventor had wanted a distraction, thinking that Lysimachus would be on the island for the miracle. With the way the enemy fell back to positions on the other side of the island, Vestalis doubted he'd be present.

"Send a couple of men up to the supply entrance of the Lighthouse," he told Calder.

It took them longer than he would have liked. The distance between the land bridge and the Lighthouse was almost as wide as the city, but he didn't want to give up his escape route by leaving the safety of the land bridge. Vestalis worried they might have hid a counterattack force inside the Temple of Isis that was along the way to the Lighthouse.

When the men finally returned, the scouting report confused Vestalis as much as the lack of a counterattack. The entrance to the supply area which led to the elevator and went up to the beacon level was bricked over, along with the archway on the ramp that led up to the observation level; and recently, by the fresh mortar between the stones. Access to the upper levels of the Lighthouse had been blocked off.

The old soldier spun around on his heels, taking in his surroundings, expecting to see something out of the ordinary, something to indicate what was going to happen next. It was as if the world had been emptied of people and they were the only ones left.

"We've taken the island. Where is the *Michanikos*?" asked Calder, leaning on his axe, seemingly disappointed for the lack of battle.

"The inventor is supposed to rescue Sepharia, but I don't see her. Do you?" he asked.

"Maybe she's already here," said Calder.

"Maybe," replied Vestalis.

Calder stretched his neck back, peering at the top of the Lighthouse. The sky behind the monument simmered a deep orange like the tip of a blade left in a fire. Night was falling fast on Alexandria.

"What do we do now?" asked the Northman.

Vestalis rubbed his stubble chin. "By all the gods, old and new, I haven't a clue."

FORTY TWO

The best misdeeds were performed in plain sight. Hoth the Black had raided many a village, not by landing on the beach like a pregnant whale scaring the folks and bringing out the song of steel with two blades for every fist, but strolling down the nearest dirt road as if he owned the place. And pretty soon he usually did.

The mess of soldiers, both Alexandrian and Roman, made their way across the leagues between the city and the pyramid by blending in with the pilgrims streaming across the dirt and sand. The Terrors had forced the citizens of the city to only take what they could haul in their arms or small horseless wagons, and sent them marching across the hot desert to their new tent home.

Along the way, the people found they couldn't carry everything they wanted, and many began to realize they weren't going to need these possessions at the pyramid. Bits of people's lives collected along the make-shift road that led to the pyramid: butter churns, bread boards, extra clothing, all sorts of things. A stuffed doll the size of a grown man lay against a dead shrub as if it'd fallen over and died there.

They couldn't bring weapons, but that was fine with Hoth. It was easy enough to hide a blade in a bedroll. The sparkpowder globes had been sown into empty water pouches. They could cut them out later at the pyramid. One of the men even carried a small keg of sparkpowder, the last of the stores Vestalis had brought with him from Rome.

Hoth hadn't seen the pyramid before. Or at least he hadn't seen the finished pyramid. He was keeping his head down, trying to blend in with the locals - he'd rubbed his hair in foundry ash to hide the pale - when he heard a grunt and a slow whistle.

The Kushite Prince walked beside him, looking nothing like a commoner with his chin raised and shoulders back, and nodded ahead. Hoth didn't see it at first. The horizon had a metallic rain quality, as if a shimmering veil of water hung from a cloudless sky. Then it parted, peeling back reality, first a miniature golden pyramid hung an impossible distance from the earth, before the rest filled in beneath it, a stone mountain that had been built in only one year.

His voice caught in his throat. He hadn't realized it would be so large. Not even big like something easily grasped, a large army arrayed on a field, or a chariot stadium housed with thousands of cheering fans. This sense of bigness matched the feeling he'd gotten so long ago when he was a young sailor on his first ocean trip, when the ship had lost sight of land and they'd been surrounded by water and only water, the primeval ocean in all her power and glory. That sense of scale that made one nervous like an itch on the bones.

The tent camp around the pyramid filled in last, as if the stone structure was merely a tarp and the corners of it had been pealed back. The dust and sweat of thousands filled the air, a cacophony of humanity.

The people had stern faces. Some of the pilgrims had tried to head east to Memphis and had been herded back by steam chariots. The crocodile soldiers had been surprisingly restrained.

Hoth moved through the tents, Algoni behind him. Unlike the slums outside of Alexandria, these were hastily set, and no pathways suggested themselves to his nimble feet. They stepped over ropes and sleeping dogs, moving with a wary gaze.

He cut out onto a dirt road that split the camp, headed to the gate. The inner city was blocked by a wooden palisade, a barrier Hoth didn't think he'd have trouble getting through when the time came.

Nearby, an older woman in dirty robes was screeching as two Parthians pulled a dead chicken from her hands. She kicked at them, until one of the men punched her in the face, knocking her out.

Distracted by the commotion, Hoth didn't see the mounted crocodile soldiers until a whinny startled him.

"By Sobek, out of my way," said the crocodile soldier.

Hoth kept his head down and feigned a limp as he moved back to the safety of the tents. He glanced to Algoni who'd stayed back, but did not avert his eyes from the soldiers.

"Apologies," Hoth mumbled in Greek.

He sensed the soldiers hadn't moved on. Algoni stood like the Prince that he was, chin high and chest puffed out. Hoth whistled softly through his teeth, trying to implore his companion not to incite the soldiers.

Hoth turned his head carefully, trying not to catch the notice of the soldiers. The bedroll containing the sword was clutched in his arms.

He counted five soldiers. With the Prince's help, he knew he could take them, but that would alert the Terrors that they had rebels in their midst.

"Tell your friend he should learn deference," said the soldier behind Hoth.

Hoth kept his shoulders hunched and spoke through his hair, so not to reveal his face in case they might recognize him. "Apologies. He was dropped on his head as a child. He thinks he's a Kushite Prince."

Laughter ensued, which brought frowns from Algoni. Hoth bared his teeth at his friend.

"Tell your friend the Kushite Prince, we have a Princess in the pyramid. They say the Will of Sobek lets you sleep with her if you cut off a finger, that's why hardly anyone even has a hand left," said the soldier.

The laughter turned riotous. Algoni's eyes bulged and he stepped over the tent rope and started to reach inside his bedroll. Hoth jumped forward, and tripped Algoni, falling on top of him in the dirt. The Prince tried to push him off, but Hoth was a skilled wrestler and kept the Kushite from rising up.

"I told you he thought he was a Prince," said Hoth, trying to fill his voice with laughter.

The men chuckled, though Hoth heard the sounds of curiosity in their mirth. He hoped they weren't starting to believe the Prince.

They were saved when a bell rang its dull tune across the shanty town. The bell sounded misshapen, but sweet, since it'd saved them.

From a position on top of Algoni, who was still trying to scramble to his feet, Hoth watched the soldiers on horse plod away. Hoth let the Kushite Prince get up, but by this time, the soldiers were passing through the gate. On the inside, Hoth caught sight of an array of Manticores lined up in neat rows.

"You should have let me kill them," said Algoni.

"You're worse than my friend Jarngard," said Hoth. "Too proud to be smart. Yes, we would have killed them, but we'd have alerted Lysimachus."

"He knows we're coming," said the Prince.

"Well, that's true, but no need to make it obvious. Especially when I have an idea. How tall do you think those palisades are?"

While dusting himself off, the Prince shrugged and said, "Maybe twice the height of a man."

"I thought so," said Hoth. "Let's go."

They moved to the wall, behind a stretch of tents. The soldiers hadn't thought to keep the tent city from bumping against the wall. After checking for more soldiers, Hoth climbed on Algoni's shoulders and made the top of the wall by pulling himself up, at least high enough so he could see over.

Right inside, he could see rows of Manticores and other steam chariots. They had at least forty of them. A huge hall had been built nearby and when a soldier went inside, Hoth saw it was full.

Behind the Manticore yard, Centaurs wandered around on patrol. Hoth counted hundreds of soldiers, and that was only what he could see. There had to be more on the other side.

Looking at the pyramid, Hoth noticed a silvery rail that stretched upward along the slope. Coming down from the top, a wagon rode on the rail, being lowered down by pulleys and ropes. There'd be a steam mechanical at the top, Hoth assumed, driving the pulleys.

From the angle looking up, Hoth realized the golden tip of the pyramid was not solid. It was only a roof over an upper level. The most important prisoners would probably be kept up there within reach of Lysimachus' Terrors. How Hoth would get himself and the others soldiers up there without being noticed was a problem for later.

Hoth jumped down from the Prince's shoulders.

"What did you see?"

"An opportunity," said Hoth.

"For what?" asked Algoni his dark face an unreadable calm.

Hoth winked at the Prince. "Mischief," said Hoth. "Don't worry, I'll explain along the way. First, we need to find the rest of our soldiers before it gets too dark."

Hoth looked west to the endless desert stretched before them. The sun was on the last arc before crossing the horizon. The shadows had almost lengthened to night.

"Let's go, my friend," said Hoth, knocking his ash dusted hair out of his face. "We've got a war to win."

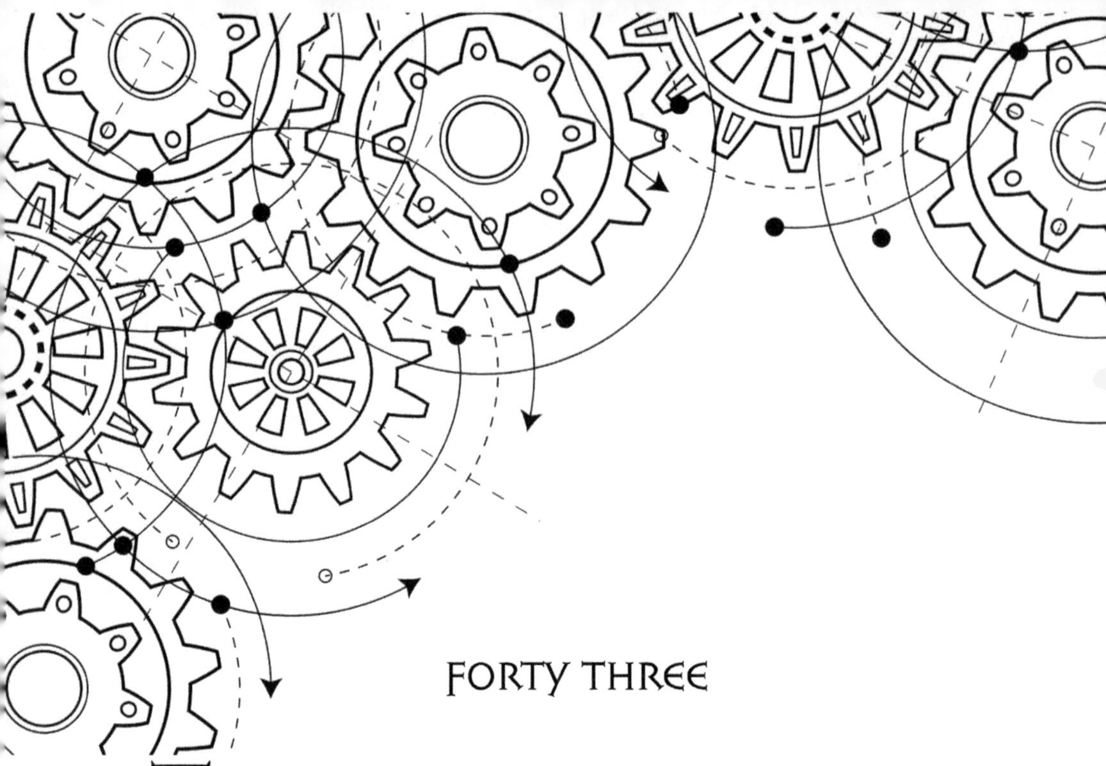

FORTY THREE

The blacksmith Punt, ever the tireless worker under the storied roof of Heron the inventor, looked upon the air ship as if it were a pustule on his private parts. His bald head, which in this heat, would have been beaded with sweat like a waystone marker at first dew, was parchment dry, as if the skin had sucked in the moisture from nervousness.

"I'd rather lie in my grave and pull the dirt over myself," said Punt to the woman who'd once been his employer.

Though it was the same person, now that she called herself Ada, and made her femininity known, it felt like he'd worked for a different person than the one standing before him. There was something different about Ada, like she wasn't wearing armor anymore. Not that he thought she'd grown soft. Her gaze still carried steel.

"It's the only way, my friend," said Ada from inside the basket, checking the positioning of the levers on the steam mechanical as its pistons thrummed. The massive leather bladder reached impossibly towards the sky, while a team of gray robed sages from the Library kept the air ship from joining the clouds with long ropes. If a few of them suddenly lost their grip, Ada would go on without him, a twist of fate he silently prayed for.

Punt swallowed, wiping sweaty palms across his bald head. "Men were not meant to fly, or the gods would have given us wings."

"They didn't give us flippers, but we sail the seas," said Ada with her back to him.

The blacksmith paced back and forth. "What about one of the scholars? They seem eager to go."

"None of them can wield a hammer like you and we're going to need to do some fighting to get Sepharia back," said Ada. "I'm sorry, Punt, but it's the only way. There's room enough for three: you, me, and Sepharia, when we rescue her."

He wasn't used to the inventor's tone. He wasn't sure if it was that he heard her differently now the she displayed her womanhood, or that she'd gone through a real change. The old Heron would have made cutting remarks designed to goad him into excellence, or in this case, climbing into the basket beneath the air bladder. Ada seemed more concerned about him, or at least that concern came through in her voice.

Ada turned to him after glancing at the sun, which was nearing the horizon. "Get in, Punt. We have to get moving."

Before his limbs could turn to stone, Punt climbed into the basket using the rope ladder hanging over the side.

"Hand me that sack," Ada called to one of the scholars.

A snow-bearded sage brought the sack over and handed it up. The objects inside shifted, eliciting a sharp *tinct*.

"What're in them?" asked Punt.

"Sparkpowder globes," said Ada. "I don't think we'll need them, but I asked for a few, just in case."

The hard weave beneath his feet sagged distressingly when he moved.

"So when are we going to—"

He swallowed his voice when Ada made a signal to the scholars and they released the ropes, letting the air ship surge into the sky. Punt sunk to his knees and clamped his eyes shut.

"You could have given me warning!" he said through gritted teeth.

The suffocating heat on the ground washed away and cool breezes kissed his sweat-drenched flesh. Punt pulled himself upward and opened one eye, ready to close it right quick, should he not be pleased with what he saw.

The view from the air ship was not unlike a trip to the apex of the Lighthouse, except there, a solid structure lay beneath his feet. Having nothing but thin sky beneath his feet turned his knees to kelp.

Ada was messing with the levers on the mechanical, adjusting the force of hot air being blown into the bladder. To the east, and rapidly approaching, was the city of Alexandria. Their path pointed them to pass the city on the southern side and they were only the height of half the Lighthouse, not that Punt wanted to go any higher.

"We're not going to make it over the island," said Punt.

Ada glanced over her shoulder, displaying a disappointed countenance. The inventor's lips were pursed into a sigh.

"When have I ever been wrong before, good Punt?" asked Ada over the noise of the mechanical.

Punt almost pulled his hand from the rim of the basket to count, but thought better of it. "Well, there was the time when you nearly blew up the workshop with your first mechanical. When you picked the wrong way in the Temple of Alexander and only Hoth's quick hand saved you. And then there was—"

Ada's musical laugh silenced him. "Plato have pity, I know. There's not learning without failure, but don't worry, Punt. I have a plan."

She seemed to be finished with whatever adjustments she'd been making to the mechanical. Ada reached up, the sleeve of her azure tunic falling around her shoulder, and turned a long rod that looked like a boat rudder.

A round cone with the top cut off swung into the air stream that blew from the mechanical, diverting part of the hot exhaust. The air ship lurched northward, sending Punt's stomach into a dive.

"That'll be enough of that," said Punt, swallowing back bile.

Ada glanced over the side a few times and hit more levers with the palm of her hand, nudging them, just so, until she seemed pleased with the result. When she was finished, the air ship drifted northeasterly towards the top of the Lighthouse of Pharos.

"We'd better hit the beacon level first try," said Ada. "I'd rather not try to maneuver around." She glanced into the bottom of the basket. "Get the crossbow ready. There's sure to be guards at the top."

"Then what do we do?" he asked.

Ada shrugged. "We'll figure it out when we get there."

The air ship moved at a tidal pace, the Lighthouse growing larger as they passed over the city. The normal haze of foundry and cooking fires was conspicuous by its absence.

As they neared, Punt judged they were going to hit right on. Two guards stood on the beacon level, but both of them seemed immobilized by the appearance of the air ship. In fact, neither had drawn their swords.

Ada was making minor adjustments to the mechanical when a sudden gust blew them sideways a length, putting them off course.

"Curses!" said Ada, jamming levers and turning the directional cone so the air ship would move perpendicular to their current direction.

The soldiers sensed the impeding danger and pulled their swords. It didn't look like the air ship was going to get close enough to the beacon level. The fire that normally burned at the center in front of two huge brass mirrors had been dulled to grayish-orange embers.

"We're not going to make it," said Punt.

He made a fist. They were going to be close, skimming right by the beacon level, but not close enough to land.

"We'll have to go around," said Punt, as he noticed Ada climbing onto the edge of the basket with a guide rope in her teeth.

He didn't have a chance to say a word before she leapt from the basket into the air. It didn't look like she had enough to make it over the gap. Her arms wheeled forward and the soldier's jaws went slack.

She hit the edge and skidded onto the beacon level, crying out in pain from the impact. The two soldiers, suddenly realizing what had happened, moved to intercept.

Punt grabbed the crossbow and set it on the edge, trying to get a good shot, but Ada was in the way. The air ship was drifting past. Ada looked to the rope and then the approaching soldiers. If she didn't tie it off, the air ship would pull her over the edge.

"Adjust the directional cone," shouted Ada. "Push it back to the beacon."

She was tugging on the rope, straining against the pull and losing, as her sandals skidded towards the edge. Punt hesitated between the crossbow and the rudder that moved the cone. He didn't have a good shot at a soldier.

The first soldier moved to strike Ada with his sword. She had her back to him. Punt fired the crossbow, grimacing when Ada bent at the waist.

The soldier tumbled forward, a feathered bolt in his chest; the sword tumbled from his limp fingers, careened off the stone, and went flying over the edge. The soldier followed his weapon to land far beneath them on the observation level.

Punt didn't have time to reload the crossbow as the second soldier approached. Punt jammed the rudder to the side, propelling the air ship further away. Ada was yanked closer to the edge.

"The other way, the other way!"

He realized his mistake and slammed it to the side, hoping it wasn't too late.

When he looked up, the soldier had his sword raised above his head, preparing a two-handed strike at the inventor. Ada had both hands on the rope, pulling so hard the veins on her forehead stood out.

A cry for her safety leapt from his lips. Punt knew he was about to see the *Michanikos*, his friend, murdered at the top of the Lighthouse of Pharos, when she released her mechanical hand from the rope, aimed it at the soldier as if it were a crossbow, and flinched.

Inexplicably, the soldier froze in mid-swing, his shoulders hunched as if he'd been punched in the chest, and then he slumped to his knees and fell backwards, the sword sliding across the stone and into the ashy fire.

With the soldier out of the way, Ada took the extra rope and ran to the pillars that held up the brass mirrors and wrapped it around them. The rope pulled taut and Punt feared the pillar or the rope would break.

"Faster, this way, this way!" shouted Ada, motioning with her mechanical hand.

Punt adjusted the cone and eventually, the rope slackened and the air ship moved over the stone. Ada grabbed the other ropes and tied them off, though the air ship fought against them like a wild horse.

Ada stood with her mechanical hand rested against her hip, the azure tunic and silver belt looking resplendent, gazing up at the air ship with thoughts passing across her face like clouds. She looked like a heroine out of myths, thought Punt.

"How did you kill that soldier?" he asked.

Ada held up her mechanical arm. "I learned a trick from the Senator's assassin, though I'm afraid it only works once. I'd need my tools to reset it."

Understanding the inventor had never been Punt's strong suit, so he shrugged and threw the ladder over the edge to join her.

"I'm afraid you're going to have to stay in the air ship," said Ada. "Someone needs to keep the ropes slack. I'm afraid if we left it here untended, it would snap the pillars in half and escape to the sky."

Punt grumbled. "Let me get Sepharia. I brought my hammer."

Ada shook her head, looking towards the stairs with a frown on her lips. "I'm afraid I need to go. You'll have to stay here."

Suddenly, though he wasn't sure why, Punt realized it'd been Ada's plan all along to leave him. She moved to the stairs and put a sandaled foot on the first one.

"If I don't come back, don't wait for me. Cut the ropes and try to land somewhere east of Alexandria."

"I'm not leaving," said Punt, turning the rudder to move the air ship back towards the center.

Ada shook her raven hair out of her face. The wind was having its way. When she'd cleared it, she fixed him with her gaze. It was part steel and part motherly concern.

"I'm sorry, Punt. If I don't see you again, thank you for your service. There'll never be a better blacksmith, or friend. None of this would have been possible without you."

Never a fount for words, Punt choked on his reply as Ada left him in the air ship hovering over the Lighthouse of Pharos.

"The world will never know a better person than you, Ada of Alexandria," said Punt, finally, to the empty air.

FORTY FOUR

The stairs coiled around the beacon level, leading Ada downward. Her feet, flesh and mechanical, found their purchase easily. It seemed her limbs had called a truce.

She regretted leaving Punt in the air ship. It was possible she might be wrong, but when she'd looked over the edge of the basket to see ships on the back side of the isle of Pharos, she knew she would only encounter token resistance.

The echoes of her footsteps matched her heartbeats, speeding up as she went further down. She suspected a trap from Lysimachus; why else had he sent everyone from the city?

She paused before she entered the observation level, absently touching the empty slot where a blade had been, before she'd shot it into the guard's chest. The surprise had been intended for Lysimachus. She knew eventually she would see him, and he would have never guessed at her weapon.

It wasn't the only weapon she had hidden in her mechanical arm, but using the second would be death for them both. She'd packed a globe's worth of sparkpowder into the center. She only needed a flame to light the fuse on the end. She figured if she was close enough to Lysimachus and close enough to a flame, with room to move, she could light it and wrap her arms around him until it exploded.

With a sigh, she continued down the stairs. It was an option she didn't want to undertake, but if it ended his Empire, she was willing.

Ada knew something was wrong the moment she stepped onto the observation level. It seemed even the waves against the island had lost their voice. The tables and chairs for visitors to lounge upon and watch the boats gain the harbor were missing. The booths that held spiced meats, sweet drinks, and trinkets to memorialize the Lighthouse were absent.

The whole level had been cleared out except for a grand iron cage that hunched over the middle, including the hole in the center for the elevator. Ada's heart went cold when she saw the contents of the iron bars.

"Father. Heron," said Sepharia, tears streaking her cheeks, "go now. Run. It's a trap."

"I'm Ada, now. And I know. It's why I came."

Sepharia beat her fists against the iron bars. "No, you can't know. You can't know what he's done. Please go."

Ada approached cautiously, not because she feared the cage, or some trap left by Lysimachus. She took tentative steps because of Sepharia's voice. It sounded like it'd been broken and pieced back together.

"Remember," said Ada, "I spent time in his pit, beneath the temple. I know what he's capable of and I can't leave you to him."

The flat strips of metal that made up the cage impeded her view. As Ada approached, she feared that Lysimachus had done to her what he'd done to so many. When she moved close enough, she saw that Sepharia had all her limbs.

"Sepharia," breathed Ada with relief, "you're whole."

As she said the words, she knew she was wrong. Sepharia stared back through the bars with hollow eyes.

"What did he do to you?" asked Ada.

Sepharia stepped away from the bars, grimacing at each movement. "It doesn't matter. Go now. There's no surviving this trap. If you leave, you'll live."

"I'll never leave," said Ada, as a mechanical click sounded through the air.

Her daughter pushed her sweat soaked hair out of her face. Even though a sea breeze whisked through the level, Sepharia looked like she'd been kept in a hot box for weeks.

As Ada moved to the bars, the contents of the cage became clearer. It wasn't one cage, but four, and between them a strange device full of gears and pulleys and levers connected to various parts of the cages. It was a mechanical spider connected by an iron web.

Her mind whirled with the implications of the design. It was a cunning trap, more devious than she would have given credit to Lysimachus.

"How could he have made this?" she asked.

Sepharia shook her head and pressed her hands against her mouth as if she feared to say the words. "Nektam made it."

"I thought he was dead," said Ada.

"I did, too. But Lysimachus kept him somewhere. I saw him before he died. There was almost nothing left of him when they brought him to supervise the installation." Sepharia shut her eyes and stamped her foot. "Please, go, Heron. By the gods, Lysimachus wants his revenge. Can't you see it? That's why he put me here, why he's kept me alive all this time."

"I said, it's Ada, now. I can't pretend to be your real father anymore. But I'm here for you," said Ada.

"Can't you see what's in the fourth cage?" asked Sepharia and then added quieter, "And you are my real father *and* mother. You're the only one left."

The overlapping bars hid the contents, so Ada moved to the side. She gasped when she saw the barrels. Hundreds of them.

"See," said Sepharia, her voice cracking, "he wants to destroy the Lighthouse and you with it. The final symbol of Alexandria, before he conquers the world."

Ada studied the gears and pulleys, following their designs, teasing out their purpose with her mind.

"Not entirely," said Ada as she moved to a door on the second cage, the one next to Sepharia's.

The door wheezed open, hints of rust already touched the iron of the cage from the moist sea air. Ada moved to a lever that stuck through the bars of the cage on the other side.

"No, Heron, Ada, don't," said Sepharia.

Ada ignored her and pulled the lever. A gear locked her door closed, while the door that trapped Sepharia clicked and breathed open.

"Go Sepharia. Quickly. Vestalis and his men should be at the base of the Lighthouse. He'll get you to safety," said Ada.

Sepharia looked like she was going to stay in the cage, until she shook her head and moved through the door.

"I don't understand," said Sepharia eventually.

"This has to happen," said Ada, "Lysimachus and I. This all began with him and I have to finish it."

"But what about his god and the Terrors? What about this new Empire? We need you to stop it. I can't do that," said Sepharia.

"No," said Ada. "You can't. That's not your job. But I think I can. Or I hope I can. I don't know if I'll survive this. But it's your job to put the city back together when it's over."

"What if Lysimachus wins?"

Ada bit her lower lip, not wanting to contemplate that future. "Then flee the city. Go east, somewhere else. I made plans that might counteract him in the future, but they'll take time to grow."

"But he's immortal. Or at least he's learned some secret of life. I've seen it." Sepharia shook her head. "Is it possible?"

"Some say it is. Some say it isn't," responded Ada.

Sepharia studied her face. "What do you say it is?"

Ada gave a maudlin smile. "Did you see anything while you were in his care? Anything that might tell you how he was doing it?"

The initial response was a shake of the head, then Sepharia opened her mouth, paused, and finally spoke: "Once I saw a drawing of him naked in a scroll, with instructions, as if it were some kind of spell."

Ada thought on it. She had her ideas about Lysimachus' immortality, but nothing conclusive yet.

"You must go," said Ada finally.

"What plans? You spoke of plans before. What's going to happen?" Sepharia asked.

"It doesn't matter. I gave that task to Plutarch, and I hope he's successful. Otherwise, the world is in trouble."

An audible click sounded from behind her. Ada felt the weight of it on her shoulders.

"You have to go now. There's no time left. Run down the stairs. I hope Vestalis is still there."

Sepharia moved to the bars of the cage with tears glistening in her eyes. She put her hand through the bars. Ada took it and kissed the fingertips, put the palm to her forehead.

"Go now, before I lose my nerve," said Ada.

Sepharia nodded. "I love you, Ada. Thank you for always being there for me."

She moved towards the stairs.

"I love you, daughter," said Ada, before Sepharia slipped away.

Ada turned back towards the interior of the cage. Her eyes traced the levers and gears and pulleys, teasing out their purpose. It didn't take her long to figure out that Nektam had designed an unbeatable trap.

Between the four cages, the mechanical clock ticked again. Ada knew she was running out of time. When the machine reached its end point, the sparkpowder barrels would be lit, and the Lighthouse obliterated.

The trap had four cages: one for Sepharia, one to hold her, one for the sparkpowder, and the purpose of the last did not suggest itself until Ada realized it hung over the pit that went from the base of the Lighthouse to the beacon level.

"Clever," said Ada, realizing what Lysimachus intended.

The fourth cage was not a cage, but an elevator. When she got inside and initiated the lever, it would go down. Ada assumed someone would be waiting for her down there, maybe even Lysimachus. If she didn't go down, she could let herself be annihilated by the sparkpowder. He'd given her a choice again.

The destruction of the Lighthouse, besides eliminating a symbol of science, would hide her capture. Sepharia would think she was dead, thus eliminating any chance of being freed. When Ada realized this, and what it implied, it felt like she'd been packed in snow.

The machine clicked again, goading Ada into action.

She moved into the elevator, since it was the cage nearest the machine in the center. The empty spaces between the bars gave her a moment of vertigo. She crouched on her heels and dug into a secret compartment on her mechanical leg. She hadn't come to the Lighthouse completely unprepared.

She pulled out a folded rod and quickly assembled it into its longer version. Then she stood and put her arm through the bars, pressing her face against the iron to get more reach. The whole contraption had been made without visible ways to shut it off, Lysimachus had seen to that.

But Nektam had been a clever inventor himself, turning her higher strength steel into the iron boats. When she steadied the rod against the slight depression on the side of the box, she had no idea if it would actually stop the device from detonating the sparkpowder. The only clue she had was that above the slight depression was a shape that looked like the outline of a spinning aeolipile.

With her face smashed against the bars, Ada pushed against the depression, resulting in a satisfying click. Though she couldn't know for certain, it felt like the trap had been disabled.

The only problem was that she had no way out and if Lysimachus came up to investigate, he would know that the sparkpowder wasn't set to go off. Only by pulling the lever and going to meet him would she keep the Lighthouse from being destroyed, at least for now.

When she pulled the lever, the whole cage rocked and for a moment, Ada thought it was going to fall through the middle of the Lighthouse, killing her upon impact. The cage lurched downward once, then continued onward at a steady pace. The ride to the bottom took less time than she would have liked.

When the cage kissed against the earth in the bowels of the Lighthouse, Ada saw a familiar set of beady eyes waiting for her.

"Greetings, Heron of Alexandria," said Lysimachus. "It's been entirely too long since we've been together."

Behind him stood a quad of crocodile guards, their bronze helms glimmering in the oily torch light. Ada heard distant coughs, as if other men hid in the darkness, outside the dim circle of light.

"Shall we leave?" he asked, opening the door wide. "I don't think we want to stay here much longer."

Ada considered her options before going out through the open door. The guards seemed poised for any mischief from her. Two of them took her by the upper arms, fingers digging into her flesh.

Lysimachus led them to the back of the Lighthouse. Bricks had been layered over the exit, the one facing north, the same as the exit to the south. But one of the guards surged forward and pulled on a handle sticking out from one of the bricks.

The whole door swung wide, revealing the glooming light of dusk. Night fell on Alexandria. After a short march, they boarded a small iron ship that could hold a dozen men.

Once on board, the sea rocking them gently, Lysimachus nodded to one of his soldiers. He took an ivory horn from his side, put his lips to the end, and blew three strong notes into the air.

Ada's stomach sunk when she realized what that probably meant for Vestalis, his men, and most importantly, Sepharia. As the iron ship pulled away from the island, hundreds of crocodile soldiers streamed out of the northern gate beneath the Lighthouse as if they were the flooded Nile spilling upon the plains.

FORTY FIVE

Sharp-eyed Calder spotted the air ship first, and had Vestalis not known about the inventor's creation from the war with Rome, he would have thought he'd gone mad. The air ship looked like it was going to miss the upper level, but then veered in the right direction and anchored there.

"She's Loptr, Queen of the Air," said Calder in admiration.

The Northman's declaration gave Vestalis the shivers though he didn't know why. "Couldn't have many with her in that small ship."

"The inventor has provided for their escape," said Calder, implying they had no reason to stay on the island.

Vestalis studied his companion's wrinkled brow, he was thinking the same thing. The longer they stayed on the island, the more likely they were to be attacked. Their earlier battles in the city had been like lightning, flash in to strike quickly and then disappear into the clouds.

"You're right, my friend," said Vestalis, "but the inventor might yet need us."

He turned in a slow circle from his spot at the island end of the land bridge. Only a few ships rested in the harbor and not a soul moved along its broken docks. The wooden structure lay tangled in the water like a bramble patch. The city's buildings sat like tired giants, not a flicker of light in their eyes.

With the sun kissing the horizon, Vestalis realized he had not heard the city bells since he'd landed on the island. The city was a graveyard of sound and even the lapping waves against the island seemed distant.

Vestalis grimaced. Inaction felt like surrender.

"Does that steam chariot still work?" asked Vestalis, pointing to the vehicle sitting amid broken stones and bent iron bars. "Face it towards the city and get that mechanical working again."

His soldiers jumped into action. Even if the machine was broken, it lessened his anxiety to see activity.

He motioned towards a group of idle soldiers. "You, squad. Head to the Lighthouse and climb the wall to the lower level. It's only a few stories up."

The squad leader saluted. "What shall we do when we've reached it?"

"Wait there to see if anyone comes down. If you see us attacked, abandon the Lighthouse and try to get off the island as best you can." Vestalis paused and rubbed his chin. "Better yet, Calder, go with them. I trust your judgment."

The big Northman hesitated before squeezing his lips together and nodding. The squad ran off at a brisk pace.

While he waited, Vestalis took out a damp rag and wiped off his face and bald head. His soldiers had the steam mechanical turned around and had gotten the fires relit, though the pistons would not move.

He kept turning around, expecting to see an army of crocodile soldiers charging his position. Every bit of his being told him that he'd been on the island too long and that the way the guards at the gate had retreated from the attack indicated treachery.

The air ship bobbed at the beacon level of the Lighthouse, but Vestalis could see nothing. If the ship left, he would take that as a sign and head back over the land bridge into the city. There he had numerous escape routes.

When the pistons roared to life, Vestalis smiled. At least one thing was going his way.

He stared back at the quiet city, longing for better times. When he'd come to the city to make his fortune, he thought that had been his most trying times. At this point in his life, he'd expected to be sitting in his courtyard in the shade, having a glass of wine, and nibbling on salted olives and honeyed figs.

When the war was over, he was going to retire to his villa and live out his days on the gold he had stashed there. The wounds of battle added up, the dead men in his past haunted his memories, and he no longer felt like the bold equestrian he was in the Roman Empire days.

The three blasts of a horn startled Vestalis from his thoughts. Their bold voice turned his jaw to steel as he realized he'd waited on the island too long.

Hundreds of soldiers streamed from the Lighthouse, throaty war cries sending the big black birds resting along the crenellations of the Temple of Isis into the air. Their flapping and caws reminded him of the carrion birds of the battlefield. It would take the soldiers a few minutes to reach the broken gate and leave them winded upon arrival, but their numbers made any disadvantage slight.

When he saw the air ship still hanging on the Lighthouse, his gut twisted. He wished he hadn't sent Calder and a squad. They'd had time to reach the Lighthouse, but were trapped behind the enemy, or had been ambushed upon their arrival.

Vestalis called to his men to form up. They would march across the land bridge back to the city.

His commands died in his throat as he saw the soldiers appear from the buildings around the city side of the land bridge. There were at least a hundred on that side, and counting the other three or four hundred coming from the Lighthouse, they were outnumbered ten to one.

He made his decision quickly. Any more delays would cost them tactically.

"Across the Heptastadion!"

The soldiers on the steam mechanical hesitated. They were fiddling with the levers.

"Leave it," said Vestalis. "We don't have time to fix it."

Vestalis took the lead across the land bridge. Like the soldiers behind him, the jog would leave him winded for the battle on the other side.

As they neared, the enemy soldiers moved wagons in front of the street and formed men with crossbows behind them. Vestalis slowed his pace for a moment. Few of his soldiers had shields, and if they did, they were only the small bucklers for close fighting, not the large kite shields that could protect infantry from arrows.

He thought about commanding his men to take off their armor and swim across the great harbor, but he wasn't sure how many could even swim. Going into the water would leave them vulnerable to ships and arrows and the crocodile soldiers would only have to wait until they landed without armor and weapons to kill them.

They neared crossbow range. His chest ached with the anticipation of being skewered by one.

"After they fire," said Vestalis, turning his head so the enemy couldn't hear his commands, "rush across the bridge. Crossbows take time to reload. We'll have to get there before the second volley."

His soldiers gave a cheer, as if that was something to cheer about.

Vestalis turned his head in time to hear the thrum of strings losing their bolts. Two soldiers running with him fell. He heard screams behind him, but miraculously hadn't been hit himself.

"For Alexandria!" he yelled, raising his blade and willing his tired legs to sprint.

The battle cries sent a surge of energy through him. It was still a dozen lengths before they would reach the barriers, but Vestalis knew they would make it before the reload.

He took a moment to glance behind him, his men looked victorious in their charge, weapons raised high. It gave him a spot of pride to know the men would follow him into such a battle.

They crossed the hard stones, feet pounding the earth, voices lifted in battle. Vestalis was only strides away from the wagons. He could see the widening eyes of his enemies. He could taste their fear, knowing the Alexandrian's courage would carry them in battle.

Vestalis let loose a roar that would have impressed Agog, preparing to burst through the gap, when the crossbows returned to the tops of the wagons.

A punch to the chest knocked him from his feet. He rolled onto his back, something snapping as he rolled over.

Suddenly, he couldn't breathe. It felt like he was breathing through a reed clogged with mud. Crocodile soldiers stepped over him as if he were a corpse and met the charge of the Alexandrians.

His vision had reduced down to a point, no larger than his hand. He couldn't move his head to see his chest, but he felt a growing wetness there.

Vestalis had no time to gather his thoughts when a soldier leaned into his vision. The crocodile soldier had lost his helm. His hard eyes and missing finger betrayed his allegiance.

Vestalis tried to wheeze out a call for mercy when the soldier lifted his gladius. The blade came down, piercing the old Roman soldier's neck, and the world disappeared from view.

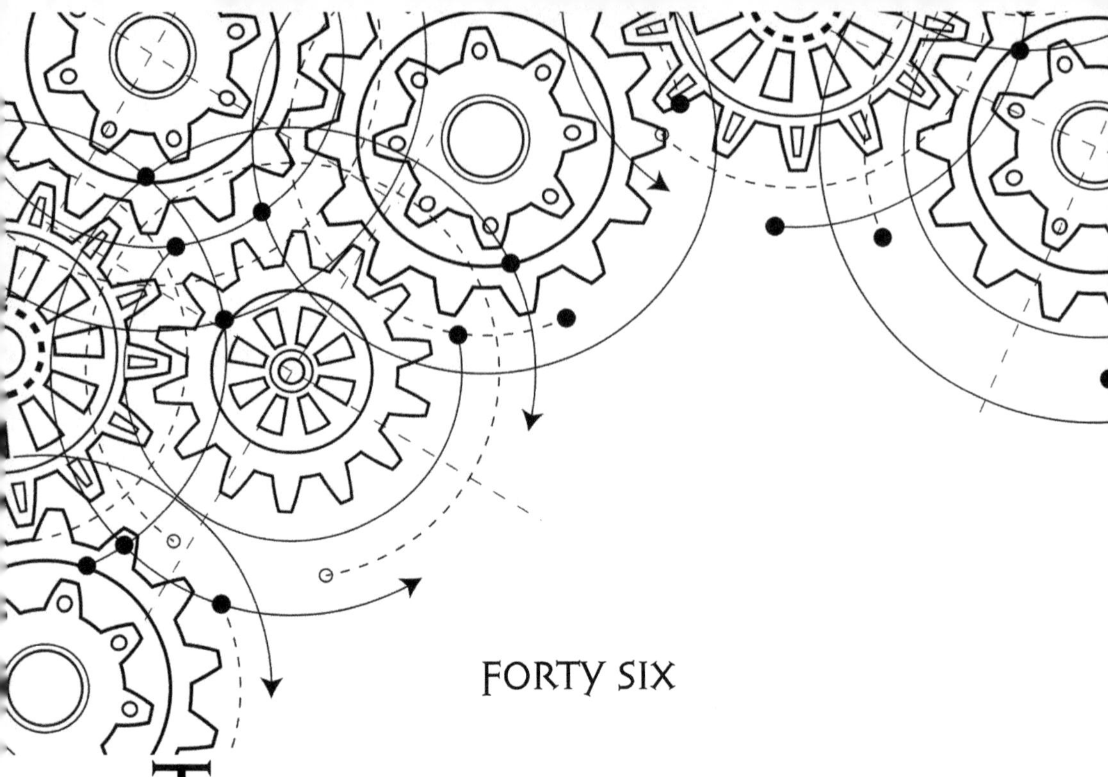

FORTY SIX

The Alexandrian soldiers had assembled in the depths of the tent city, far from the prying eyes of their oppressors, the sky above stained with the rusted light of dusk. Nervous coughs and hushed laughter tittered through the men, the unfamiliarity of three fighting forces joining together leaving them without a strong bond.

Alexandrian, Roman, and Kushite, an odd grouping to wage a war against an upstart god in the shadow of a newborn pyramid. The gold tip glowed like an ember in the dead sky.

The guard on Hoth's blade bit into his hip. He fingered it nervously, waiting for Algoni to return from his scouting.

Hoth would have preferred to send one of his soldiers, but the Kushite Prince had insisted. Their make-shift army of two hundred was ragged enough, Hoth didn't want to argue in front of the men, so he acquiesced to the Kushite.

The dark-skinned Prince appeared like a grim shadow. His skin shone like onyx.

"The croc soldiers have returned to the inner walls, while a force of a dozen Manticores went north to Alexandria. The time is ripe for us to attack," whispered Algoni.

All at once, the overlapping tents surrounding them became confining. Stifled by the lingering heat, Hoth tugged at the neck line of his tunic. Somewhere in the distance, a woman screamed.

Hoth squeezed Algoni's muscled shoulder. "You lead the men on the attack. I'll take a small team to climb the pyramid while you distract them."

The Kushite Prince hardened his face. "I was going to be the one to climb. It's my sister up there."

"Which means you won't be thinking rationally, should something go wrong," said Hoth. "And I'm better at sneaking. You sneak like an elephant."

He thought the Prince was going to be insulted, but he smiled, showing his white teeth and patting Hoth on the shoulder.

"You are right. It is my way to lead the charge, not sneak." Then the Prince grew serious, his eyes like daggers. "But if you let them kill my sister, my beloved Bani, I will tear out your entrails with my bare hands."

Hoth tried to hide the flinch when Algoni patted him on the shoulder.

"Right. First to be rescued," said Hoth, clearing his throat.

The Prince looked away for a moment, though Hoth didn't hear anything. Hoth tapped Algoni in the chest with his finger.

"Don't forget our little trick," said Hoth to a distracted Prince. "It'll help you get through the palisade and create enough confusion so you can hit them hard. Just remember to give me about twenty minutes to get to the wagon that goes up the pyramid."

"And how will you get past the guards?" asked a distracted Algoni, his head tilted.

Hoth kicked a sack at his feet. "I have disguises."

He was about to gather his men when he noticed that the Prince wasn't the only one looking around. Hoth concentrated, trying to pick out anything above the din of humanity surrounding them.

"Freya's frozen tits," he muttered, before throwing himself to his knees and putting his ear to the ground.

The tumbling vibration put a spear of worry into his gut. He jumped to his feet.

"We're being ambushed," he shouted as screams reached them.

To the south, tents and pavilions fell like wheat before a scythe. It looked like a tidal wave approaching, or a herd of horses rushing forward.

When Hoth saw the first crocodile soldier riding above the tents, the gleam of brass reflecting in the distant fire lights, he knew what was approaching.

"Manticores!"

His shout came too late as the vehicles trampled screaming men, women, and tents. The Alexandrians pulled their weapons.

"Run!" he shouted, not knowing if anyone had heard him. The soldiers turned in circles. It seemed Manticores were closing on them from every direction.

Algoni was reaching for his weapon, when Hoth grabbed his arm, pulling him towards the tents. With his other hand, he grabbed the sack. He aimed them for a gap between two approaching steam chariots and when they converged, Hoth threw himself to the ground, pulling Algoni down with him.

The iron-banded wheel cut through the tent nearest him, the muffled scream of someone inside being run over. The air was filled with shouts and the growling of the mechanicals, followed by the thrum of arrow launchers.

The soldiers in the Manticore did not see them as it rumbled past. Hoth scrambled on his hands and knees forward as a second Manticore bore down on them. The fallen tent was uneven, he put a hand on an empty pot, a dead body, and kneed a tent post in his mad scramble.

Another wheel narrowly missed him. Hoth glanced back to see the Manticore headed right at Algoni's prone form. The vehicle burst right over him, and when it was past, the Prince looked up wide-eyed.

A path of trampled tents gave them a way out. Blood curdling screams and fighting punctuated the night air behind them. Hoth got to his feet and started running, leaping over lumps and broken bodies, trying not to get his feet tangled in the lines.

He was certain a Manticore had seen him. Hoth kept running, until he leapt a second too late and caught his foot on a stake. He hit the ground hard, breath fleeing his lungs.

Someone was there helping him up. It was Algoni. Together, they looked backwards. No Manticores followed. Through a field of fallen tents, his men were being rounded up, the battle over so quickly.

They reached the dusty road between the tents and immediately moved to the other side, stepping past the hastily arranged deer-hide abodes. Away from the carnage, Hoth couldn't hear anything other than the normal clang and chatter of living. The rest of the inhabitants didn't know about the attack, though he was sure they would soon enough.

When they were far enough away to ease the discomfort in his chest, Hoth pulled to stop.

Between heaving breaths, Algoni said, "Those Manticores leaving must have circled around. A decoy."

With his hands on his hips, and bent slightly at the waist, Hoth said, "They knew we were coming. Knew where we were going to be."

"Someone betrayed us?" asked Algoni.

Hoth half-shrugged. "Or they saw us from up there." He nodded towards the top of the pyramid.

"What do we do now?" asked Algoni.

Hoth wiped the sweaty hair away from his forehead, finding that he still clutched the sack of disguises. "Head back to Kush, if we can. It's over. Even if Vestalis was successful in the city, we're lost without freeing the noble prisoners. We needed their support against Lysimachus."

"You have my support and they have my sister," said Algoni forcefully.

"Yeah, well...but, uhm, you see," said Hoth, rubbing the back of his neck.

"What do I see?" asked Algoni, staring into Hoth.

Hoth looked away in the direction of Alexandria. He'd come to these lands in support of Agog and his wergild empire. Then he'd stayed because of the iron ships and then the *Jörmungandr* was lost along with the Alexandrian Empire.

What did he have left tying him to these desert lands? He could strike out on his own, head east to the lands of Indus, or back north to his home in the snows. Anywhere but this land of crocodiles. He enjoyed the company of all his limbs.

But thinking of that made him think of Heron, of Ada. His chest grew heavy with regret. If he left, he'd be leaving her, not that he hadn't left a woman before. He'd left them all.

Something about Ada left him grasping for purchase. Like falling from a great height only to grab onto a rope that seemed magically there. Women had always been an object to be conquered, and conquer he did. Ada had never been like that, and maybe that's what intrigued him.

Hoth sighed, pinching his nose between his fingertips. Maybe Ada had rescued Sepharia and they were back in the city, at the tomb. If he could help Algoni rescue his sister, they could go back to Kushite. It was a prosperous land with a fair Queen. It would be a good place to rest for a time.

The Prince was still staring at him. Hoth shook his head. There was another reason he'd never stayed with a woman. Staying in one place usually got you killed.

"You want to rescue your sister?"

Algoni nodded, his sweaty forehead looking like smooth black stone.

"We'll rescue her and then head to Alexandria for Ada and Sepharia. Maybe we can salvage something from this."

"Proper thinking you are now," said Algoni. "Tell me how we rescue her."

Hoth reached into the bag and pulled out a wig of long dark hair.

"I hope you don't mind makeup," said Hoth the Black.

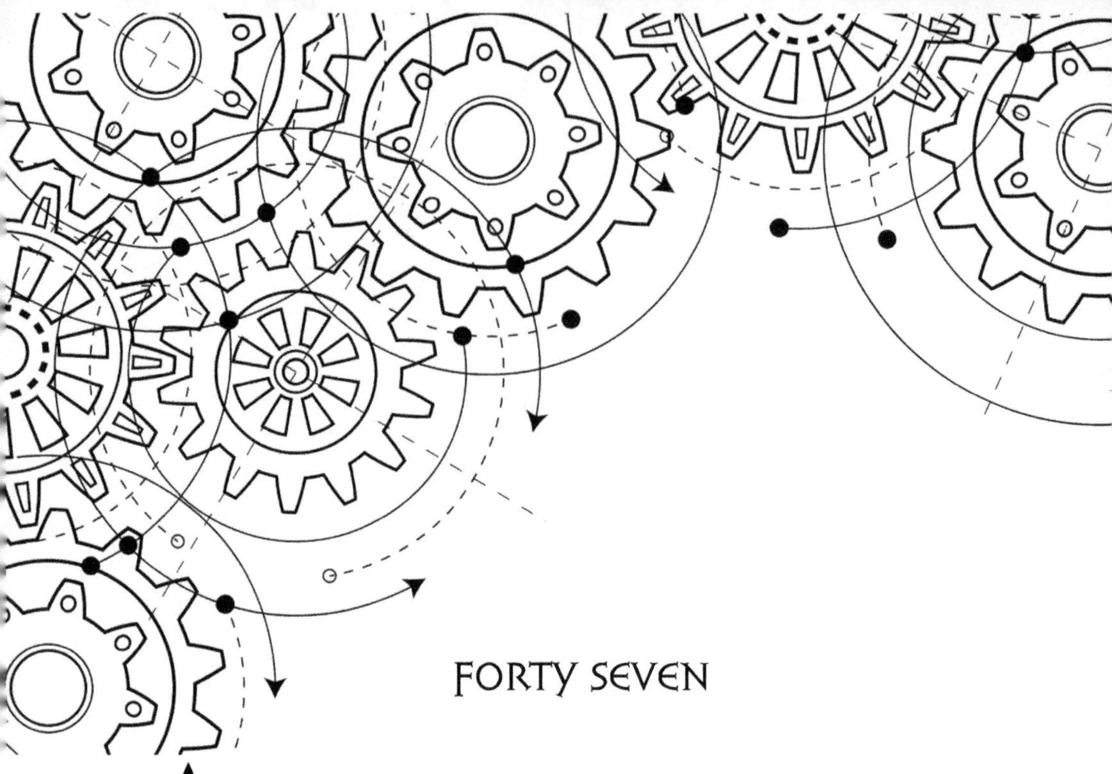

FORTY SEVEN

Ada didn't bother telling Lysimachus that he was calling her by the wrong name. She frankly didn't care.

The only thing she listened to was the wind whipping past her face as the steam barge headed to the pyramid. They'd taken the boat to the royal pier and then boarded the steam barge. The former Alabarch was lecturing her about how Sobek had foreseen this moment.

When a sharp silence hung between them, Ada glanced back to find Lysimachus' cheeks pink with anger. An itch distracted her and she tried to scratch it, but the chains around her wrists rattled in the attempt.

"I can make you talk," said Lysimachus as if he were a boy making demands of his mother.

Ada went back to staring at the sand going past the vehicle. Occasionally a tortured shrub went by, twenty three of them to be exact, breaking up the view, but otherwise it was better than looking the other direction. She knew the pyramid would be there when she turned. She'd see it soon enough. He was taking her there. That much was obvious.

A slap brought her head around. Ada blinked hard and tried to flinch off the sting.

"You are in my control. You will listen to me," said Lysimachus.

He pulled his dark green robes tighter around his body. The glow from the fire chamber turned his beady eyes into coals.

"Or you'll cut my ears off?" asked Ada. "To the Underworld with your demands."

Lysimachus locked her in his glare. She looked over his shoulder at the field of tents and fires surrounding the pyramid. Even though it was dark, the stone mountain made its presence known, and try as she might, she felt no connection with the monument she'd built.

The former Alabarch followed her gaze and let his lips curl back like a jackal. He chuckled low.

"The Tooth of Sobek will be my capitol, not Alexandria. I'll use it as a port, of course, but the rest of the city will turn to dust. This will be the center of the Empire," said Lysimachus.

The steam barge passed the outer tents on a dirt road, pressed in from both sides. Ada said nothing, because they approached a line of men being led towards the inner city. She recognized some of the men.

"Your rebellion is dead," said Lysimachus, his chin raised. "One of your men gave you up for a few silver drachmas."

The faces of the men flew by. Ada's chest tightened as she looked for Hoth's face amongst them. As they passed the inner gate, she wasn't sure if she'd seen him or not, they'd passed too quickly.

After unhooking the chains, the soldiers jerked her off the barge and shoved her into a wagon at the base of the pyramid. One of them tugged on a rope and after a few seconds' wait, the wagon lurched and began moving upwards at a steady pace.

Her hands were still bound, but Ada used the moment to relieve the itch on her nose. It would be one of the few remaining moments of comfort in her life.

Ada leaned over the edge, looking down at the new city forming around the pyramid. It looked like mange on a dog. Even the slums around Alexandria hadn't been this haphazard.

"It'll never work," said Ada.

"What won't work?" he asked, catching himself after he said the words.

"Your Empire," she said.

He snorted derisively, looking away. "He Who Dwelleth Amid Terrors has shown me a future in which my soldiers march on every country. I will be a new Alexander."

"Everyone wants to claim his legacy, but only one can," she said.

He didn't catch her meaning, his brow rippling. "Was that all you had to say? I thought I'd hear something more scientific from your lips, something more specific."

"It's a gut feeling," she said, a smirk in her voice.

This upset Lysimachus, who darted upright and leaned forward into her face. "Not only will the Empire of Sobek stretch to every country, but I will rule over it for all time. I will be a new god. Immortal. Sobek has given me that gift. Could have given it to you as well, if you'd learned to bend the knee."

"I've accepted a finite life, and I don't believe in immortality. Not your kind, anyway," she said.

Ada glanced behind her, forgetting they'd been traveling up the slope of the pyramid while they sparred. The distance took her breath away.

"Look at me," he said, a dangerous rage hiding in his tone. Ada looked back, keeping her face neutral. She'd been trying to antagonize him, to get him to reveal his secrets of immortality, that maybe he would brag, or slip up.

She didn't really believe he'd found the secret of immortality, but she hadn't ruled it out either. Every civilization, and every religion, had its myths about it, all the way back to the story of Gilgamesh. That was the only truth she'd found in the Great Library. Was immortality merely a dream like the gods, or something tangible like a root bark that could be ingested to extend life?

"Why did you bring me here?" she asked, hoping to distract him. "You could have killed me at the Lighthouse, or when I was in Rome. Why not?"

Lysimachus leaned against the bench. They were almost to the top. His beady eyes regarded her with suspicion.

"I told you," he said, the rage gone. "I wanted you to join me. How can you not see that it's been Sobek guiding you this whole time? How can you not know that?"

The sudden even temperament disarmed her. He believed what he was saying. He believe in Sobek, that truth was threaded through his words by an unshakable bond. But she could see he was still the Alabarch, a man of power and greed and cruelty.

Before, she'd thought him a mad man, but he was not one of them. His time beneath the Temple of Sobek had skewed his view on reality, changed his thinking, but not his methods.

But if he wasn't mad, why was he bothering to keep her alive? She was his greatest enemy, the one who'd placed him in the care of the priests of Sobek.

"If there are gods," said Ada, "I don't believe they'd waste time interfering in our lives. Do you spend your time arranging elaborate parties for insects?"

"You don't understand," he said with a sigh.

"No, I don't."

The wagon reached the top, shaking upon impact. He seemed disappointed by their conversation thus far.

"A demonstration," said Lysimachus. "Only with your eyes will you know the truth."

His low tone chilled her to the bones, as he opened the gate on the wagon and led her onto the Tooth of Sobek.

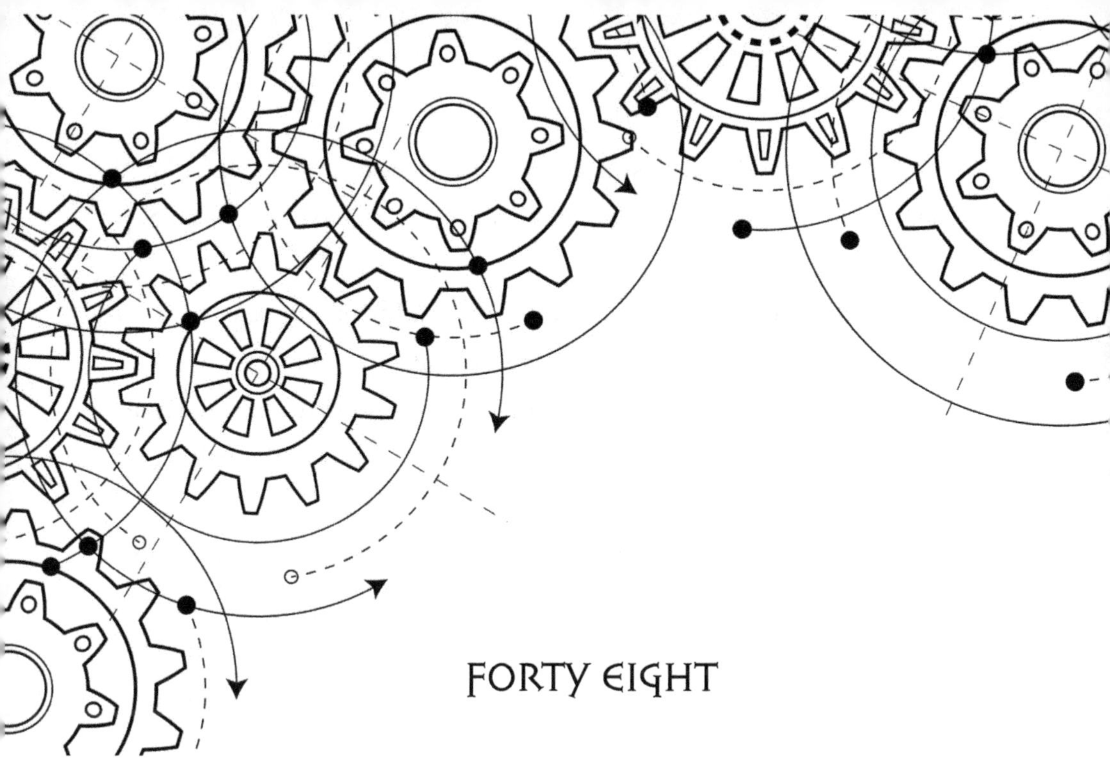

FORTY EIGHT

After letting Ada take her place in the cage, Sepharia watched the crocodile soldiers slaughter Vestalis and his men from the Lighthouse.

They hid in an alcove on the lower level. It must have once been a place for guards to stand, either to stay out of sight, or out of the rain. Worn wooden brackets on the back wall were once made for holding weapons. Time and the salty air had reduced them to nubs. Sepharia had been to the Lighthouse dozens of time, but had never noticed the alcoves before.

"Thank you, Calder," she told the Northman. The words felt ashy in her mouth after watching Vestalis die. Calder made the briefest of nods, almost a flinch. He mourned the old Roman soldier in his own way.

"We need to get off the Lighthouse," said Sepharia. "It might fall soon."

Calder made noises of disagreement as he looked up to the top of the Lighthouse.

"How?"

"Sparkpowder. There must have been a warehouse of it shipped here after the war. The upper level is packed with it. We have to go," said Sepharia.

The Northman nodded. The land bridge had been cleared of crocodile soldiers, probably headed back to the pyramid.

With the island empty, and night fallen, Calder led them past the Temple of Isis and to the land bridge. They could have swam to the Palace, but Sepharia had told them there might still be soldiers there.

To their surprise, they found the fire chamber on the steam chariot, the one that had been used to break the gate, still warm. It took Sepharia only a minute or two to get it running again. The levers had been knocked out of adjustment upon impact. The six of them climbed on, with Sepharia at the steerage.

"Where do we go?" she asked Calder.

The big Northman picked at his teeth with a fingernail, looking at his feet. Sepharia never recalled Calder in any of the war council meetings, which meant it was doubtful he'd been a captain. Rather, he was one of the few Northern warriors left in Alexandria. Which probably said something about his character.

"Right," she said, biting her lower lip. "Can you at least tell me where everyone else is? What about Hoth?"

Calder brightened up, pleased that someone else had taken control. "He's at the pyramid with the Kushite."

She looked at their meager band. "I guess we'll go there. I think that's where Lysimachus will take Ada."

"Wait," said Calder, grabbing her arm with his coarse hand. His hand was a gnarled root of old broken bones and scars.

He pointed to the top of the Lighthouse. It was night and the beacon wasn't lit. Only the slivered moon reflected whiteness against the tall monument.

"What? I see nothing," she said.

"The ship of air. Ada and the blacksmith rode in it," he said, perplexed. "It's gone."

Sepharia's heart momentarily leapt as she thought that her father might have escaped. The feeling didn't last long. She knew Lysimachus wouldn't let her go that easily, and the trap Nektam designed had been devious.

"To the pyramid," she said, setting the steam chariot in motion.

The vehicle had been damaged in the impact with the gate. The iron-wrapped wheels wobbled as they went. Pipes had been pinched, leaving the mechanical permanently out of adjustment. The whole thing wheezed across the land bridge like a dying horse. By the time they reached the other side, she wasn't sure it'd been worth the extra speed for all the noise it made.

She turned the vehicle east towards Canopic gate. It would take them the longer away around Lake Mareotis, which meant they were less likely to encounter crocodile soldiers.

The coarse echoes off the emptied buildings made her jumpy. The only signs that the city had once been inhabited were the hastily left items in the doorways and the packs of dogs roaming freely.

She could have been Charon piloting a boat on the River Styx for all the life surrounding her. The emptiness reminded Sepharia how much the city was a city because of its people.

Passing the Great Library, she could almost taste the dusty scrolls on her tongue. A wind gust blew straw across the steps of the hallowed place of learning. A host of black birds roosted on the corroded copper dome, cawing and shitting down the curved sides.

Too busy trying to picture the scholars of the Library arguing philosophy on the steps, she didn't see the ragged men draw a wagon across the street, blocking the way. Hard-eyed men with crossbows and short swords surrounded the steam chariot after she made it stop.

Behind her, Calder growled and hefted his battleaxe, looking ready to charge into battle. The other soldiers kept their hands off their weapons.

Sepharia thought they were being robbed, bandits left in the city after the population had been emptied out, until she saw the old man stroll from behind the wagon. Calling him old was to assume frailty. He was old like meat left in the oppressive desert sun for weeks. His gray hair was wiry and his eyes, the blackest night.

He made his way onto the cobblestones, the air of kings and pharaohs surrounding his simple walk. It was Black Omari. Sepharia had never met him, but knew enough from Ada's stories. The moral of all of them had been: *do not trifle with this man.*

She'd spent the last year and a half in the care of Lysimachus, the priest of Sobek. She'd thought the whole time that it couldn't get any worse. That the former Alabarch was the worse person to have been captured by. In this moment, she felt that she might have gotten that wrong, very, very wrong.

"Greetings, daughter of Heron," said Black Omari, in heavily accented Greek. "Is Sepharia, I understand?"

Sepharia squeezed the brass bar that made up the steerage until her knuckles turned white.

Calder muttered under his breath, "He works with Lysimachus."

Her shoulders deflated slightly, before she pushed them back up. It wouldn't do any good to appear weak to the crime lord.

"Yes, I'm Sepharia. Daughter to the *Michanikos*, and the great inventor of Alexandria, friend to the Rhakotis District," she said, hoping to remind Black Omari how much her father had contributed to the city.

His cold eyes and pinched mouth made no movements to indicate his thoughts. He was an ancient mummy, poised to offer death.

"Crocodile Man kill you many times. Now you live. How?" asked Black Omari.

Was he testing her? If he worked with Lysimachus, why didn't he know? She hesitated, fearing to speak and say the wrong answer.

"Tell me, daughter of Heron," said Black Omari, the threat hanging in the air.

She cleared her throat, starting tentatively, "I...I, uhm..."

His gaze narrowed. His patience was thinning, but why did he want to know at all? If he worked with Lysimachus, the only reason could be that the priest of Sobek had not told him. Kept it a secret.

But Sepharia didn't know either and was about to tell him so, when she remembered how old the Egyptian man was. Had he sided with Lysimachus to get a taste of immortality?

Sepharia didn't know how Lysimachus had made it appear she'd been killed and resurrected so many times, she'd been drugged most of them, but she knew what Black Omari wanted to hear. So she lied.

"It was a trick," she said.

"Trick?" His head tilted slightly to the right. He seemed to not expect this answer.

"Lysimachus made me his slave because I'm the daughter of the *Michanikos*. I know her secrets, the ones she used to create miracles in the temples," she said.

His brow pulled tight, his lips thinned. "What is trick?"

"The miracles in the temples. They weren't real. Heron just made them look like they were. We used things like this steam mechanical," she said.

Black Omari shook his head. "You are wrong. I see with my eyes."

The crossbowmen sensed his mood and leaned forward. Her ploy was going nowhere.

Sepharia closed her eyes and summoned memories of the workshop, trying to piece together a convincing story.

"We used mirrors, and smoke. When they cut my head off," she said.

"That wasn't me. They'd taken a dead body, put a wig on it that made it look like me, and when I finished circling the platform and the Terrors collapsed around me, I dropped through a trap door and they put the dead body on the stump to have its head removed."

Black Omari worked through the plausibility of it. "It is possible, maybe."

"Every one of them," she hurried out. "All tricks. That's how Heron made her gold in the temples. Lysimachus is just doing the same thing. Except instead of gold, he's gaining followers."

With the words out of her lips, it made sense. Even she hadn't completely seen it in the middle of it all.

Black Omari shook his head. "I do not believe this."

She threw her hands up. "No. Don't you see? He promised you immortality, right?"

By the wide-eyed look on his face, she knew she'd hit true.

"That's why he won't tell you. Because it doesn't exist. He's just a man with a well placed lie," said Sepharia.

The image of the naked drawing of Lysimachus passed through her mind. She realized what it was for, though there was nothing she could do about it now. He was making other priests in his image, and sending them into the wider world, to proselytize his cult of Sobek. In a way, he would become immortal, or at least the idea of him.

"This priest of Sobek lied to me?" asked Black Omari.

Sepharia didn't answer. She gave the smallest of nods instead.

Black Omari smiled, and despite his age, his teeth were strong and bone white. The rictus of his smile curled upward, deepening valleys in his wrinkled face. Sepharia wanted to recoil, but dared not move a muscle.

When Black Omari finally spoke, it sent chills through her gut.

"Let us go ask the high priest of Sobek."

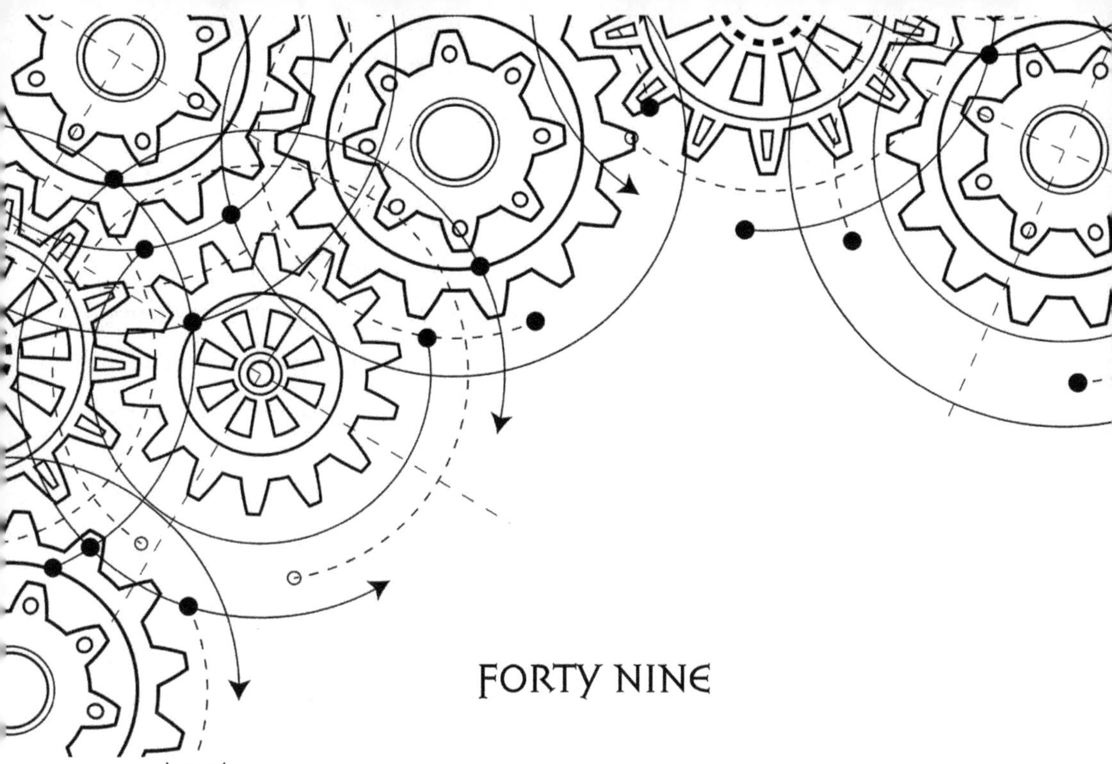

FORTY NINE

The Kushite Prince stamped around in a small circle like a child splashing through water puddles, before coming back to stand before Hoth the Black. The tantrum had tilted the dark wig on the Prince's head.

"I won't wear it," said Algoni, arms crossed.

Hoth held the brush tipped with burnt red ochre. The earthy scents from the clay jar tickled his nose as he held the brush out between forefinger and thumb.

"You're the ugliest woman I've ever seen without it," said Hoth. "And that's saying something."

"I'm not trying to find a mate," said Algoni, tugging on the wig, trying to set it right and only succeeding in knocking it into the dirt.

Hoth snatched it up, dusted it off, and made the Kushite Prince sit on the block of stone behind the row of tents. A zephyr of wind knocked the lantern out, so Hoth pulled out his flint and steel and relit it, this time remembering to close the glass pane on the front.

When Algoni tried to keep him from putting the wig back on, Hoth set him in his sights. "You said you wanted to rescue your sister. If you want to do that, you're going to have to put this on."

"I won't. I'm a Prince," he said with his chin high.

Hoth pressed his forehead into a sweaty palm. "Fine. No makeup, but you need to wear the wig. You'll just have to keep your head down."

From somewhere on the pyramid, the sound of squeaking pulleys made its way to them. The wagon was transporting people up the incline to the platform at the top.

When Algoni looked up to the faint light high above them, he sighed, slumped his shoulders, and nodded. "Wig only."

Hoth got Algoni set, not before slapping his hand once for tugging on his stola. It'd taken three normal sized women's clothes to make one outfit for the Kushite Prince.

As Hoth applied the black kohl to lengthen his eyes and the green eye paint beneath them, Algoni tilted his head at him.

"You do that with much practice, Hoth the Black. Are you a shape-shifter like the *Michanikos*?" asked Algoni.

Hoth exhaled a short laugh out his nose, trying to keep his face still while he looked upward and painted the soft area beneath his eye.

"When you spend a winter trapped in a hall with four beautiful wom-en, you do a lot of things to spend the time," said Hoth.

Algoni clapped his hands softly together. "I would have thought of much better things to do."

"Trust me, my Princely friend. I did all those and more, but eventual-ly, one gets a bit worn out. We spent our time not in bed acting out stories and my supple companions wanted the full experience," said Hoth, putting the brushes and jars back into the sack.

The Kushite Prince shook his head while rubbing his hands together. "I would not have worn out. Never."

Hoth chuckled. "You might not have, my friend, but these talents have kept me alive. I once played the part of the long lost sister when caught in bed by an angry husband and his five brothers, but that's a story for another time."

The squeal of the wagon at the pyramid stopped, summoning a moment of grim contemplation.

"I am ready, sister Hoth. Better we find Bani and be done with this," said Algoni, indicating the disguise with a sharp sweep of the hand.

With his face cleanly shaven and wearing enough makeup that he felt like he had armor on, Hoth grabbed the basket of breads he'd paid a woman in a nearby tent for. The press of people around the pyramid didn't have the facilities to feed themselves, so the bread was only a few hard, moldy pieces. The rest of the basket held his clothes.

His sword he had stuffed into the stola. It kept him making stiff-legged steps, which only enhanced the disguise.

When he looked at Algoni, he almost decided to leave the Kushite Prince behind. He looked like a man that had fallen into a pile of women's clothes, only to come out with cloth and wig hanging haphazardly on his body. Only the realization that the Prince would not stay kept Hoth's lips closed.

"Keep your head down and let me do the talking," said Hoth under his breath as they shuffled down the dirt road between the tents that led to the inner gate. "And walk like a beaten animal, not a Prince."

Prince Algoni, much to Hoth's surprise, let his shoulders slump and his massive body deflate, until he seemed half the size he was before. To Hoth's eyes, the Prince didn't look like a woman, but expectations were a powerful thing.

Four guards waited at the inner gate. The way was open and any invading army could sweep right through, except for the two Manticores sitting inside with their arrow launchers pointed up the road.

Hoth swallowed the beating of his heart as he approached. The closer he got, the foolishness of his disguise became more apparent. If they had to run, he'd trip over the tightly bound fabric around his legs, say nothing of the sword strapped to his chest and running down the inside of his left thigh. If he moved too fast, the bouncing of the blade would serrate his flesh to ribbons.

Only the knowledge that he'd seen other women passing though the gate kept his feet shuffling forward. They reached the gate and the first guard miraculously motioned them through without so much as a glance.

Hoth inclined his head demurely as possible and continued on. They'd made it nearly past the Manticores when one of the guards called out: "Halt."

The world slowed and a rivulet of sweat ran down Hoth's back. The guards had been laughing and talking before. They were deathly silent waiting for a response. Hoth turned, trying not to topple as he circled around.

"You're one big woman," said the guard that had strolled forward, indicating Prince Algoni.

The guard was a Thracian with thick, dark hair, including coarse curls that stuck from the neckline of his tunic. He had thick features and a forehead like a brick.

The guard looked back to his friends, "And I like big women."

They erupted in laughter and though the guards didn't see it, Algoni had stiffened in response to the remark, growing larger, like one of the inventor's air ships inflating.

The Thracian guard made his way to the Prince and slapped him on the ass, grabbing a handful. Hoth prepared to run, or somehow untangle his sword from his stola. His every nerve was set to twitch.

For a moment, the Prince started to rise up like a bull sensing its freedom. Even the Thracian guard seemed to sense something, his brow rippling in a fear he didn't quite understand.

"I am a Bride of Sobek," came the words out of Algoni's mouth, in a surprisingly high tone.

The announcement that "she" was already pledged to the crocodile god took the spark out of the guard's fun. He backed away holding his hands up, while the others laughed politely, though Hoth could hear the unease in that tone.

With disguises intact, they made their way into the compound. There were three parts to it: a series of clay brick halls that made up the soldier's barracks, the marshalling yard for the Manticores and other steam mechanicals, and a small town's worth of buildings made up of the artisans and bakers that had first come to the pyramid.

The wagon that went up the pyramid was next to the artisan buildings. Hoth was able to get a good idea of the layout when Algoni had hoisted him to the top of the palisade.

"We need to find our friends first," said Hoth under his breath. He didn't dare speak much louder, as crocodile soldiers seemed to be everywhere, peppered occasionally with a priest in dark green robes, some with a hand, foot, or ear missing.

It didn't take them long to find their captured friends. A series of pens behind the barracks had been set up. They were packed with more than the Alexandrian soldiers captured on this night. The pens were not built with high walls, but four Manticores kept the prisoners from even thinking about escape.

Hoth moved close enough to see his men littered with bandages, sunken eyes, and bruised faces. They sat in clusters on the ground, or leaned against the palisade that made up the back wall.

"Now what?" asked Algoni, his eyes shifting warily.

The wagon had returned to its position at the bottom of the pyramid. It was heavily guarded. Even if they could kill the soldiers stationed there, which doing so without bringing the whole camp down on them seemed unlikely, there would still be too much time while they rode up in the wagon.

Hoth shifted, trying to keep the sword from resting against his balls. That would be an unfortunate accident.

"We can't free our friends and we can't make it to the top of the pyramid," said Hoth.

The enormity of the task crushed him with its imposing weight as if the pyramid had been dropped upon him. He would have fled the region already had it not been for Algoni's insistence on rescuing his sister.

Was it all worth it? Probably not, he decided. Especially if he ended up a cold corpse in a ditch somewhere, a possibility that seemed like it had a high likelihood.

And then he realized he hadn't put on his disguise and snuck into the inner sanctum of the crocodile god because of the Prince. Hoth knew then that he endured because of Ada.

Hoth sighed, wondering how he got himself into these situations, and knowing the answer, all at the same time.

"Can you climb, my friend?" asked Hoth.

"Climb what?"

Hoth nodded towards the looming structure, the mountain of stone.

"But the sides are sheer and smooth. I saw it when we walked by. I do not know what sorcery made them, but there's nothing to climb," said Algoni, the volume of his voice raising higher than Hoth would have liked.

"Where there is stone, there are cracks," said Hoth. "I've climbed worse."

Algoni shook his head. "I cannot climb it."

"Then it seems we must part ways," said Hoth. "I'll make my way up the pyramid, while you stay here."

"And what will I do?" asked the Prince, his broad face dipped in shadow and sadness.

"You remember that barrel of sparkpowder we dropped into the coal bins?" asked Hoth to a nod from Algoni. "With that distraction, you might be able to free our friends."

It was a terrible plan, and even Algoni knew it, but to his credit, the Prince nodded and agreed.

Hoth left the Prince's side, moving towards the artisan town with the basket of moldy breads in his arm. When he looked back to see the Prince moving in the direction of the steam chariots, he muttered under his breath.

"We're both going to die here tonight."

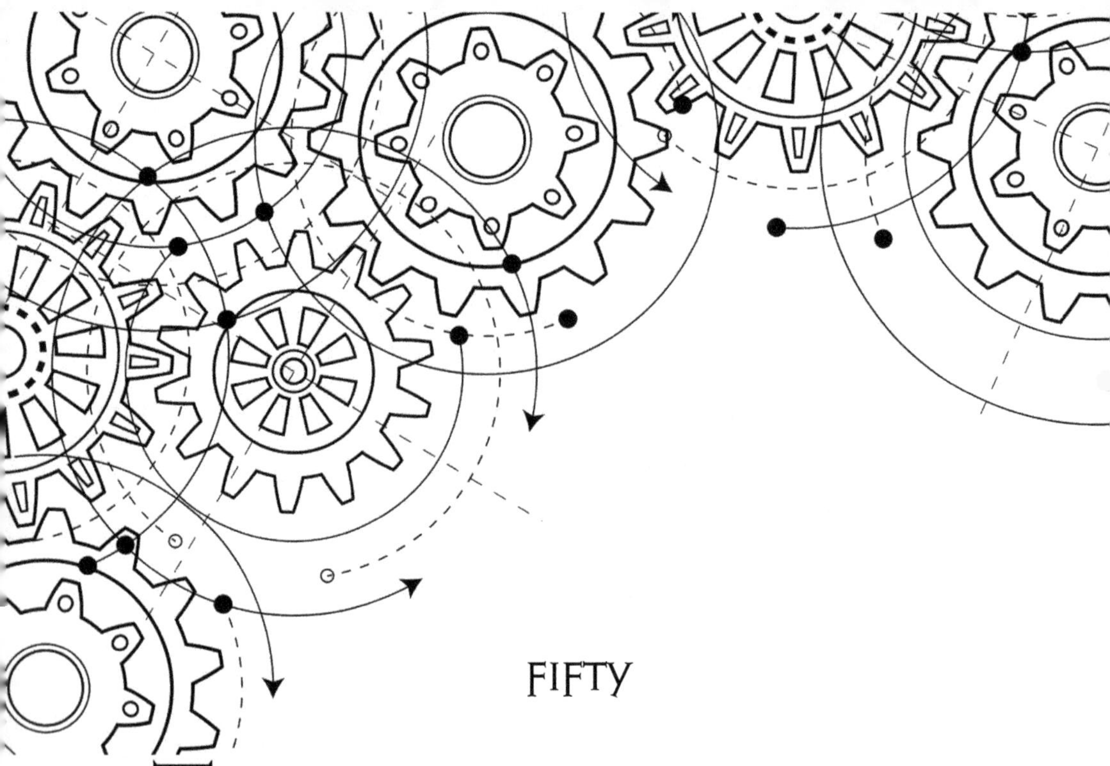

FIFTY

The air had a sullen, old water smell to it, despite the high breezes whisking across the upper surface of the pyramid. Ada knew what the smell indicated, knew it in her beating heart, that had thrummed to full once the first tastes of blight had hit the back of her throat.

The sounds of splashing had come after, of tails swishing through water. Ada had stepped off the wagon at the top of the pyramid, and stepped into a nightmare.

At the center, a huge pool commanded the space, the water contained by a rock wall half as high as a man. Reeds and gnarly bushes choked the pool that was as wide as she could throw a stone.

It must have taken hundreds upon hundreds of trips in the wagon to bring enough water for the pool and to keep it full despite the summer heat. The golden roof, which in the night was a blight on the populous stars, blocked the worst of the sun's effects during the day.

On the far side, a cage had been built. Dozens of shapes moved inside the cage. Bani's dark face stared back from the bars, illuminated by flickering lantern light. Ada hoped Polyxena was somewhere in there, too.

Shapes in dark green robes moved about the level, like souls milling about at the edge of the River Styx. The dim light and contradictions of swampy rot and clear desert air left her dizzy with vertigo. One priest with a hood pulled over stood on the stone wall staring into the pit of crocodiles. Something about the priest gave Ada shivers.

"Every ruler in the histories, from Caesar to Alexander, would be envious of my throne. The Tooth of Sobek will be a capitol like no other," said Lysimachus.

"If you think those men cared about such monuments, then you know nothing of them," said Ada.

"Of course they did," said Lysimachus, wandering to the edge of the platform. A wooden fence lay between the priest and the yawning edge, or Ada would have rushed over to throw him off. There were also a pair of Terrors lurking nearby, one as large as a Northman, that kept her from acting.

"All men who seek power want their story marked in history immemorial," said Lysimachus.

"But they understood the people meant more than the monuments," she replied.

Lysimachus chuckled lightly. "Lord Sobek's ranks grow with new followers by the day. I expect even tomorrow, I will have new believers from the ranks of your soldiers. The alternative is quite permanent."

"Fear," said Ada, "you rule by it while those you admired ruled with love."

A splash in the pool made her flinch, widening Lysimachus' eyes with glee. She felt betrayed by the reaction.

"Why, Heron, you're blind if you think they didn't rule with fear," said Lysimachus.

"Their enemies feared them, but never their followers. Alexander was loved like a god. And the people of Rome adored Caesar. It's why the Senators feared him and they became his enemies when they allowed that fear to rule them," said Ada. "And I am no longer Heron. That was my twin's name. I am Ada."

His eyes flashed with darkness. "Do not presume to tell me what to call you. The only person I need here is Heron of Alexandria. Anyone else I would have fed to Sobek's children already."

The burst of anger staggered Ada. She said under her breath, but loud enough for him to hear: "I am Ada."

Lysimachus ignored her and turned to gaze to the north. He motioned for her to join him at the edge. The big Terror moved within range to dissuade her of any foolishness, which only reminded her that she had enough sparkpowder packed into her mechanical arm to kill a pack of Terrors.

While feigning interest in whatever Lysimachus was looking at, Ada tried to find a nearby torch, or a lantern with easy access. She needed to pull the wick out of the mechanical arm and light it. After that, she didn't think it'd be too hard to stay near Lysimachus. Even if he stabbed her, she could hold on long enough for the sparkpowder to detonate.

When Lysimachus burst out laughing, fear for her life flowed through her limbs. It took a moment for her to realize he was looking at something out in the desert.

"See those glowing lights moving across the desert towards my city?" asked Lysimachus with his stump extended to the north. Dull orange smears, the glow of fire chambers, moved in a southerly direction. "Those are steam chariots, gifts I gave to Black Omari for his loyalty. Yes, yes, I see by that look on your face, you know him. Do you think it is fear that drives a man like him? No. No one could make that man afraid. He desires immortality, a gift he believes he can earn from me."

Ada watched the lights move across the desert. She spoke under her breath, quiet enough the Terror nearest couldn't hear, "Your immortality is a lie. Don't think that I don't know it. I spent too many years making miracles for the temples not to know what you're doing."

He gave her a sober glance. His thin lips relaxed from their normal arrogance.

"Dagius," he said to the Terror, "step away for a moment. Not too far. I must speak to Heron in private."

Ada's face suddenly flushed with heat. Lysimachus turned to address her and a smirk formed on his lips. "Perception is reality. A lesson I learned from you. If they believe the gift of immortality, then it makes it real."

The admission startled Ada. At first, she couldn't understand why he would admit such a thing to her, but then she realized, she could do nothing to stop it and that he probably wanted some sort of acknowledgement for his cleverness.

"So this piety is an act? All this business with Sobek?" she asked, trying to distract him while she looked for a convenient flame. An open torch lay not far from them.

"Of course not. I've given my life to Sobek." He held up his arm. "I toil in his name, using what tools are available to me. And I have achieved immortality, just not in the way that most people want it. There will be certain sacrifices, even by me."

In that moment, Ada knew exactly what he was trying to do. The comment from Sepharia about the scroll made perfect sense now. What Lysimachus was trying to do wasn't so different than what she wanted to do to oppose him.

"You're going to appear to live forever using men that look like you," said Ada. "The cult of Sobek will always be led by its high priest Lysimachus, though it might be another person in your robes after you die."

Lysimachus grinned triumphantly. "And now you understand. I cannot be stopped. This movement will take over the world, on the backs of your machines, and using the lessons that you have taught me. As I have said many times, you are Sobek's champion. Whether or not you enjoy the fruits of your labors is up to you."

The realization felt like ice in her soul. She felt the need to strike back in any way possible.

"I have my own plan for immortality," said Ada, "but not for me. For my works, and the works of the Great Library. My plan is already in place, and you will find opposition united against you in every corner of the world."

Lysimachus stared her down. He reached into a pocket in his robe and handed over something small. As soon as the object touched her palm, she shuddered. Opening her hand to see what was in it was like stepping into a noose.

Resting on her palm was the wooden carving of the two dragons that she'd made in Arethussa's tavern. She'd given it to Plutarch along with the drawings to make her machine.

"My spies uncovered your operation in the noble district a few days ago. I have your friend, Plutarch. He's in the cage with the others," said Lysimachus.

Ada glanced in that direction. Her view was blocked by a curtain that had been pulled in front of the cage, but she believed him. He could not have this carving of hers unless Plutarch had been captured. Which meant that all her plans had been destroyed.

"Thank you for your machine, Heron of Alexandria," said Lysimachus. "It's quite ingenious. Another gift for Lord Sobek to propagate his message across the world."

Pain wracked her bones as if they'd been snapped and hastily jammed back together. All her life's work was being twisted by this man. Ada took a step towards the torch spewing its greasy black smoke into the night.

"And this is where I make one last offer for your fealty to Lord Sobek. While I expect I know your answer, I will ask just the same," said Lysimachus.

"Why would you even want it?" she asked, her voice cracking.

"I would hate to throw away a good tool, especially one that has provided so much. And your allegiance would do much to sway the nobles, to convince them that they should join me," he said.

"What if I refuse?"

He made a lazy-eyed shrug that belayed his confidence. Then he snapped his fingers and motioned for the hooded Terror who had been standing on the edge of the pool to attend to them.

Ada expected to see some demonstration of loyalty from the priest. Proof that Sobek had total control. Or maybe an example of mercy.

What she wasn't ready for was the image of herself when the Terror flipped back her hood with one good hand and one stump. The woman wasn't a twin by any means, but there were enough similarities that those who didn't know her well would never guess otherwise.

A pit grew in Ada's stomach.

"You see, I do not need you at all," said Lysimachus.

She also knew what it meant to her closest friends. If he had to use her double to fool them, no one who knew her well would be allowed to live.

"So I ask one last time, will you join Lord Sobek? If your answer is no, then I'll have you thrown into the crocodile pit. And do not think that you can fool me if you choose to say yes, thinking you will turn on me later. I will test your loyalty in ways you cannot imagine."

The question hung in the air like an executioner's axe. She knew how he would test her. He would force her to kill her friends to show loyalty. Or worse. Either way, she knew there would be great suffering. Death, even a horrific end in the toothy maw of a crocodile, would almost be a blessing.

Ada eyed a torch near the pool. She moved in that direction. Dagius lurched forward to stop her, but Lysimachus waved him away.

She climbed onto the edge. The flat stone was easy enough to balance on. Behind her in the water lurked huge Nile crocodiles, but she kept her gaze forward despite the interested splashes.

Though it unbalanced her slightly, Ada put her hands behind her back, so she could open up the hatch on her mechanical arm without being seen to do so.

"You knew what my answer would be even before you brought me here," said Ada. "Otherwise, you wouldn't have made her."

The thin lips of the high priest of Sobek twitched with the hints of a smile.

"This is not just a battle between you and I, Lysimachus," said Ada. "This is a clash of civilizations. Fear versus science. The Temples against the Great Library."

She had her fingernail dug into the gap on the hatch, but it wouldn't budge. She tried to pull it open without giving away that she was straining. Once it was, there was almost no way they could stop her before she put the wick into the flame.

"You know I cannot stand with you," said Ada. "Even if I said yes out of fear, which is the only way those words would cross my lips, I would never truly believe it."

"I thought nothing less," said Lysimachus flatly. "If so, throw your-self into the pit, or I will feed you to them slowly."

Ada jammed her fingernail harder, trying to get it open. The nail felt like it might snap before she would succeed. Right as the hatch gave way, Lysimachus said, "Seize her. Remove her mechanical limbs. I don't want Sobek's children to break a tooth."

Ada lunged toward the torch, but the Terror Dagius grabbed her before she could get there. Two other Terrors descended on her, fingers clutching and ripping at the buckles until the mechanical limbs had been removed.

She felt naked once they were gone. Lysimachus had the arm in his hand. He didn't even notice the open hatch with the wick sticking out.

"I don't think you'll need this anymore," he said and threw it over the edge of the pyramid. The leg went right after it.

The thin hope of survival drained away until she was an empty husk.

"Now," said Lysimachus. "Throw yourself in the pit, or I'll feed you to the crocodiles piece by piece."

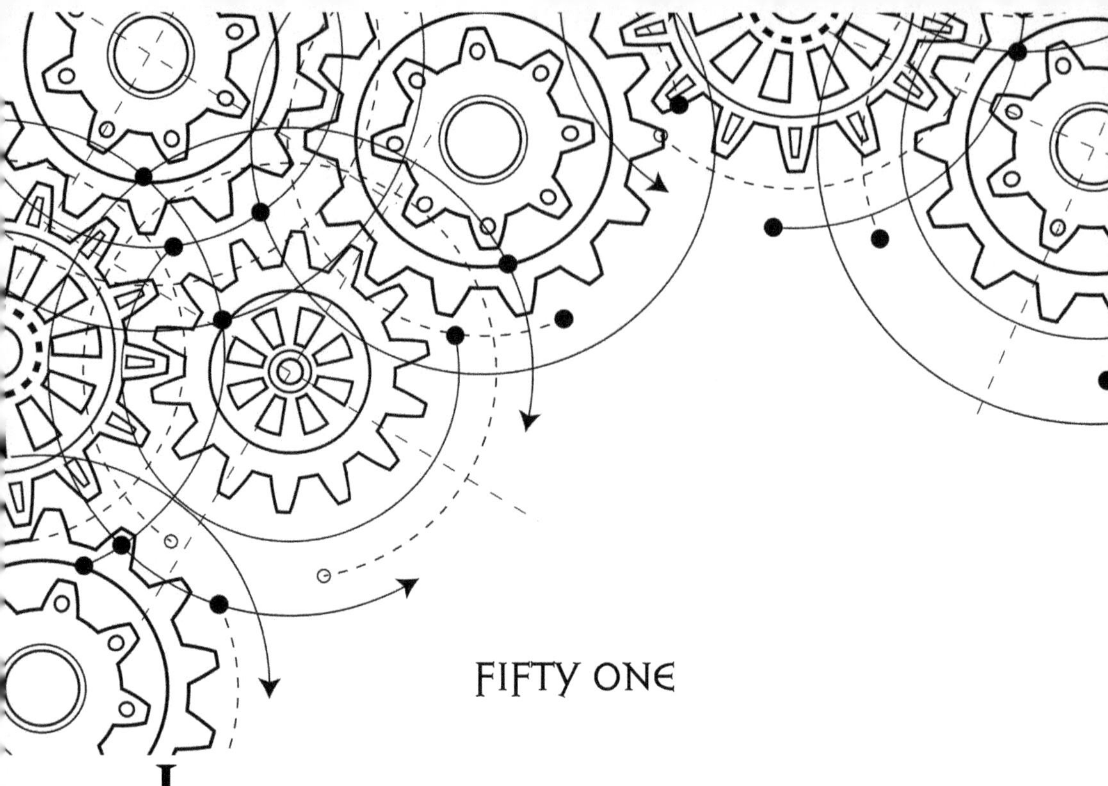

FIFTY ONE

Long after Ada had left him at the top of the Lighthouse, Punt had cut the rope tethering him to the beacon level. He'd watched Ada led onto a ship by a contingent of crocodile soldiers. Then as he drifted to the east on the mercurial winds, the rescue at the Lighthouse came to a brutal end.

Punt sunk to the bottom of the basket, head in his hands, fingers digging mercilessly into his skull as if could rip those memories from his mind.

It seemed the world he knew had been annihilated. Even the bottom of the basket refused to shield him from this new reality as he watched the empty streets of Alexandria pass beneath him, bereft of even one foundry fire.

He squeezed his fists until they were numb. Punched the sides of the basket until his knuckles were bloody.

When he could rage no more, he climbed to his feet with the thought of throwing himself from the air ship. He knew he really couldn't, but just the idea snapped him back to reality.

When he looked over the edge, cheeks stained with dried tears, he could see nothing. While he drifted, night had fallen, surrounding him like spilled ink. Only when he looked up to the night sky did he see light sprinkled across the heavens.

The air had gotten colder and Punt reflexively put more fuel into the steam chamber. A chill wind blew from the northeast and the air ship shifted.

Punt rubbed his arms and stared into the night, wondering what he would do once he landed. Should he go east to Memphis, or was that too near? Maybe he could head to Kushite, or further east, past ancient Babylon. Maybe he would end up like the blacksmith in that fallen city, practicing his craft making simple tools for mud men and hermits.

The aching of his heart told him how much he would rail against that life. Better to not practice at all, rather than live that wasteful life.

With elbows resting on the hard woven edge of the basket, Punt realized his first problem was landing the air ship. Ada had not explained how it got back down to the earth, nor how to do so in the night.

If he could land, he decided he would find Plutarch, and the two of them would head off together. Even without the inventor, they could carry on in her name, spreading her inventions in the east to fight against the Empire of Sobek.

Punt looked around him and then to the stars to determine which direction was north. He spied a faint orange glow that had to be the beacon on the Lighthouse of Pharos. It was both northerly and below him. He was surprised he could see it from this distance.

Using the directional cone, Punt diverted the exhaust of the mechanical. The air ship lurched in that direction and moved like the tides to the north.

Diverting the air stream made the air ship drift downward, which Punt was grateful for, since he had to land eventually. As he neared the glowing lights, he saw more fires scattered and for a brief moment thought Alexandria had been reborn.

His excitement was quenched by the pyramid appearing out of the gloom, outlined by the reflections of fire light. The glow that he'd mistaken for the beacon was the upper level of the pyramid.

Digging into the sack that Ada had brought, Punt produced a trio of sparkpowder globes. He could at least cause some havoc before he headed away. It would give him that much pleasure.

So he adjusted the directional cone, trying to move the air ship over the top of the pyramid, but no matter how he tried, the air ship drifted past. An updraft from the sloped walls kept pushing it away and making it too difficult to go directly over the top. Realizing that he only had so much fuel and that he couldn't circle the pyramid forever, Punt maneuvered the airship into a position above the camp and readied a globe.

As the air ship shuddered through the darkness, Punt lit the wick, let it burn down a little, and dropped it over the edge.

The sparkpowder globe exploded in mid-air above the camp. Shouts erupted, and before they could figure out where it'd come from, Punt dropped another.

He was halfway across the little village when the second globe exploded above a group of soldiers, throwing them to the dirt. Punt couldn't make out many details, but the camp looked like an ant colony unearthed.

Realizing he was about to drift away from the camp and over the tent city, Punt dropped the last sparkpowder globe. In his hurry, he didn't wait, letting it slip from his fingers as soon as the wick sparked to flame.

When no explosion followed, Punt assumed the globe had broken upon impact. He leaned back into the basket, preparing to adjust course for Alexandria.

Punt's fingertips scraped the sharp edge of the brass lever the moment the last sparkpowder globe ignited. The explosion sent up a fireball that blew a heat wave up and through the basket, making Punt wonder if he would catch flame. It was like standing before the hearth fires of Vulcan for one brief fiery moment.

The deafening boom shook the air ship as a wave of air passed it. Punt shook his head, trying to get the ringing out of his ears, realizing that he must have thrown the globe into a reserve of sparkpowder that the crocodile soldiers had captured.

Punt glanced over the edge to see the destruction he had wrought. It looked like the explosion had ripped a hole in the earth. The palisades were flattened and the rows of Manticores had been thrown like a child's toys. In the middle of the camp, men were fighting.

Satisfied that he'd done the best he could, Punt set the air ship on a course for Alexandria.

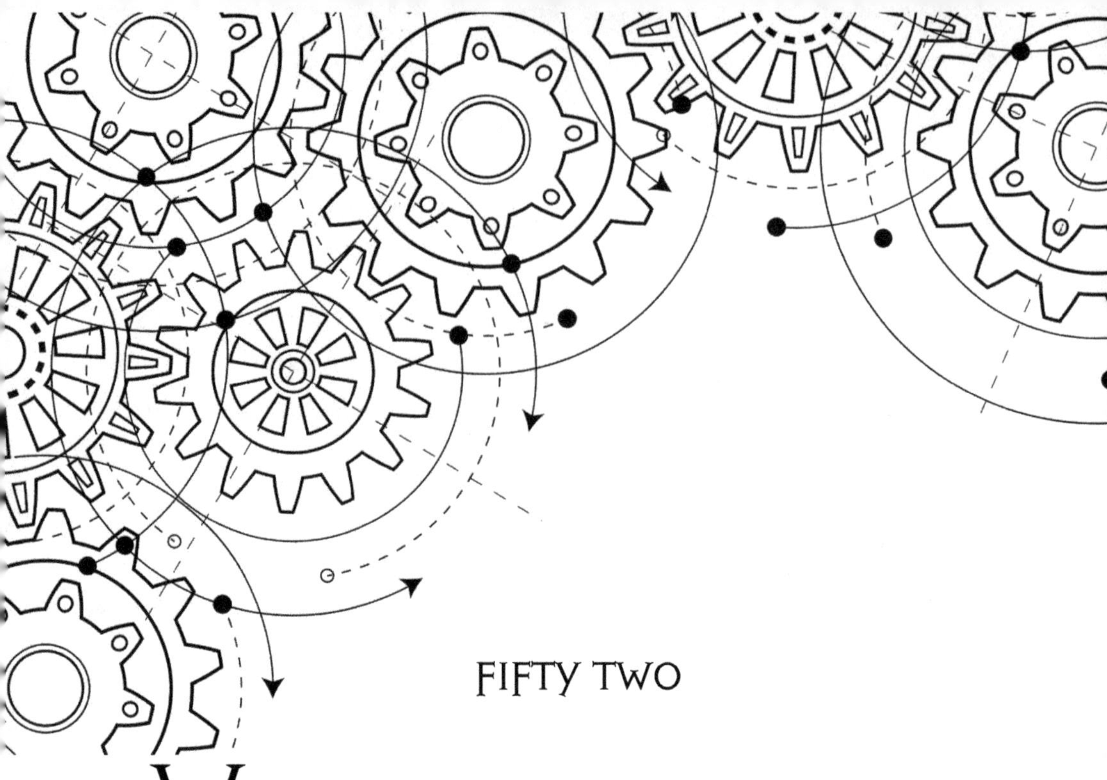

FIFTY TWO

When the explosion rocked the camp, the Terrors left her and moved to the edge of the platform. Ada looked around for a means to escape. Nothing suggested itself.

The Terror who would take her place had not moved away. Ada looked at the woman, face illuminated by flickering flame, eyes hungry with malice. This woman wanted her dead, so she could take her place.

The Terror twin lunged forward and grabbed Ada's arm. Ada was unbalanced without her mechanical limb and the woman pushed her against the stone wall, bending her backwards.

The second explosion startled the Terror, who glanced over to Lysimachus and the other Terrors watching the destruction below. Ada kneed the woman between the legs, eliciting a grunt. Then she slammed her forehead into the woman's nose, breaking it. This woman may have endured having her hand removed, but she'd not been through what Ada had been through.

Ada fought with the woman Terror with all her strength, clawing and fighting. She turned the woman and pushed her against the stone wall. Her strength was no match for Ada's. Behind the wall, the splashes of crocodiles coming to investigate gave the woman wide-eyes.

The woman who would replace her scrambled away, pulling herself across the stone, dangerously near the crocodiles waiting beneath her. Ada did not pursue as she had no intention of killing the woman.

When the third explosion rocked the pyramid, sending a fireball high into the sky, the woman lost her balance and fell into the pool. The crocodiles seized her in their powerful jaws immediately. Her screams rent through the night air.

The sounds of fighting reached them from the camp below. Lysimachus turned, eyes like hot coals, his lips peeled back.

"You, what have you done? Kill her now. Throw her in the pit. I want her dead," said Lysimachus, pointing in her direction.

The two Terrors advanced on her. The big one named Dagius produced a longsword, while the other pulled a pair of knives.

Ada backed against the stone wall, knowing her end was near. She could do nothing to stop them limbless and unarmed.

When a strange creature slipped over the edge of the railing, Ada thought she'd lost her mind. The creature had a human shape, but its eyes were elongated and colored strangely. In its fist was her mechanical arm.

To Ada's surprise, the creature put the arm into a nearby torch and threw it towards the feet of the two Terrors. The big one, Dagius, looked down at the mechanical arm reflecting fire and darkness, with a wick sparking like miniature spits of lightning.

The explosion knocked Ada hard against the stone wall, head ringing with bells. She looked up to see nothing where before there had been the two men advancing.

Ada shook her head. Her vision had doubled and blood gushed from her forehead.

The strange creature that had thrown the arm lay unconscious against the fence at the edge of the platform. Ada looked to her left in time to see Lysimachus staggering towards her.

The priest of Sobek punched her in the mouth. She felt her consciousness dim, already damaged from the explosion. He lifted her up and pushed her onto the ledge.

Ada regained enough strength to fight back. He was trying to push her into the pool. One of the crocodiles lurked right behind, its snout pushing onto the edge, the smell of rotten meat wafting from its open mouth.

She tried hooking her leg around the stone wall, but Lysimachus was stronger. He punched her twice in the face, spilling blood into her eyes. Ada clawed at his face and succeeded in only grabbing his tunic.

He kept pushing her backwards. His knee was on the edge of the ledge and he was trying to roll her over. A hard snout bumped her in the back and a tooth scraped her spine.

Lysimachus had his full weight pressing forward. He was winning. She could feel herself sliding towards the crocodile. The lights of victory reflected in his eyes.

He would get his revenge and there was nothing she could do about it. She looked back to the motionless form against the fence. She would get no help from that quarter.

Lying on the edge of the stone, with the crocodile waiting to tear her apart only a breath away, Ada realized it was useless to fight against a stronger opponent. She would never keep him from pushing her into the pool.

But she didn't need strength, or fear. She needed the tools she'd learned in the Great Library.

In one violent motion, Ada stopped pushing and with her fingers gripped firmly into Lysimachus' tunic, she shifted her weight, rolling over and—pulled.

For one brief instant, Lysimachus thought he'd won until he realized his momentum was bringing him into the waiting maw of the crocodile. He gave one last scream before the crocodile bit into his face.

Ada rolled off the ledge, away from the kicking legs of Lysimachus, as the crocodile pulled him into the pool. The other beasts in the water converged on him and tore him to pieces.

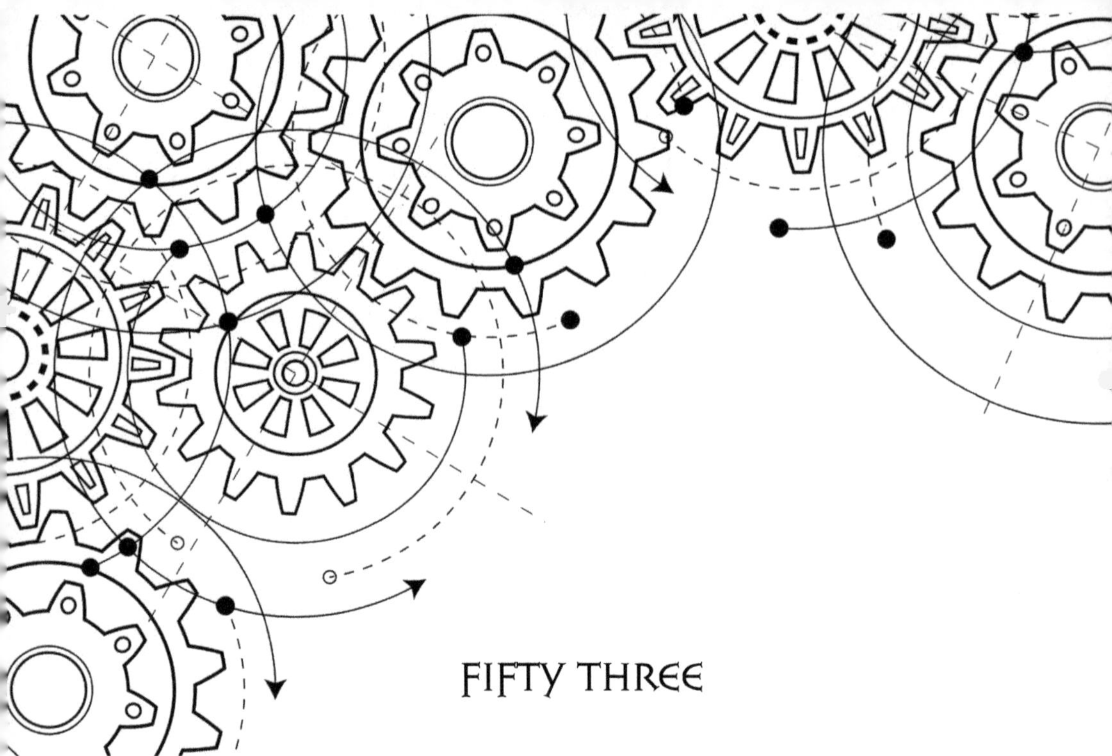

FIFTY THREE

Hoth rolled onto his hands and knees, and vomited out the meager contents of his stomach. The explosion had thrown him against the fence and knocked his head against the stone.

Cradling his head in his hands, he looked through his fingers to witness Ada crawling across the stone towards him.

When she neared, she spoke in a quiet voice, "Hoth?"

"It is me," he said weakly.

"What's on your face?" she asked, wiping away blood from her forehead.

"War paint," he replied.

"That looks like makeup to me."

Hoth chuckled, though it nearly made him vomit again. "You're not the only shapechanger around."

Using the hem of her tunic, Ada wiped the blood from her face. "The secrets you keep from me."

He nodded. "Help me up."

Together, they staggered to their collective feet.

"Did you climb up the pyramid?" she asked.

"I did. Do you typically throw your limbs from the side of it?" he asked.

"Lysimachus did that," she replied.

"And where is he?"

"Dinner for his god."

Hoth grimaced, understanding what she meant. They moved to the corpse of the big Terror. Hoth took the sword clutched in the dead hand by peeling back the fingers.

"Any more Terrors up here?" he asked.

Ada tilted her head. "A few. Do you hear that?"

"All I hear is ringing."

"The mechanical. Someone's coming up in the wagon," she said.

Together they limped towards the edge of the platform on the other side of the pool. A priest in dark green robes ran away from the mechanical as they neared. He looked like an old man without any fight in him.

Hoth was about to shut off the mechanical and halt the wagon's progress up the side when he saw it cresting over the edge.

"Too late," muttered Ada.

With Ada on one side, Hoth gripped his sword and prepared to fight, which seemed laughable since he could barely stand up.

When he saw the hard old Egyptian man at the front of the wagon, Hoth's heart sped up. It seemed he would have to fight after all.

"Black Omari," whispered Ada with considerable regret.

Behind the crime lord were four thugs, each who looked comfortable with his weapon, and a lot sturdier on their feet.

When the wagon door opened, Hoth clench his sword, feeling the rough grip against his callused hand. He planned to go down fighting.

Next to him, Ada said, "Wait."

A figure pushed through the crowd, stepping onto the platform with a smile on her face. It was Sepharia.

Sepharia rushed into Ada's arms, taking the burden from Hoth. Confused, Hoth lowered his weapon.

"Where's Lysimachus," said Black Omari.

"In the belly of a crocodile," said Hoth.

The hard-eyed crime lord nodded appreciatively. "A fitting end."

Ada turned to face Black Omari, half-hugging Sepharia with her handless arm.

"What do we do now?" asked Ada to Black Omari.

The old man looked around. Hoth could see him considering his options. Hoth hoped that included them living, since he could do nothing to stop the four thugs.

"Return to Alexandria," he said.

"Just return?" asked Ada. "As simple as that."

"All this piety is bad for business," said Black Omari.

"What about your immortality? I thought you wanted that from him," said Ada, nodding towards the pit.

"Clearly, it didn't work," said the crime lord. He paused and then smiled. "I will, of course, expect certain concessions for my help."

Ada thought for a moment and nodded. "We shall enshrine them in our charter."

An interested eyebrow went up on Black Omari's face. "What finally did him in?"

Ada smirked. "His lack of understanding about science."

No one but the inventor seemed to understand what she meant, but everyone laughed, just the same.

FIFTY FOUR

The cacophony of the workshop: the tapping, hammering, sawing, shuffling of feet, laughing cadence of work, the hiss of steam, the thump of stone against stone, Plutarch shouting commands in his high, willowing voice, the crunch of gravel, grunts from Punt molding steel into shape, the syncopated click of gears from the wind catchers, iron cracking from a mold spilling black sand across the stone floor. Ada sat at her desk and listened to the workshop sing to her in its sweet, industrious tones.

It'd been three weeks since the events at the pyramid and today was the first day the workshop had really come alive. The others had been busy with the affairs of the city. Ada didn't care about that. They could decide who would rule. She had work to do.

She was not so enamored by the sounds of the workshop not to hear the scuff of boots against the stone.

"Hoth?" she asked, not bothering to open her eyes.

"How did you know?"

Ada allowed a smile to grace her lips. "I don't know. Maybe your footsteps sound arrogant. As if every place you walk into, you think you own."

"I think that knock in the head might have damaged you," said Hoth.

She lifted an eyebrow, peering at him through a half-lidded eye. Despite the heat, he was wearing the black outfit with a fur cloak that she'd seen him wear on his ship. His pale hair had been brushed and fell like silk against his shoulders.

"This is Alexandria in summer, you know?"

Ada opened her arms and Hoth slid into them, the fur around his shoulders tickling her chin. He pressed his lips against hers and she wrapped her legs around him, pulling him close. She was ready to take him upstairs when he pulled away.

"You're a cruel man, Hoth the Black," she snickered.

Hoth gave a short bow. "I'm here on business. Business of the city-state of Alexandria."

"Is that why you're wearing that outfit?" she asked.

He winked and pulled a scroll from the inside of his cloak.

"It's from Senator Dominitus," he said as he handed it over.

"And what does it say?" she asked, crossing her arms. "I assume you know."

Hoth looked away and cleared his throat. "Yes. He's asking if you'll take the position of Consul of Alexandria."

The noise in the workshop grew louder. Ada turned back to her desk, grabbed the quill with a swift motion, and made purposeful marks across her drawing.

"I told that old fool last week I wasn't interested. Find someone else to be his figurehead. And why hasn't he come to visit himself?" she asked, pressing the quill into the parchment hard enough to smear the ink.

"He's not doing so well," he said. "The last few months were hard on him."

Ada whipped around. "Hard on him? I was nearly fed to a pool of hungry crocodiles."

"He is an old man," said Hoth, opening his hands.

She glanced up and sighed, feeling the inexorable tug of responsibility. "I can't. I won't. I'm going to help Alexandria in the best way I can, from my workshop."

Hoth opened his mouth when footsteps rang from the hallway. Prince Algoni and Princess Bani stepped from the gloom as the golden warriors of Kushite, bangles and bright garments bringing riotous color to the workshop. The Prince limped from a mace blow he'd taken at the pyramid, while the trials of Bani's imprisonment haunted her gaze.

"*Michanikos*," said Bani, bowing. Her brother matched the gesture, though his gaze was less amiable.

Ada climbed to her feet, though she felt unbalanced by the simple brass leg. Sepharia and Plutarch were making her new limbs, which would be finished in a week.

"Greetings, heirs of Kushite. I welcome you to my humble workshop," she said with a sweeping gesture.

"It is we who are honored," said Bani, touching her fingertips to her generous lips and then her forehead. "Without you, I would still be subject to Sobek's rule."

"Thank your brother and our rakish Northern friend," said Ada. "They had the bigger part."

Bani shook her head softly. "No. Maybe that day they had some part, but you have been Alexandria's protector for a long time. Even when exposure of your secret would have put you in danger."

The Kushite Princess winked, sparking the memory of their encounter at the top of the Lighthouse many years ago. Ada wondered if Bani would have been surprised if she'd taken her to bed.

"I give service to the city which has given so much to me," said Ada.

"Which is why, Ada of Alexandria, you should accept the position of Consul," said Bani. "There's no one else who can put the city to rights in these dark times."

The words lay heavily across her heart. "You honor me with your suggestion, but I cannot. I proved inept in Rome. I would not endanger Alexandria, too."

"Even we Kushites know that Rome was a den of backstabbing. Caesar did not survive there," said Bani.

"No. I can't. My place is in the workshop," said Ada. "I cannot help with those things the city really needs right now, like food for the winter. Lysimachus in his arrogance thought he would conquer Egypt to feed his new army. Now the city will go hungry."

"So if the city was fed, you would consider it?" asked Bani hopefully.

Ada hesitated before speaking, not wanting to insult, "I would consider it."

From the archway came more figures wearing the livery of Egyptian priests. Ada didn't recognize them at first, but when she did, she glared at Hoth who seemed entirely too pleased with himself. Ada sensed his plotting and reminded herself to punish him later for it.

"High Priest Hotep and Keeper of the Records, Xan-Ra," said Ada feeling besieged on all sides. "You do me great honor by visiting."

As the two priests of the Temple of Ptah joined the burgeoning circle, Ada began to suspect this procession of visitors had been choreographed.

"The honor rests with us, O Broken One," said Hotep, stroking the gold wire wrapped beard hanging from his chin. "We have come to Alexandria on behalf of the Northman."

"Greetings, Ada," said Xan-Ra, tasting her name on his lips for the first time and seeming pleased by it.

The initial impression she'd had of Xan-Ra, of a kindly innkeeper had not changed with the years, though she thought she might add *wise* to the descriptor.

Ada shot a withering glance to Hoth before addressing the priests of Ptah. "I do not gather you're here on a simple visit."

Both priest's eyes flashed with conspiratorial vigor, though they kept their lips flat with piety.

High Priest Hotep stepped forward, his bald head gleaming even in her window-lit workshop. "We're here to beg of you to take the Consulship of Alexandria."

"I thought as builders and makers, you would want me in my workshop," said Ada, frowning.

Xan-Ra touched his forehead with two fingers. "I'm certain the great *Michanikos* would want the peace to be secured before birthing new inventions that could be misused."

The Keeper kept his gaze low, though the shiver of self-indulgence on his lips revealed his inner state. Ada decided to add impetuous to the descriptor for the Keeper of Records.

Ada clasped her hands, flesh and metal, in front in the lecturing position of the Great Library. She lifted her chin and spoke in her battlefield voice, "Is there anyone else lurking back there that has an idea of what I should be doing here in Alexandria?"

When Senator Dominitus shuffled in with Polyxena on one side and Sepharia at the other, the conspirators shared a chuckle. The Senator was using a cane and grimaced at each step, even with Polyxena and Sepharia's support. His right eye had gone dim and he had to turn his head to look at her. The last few years had been very hard on him.

"Greetings," said Ada in an exasperated tone.

"Greetings," replied Polyxena, wearing a light blue stola, pinned up with a familiar brooch. "The League of Corinth sends its greetings."

"A Roman Senator arm in arm with a member of the League," said Ada with a sigh. "What has the world come to?"

The crow's feet around Polyxena's eyes deepened. "The chaos after the fall of Rome hit the members of the League hardest. Refugees and bandits overrun our lands, and the Germanic tribes are restless without the Legion to keep them in check. While we were no friend of Rome, the alternative at this point is worse."

Ada grit her teeth. "And what would you have me do about it?"

"As the heir of Alexander the Macedonian—" a few of the workers within earshot stopped hammering and Plutarch moved closer to the circle of conspirators, "—you are the most capable and the most palatable to the League to lead us through this crisis."

Ada slapped her hand on the table. "The League wants to crawl back in bed with Rome, to be its slave again?"

"No," said Polyxena and Dominitus put a hand over hers. She gave him a comforting smile.

Senator Dominitus cleared his throat and began speaking, though he did not look up and his voice was like watered down wine.

"The world needs a dominant empire. If too many countries are opposed but equal, it will result in destructive war, and forgive me if I say it, Ada of Alexandria, but your inventions have made war most calamitous," said Dominitus.

"But who will be the dominant empire? Who will decide who will rule over the others? Surely the League cannot accept Rome," she turned to the Kushites, "and surely you cannot want rule from a foreign empire? What of your sovereignty?"

Prince Algoni touched his arm across his chest. "War is bad for trade. Even I know that. I've spent half my life warring with the tribes to the south. Someday I would enjoy time to take a wife." The Prince glanced towards Sepharia.

"It will be an empire of equals," said Sepharia, "much like the League of Corinth, but with a Senate and a Consul. And roads and steam barges to join us together, and for mutual protection."

"You've thought this through," she said. "But why me as Consul?"

Hoth chuckled. "Who else could it be? Name one person who is better known by all parties that they could trust? Yes? I didn't think so. There is no one else. It has to be you. We came to that conclusion weeks ago, but now we need you to accept."

She rolled his argument around in her head and could find no flaws. She hated to admit it, but she was the best choice, even if she had no intention of accepting.

Bani spoke up, "If you are Consul, my Queen has agreed to help feed Alexandria and Rome, because I can vouch for your trustworthiness."

High Priest Hotep stepped forward, "If you are Consul, the Temple of Ptah will offer its services to you to burgeon the capabilities of your workshops. What you wish to have made, we will make."

Ada fell against her seat, feeling hemmed in by the conspirators. Hoth held his hands out pleadingly. "We knew you wouldn't want to accept."

She massaged her forehead. "If I'm going to be Consul, again, I will do it under two conditions: the first that my sentence is only for a year and a day, and the second is that slavery will be outlawed in the empire."

The way they glanced amongst themselves told her that this point had already been discussed. They anticipated her at every turn.

"Done," said Hoth without even consulting the others.

Suddenly, the workers who had all stopped working during the last bits of discussion, started applauding wildly. The conspirators joined the applause, and moved to salute her, or give her a bit of affection.

Sepharia wrapped her arms around her and gave her a peck on the cheek.

Ada whispered to the world, "Oh, what have I done?"

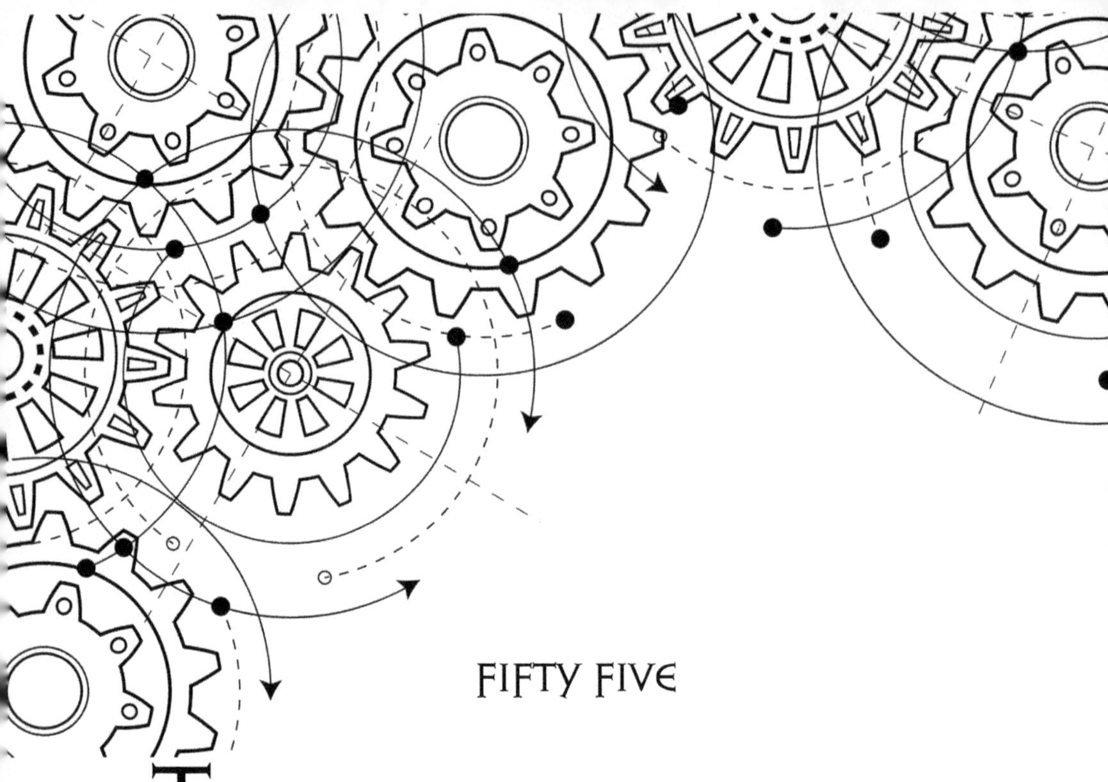

FIFTY FIVE

The Great Library, despite the burning of some of its books, had recovered since the rule of Sobek. When Ada graced its marble steps a few weeks after being named Consul, she was pleased to find a trio of scholars in their customary togas arguing about the nature of Man. She'd heard this argument before, and it was waged between: the Naturalists, Man as Tyrant, and the Lion Walkers.

The three scholars upon seeing her, gave a nod and a smile, though so embroiled in philosophical battle, they could not unengage to greet her. Which was fine by her, she was waiting for Sepharia, who appeared in that moment as if by divine intervention.

"Greetings, daughter," said Ada, taking Sepharia's arm.

Her daughter would have made Athena jealous with the bold combination of striking beauty and piercing wit. The light of wisdom in her eyes turned the golden curls of her hair into dangerous coils.

"Greetings, mother? Father? I still don't know what to call you," said Ada with a smile.

"Whatever you'd like," said Ada. "Shall we go?"

The two climbed the steps and no one stopped them from entering, as would have been customary even a few months ago. The leaders of the Library had not yet passed laws allowing for the attendance of women, but no one was going to stop the pair of them.

They passed through one of the bright halls with stark white columns and trees planted in stone boxes. Scholars sat amid the benches with scrolls and tomes, many murmuring to themselves. The fresco of Zeus wielding his lightning bolt showed craters across the bottom, where someone had smashed it with a mace. On the marble floor, the stone was cracked with faint ideograms of umber overlapping where fires had burnt. The ceiling had clouds of darkness and the windows that let the light in had been recently replaced.

The worst crimes to the Library had been the burning of its books. The scholars had done what they could to preserve the knowledge within, but Lysimachus and his Terrors had been quite systematic with the burning of those scrolls.

Which was why Ada had come to the Great Library, to check on her invention that would thwart future attempts to destroy knowledge.

She found the machine and its scholars in one of the empty scroll rooms. It was as large as a steam chariot with four scholars attending to it. Ada watched from the entrance, having not yet been spotted.

When the machine opened its maw, one scholar, tunic speckled with ink, swept in and took a brush to the plate contained on the upper side of the insert and afterwards, wiping down the ink that had fallen on the lower. Once he was free of the machine, another scholar darted forward and placed a parchment on the bottom, and then two scholars pulled on a huge lever that stamped the plate onto the parchment. When the machine opened its mouth again, a scholar removed the freshly printed document.

"*Michanikos!*" came a cry from right inside, and a scholar that she partially recognized came scurrying up. One eye of his was scarred closed from the attentions of the Terrors.

"Gnaeus," said Ada, remembering his name. "It has been a long time."

"Too long," said the scholar. "You still owe me some information about those barbarians."

She laughed. "You have a good memory. What are you doing here?"

He indicated his missing eye. "Without this, I'm a little clumsy, so I keep them organized. My eye is gone but my mind is still working."

"Excellent," said Ada, "and how is the machine?"

"Great," beamed Gnaeus. "We shipped out fifty copies of the drawings of your machine and the instructions to operate it a few days ago. In a year, I'm sure, every library in the known world will be producing books at the pace we are." Gnaeus hesitated, a worry rippling across his brow. "One question, *Michanikos*, did you ever give it a name? We can find nothing in the specifications and we keep calling it the machine. Seems rather uninviting."

Ada patted him on the forearm, remembering her conversation with Lysimachus, "I call it the Immortality Machine."

Gnaeus seemed confused for a moment, "Ahh! I get it. What a catchy name. I'm sure that's what it shall be called from this moment forward."

"Good, I'm pleased," she said. "But I came not to name this metal creature, but to let you know my workshop will be delivering three more next week. And these will be able to stamp multiple parchments at the same time. Can your woodcarvers keep up?"

Gnaeus put a hand to his chest. "Probably not, but I can recruit more. The scroll room next to this one is filled with wood chips. We have dozens working already making the original plates."

Ada tilted her head. "I have some ideas there, but it might take some work. Maybe the next iteration of the machine after this one. More importantly, are you copying the important works yet?"

"You realize the enormity of that task? The Room of Debate has been busy, deciding which books should be copied next. First Archimedes, or Aristotle? Socrates or Pythagoras? The number of works is staggering."

"Which makes it all the more important that we increase the rate of copying. Every library in the known world should be Alexandria's equal. It's the only way to preserve it, to make it impossible to destroy it all," said Ada. "It's the lesson every new civilization should take, to preserve its knowledge against the ravages of time and catastrophe."

Sepharia, who had been standing quietly to the side, asked quite pointedly, "But what of the tomes of Ada of Alexandria? Surely you are copying her first?"

Gnaeus chuckled and bowed low. "Of that, there is no doubt. It's the one thing the leaders of the Great Library agreed upon. No one shall forget what Ada of Alexandria has done. You are a goddess to the Library."

Ada blushed, feeling overwhelmed for the moment. "Please, let us not use that term. We've had enough trouble from gods and goddesses."

Gnaeus smiled.

"I should be returning to the Palace," said Ada. "Dominitus and Polyxena are probably still arguing about the proper way to distribute representation."

Sepharia grabbed her good hand. "Let them argue a little longer. I wish a proper tour of the Great Library from its most famous scholar."

"As you wish," said Ada, sighing, "I suppose it won't hurt them to argue a little longer and it'll do me some good not to have to hear it."

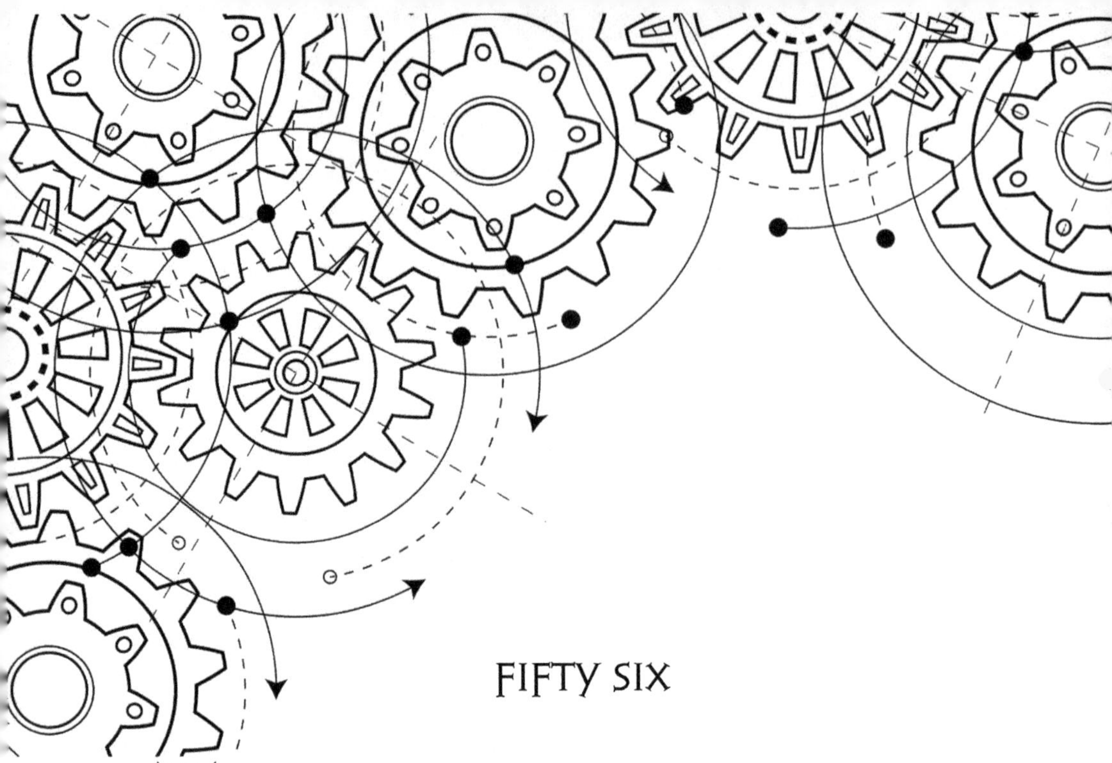

FIFTY SIX

The summer had faded to autumn, though someone had forgotten to tell the sun, as Ada wiped sweat from her brow. She shook her hair away from her neck, wishing she could cut it again, but Hoth begged her to keep it and she enjoyed letting her femininity be known, even while she wore a man's tunic.

The steam rail to Memphis was nearly complete. Ada sat astride the roan horse, gripping the reins quite comfortably with her metal hand, the tiny gears responding to the movements of her stump.

In the distance, workers toiled, laying more rail that would connect Alexandria to Memphis. Another line went North around the coast of the Mediterranean. It would have stops at every city along the way: Jerusalem, Tyre, Sidon, Antioch, and so on, until it reached Rome. It would take many years to connect them and another team worked from the Rome side, but when it finally met, it would transform the Empire.

Hoth galloped up from the direction of Memphis. He'd gone ahead to speak to the foreman while Ada had stayed back, wanting to have a moment of solitude. As Consul of the resurgent Alexandrian Empire, she had little time to herself, between the needs of the workshop and the needs of the government.

Still, it wasn't as bad as it had been in Rome. There was political infighting, but each side knew that the Empire had to be strong. Already, raids had been made on Ravenna, a populous city north of Rome. Further west, the Gaulic tribes were consolidating and in the east, Persia was ascendant.

Ada hoped to temper the ambitions of the Persians with trade agreements, but she didn't think the Gauls or Germanic tribes would accept those terms just yet. Which was why they'd sent Manticores by iron ship across the sea to support the Roman province.

"Hail, beautiful Ada," said Hoth, wearing breeches only, his muscled chest glistening in the sun. His pale hair had never been whiter, and almost hurt her eyes to look at.

"You just left me, you dolt," said Ada.

"And each time I return, it's like seeing the sun for the first time after a long, cold winter in the North," he said, as his dark stallion pranced.

Ada turned her horse so she faced him. "Did those words actually work on the maidens you seduced?"

"Sometimes," he grinned. "Did it work on you?"

She let her shoulder shrug ever-so-slightly, as if she could barely be bothered. "You already share my bed. Does it matter?"

"I just want to make sure you don't leave me," he said, seriously.

"I said I would stay in Alexandria as Consul for a year and a day," she said. "I'm not going anywhere, just yet."

"And when your time is up?" he asked, pouting.

"I haven't decided," she replied. "The affairs of the Empire keep me too busy for thoughts such as those."

"You'll take me with you?" he asked.

She winked. "If you're good. You fell asleep after the second time last night. That just won't do."

Hoth opened his mouth to give her a pithy response when he stopped, looking past her into the distance towards Alexandria. A steam chariot raced towards them, a streamer of dust billowing out from behind it. At the wheels, the dust only formed a small cloud, but as it blew away, the cloud grew larger until it took up half the horizon. Her life and inventions had been much like that.

A cold stone formed in her gut as the steam chariot approached. She wasn't expecting any important messages, so when it skidded to a halt, and the soldier jumped off to run up, pushing his bronze helm back on top of his head as it had slipped off, she steeled herself for bad news.

"What is it?" she asked. "Have the Gauls invaded Rome? Did the Persians reject our offers? What's wrong?"

The soldier couldn't meet her gaze and stared at his feet. "Consul Ada, my apologies. Senator Dominitus has passed."

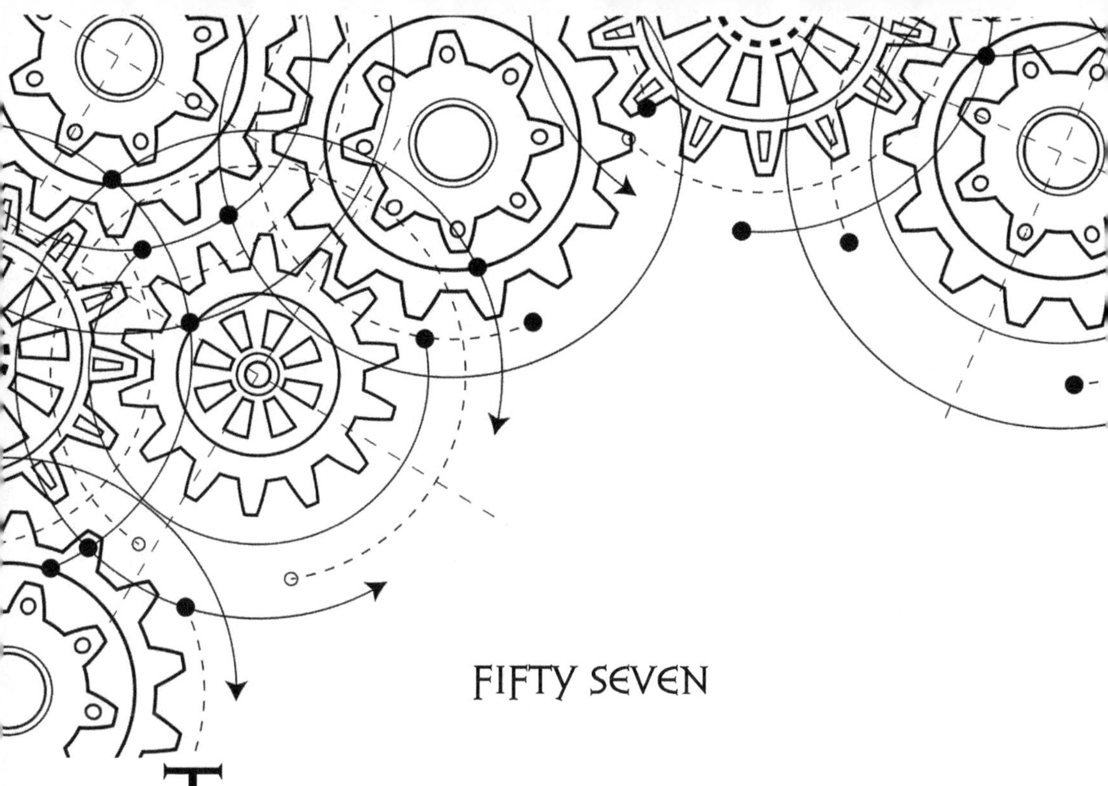

FIFTY SEVEN

The funeral for Senator Dominitus did not occur until one month after his passing. It took time to bring the important dignitaries from across the Sea, even by the standards of the speedy iron ships that criss-crossed the water on a regular basis.

The funeral would be Roman, with touches of Egyptian and Greek to give it a more multi-cultural feel. Senator Dominitus had been quite specific in his instructions.

Ada stood at the head of the procession, wearing her dark tunic and silvery belt. Her mechanical arm and leg, a mixture of brass and steel, had been polished to a shine. A steam chariot had been rededicated for the funeral, making it appear to be a simple wooden boat with markings of the dead carved into the gunwale.

Even the most uneducated Alexandria knew that it was Charon's boat, which only made Ada smile when she thought of her sparring with the old Senator at his villa in Rome. Before the procession began, Ada climbed upon the steam chariot, knee clicking with gears, and placed a Roman golden eagle coin in his mouth.

Though he'd died a month before, he looked quite preserved in his toga. His organs had been removed and placed in clay jars by his side. His skin looked like thin parchment and he smelled faintly like lilacs, a perfume used to hide the odor of decay.

Ada stayed with the body, standing at his head, as the steam chariot drove through the Alexandrian streets. They started at the Temple of Saturn, west of the Great Library, and would reach the Soma of Alexander after a slow, rattling ride down Canopic street. His mausoleum had been constructed near the Soma, a request that normally went unanswered, but Ada's acceptance as heir of Alexander had been enough for the city planners. His grave would lie near Vestalis, whose burial had received less attention in the aftermath of the battles.

The streets were lined with the citizens of Alexandria, and of the new Empire, and beyond: Romans, Thracians, Kushites, Persians, Egyptians, and so on. Ada suspected they'd come out to see her rather than the old Senator, who'd done most of his business behind closed doors. Which was why she'd take position in Charon's boat; so that Dominitus' body would receive a proper tribute on the way to its burial.

To her relief, lamentations of the Senator's name rung out with increasing frequency, making Ada wonder if Hoth had handed out ha'pennies to the poor for their parts. Cries of her name were interspersed with the Senator's name, either as: "Heron!" or "Ada!" or "*Michanikos!*" and even a few, "Alexander's Daughter!"

The last seemed especially embarrassing, as Alexander would be her ancestor removed by many generations, but the commoners did not care. They seemed to like that the city was led by a descendant of the very man that had founded it.

Riding through the streets also gave her perspective on how much the city had changed these last few years. She'd spent so much time either locked in her workshop, or out of the city, that she hadn't realized how the city had been transformed.

It seemed every other rooftop had spinning cups for turning wind energy into power, churning butter or kneading bread, freeing those makers to other tasks. After years of war, the pieces of broken steam chariots left in the streets or on the battlefield had been repurposed. A man in a mechanical Centaur gave a salute as Dominitus' funeral precession passed.

The city had a natural paleness, white stone walls against desert sand, while colorful banners snapped from every parapet and tower. Signs, once faded with sunshine, had been retouched in preparation for incoming trade.

And that's when Ada realized what had changed about the city. With the specter of war banished, and the new government formed, the city anticipated its reemergence as the center of the known world. Even when Rome had been whole and the head of the Roman Empire, Alexandria had bled away trade. The city vibrated with the anticipation of its future, like a host waiting nervously for a party to start.

It wasn't the Senator's funeral that had brought them out, or Hoth's ha'pennies, but a celebration of the city. As the steam chariot passed the Emporium, the wind shifted, throwing her hair into her face unceremoniously and bringing the scents of a thousand lands: sage, thyme, cinnamon, cassia, chilies, turmeric, ginger, myrrh, cardamom, and so many others that Ada felt delirious.

Beyond the spices, fresh breads cooked in hundreds of ovens and foundry fires leaked black smoke into the sky. The scents of horse and mechanical, desert and sea, fire and clay, came together at this intersection of the world. Ada couldn't help but be buoyed by the knowledge that her city had survived everything that had been thrown at it.

Which was why she'd ultimately accepted the position of Consul. Because it was her city, the City of Wonders, a city like no other, and she couldn't let it fail.

It would not fail. She saw into the Emporium as the goods passed between the traders: ivory, tortoiseshell, cotton, silk, sugar, ointments, perfumes, cosmetics. Goods from across the world meant that the world had accepted Alexandria's return.

Upon reaching the Soma of Alexander, and the grave site of Senator Dominitus, Ada felt a moment of embarrassment that his funeral procession had been more like a victory parade.

The dignitaries that had come for his funeral were gathered around the mausoleum. Some were former Senators of the old Empire, although none that had been involved with the conspiracy in Rome. Prince Algoni and Princess Bani were there. The Prince had been inquiring about Sepharia's hand. Ada had told him that was up to Sepharia to decide, because she was a grown woman who had survived so much.

The ranks had swelled with nobles, as each family of Alexandria wanted to be a part of the new Empire. There were others: representatives from Persia, priests from Egypt, members of the League of Corinth, the remaining Northmen still in the city wearing fashions more local than the ones that they had come south in, scholars from the Great Library in togas, Black Omari standing apart, the magistrate of the Rhakotis district in his purple-lined toga, Arethussa in a sapphire gown of exquisite craftsmanship, and even Takul in his colorful attire who'd been sent by the Queen of Sakrur to open up trade with Alexandria.

After the body was placed on the earth, and libations were poured to honor the former Senator, words were spoken by the representatives of the old priesthood. His body was carried into the tomb and his body sealed within.

As the gathering broke up, Ada took a place by Hoth's side and they walked to the pair of horses he'd brought. Neither spoke, and if she would have guessed at what he was thinking, it was probably the same as she. For it felt like the funeral hadn't been just for the old Senator. She mourned those who had brought them to this point, the names as numerous as the stars, many simple soldiers whose names she would never know.

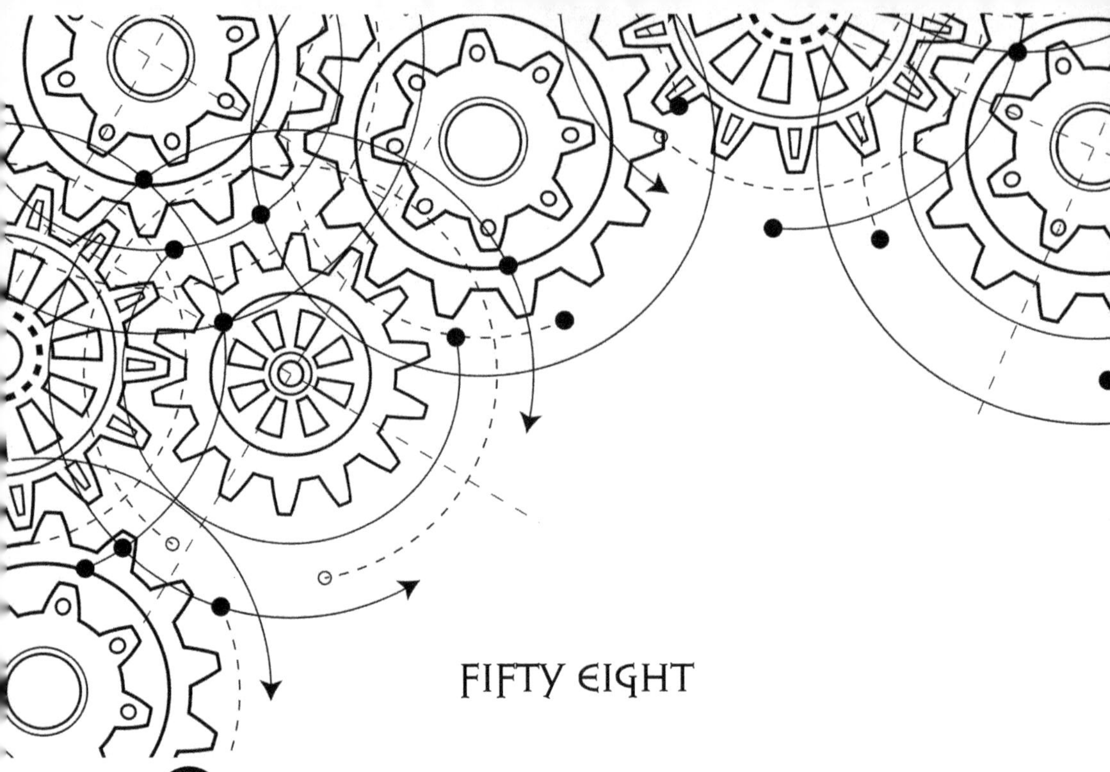

FIFTY EIGHT

On an early spring morning in Alexandria, Ada found herself wandering down Canopic street towards the Great Library. Hoth had shared her bed, which was most nights, and had been sprawled across it diagonal, forcing Ada to wake.

A cart merchant wearing mechanical arm guards that clicked when he moved, gave her a hunk of fresh bread as a gift. She thanked him and nibbled on the flaky crust that broke apart when she touched it, and shoved the sweet insides into her mouth, to dissolve as she strolled.

She could have taken a horse or steam chariot, but wanted to be closer to the city. She passed two young boys with dark skin and pale eyes who had made a pair of cloth and metal puppets out of gears and other things they'd found in the streets. The performance entailed the story of her fight with Lysimachus at the top of the pyramid, though it had no relation to the truth. In the puppet version, she flew up the pyramid (as it was commonly held that she could fly due to the Lighthouse story and her air ship) and killed the priest of Sobek who was represented by a metal crocodile. They'd made the puppet out of an old crocodile soldier helm, which meant it was mostly teeth and the boy's arm had been painted dark green.

She gave the boys a pair of ha'pennies and continued, the echoes of her fight with Lysimachus a shadow on her memory. Rather she thought about the news she'd received the night before that the iron rail had reached Tyre, a month ahead of schedule, though the Rome side was having problems due to attacks by raiders that melted back into the forest when Manticores arrived. The world would never truly be safe.

After a quick visit to the Great Library, she planned a visit to the shipyards to examine progress on her iron boat. As she'd told everyone before, she had no intention of staying on as Consul past a year and a day. The iron ship, yet unnamed, would take her and Hoth on an unspecified journey once her term was complete.

As to who would take her position, it seemed much of the talk centered around her daughter, Sepharia. Ada had not given her opinion on the matter, though her private thoughts were that picking Sepharia gave too much credence to a family name.

On the good side, Sepharia had taken Algoni to her bed, and the sometimes grim Kushite Prince had lightened in mood. The three of them, Sepharia, Algoni, and Bani, were in constant conspiracy, and the nobles of Alexandria loved them. They could do worse than her daughter.

Ada was picturing Sepharia as Consul, when a vagrant sitting in the shadow of the marble building called her old name. This was not an uncommon occurrence, as the citizens of the city enjoyed familiarity, but something in the way her name had been spoken by this man summoned raised hairs on the back of her neck.

The vagrant was sitting with his back against the building, the old Office of the Empire, and had it still been, the vagrant's presence would have not been allowed. He wore dirt smeared traveling robes and had a cowl pulled over his head, hiding his face in shadow, though edges of a long gray beard rested against his pulled up knees. Despite being seated, the vagrant had size that implied he was no mere wanderer.

Ada had the impression that she should flee. Her heart had doubled in time and a sweat appeared on her forehead. Yet, something in that voice tickled memories that she thought were long dead.

She took steps forward until she stood just out of reach, then took a step back. Something in the man's hunched form told her he could grab her before she moved away. He had the presence of a lion, or maybe one of those great bears she'd heard about in the North.

"You never made my metal soldiers," said a low voice, sending a moment of panic through Ada.

Her metal hand raised to her quivering lip. "Agog?"

Hands the size of plates pushed back the cowl until a familiar face, though covered in coarse gray hair around the mouth and chin, was revealed. Hard lines traversed the weathered skin.

"No longer," he said. "I go by Woden these days."

"I thought you were dead," she said, moving closer so they could speak privately.

"I did, too," he said. "I woke later under the fallen tree, my neck bruised, my side leaking blood, and made my way from the burning city."

"Why did you not reveal yourself to us? We could have used you in our fight against Lysimachus," she said.

He waved her off. His hands were dirty and rough like bark or roots. "Clearly, you did not need me. And I needed time. Once Rome was burnt, I felt strangely at peace, not caring about what happened after."

"You had your revenge," she whispered, understanding.

"In a way," he said, waggling his snowy white eyebrows.

"What have you been doing? And why did you come back?" she asked.

"Traveling. Staying off the roads, moving through the world mostly unseen, finding the hidden shrines and places that reminded me of the north," he said. "Places Aurelia would have loved to see."

"You came back to see Alexandria one last time," she said.

"I came back to see you," he said.

"Me?"

He picked at a bit of dirt under a fingernail. "I wanted to know you were well before I returned north. Are you?"

His gaze seemed to bore right into her, as if he could see her inner-most thoughts. He'd always had that quality about him.

"I am, better than I thought I'd be," she said. "The world is chang-ing."

"And that's why I have to go back north," he said.

"Why not stay? Hoth, and the other Northmen, it would warm their hearts to see you," she said.

"No. No, it wouldn't. They came because of me, some against their will. Better that I fade into memory." He knotted his brow and rubbed his hands together. "The name Ada wears on you well."

"I never liked the name Agog," she said.

"We play the parts we have to," he said. "Though I always wondered, do the names transform us? Or do we take them when we are trans-formed?"

He asked it in a way that said he wasn't expecting an answer.

"What will you do in the North?" she asked.

A smile quirked to his lips, one filled with memory and mystery, of light and laughter.

"There's an old walking house I need to find, lost without its mistress. I need to put things to right," he said, maudlin. Then, "What of you?"

"I want to see the lands of Indus," said Ada. "I'm making Hoth take me against his will."

"I doubt that," chuckled the man she'd once called Agog.

They stood in silence and in shadow. Eventually, Ada realized she had nothing more to say. The world they had transformed together did not need them anymore, so it was nearing time to leave. For the first time, and probably not the last time, it ached in her bones that her term as Consul was not yet complete. The end of summer would come like the tides.

"Farewell, Woden of the North," she said, with a deep bow that confused many a passerby.

"Farewell, Ada of Alexandria," said Woden, eyes like the cold, dark sea creasing at the corners.

She did not look back until she'd gone up the street, and when she did, he was gone. Ada knew in her heart that she would never see him again.

FIFTY NINE

A year and a day had gone too quickly for Sepharia. Sunlight leaked through the curtains on the eastern windows, forcing her to put a hand up. A grunt beneath the covers made her smile. A dark muscled leg stuck out from the thin sheet and she had to resist running her hands up the thigh.

Shaking off her erotic thoughts, Sepharia got out of bed and wrapped a cream stola around her naked body. She didn't want to miss the *Alexandria* leaving.

With her hair a tangled mess, Sepharia hurried to the royal pier, receiving smirking glances from the guards on the way. As she passed the cliff's edge, she had a moment of heaviness hang on her shoulders in remembrance of the day she nearly leapt off them to her death.

Those thoughts passed quickly, as she spied the gray, sailless ship waiting at the dock. Men carried cargo onto the deck and into the hold. A flag ruffled in the breeze, coming south over Pharos island. The design was something Ada had created after her journey around the African continent. It was two dragons, one fire and one water, wrapped around the world. The significance of it was lost on Sepharia, but seeing it made her smile, just the same.

Before she descended the winding wooden stairs, Sepharia admired the main docks, once destroyed by Ada, filled with ships from all over the Mediterranean. Except there was something different about the docks and it took a few moments of contemplation to figure it out.

It used to be that the runners that made their way from the ships to the book warehouses had their arms full of scrolls, which would be copied by scribblers for the Great Library expanding its catalog. Today, the runners returned with tomes as well as scrolls. Alexandria was sending books on the ships as payment for the copying of others, in an attempt to spread the knowledge of the Library.

The last time she'd visited the copy rooms, twelve Immortality Machines stamped away at dizzying speeds, making copies faster than Sepharia could comprehend. Rooms filled with binders and gluers worked from dawn till dusk.

Word had come back to Alexandria that the other important libraries of the world like the Library of Celsus in Ephesus had built their own Immortality Machines. Even the Library of Pergamum had been reinstituted, though it would take some time to refill the racks of the 200,000 scrolls that had been given to the Great Library by Mark Antony as a wedding present for Cleopatra.

Sepharia reached the iron ship *Alexandria* as her stomach noised its complaint that she had not yet eaten. Hoth hailed her from the steerage, wearing a tunic, and dressed in local styles with stamped leather armguards.

Ada appeared moments later in dark tunic and silver belt, having been summoned from below. The brass and steel mechanical limbs clicked like living things upon approach. Sepharia and Ada exchanged greetings with a kiss.

"I feel like I should be joining you," said Sepharia. "This ship reminds me of the *Gray Cetus.*"

Ada's eyes creased with thought. "It's larger and rides higher in the waves, made for traveling across the deeper oceans."

"Does that mean you're going to try to reach Indus by going west around the world?" asked Sepharia.

Ada nodded. "It is. We've got a crew of ten, including scholars more studied in astronomy than I."

Sepharia tilted her head. "I thought you would have preferred to do that yourself?"

The sigh that left Ada's lips was filled with the efforts of the years. "For once, I prefer to observe. I've spent the whole of my life toiling in the workshop, or scribbling on parchment. I plan to spend this simple journey above deck and I hope to see more whales."

"Did you really see an ocean full of them?" asked Sepharia, though by the light of Ada's eyes she knew the answer.

Sepharia laughed. "You call this a simple journey, but if you are successful, you'll open up shipping lanes to the lands beyond the Indus. That's nothing like simple."

Ada ignored the comment. "What of you, daughter? Are you ready to take the mantle of government?"

"No," smiled Sepharia, "but I expect that's normal. Only fools expect to wrestle privilege from power. It'll be a burden, but a worthy one to bear."

"What of Algoni? He still shares your bed," said Ada.

"While I am Consul and he's the Kushite Prince, we plan no further entanglements, so as not to have the appearance of royalty at the head of the Empire." Sepharia hesitated, having not voiced this to anyone but Algoni. "If after my two year term is complete, he still shares my bed..." Sepharia gave a half-shrug, indicating that anything might happen.

"A wise course," said Ada, smiling. "Maybe in two years, I will have returned and can enjoy your wedding."

"What if you don't come back?" asked Sepharia, suddenly maudlin.

Ada drew serious, then the lines in her face softened. "Then imagine we're having grand adventures on the other side of the world and we're too busy to return."

"I will," said Sepharia.

They gazed into each other's eyes for a long spell. Sepharia broke away when she felt dizzy from the eye contact. Without speaking, each turned away, Ada up the gang plank, and Sepharia to return to the Palace.

By the time she reached the top of the stairs, the *Alexandria* had pulled away from the royal pier. Sepharia watched as it headed out of the harbor, past wooden ships full of white sails carrying trade to and from the city. Sepharia waved as the figures on the deck of the boat grew smaller, and one small figure returned the gesture, a glint of sunlight reflecting from her arm.

Then the *Alexandria* turned course to the west, black smoke trailing behind it. Before long, the ship disappeared from the waters of Alexandria, and into memory, carrying on it the greatest inventor who ever lived.

§§§

ABOUT THE AUTHOR

Thomas K. Carpenter resides in Colorado with his wife Rachel. When he's not busy writing his next book, he's hiking, skiing, and getting beat by his wife at cards. He keeps a regular blog at www.thomaskcarpenter.com and you can follow him on twitter @thomaskcarpente. If you want to learn when his next novel will be hitting the shelves and get free stories and occasional other goodies, please sign up for his mailing list by going to: http://tinyurl.com/thomaskcarpenter. Your email address will never be shared and you can unsubscribe at any time.

OTHER BOOKS BY THOMAS K. CARPENTER

The Hundred Halls Universe

SEASON ONE
THE HUNDRED HALLS
Trials of Magic
Web of Lies
Alchemy of Souls
Gathering of Shadows
City of Sorcery

THE RELUCTANT ASSASSIN
The Reluctant Assassin
The Sorcerous Spy
The Veiled Diplomat
Agent Unraveled
The Webs That Bind

GAMEMAKERS ONLINE
The Warped Forest
Gladiators of Warsong
Citadel of Broken Dreams
Enter the Daemonpits
Plane of Twilight

ANIMALIANS HALL
Wild Magic
Bane of the Hunter
Mark of the Phoenix
Arcane Mutations
Untamed Destiny

STONE SINGERS HALL
Song of Siren and Blood
House of Snake and Tome
Storm of Dragon and Stone
Sonata of Shadow and Thorn
Well of Demon and Bone

THE ORDER OF MERLIN
The Order of Merlin
Infernal Alliances
Tower of Horn and Blood